Praise for

In Search of
The Beloved

Truth be told, I am not a novel guy. But I have to admit, Marian Rizzo's In Search of the Beloved drew me in from the first page. I love how she weaved her characters in and out of the search for the Apostle John. Great read.

Dr. Woodrow Kroll
Creator of *The HELIOS Projects*
Radio host, *Back to the Bible*

A gripping and engaging exploration of what it would be like if John, the beloved Apostle, were still alive and living in the island of Patmos. Marian Rizzo takes us on a delightful journey through the eyes and experiences of two thought-provoking and inquisitive characters, Mark, a professor, and Julie, a newspaper reporter.

Tom Mabie
Ordained United Methodist Pastor
Appointed to work with The Navigators

Marian Rizzo is a gifted storyteller, whether it be for news reporting or fiction. She has a keen eye and ear for the intricacies of a story, which translates into very powerful narratives. Marian can turn the mundane into the magnificent through the masterful weaving of character, context, and scene-setting.

Susan Smiley-Height
Longtime journalist and editor in the newspaper industry

IN SEARCH OF THE BELOVED

To Donna,
So good to see you again.
Stay in touch.
Love,
Marian Rizzo

Also available from

Marian Rizzo

Angela's Treasures

IN SEARCH OF
THE BELOVED

a novel

Marian Rizzo

WordCrafts

In Search of the Beloved is a work of fiction. All References to persons, places or events are fictitious or used fictitiously.

In Search of the Beloved
Copyright © 2019
Marian Rizzo

Cover concept and design by David Warren.

Published by WordCrafts Press
Cody, Wyoming 82414
www.wordcrafts.net

To Joanna, my daughter, my friend, my sister in Christ. Without your help this book would never have been completed..

JULIE

Julie Peters had a pretty good idea why the senior editor had called her into his office. Once again, Jason Redding, the most obnoxious, conceited TV reporter she'd ever known, had scooped the public works story out from under her and had featured it on the 12 p.m. news an hour ago.

Now she sat in front of the broad mahogany desk that separated her from the balding man on the other side.

"I'm sorry, Andy. Jason beat me to the mayor's office and somehow he convinced them to shut the door in my face." She shook her head. "I didn't have a chance to—"

Andy raised his hand and cut her off. "Do you think I'm upset with you?"

Puzzled, Julie narrowed her eyes at the big man. Seriously? Was he brushing off her failure, or was he about to lower the proverbial axe? Andy had already fired two reporters and a photographer. The whole office sat on pins and needles. Print media was on its way out in a day when most people got their news from the internet. Even the TV reporters could expect a cut—Jason Redding included.

"I'm fully aware of how WPIX operates," Andy said, his voice uncharacteristically mellow. "If Redding ever stopped hobnobbing with government officials he'd lose his connections, and maybe his viewers too. You can chalk this one up to experience, Julie. You're not the first reporter to blow a story because of that man's unscrupulous tactics."

She let out a relieved sigh. "Then, I'm off the hook?"

"Not entirely," he said, a firmness slipping into his tone. "But," he added, as he leaned back in his chair, "you may be able to redeem yourself."

Julie slid to the edge of her chair. "How? Just say the word. Whatever it is, I'll get right on it."

Andy nodded. "Okay then." With the hint of a smile, he held up a manila envelope that had been lying on his desk. "It's a simple assignment, Julie. But it involves some long-distance travel. You'll be away from the office for a week."

Julie eyed the envelope with an inkling of suspicion. Long-distance travel? Several possibilities ran through her mind. *New York City?* She could drive the distance. *Florida?* Sounded too much like a vacation. *How about California?* She brightened.

"You're going to the other side of the world." Andy shoved the folder across his desk toward her. "You'll fly to Ephesus and spend a couple of days in research, and then you'll head for the isle of Patmos where you'll complete your assignment." He shrugged. "Think of it as a paid vacation with a little work attached to it."

Julie picked up the envelope and lifted the flap. Inside were an airline ticket, a couple of travel brochures, and—she frowned as she pulled out a small New Testament.

"What—?"

Andy bobbed his head. "Open it to the bookmark."

She located the marker and opened the book to the last chapter of the Gospel of John. A yellow highlighted verse leaped out at her. She silently read it. *Jesus said to him, "If I want him to remain until I come, what is that to you? You follow Me!"*

She searched Andy's face. "I don't understand."

"That passage contains a conversation between Peter and Jesus," he said. "Peter has just learned he can expect to die a martyr's death. Then, he points to John and asks, *'What about him?'* Look again at Jesus' response, Julie. Jesus has told Peter that John might live until He returns."

She raised a shoulder. "So? What does that have to do with us?"

"Jesus hasn't returned yet," Andy said with a casual air.

As usual when he expected to have a lengthy conversation, he drew a handful of paperclips from the ceramic bowl on his desk and started linking them into a chain. Julie braced herself. This could take awhile.

He fastened another clip but kept his eyes on Julie. "There's a religious sect who think John might still be alive," he said. "In fact, someone's claimed to have seen him."

She closed the Bible. "That's ridiculous."

He added three more links, and the chain grew longer.

Julie let out a sarcastic chuckle. "What are you telling me, Andy? That a 2,000-year-old man is alive and kicking and strolling around the Mediterranean? And what am I supposed to do; get an interview with the guy and write a big story about it? Come on, what's this really about?" She slid the New Testament back inside the packet.

Her editor slipped another clip on the chain. "You're right, Julie. This is as ludicrous as those claims people make that they've died and come back from the other side. Regardless, I think there's a story there worth investigating. Even if you come home with a human interest feature about some loveable old guy who helps his neighbors, it'll make good copy. On the flip side, what if it turns out to be true? You'll have the scoop of a lifetime."

"Andy, I'm a journalist, not a novelist," Julie settled back in her chair and placed the envelope on her lap. "And this is a respected newspaper, not the National Intruder writing about *The Incredible Two-headed Sheep* or *My Baby's Father was an Alien*. Why don't you give this to a reporter who believes this stuff? Mary Beth Simmons or Roger Cappella, for example. They claim to be *Christians*."

She realized she'd uttered the last word with a touch of bitterness. The truth was, she'd known plenty of Christians, and it was because of them that she'd stopped believing a long time ago.

She shook her head. "I haven't set foot inside a church in six years, Andy. Even if God *does* exist, which I doubt, He's out there somewhere, minding His own business." She waved her hand toward the ceiling. "He doesn't care what happens to m— to us."

"Julie, it was because of your skepticism that I chose *you* for this assignment. You can be objective. I don't have to worry about you letting any preconceived religious beliefs interfere with your job." He tapped his desk with his index finger—one tap for every other word. "I *need* an investigative *reporter* on this, someone who will *look at all the facts* and either *prove* or *disprove* that rumor." He grinned like a Cheshire cat. "Plus, there's a bonus attached. And who knows? Maybe some awards."

It was a no-win situation. If Julie turned down the assignment, her career would end faster than Andy could attach another link to that foot-long chain of paperclips. If she went, she could be laughed right out of the newsroom. Scowling, she withdrew the airline ticket.

"You leave Wednesday morning," Andy said.

"That doesn't give me much time to prepare."

He started pulling clips off the chain and dropped them, one-by-one into the bowl—a sure sign their discussion was coming to an end. "You only need to conduct an internet search of your two destinations, Ephesus and Patmos," *plink, plink,* "and be sure and get a little background on John the Apostle." *Plink, plink, plink.*

With a sigh of resignation, Julie slid the airline ticket back in the envelope. The whole thing reeked of failure; one more flop on her way out the door.

She stared at Andy. The overhead light bounced off his shiny scalp. If she didn't know better, she'd swear he had a halo.

"You say somebody actually saw this guy?" she said.

Andy bobbed his head and his halo dissipated. "None other than Peter Pike."

"The TV evangelist?"

"That's right."

She allowed a smirk to cross her lips. She'd caught the man's show once, several months ago, while she was changing channels.

"It seems Peter recently traveled to Patmos," Andy continued. "He claims he caught sight of this wise, old man ministering to people in the village. He said the guy feeds the poor, heals the sick, and counsels the hurting. The locals call him a miracle worker."

"Well, I suppose I would need to give Peter Pike a call."

Andy nodded toward the packet still in Julie's hand. "You'll find his contact information in there. Though his TV shows come from a studio in New York City, he happens to be here in Springfield at this very moment. He owns a summer home by the lake." Andy raised his furry eyebrows. "We're gonna have to move on this, Julie. This is the kind of piece Jason Redding will pounce on, once he gets wind of it."

Julie doubted Jason would have any interest in this biblical wild goose chase. He was so caught up in politics he stank of the swamp. It was obvious what Andy was trying to do. By mentioning her worst adversary, he thought he could motivate her into taking the assignment.

She considered her options. If she refused, she'd probably get stuck with calendar entries, obituaries, and a boring city council meeting. *What were they discussing these days? The municipal sewer system? Next month's Fourth of July celebration?* On the other hand, an overseas assignment carried a flavor of intrigue and adventure. *Like a vacation*, Andy had said, *with a little work attached to it. And maybe a bonus.*

Another thought struck Julie. "Our newspaper's been in a budget crunch for more than a year. How do you expect to pay for this trip?"

Her boss's visage channeled the Cheshire Cat again. "Other than your salary, we're not spending a dime. St. Paul Bible Institute is picking up the tab." His steel gray eyes softened momentarily. "Melanie Stevens, the school's director, came to see me last week. It seems two of the institute's board members attend a church where this rumor caught on. They came up with the money and insisted Melanie take on the project."

"So, why did she come to you?"

"She believes newspaper coverage can put a favorable spotlight on the college, especially if something big comes out of your search." Andy cleared his throat. "By the way, Julie, you're not going alone."

She froze. There was something odd about the expression on her boss' face.

He looked her in the eye. "Melanie will be sending along one of her professors, an expert in biblical history and archaeology."

Julie didn't even breathe.

"You know him," Andy went on. "His name's Mark Bensen."

A surge of heat rose to Julie's cheeks.

Mark Bensen.

She'd been trying to forget that guy for more than a year.

She gazed at the envelope. It held a much-needed break from the daily grind, maybe even an adventure of sorts. It meant a week of freedom from Mary Beth Simmons' nasty remarks. It was a chance to visit an exotic land, an opportunity to redeem herself for having failed.

But she'd have to face Mark again. She'd have to acknowledge some unanswered questions. She might even have to unearth a past she had buried long ago.

Rising to her feet, Julie dropped the envelope on her boss' desk with a thump. "You'd better give this to someone else. I can't do this."

Andy's lips parted in a patronizing smile, but his eyes had turned to ice.

"I thought you'd moved on, Julie. It's been over a year. Melanie believes Mark is the right person for the job, and she specifically asked for you."

He stood up and leaned over his desk toward Julie. A lump came to her throat, but she stood firm.

Andy was frowning now, the Cheshire Cat grin nowhere to be found. "I don't care what happened between the two of you. Get over it. You're supposed to be a professional, Julie. Start acting like one." He huffed and returned to his seat. "Besides, you already know each other. That could be a plus."

She waited for the flush to drain from her cheeks. She could thank her Irish mother for the instant blush that hit at the wrong times.

"We're moving on this story, with or without you, Julie. I need an answer. Are you in, or out?"

She took a breath. "I'd like to think it over."

He nodded. "Tomorrow. I want an answer tomorrow."

Julie left Andy's office and hurried past the clicking keyboards and muffled phone conversations. She ignored the glances, the whispers, the stares that followed her down the aisle. Without stopping to acknowledge Roger Cappella's "Hey," from the cubicle next to hers, Julie grabbed her purse and fled from the newsroom, down the stairwell and out the front door of the Springfield Daily Press. She took a deep breath of outside air, then pulled out her cell phone and called the one person she could depend on. Her best friend, Lakisha Davis.

"I know it's only 3 o'clock, but how about an early dinner?"

Lakisha didn't ask any questions, but merely responded to the urgency in Julie's voice. "I'll lock up right away and meet you at the Olive Garden in ten minutes," she said.

Julie pictured the girl turning her back on a pile of real estate contracts and rushing out the door. She was a true friend. The night Julie broke up with Mark, Lakisha left a dinner party in order to comfort her. They spent the rest of the evening laughing and crying and cursing men. She could trust Lakisha to give her an honest opinion, which she could accept or reject. Hadn't the girl urged her to give Mark another chance? Hadn't she backed off when Julie refused?

Call it chemistry or a convergence of sun signs, whatever

the reason, Julie had connected with Lakisha from the day she moved to Springfield three years ago. It was hard to imagine what her life might be like if she hadn't walked into that real estate office, if Lakisha hadn't been the one sitting behind the desk, and most of all, if they hadn't nurtured a budding friendship over afternoon lunches and early morning jogs at the park.

They were as different as apples and oranges. Julie, with her flaming red hair and her Irish/English heritage, had grown up in the suburbs of a small town. Dark-skinned Lakisha had begun life in an elite section of Boston, the daughter of a man who practiced corporate law and a woman who taught college physics. Julie had one sister, Rita. Lakisha had seven siblings. Julie went to a public high school and depended on a scholarship and a part-time job to get through college. Lakisha attended a private academy, spent summers on Cape Cod, and had servants to care for her daily needs. When she left home, she plunged into an unfamiliar world where she earned her own money and cleaned her own apartment— when she felt like it.

While Julie kept a neat condo and could locate whatever she needed, even in a dark room, Lakisha's home looked like the end of a three-day party, yet she also claimed she could find anything she needed in the dark.

Somehow, despite their differences, they found common ground in a lasting friendship of loyalty and support. Julie could expect nothing less from their dinner meeting. She smiled as she maneuvered her immaculately clean compact car through traffic and imagined Lakisha slipping into her minivan's front seat beside a pile of real estate magazines and fast food wrappers.

At the restaurant, the two women sat across from each other in a booth. Julie ignored her friend's quizzical stare. She took a couple of bites of her salad, then pushed aside the plate. Lakisha bit into a breadstick. Her dark eyes moved to Julie's half-eaten salad.

"Aren't you gonna finish that?"

Julie lifted a shoulder. "Not hungry."

"Not hungry? You're the one who suggested dinner." Lakisha reached across the table and took hold of Julie's hand. "Okay, girl, something happened. You didn't call me away from my clients so we could sit here and stare at each other. What's going on?"

Julie shook her head. A crimson lock fell across her brow. She brushed it back. Then her eyes misted over. The words she'd planned to say caught in her throat.

"Did something happen at work?" Lakisha's brow wrinkled with concern. "Did that monster fire you?"

Julie shook her head. Tears spilled from her eyes. She managed to say two words. "It's Mark."

"Mark?" Lakisha straightened. "What's going on?"

Julie glanced at a couple seated at a nearby table. They were engrossed in their own conversation.

She turned back to Lakisha. "I—I don't know what to do. Andy wants to send me—what I mean is, I have this opportunity—but, then I'd have to—but the truth is, we could be thrown back together again and I don't know if I can handle it."

Lakisha's dark eyes grew wide. "Thrown back together? What do you mean? Say something that makes sense. *Please.*"

Julie withdrew her hand from Lakisha's gentle grasp. She took a sip of water, then she went over her conversation with

Andy in an emotional roller coaster ride that finished with a sigh of defeat. Lakisha listened intently, her only response an occasional nod, a pensive "um-hm," and ultimately, a wince when Julie said she was planning to turn down the assignment.

"What? You want to turn it down?"

Julie stared back at her in puzzlement. "You think I should go, don't you?"

Lakisha raised one eyebrow and straightened her back. "Why not, girl? It's a chance of a lifetime."

"Yeah, I guess it is, but—"

"But, nothing. You need to forget about Mark and think about your career. Andy promised you a bonus, right? And, there could be some awards? Why, you might even win a Pulitzer Prize."

Julie shifted in her seat. "Right. The top prize in the industry. Get real."

"Well, you might win *something*."

"Lakisha, I'm not thinking about prizes or bonuses or even my career at this point. You're forgetting one thing. Mark is going."

Lakisha crossed her arms. "Uh, huh. So what? It's been a year since you guys broke up. Haven't you gotten over him yet?"

"Well, yes, except—"

"Except what? You told me you'd put that relationship behind you and had moved on." Lakisha leaned toward her and softened her tone. "It's a job, Julie. You're not going on a honeymoon."

Julie's lips parted in a weak smile. "I guess you're right. It's just..."

"Yes?"

"Well, I don't know how I'm going to feel to be around him again. I don't know how I'll act, or what will come out of my mouth. I've done okay without him. But this trip—we'll be traveling together. We'll be staying at the same hotel. It may not *be* a honeymoon, but it's sure gonna *feel* like one. I don't know if I can handle being that close to him again."

"You *can* handle it. Remember, you can do all things through Christ who strengthens you."

The Sunday school verse came flooding back to Julie. She'd first recited it when she was ten years old. Back then, that slice of Scripture meant something to her. But she no longer believed in that promise, so how could it help her now?

"You're gonna have to think before you speak," Lakisha said, then she chuckled. "Or don't speak at all. You may be a talented writer, Julie, but let's face it, when you talk you tend to put your foot in your mouth."

Julie blushed, but laughed with her friend. "Yeah, you're right, Lakisha."

"You know I am. I'm telling you to focus. Get your story and enjoy the trip. You don't have to pay any attention to Mark. He'll be working on his own project." Lakisha tilted her head to one side. "Think about what you'd be giving up. Are you going to let a broken relationship ruin this opportunity?"

Julie gazed with admiration at her friend. Lakisha was trying to revive a fighting spirit within her. Julie had never let emotions get in the way of her career before. So why now? Why should she give up an opportunity like this simply because of some guy?

"You're absolutely right, Lakisha. And, with my luck, if I don't take the assignment, Mary Beth Simmons will probably jump on this thing."

"And you'd let that annoying Southern belle rob you of the most exciting assignment you ever had?"

Julie giggled. "That would be a low blow, wouldn't it? She'd never let me forget it. I can almost hear her drawling description of the wonderful trip she had and how dumb I was to let it slip through my fingers."

The conversation stalled for a few seconds, then Lakisha pressed Julie. "When do you have to decide?"

"Andy wants an answer tomorrow."

"And?"

Julie smiled with renewed confidence. "And—it looks like I'm going on a trip."

Lakisha shoved Julie's half-eaten salad toward her. "Now, eat up, girl. You're gonna need lots of energy for this one. And don't you dare change your mind. You're going to Patmos, and I'm gonna help you pack."

2

MARK

Mark Bensen wondered whether the lunch meeting with his boss would be nothing more than another brain-storming session, like all the others. He and Melanie Stevens had had many such meetings during his tenure at the Bible institute, and none of them had gone beyond course schedules and exams. But Melanie's charged demeanor that morning led him to suspect this meeting would be different.

The cafeteria clattered with activity. The aroma of sizzling burgers and fries filled the air. Along with the rest of the staff, Mark and Melanie crashed the line of students, slid their trays along the metal bars, and selected their personal favorites from an array of soups, salads, and sandwiches. Like programmed robots, they headed for their usual table in a corner away from the hubbub.

Melanie set her tray on the table and placed a white envelope in the center. She mumbled a silent blessing, then dug into her Cobb salad, all the while ignoring Mark's inquisitive stare. Between bites of his burger and fries, Mark's eyes moved to the strange packet, then to Melanie's face, then back to the packet again. Knowing Melanie, he'd have to wait until every last bite had disappeared off her plate. He swallowed the last of his burger, ignored a few stray fries, and checked his cell phone messages. They were all from Katie. He chose not to answer any of them, even though his boss was still eating her lunch.

A tall, attractive woman, Melanie could have posed for a fashion magazine. She had that same sweep of blonde hair that was a trademark of Lauren Bacall. Her dark eyes flashed with wisdom, and her makeup and nail polish were impeccably applied.

The woman had skipped marriage and children. opting instead to move up the ranks at St. Paul Evangelical Bible Institute. One thing was certain about Melanie—she was dedicated to her job. She worked twice as many hours as anyone else, even extended her labors into the weekend. But she always returned on Monday morning looking refreshed, like she'd been to a health spa.

Being twenty years older than Mark, Melanie tended to mother him a little, but he didn't mind. His own mother had died when he was twelve. His father never remarried, so he'd grown up without a doting female to nurse his cuts and scrapes and pamper his bruised ego.

After he took the job at the Bible institute, he was pleasantly surprised when the director took him under her wing. He didn't know why Melanie had singled him out from among the other instructors, until he saw a family photo on her desk. He had the same tussled, sandy hair and sky blue eyes as Melanie's younger brother. He later learned the young man had died in a traffic accident. Mark was without a mother, and Melanie had lost her only sibling. It began to make sense why she favored him.

Which is why he suspected the white envelope had to have something to do with his job. But it wouldn't do him any good to ask about it. Like a big sister, Melanie was in control and she'd let him in on the secret when she was good and ready. Until then, the most he could do was make idle conversation.

"I see a lot of students have signed up for summer classes," Mark said, keeping his voice casual.

"Yes, about 500."

Melanie stabbed a piece of lettuce and slid it off the fork with her front teeth.

Mark grinned. "Why do women do that?"

"Do what?"

"You know—put on lipstick before they eat lunch, knowing perfectly well they're gonna eat it off, or wipe it off, or leave it on the rim of a glass. Then, they take dainty little bites as if they're afraid of their food."

Melanie's eyes crinkled from behind her designer eyeglasses, and a smile tugged at the corners of her mouth.

"I think it's because we want to stay pretty for the men in our lives," she said with a wink.

The mock flirtation didn't faze Mark. He smiled back, furrowed his brow and said, "Well, whatever you gals are trying to accomplish, it works."

Though he tried to appear nonchalant, he couldn't help but eye that envelope. It was broad and thick and it had an interesting bulge in the center. Curiosity got the best of him. He pointed at the envelope.

"What's that, Melanie?"

She gave it a glance, then went back to her salad. Disappointment washed over him. He flopped back in his chair.

"How are things going in your department, Mark?" she said, without looking up from her plate. "Are you ready for summer classes?"

"Yeah," he said with a touch of irritation. "I've asked Jimmy Nolan to come in to teach in my place while I take a couple of weeks vacation. But, don't worry. We're right on track. I've already put together a course syllabus. I'll have it on your desk this afternoon."

"Have you included any new materials I should know about?"

"The usual," he said.

"So, I guess you're available for a side project that will involve a little travel?"

Mark perked up. His eyes darted to the packet again. "I read an internet report about a dig in ancient Samaria," he said. "And there's been talk that St. Catherine's Monastery has gathered more artifacts from the desert."

"Those reports bear interest, but how do you feel about hands-on involvement?" She raised her head and locked eyes with him. "What I mean is, do you want to get an up-close look at some fascinating biblical history?"

Here it comes, Mark thought with relief.

"Is there any reason you can't make time for a trip to—say—Ephesus? And Patmos?"

Mark nodded with enthusiasm. "I'm game."

"Is your passport current?"

"Yeah, it is." Why did he feel like a kid whose mom was about to hand him a cookie? He regrouped and assumed a more professional air, his shoulders back, his chin raised, his eyes on Melanie instead of on the envelope.

She set her fork on the table, dabbed her lips with a paper napkin, then launched into a detailed explanation about a project that would take Mark on the ride of his life. By the time she finished, he was nearly leaping out of his chair. Off went his professional facade. On came the little boy who just discovered he was getting a puppy for Christmas.

"Are you kidding me?! Patmos? Ephesus? All to search out

some off-the-wall rumor that the apostle John is still alive? That's nonsense, of course. But to travel to places where John once walked, where he wrote some of the most beloved books in the Bible? You bet!"

Several students at a nearby table suddenly grew silent and gawked at Mark.

Melanie laughed. "Settle down," she whispered. Then she cast a warning glance at the students, who immediately went back to their own business.

Mark's mind was racing. "I'd love to bring back a memento from that trip," he said.

Melanie shrugged. "Who knows? Perhaps it's all nonsense; perhaps not. The mystery man in Patmos may have accumulated some precious artifacts. Use your own judgment."

Finally, Melanie smiled and nodded toward the packet. Mark grabbed it and tore open the flap. Inside were tickets for a commuter flight to JFK and a connection with Turkish Airlines to Izmir.

"Wednesday morning?" Mark groaned. "I can't possibly be ready by Wednesday." He ran his hand through his mop of hair. Then, he caught the frown on Melanie's face. He didn't want to miss this opportunity. "But nothing is impossible with God, right? I can try," he quickly added.

Melanie's dark eyes sparkled with amusement. "You can do this, Mark. I'm taking you off schedule immediately. Jimmy's going to cover for you until you return."

She removed her eyeglasses and set them on the table, a move his boss often used to get someone's attention. The tactic worked. Mark listened intently while she laid out her plan.

"You still have a few days to prepare for the trip. Use your time wisely. Do what research you can here, then you can gather whatever additional information you need at the sites. The middle of June is a good time for you to be going there. The rainy season has ended, everything is in full bloom, and the northern Europeans have not yet overrun the islands. The tourist season won't begin until after you return home."

"Wednesday." Mark muttered. He examined the airline tickets, then he smiled at Melanie and shrugged. "Okay. I'm in."

With fresh enthusiasm, Mark pulled everything out of the packet. He found several brochures containing detailed descriptions and photos of the places on his itinerary, plus hotel reservations, land transportation, and a list of restaurants. And there was a credit card. He raised his eyebrows at Melanie.

"It has a designated amount of money for the trip," she said. "And, upgrade your cellphone for international calling. I want you to stay in contact with me the entire time you're away."

Mark nodded and stuffed everything back in the envelope. Feeling a sudden sense of euphoria wash over him, he relaxed and reached for a wayward French fry.

"There's one more thing," Melanie said.

Mark bit into the potato. "Aaand here's the catch."

"No catch, Mark. I've collaborated with Andy Jacobs at the Springfield Daily Press. This could mean big news for us. He's agreed to send a reporter along."

The masticated potato formed a lump in Mark's throat.

"He's sending Julie Peters," Melanie said, her eyes on Mark's face.

An electric current flowed through Mark. He swallowed hard.

Years ago, his mother's death had taught him how to mask his emotions. But this? He still wasn't over losing Julie. He stared back at Melanie, defying her to say anything that might embarrass him.

"I trust you will maintain a professional image," she said, her tone cool.

"Of course, Melanie. Julie and I parted amicably. You don't have to worry about me."

Mark couldn't believe he was getting another chance with that red-headed firecracker. This time he wouldn't push her away. He'd take it slow, give her plenty of space, and see what happens.

"I'm up for this, Melanie," he said. "Believe me, it's strictly business."

That night, on the second floor of Mark's townhouse, his bedroom light glimmered until three in the morning. Sleep? Who could sleep? Pamphlets, brochures, and guidebooks lay strewn across Mark's bed. On the kitchen table was an extra-biblical study on the life of John the Apostle, plus Mark's favorite Bible, which had commentaries at the bottom of each page.

He turned his attention to the materials Melanie had given him, scanned through the lists of hotels, restaurants, and transportation options. Then he examined a detailed map of the streets of Hora and the Patmian village where people were supposed to have seen John—or his doppelganger.

Julie's image came to mind. What about clothes? He rushed to his closet and surveyed his assortment of shirts and pants. "She's seen all of these. I'll go shopping tomorrow," he murmured. "Maybe get some shirts, and a couple pairs of shorts. And I'm gonna need a good pair of walking shoes."

The excitement kept Mark's eyes open long after his head hit the pillow. His mind scrambled through visions of his upcoming trip. Such a project could bring about a major breakthrough in biblical research. Maybe not worldwide fame and fortune, but at the very least recognition among his peers, not to mention a huge research grant for his department. He'd have papers to write, maybe a PowerPoint presentation to take to colleges across the country. He might even publish a book. It didn't matter to him if the rumor about John was true or not. He could gather enough fodder from this trip to nourish a whole garden of possibilities.

Before sleep overtook him, Mark's mind settled on the other reason for his enthusiasm—a reason he'd been trying to avoid thinking about since his lunch meeting with Melanie. Despite his resistance, Julie's image resurfaced. Letting her go was the hardest thing he ever had to do. Now they were being thrown back together on a job half-way around the world. Could fate be working here? Or God? Was it coincidence? Or the inevitable destiny of two soulmates?

Mark lay in bed staring at the ceiling. Katie Marshall came to his mind, and he bit his lower lip. He'd forgotten to call her back. His current girlfriend knew about his past relationship with Julie, and she occasionally badgered him over it. This news would surely send her over the edge.

I'll tell her tomorrow night, while we're eating dinner. In a public restaurant. With lots of people around.

But Mark had had enough experiences with women to know that time and place didn't matter when it came to an emotional outburst. He wanted to say the right words to help Katie understand. When it came to talking about other women—especially Julie—the girl literally fell apart. He began to rehearse what he might say to convince her that there was nothing between him and Julie.

Yet, as Mark's eyelids fluttered shut, Katie's pouting face faded into oblivion, and he drifted off thinking only of Julie.

3

JULIE

The next morning Julie entered the newsroom still undecided about the trip. Lakisha had nearly convinced her to accept the assignment and she'd do almost anything to keep her job.

Yet she felt nervous about seeing Mark again. If only she could pull this off without all the drama.

As she approached her desk, she caught sight of Andy Jacobs waving his hand and pointing toward the conference room. Julie stared at her desk. She'd left the office in such a flurry yesterday she hadn't cleaned up her mess. Reporter notebooks lay open next to her tape recorder, along with her headset, pens, and research papers. Julie's throat tightened. She rarely left her workplace in such disarray. She gazed at her sister Rita's photo, the only item that had a permanent spot on her desk. She needed to clean things up, put everything back in order so she could think.

"Julie!" Andy's impatient voice sailed over the cubicles. She stood on tiptoe and peered over the divider as her boss disappeared behind the double doors to the conference room. Heaving a long sigh, she forced herself to turn away from the clutter. Hopefully, the meeting would be brief.

She entered the conference room and settled in a padded chair on one end of a 20-foot-long table, as close to the exit door as she could possibly get. The meetings usually involved a handful of reporters and editors. But to her surprise the entire staff came in—three city desk editors, plus department heads from sports, features, and city government. Even Morris Bradley, the aging editorial page editor, had come to this meeting.

Julie cringed when Mary Beth Simmons grabbed the seat to her right. It was way too early in the day to listen to that woman's ranting. Carl Flagle, from photo, settled on Julie's left, boxing her in between her two least favorite people in the newsroom. Not only did she feel trapped, she could smell the residue of Carl's last cigarette.

Across the table, Benny Foster fiddled with a broken pen. A court reporter with a self-righteous attitude, Benny had a nasal voice that irritated Julie. Other familiar faces flocked around the table. Some she'd come to know and like. Others were like strangers to her.

As soon as the door clicked shut, the buzz of conversation dwindled, and Andy launched into a monologue about Julie's assignment, as if she'd already agreed to go. By the time Andy finished, all eyes had settled on Julie. She remained stoic, determined not to react to the unwanted attention.

"That is a *terrific* story," Mary Beth drawled, her face lighting up like a Chinese lantern. "Just think what this could mean to the Christian community. Why, it's the most astounding discovery of the 21st century."

Benny scowled from across the table. "Oh, puh-lease," he sneered. "First it's the Shroud of Turin, then it's Solomon's stables, and now what? Oh, yeah, a ridiculous theory about the excruciatingly long life of the apostle John. What will you church people try to prove next, Simmons?"

Mary Beth nearly lunged out of her chair. "Ah'll have you know, those things you mentioned have been proven through scientific testing."

"Right," Benny said, with an air of sarcasm. "So has Hangar 18."

Mary Beth's support came, as always, from Roger Cappella, a soft-spoken features reporter who kept a Bible on his desk. "Anything's possible," Roger said, his voice barely audible. "Don't forget, the book of Genesis speaks about people who lived to be 900 years old. God can do anything. Even today."

"Sure, if you believe the Bible to begin with," countered Benny.

"Yeah," said Carl. "In those days they didn't follow the same dating system we have today. They didn't have calendars. Who's to say those numbers in Genesis refer to years and not months? Or some other time element?"

Parker Muldowny raised his hand. "I read somewhere that John is buried in a tomb in Ephesus. Ain't you goin' there, too, Julie?" His eyes sparkled with mirth. "Maybe you can dig 'im up."

Julie glared at him but said nothing. She didn't have to. Mary Beth nearly jumped down Parker's throat.

"You are so wrong," she snapped. "Ah'll have you know, no one has evah found any bones there. In fact, there's no physical evidence and no written proof that John evah died. Mah pastor preached on this very subject a few Sundays ago." She glanced around the table, like she was making sure she had everyone's attention. "Ah, for one, believe John is still alive, and Ah'd so loooove to meet him."

Eyes rolled, a few snickers erupted, and the graphics trio put their heads together in whispered tittering.

Again, Roger came to Mary Beth's rescue. A gray-haired, bushy eye-browed veteran reporter, Roger had earned the respect of his co-workers. His one annoying habit? He didn't hesitate to speak openly about his faith. Julie had avoided him as much as she could. Having his cubicle right next to hers didn't help. She would have relocated to another desk, if moving had been an option.

Even now, Roger took the opportunity to do some preaching. "That verse in John isn't the only place where Jesus implied that some of his followers might live until He returned. There's a similar passage, in Matthew Chapter 16."

Benny yawned loudly. Roger ignored the interruption. "All I'm sayin' is, anything's possible," he insisted.

Parker tapped the table and grabbed everyone's attention. "You mentioned two verses, Roger. Are you telling us you're building an entire premise on two verses? You'll have to do better than that."

Other voices erupted and merged with theories on a topic that had been, until now, alien to newsroom debates. The discussion cascaded into a thundering waterfall of opinions—some in favor and some against. Determined not to join in, Julie pinched her lips together and crossed her arms. She turned toward the head of the table. Andy had leaned back in his chair and was watching his staff, elation written all over his face. He even chuckled a couple of times. Then his eyes fell on Julie. Her face grew hot and she looked away.

When she looked back at her boss, he was still grinning. Then, he stood to his feet and raised his hands.

"People, please. Do you see what's happened here? The mere mention of this rumor got all of you debating its authenticity. And with such fervor. That's why it makes a great story. If this subject can do to our readers what it has accomplished in this conference room, it will boost our numbers. In fact, I'm considering creating a special section based on Julie's findings." He glanced around the room. "Depending on what evidence comes from her trip, the rest of you can contribute articles from your own beats. I want you graphics people to come up with designs for the layout. Roger, I want you to put together a timeline of John's life."

Then, he turned toward Mary Beth. "Ms. Simmons, get your preacher and a few other religious leaders to share their thoughts on that passage in John, Chapter 21. Ask them how they feel about miraculous life-and-death situations." He glanced at Julie and lost his smile. "One more thing, Mary Beth, be ready in case Julie decides not to go."

The girl literally squealed like a stuck pig. "Ah'm willin' and able. Say the word, and I'll pack in a second."

A prickling sensation crept up the back of Julie's neck. She glared at the girl. If for no other reason than to defeat Mary Beth, she needed to take that assignment.

"It doesn't matter who goes," Benny blurted out. "She's gonna end up proving the Bible is nothing but a work of fiction. Now *that's* an angle I can live with."

Benny's remark caught Julie by surprise. Until that moment, she hadn't considered how she might use this opportunity to verify what she'd believed for years—that God was a figment of someone's imagination and, even if He *did* exist, He probably didn't care about people, which pained her heart even more than if there *was* no God to begin with. To believe in a supreme being, to call on His name when you need Him most, only to have Him ignore you, that was the greatest tragedy of all.

Julie now saw the assignment in a totally different light. Maybe, after a week of research in that ancient land, she could prove to herself, and to everyone else, that the Bible was false and the apostles were a bunch of religious fanatics.

The meeting ended with electricity in the air. Julie headed straight for Andy's office. He was settling down at his desk when she entered.

"Well?" Her boss raised his eyebrows.

"I've thought it over, Andy," she said. "I'll go, but I have one condition."

Andy frowned at her. "A condition? Like what?"

Despite a sudden surge of anxiety, she took a deep breath and plunged ahead.

"I think Mark and I should take separate flights and meet up in Ephesus on the second day." Julie's hands began to tremble. She closed her fingers into fists. "Assuming that's all right with you," she said with less confidence.

Andy pounded his desk with his fist and leaped to his feet. "Well, it isn't all right with me, darn it. I won't change your ticket. And I doubt Melanie Stevens will change Mark's. For one thing, there's a fee when you do that sort of thing." Andy let out a sigh and dropped back into his chair. "Look, Julie, the plans are set. There's no turning back. Now, are you going to take this trip or do I have to substitute Mary Beth? By the way, doing that will cost more money, too, but I'm willing to make the change. So tell me, are you going or not? I don't have time for any more nonsense."

A tapping drew their attention to the open door. Mary Beth Simmons stood there fidgeting with a pen in her hand. "Sorry, Andy. Ah have a question about this story Ah'm workin' on."

Mary Beth's eyes darted from Andy to Julie. An uncomfortable silence settled on the room. Julie glared at the girl. Mary Beth backed away. "Y'all are busy. Ah can come back later, Andy."

Julie sent imaginary darts after the departing figure. She

remembered Lakisha's words. *"So you'd let that annoying Southern belle rob you of the most exciting assignment you've ever had?"*

She turned toward her editor. "Okay, Andy. Let me have that ticket. I'm going."

Julie returned to her desk and started putting everything away. She couldn't start a new project on a messy workspace. As she placed each item in its preassigned drawer, she breathed a little easier. When she finished, only Rita's picture remained on top of the desk. Julie lifted it and planted a kiss on her sister's face.

"Well, little sister," she murmured. "I'm gonna prove to Mom and Dad that they've been wrong all these years, dragging us to church and preaching to us from a book of outdated writings. Then maybe you'll have some freedom too."

But having said that, a contradiction crept into Julie's heart, and she feared she might be embarking on an impossible quest—one that may come back to haunt her.

What if, after all this, I find out the Bible is true, after all? Then what?

When Julie stepped into her condo that evening, her head swam with plans for her trip. She had convinced herself she could face Mark again. He was no longer a part of her life and therefore no longer a threat. Months ago, she'd tossed out his photos, burned his love notes, and donated his gifts to Goodwill. She'd completely rid herself of every vestige of Mark Bensen.

Now she walked about her living room and ran her hand over her white leather sofa without experiencing the slightest flutter of her heart. A year ago, that man had sat in that very spot with his feet propped up while he munched on his favorite snack, a bag of roasted peanuts and a Coke. He was gone now. So were the peanuts and the Coke. Her coffee table had been cleared of his college textbooks. The only piece of literature that lay there now was Julie's copy of Linda Goodman's *Sun Signs*, the only "bible" she read these days.

With her mind on the more important aspects of the trip, Julie popped a Lean Cuisine in the microwave and brewed a cup of tea. As always, she barely touched her food and was thankful that no one was there to guilt her into taking another bite. She ate absent-mindedly, then tossed the half-eaten meal in the trash and went to her computer to begin an internet search.

"Ephesus." The text said. *"One of seven churches named by the apostle John in the second chapter of Revelation. It's believed John may have written his gospel from this location."*

"So, where is he now?" Julie said aloud. "Is he alive or dead? Is he buried in Ephesus or running around Patmos?"

During her search, several theories surfaced. One source stated that the Jews had killed John. Another said he died of old age in his sleep near the end of the first century. Still another source alleged that while John was praying inside a cave in Patmos, Jesus appeared and took him straight to heaven.

Julie snickered. The only theory that made sense was that John died in his sleep.

Her eyes strayed to the manila envelope her editor had given her. Besides the brochures and airline ticket, there was that New Testament Bible. Six years had passed since Julie last opened the Scriptures. The day she packed for college she left her own Bible sitting on her dresser. She walked out the door and never looked back.

Now, she pushed away from her desk, picked up the Bible, and flipped to the bookmark and the highlighted verse she had read in Andy's office. *If I want him to remain until I come, what is that to you? You follow Me!*

She went on to the verse that followed. *Jesus did not say to him that he would not die, but only, If I want him to remain until I come, what is that to you?*

"Well, there it is," Julie said, frowning. "Jesus said, 'If.' He was speaking hypothetically."

But a flicker of doubt crept in. *Okay, so Jesus never said John would not die, but neither did he say he would die.* That word *"if"* would have chased many pastors away from the topic. Except, of course, Mary Beth's pastor.

Julie slammed the Bible shut and tossed it back on the table. "I'm going to bed," she said aloud.

It was ten o'clock when Julie snuggled underneath her quilt. She awakened in the middle of the night to rumpled blankets and a tear-stained pillow, though she had no idea how they had gotten that way. For years, she had cried herself to sleep. But in recent months, devoid of all outside influences, she'd managed to develop a stronger mindset, a fortitude that no one could ever penetrate—not even Mark, though he'd tried hard enough.

She flipped her pillow over, straightened her blankets, and lay back with a sigh. She could face anything now. Even Mark Bensen and his sanctimonious moralizing. She'd built a shield of granite around herself and he'd never be able to tear it down.

4

MARK

Mark was still thinking about Julie when he awoke to a rising sun. Immediately, he started organizing the materials for his trip. He tore through the brochures like a child opening presents on Christmas morning. Then, he hurried out the door and headed for a local fast-food restaurant. After downing an Egg McMuffin and a cup of coffee, he sailed across town to the public library.

Mark returned home with three travel DVDs and several guidebooks on Turkey and Greece. He inserted a disc in the player, sat back in his recliner, and started taking notes. When the first film ended, he inserted another. By mid-afternoon, he had reviewed all three documentaries. Spreading the guidebooks on the kitchen table, he began to outline his travel plans, beginning with the ruins of Ephesus.

From out of nowhere, he began to imagine strolling with Julie through the ancient metropolis. To be thrown together in such a magical place certainly added a touch of romance to this otherwise sober project.

Of course, Mark mused, *if I want to be a good tour guide, I'll have to brush up on my knowledge of Byzantine art and Greek history.*

He scribbled a few more notations, then switched to the guidebook on Patmos. The first page described it as one of 12 islands in the southeastern corner of the Aegean Sea. From the images, Mark thought it looked more like a tropical paradise than the desolate place of exile where the apostle had lived.

The trip had to include the old nunnery that houses the cave where John was said to have received his revelation, and there was the monastery in Hora that was steeped in history. Mark calculated the time needed for visiting the various sites. After all of the touring, they'd have three days to visit with the old man—*if* they could even find him.

Mark sat back and let out a sigh. He needed to buy some clothes for the trip. He hadn't bought anything new in ages. His closet was full of business attire. He needed to get some sporty outfits, things people wear while vacationing, maybe a couple of polo shirts and a white sport coat for evenings out.

Evenings out. That meant he and Julie could end up walking the streets together after sundown. They'd find a candlelit restaurant with soft music and good food. They might share a bottle of wine. Or maybe they could stroll along the waterfront and watch the boats come in. Or they could...

Mark puffed out an exasperated sigh. What was he thinking? He had to stop this daydreaming and get serious about the work ahead of him. Still reprimanding himself, he left for the mall with a little less enthusiasm. The trip to the mall reminded him of Katie. It was her favorite stomping ground. He should call her, but he didn't want to get into an argument right now.

Somehow that little blonde school teacher had become his steady girlfriend, but he truthfully didn't know how that had happened. All he knew was, he'd met Katie the previous summer while they were counselors at a youth retreat. The girl's platinum blonde hair and sky-blue eyes had caught his attention from across the cafeteria. Then, he kept running into her in various places—on the soccer field, in the art room, during the kids' music program. Their meetings occurred so often, he began to think they were not a coincidence. By the time camp ended, they'd made plans to go out for dinner. But, he couldn't recall if he asked Katie out, or if she asked him. Then Katie changed her church affiliation and she started attending his church. She got involved in his ministry providing food and clothing to the poor. She joined an evening Bible study at his best friend's house. She was always there. In his face. Smiling.

At first Mark found Katie's attentions flattering. It had been a long time since a beautiful girl had looked at him the way she did. But their relationship had become increasingly claustrophobic. Katie had started asking questions. "Where were you last night?" "Why didn't you call?" "What's the matter?" "Is anything wrong?"

After three weeks of it, Mark told her to stop calling him during work hours. Katie took the reprimand hard. She collapsed in a heap of tears and apologies. Mark didn't know how to handle such a display of emotion. He'd never seen anyone fall apart the way she did.

Worse yet, Mark could kick himself for having told Katie about Julie. Though he insisted their relationship had ended, Katie didn't believe him, probably for good reason. He still wore his heart on his sleeve, as they say, and any mention of Julie's name had turned him into a grieving widower. His friend Greg told him more than once he looked like a heartsick puppy dog. Now he needed to tell Katie about this upcoming trip. And he had to do it soon.

As he left the mall, he phoned Katie and asked if she'd like to go to Angelo's for dinner. It wasn't until he walked through the front door that he realized he had taken her to Julie's favorite restaurant.

As he and Katie followed the hostess to their table, Mark gave a quick glance around the seating area.

Julie wasn't there.

Without having to look at the menu, Mark ordered chicken parmesan and spaghetti. No surprise, Katie chose the same. *Why can't she be more independent,* he thought. *Like Julie?*

He quickly berated himself. Katie was his girlfriend, not Julie. They were two different people. He needed to accept Katie for who she was and stop trying to turn her into a clone of someone else.

Yet, Mark had real concerns about how Katie would react when he told her about the trip. He checked out the other tables. In the booth directly behind them sat a family of five, including three little ones who made enough noise to drown out a wild elephant stampede. Across the aisle, a young couple were so engrossed in each other, they wouldn't notice even if Katie doused him with spaghetti and screamed at the top of her lungs.

Mark took a deep breath. He had to remain nonchalant. "Hey, Katie, do you believe it? Melanie gave me the most awesome assignment yesterday."

Katie grabbed a roll from the basket on the table. A lock of hair slipped over her left eye. She brushed it back. The movement distracted Mark for a moment. He blinked away the diversion.

"It looks like I'm going on a trip," he said. "To Ephesus and Patmos."

Katie tilted her head and smiled. "Where on earth are Ephesus and Patmos?"

A sarcastic remark caught in his throat. He swallowed it. "Well," he said with as much patience as he could muster. Ephesus is in Turkey, and Patmos is a Greek island in the Aegean Sea."

"Oh," Katie said. "Really far away, huh?"

"Yes, really far away. Like the other side of the world."

"Sounds fun," Katie said. Her face lit up. "Can you take a friend along? I'll be off for the summer."

Mark scratched his forehead. This wasn't going to be easy. "It's a business trip, honey. I'll be doing a lot of research. Archaeology mostly. And history. Boring stuff. And, I'll be searching for an old man who's supposed to be living on Patmos."

"An old man?" Katie laughed, and her blue eyes sparkled.

Okay. She's in a good mood. It's the perfect time to spill the rest of the story.

At that moment, the server set their plates in front of them and offered a shower of parmesan. Katie nodded and raised her hand when she was satisfied. Mark asked for half of the block of cheese, which got the server laughing. When she walked away, Katie stared after her, and Mark was certain her cool blue eyes had turned an icy green.

The aroma of hot tomato sauce drew Mark's attention to his meal. He cut a piece of chicken and was about to lift it to his mouth when he looked up and caught Katie gazing at him from across the table, a quizzical expression on her face.

"Why do you need to find an old man?" Katie asked, frowning.

Mark set down his fork. "Well, there's a rumor he might be John the apostle, alive and well." He started to pick up his fork, but hesitated.

36

Katie's brows had knit together but her smile remained on her lips. "That's absurd," she said. "It seems like a waste of time, doesn't it?"

Mark shrugged. "Kind of. I'm more interested in the educational aspect of the trip. I want to gather enough data to apply for a $200,000 grant for the college. It doesn't matter to me whether I find the old guy or not. The information I collect on this trip will be invaluable. And, if, by some miracle, John is alive, that's frosting on the cake."

Katie nodded like she understood. Mark twirled spaghetti onto his fork and raised the ball of noodles, but he froze without taking a bite. Katie had leaned toward him, her brow creased, the sides of her mouth turned down in an unattractive frown.

"There's more, isn't there?" she pressed.

Mark nodded. His eyes followed the strands of spaghetti as they slipped off his fork and back onto his plate. He looked nervously at Katie. She stared back at him, the blue of her eyes floating in tears.

Mark's tongue felt like it had doubled in size. Still, he needed to get this over with. "You see, Katie—um—the Daily Press is sending a reporter with me."

Tears oozed out and trickled down Katie's cheeks. She choked out the name. "Julie?"

Mark nodded. He reached for Katie's hand. She pulled it back.

"It's work, honey. Just work," he lied.

Mark picked up his napkin and blotted away her tears. "There's no need to be concerned," he said, his voice tender, though a surge of guilt rose within him.

He had just told Katie another lie. No need to be

concerned? When all he could think about was seeing Julie again? What should he say? *"Oh yeah, Katie, I can't wait to see my lost love. I still care for her, and I want to dump you and start dating her again."*

In truth, he didn't know if Julie even thought about him after all this time. She hadn't called him to discuss their trip. But neither had he called her.

"Julie—I mean, Katie, please..."

With that, Katie reached for her purse, slid out of the booth, and, without a backward glance, she hurried out of the restaurant. Mark tossed a couple of twenties on the table, woefully aware that he had left a humongous tip and he hadn't taken a single bite of his food. He rushed outside where he found Katie weeping under a streetlamp.

He helped her into his car. Except for her muffled sobs, they drove in silence to her parents' home, where she'd been living since she graduated from college. Mark was at a loss for words. This time, instead of going inside the house to visit with her folks, like he usually did at the end of their dates, he planted a kiss on her forehead and mumbled a pathetic goodbye. Katie turned her face away, fumbled with the lock, and hurried inside.

By the time Mark reached his apartment, his mind had segued back onto his upcoming trip. And Julie—her fiery red hair and turned-up nose. Her impish smile and perpetually flushed cheeks. The idea of seeing her again, of spending a whole week with her, got his head spinning.

He dumped his new shirts on his bed. One-by-one, he checked the color of each shirt against his tanned skin. A couple of blue ones set off his eyes. He selected eight for the trip. Satisfied, he headed into the kitchen and grabbed a bag of chocolate chip cookies and a glass of milk. Then, he returned to the bedroom to sort through the brochures.

At midnight, Mark shoved aside the piles of clothing, research materials, books and Bibles—and cookie crumbs. Then he fell into bed and was asleep before he could utter one word of prayer.

5

JULIE

Julie could hardly believe Peter Pike's response when she called him for an interview.

"Yes, dahlin'. Just come on over at one o'clock and we'll have a nice chat."

That a man of his stature had agreed so quickly to an interview was a bit daunting to Julie. She recalled spotting the boisterous TV evangelist one morning while she was flipping through channels. The pompous, overweight preacher strode across the stage waving a Bible in the air and shouting over the tinkle of a piano in the background. His face turned beet red and the veins protruded on his neck, but he kept on weeping and wailing, until it looked like he might suffer a stroke at any moment. A lighted message appeared on the bottom of the screen along with a phone number and a request for donations. Julie immediately switched channels.

Before heading out to Peter's home on the lake, Julie went to her computer, punched in his name and surfed to his website. His bio described him as an internationally famous nondenominational evangelist, born and raised in Alabama and trained at a seminary in Texas. His wife, Willa Mae, was head of a woman's outreach to homeless children. They had five sons, all of them employed at Peter's ministry. In addition to filming numerous TV specials, Peter and Willa Mae hosted tours to the Holy Land. He had written three inspirational books, an autobiography, and several Bible studies. Through his television show, Peter sold Bibles, music CDs, tapes of his sermons, and healing handkerchiefs. The website also had a three-minute telecast in which Peter told his audience he had seen John the Apostle on Patmos. Other than that brief account, there was no other mention of the encounter.

Julie faced an uphill battle. Somehow, she was going to have to get the whole story out of the evangelist, and then she'd have to decide if there was any truth to it.

At ten minutes to one, she peered through a wrought iron gate at a manicured lawn, a cluster of flowering fruit trees, and a snaking brick drive that led to a two-story mansion with a wall of windows overlooking the lake. A Rolls Royce sat in the driveway. On adjoining acreage, a twin-engine Cessna was tied down at the end of a grass strip.

Such affluence didn't impress Julie. Her work introduced her to a variety of people at all levels of wealth and importance, from grade school janitors to government officials and celebrities. She treated them all with equal respect. Nevertheless, her hand shook when she reached through her car's side window and pushed the button for entry. The iron gate swung open and she drove in. She parked her five-year-old Kia Forte behind Peter's expensive car, then she grabbed her reporter bag and ambled up the steps to the front door.

Seconds after she rang the bell, Peter's wife opened the door and extended a jeweled hand. The woman's pink painted fingernails left a row of hyphens on Julie's palm. With a swirl of her flowered skirts, Willa Mae ushered her into the den.

Julie paused in the doorway and took in the elaborate decor, from the oiled hardwood floor and Turkish rugs to the red velvet lounge chair to the ebony desk in the corner to the massive bookshelves, neatly packed with leather-bound books that looked like they'd never been opened. The hint of a woody incense tickled her nostrils.

Peter sat in an armchair beside a plate glass window. He was drinking what appeared to be lemonade. He dabbed his mouth with a handkerchief and, catching sight of Julie, he gave her a nod, like he was admitting her to his throne room.

"Ah'm afraid Ah can't visit for long," he said with his eyebrows raised in an apologetic arch. "Ah promised to take some friends out on mah boat today, and it's almost time to go."

Julie had a fleeting image of a male version of Mary Beth Simmons. If she closed her eyes and merely listened to their voices, she'd guess they were father and daughter.

Peter grinned and revealed a row of sparkling teeth that obviously had been treated with a whitening process which resulted in an unnatural, chalky appearance.

Julie forced a smile, accepted a glass of lemonade from Peter's wife, and settled in a chair across from her host. She glanced out the window at the silvery lake bordered by a row of willow trees on the far side. Peter's yacht dipped lazily beside the dock.

"Ain't she a beaut?" Peter said, a proud twinkle in his eye.

"You have a wonderful place," Julie said. She'd learned early in her career not to plunge right into an interview but to open the conversation with compliments and pleasantries—anything to break the ice and gain her source's trust. "It's so peaceful here," she sighed.

"Yes Ma'am, Ah come here to regroup. The New York hullabaloo can wear a man down. Travelin' all over the world ain't much easier. But here? Here Ah can kick back and forget about the crowds and the fans and the TV cameras, and just be mahself."

Julie patiently sipped her lemonade while Peter elaborated for another ten minutes about his life on the lake. Sitting this close, she got a better look at the preacher. He was different from what appeared on the TV screen. Without the stage makeup, his skin looked blotchy. He had a ton of freckles, and he wore a toupee that flopped to one side in a whimsical haphazard slant.

When, at last, his monologue ran down, Julie set her glass of lemonade on a coaster and pulled out her notebook and her tape recorder. "Do you mind if I use this?" she said, lifting the device.

Peter nodded. "Just don't ask me nothin' too personal. Ah once had a bad experience with a nosy reporter. Can't go there again."

Julie imagined he was probably talking about Jason Redding, but she decided not to say anything. She turned on the microphone, shifted to a more comfortable position, and poised with her pen in her hand and with no time to waste, got right to the issue.

"As I told you on the phone, Reverend Pike, I'm interested in your recent trip to Patmos. Your website indicates you met a gentleman who has quite a mystique surrounding him, a man who some claim could be John the Apostle. Would you tell me about your experience?"

Peter stared at Julie's recorder and let out a sigh. "You're right, little lady. Ah been to Patmos, and Ah've seen the man you're talkin' about. Ah was in town souvenir shoppin' with mah wife, and this bearded old gentleman ambled into the square. As soon as those dang Patmians caught sight of him, they swarmed over him like a bunch o' ants on a heap o' honey. Ah couldn't get within two feet of the guy."

"What can you tell me about him? For example, what did he look like?"

"Far as his looks go, he's *extremely* old." Peter let out a laugh and spilled some of his lemonade. "He had a beard—neatly groomed though, but with lots of gray strands runnin' through it. His hair was pulled back in a ponytail, and his skin had the look of an old baseball glove that needed oiling. Ah imagine he spent a lot o' time in the sun."

"Did anyone say his name?"

"His name? Let's see now. Ah believe they called him Yannis, or something like that."

"Reverend Pike, did you ever get close enough to speak to the guy?"

Peter wheezed a few times, drew a handkerchief from his pocket, and coughed into it.

"Well, Ah'd like to say we played a round o' golf or went out on a fishin' boat, but I couldn't nail him down. Elusive. That's the word that describes him best. And the townspeople?" Peter shook his head so hard Julie feared his toupee might fly off, but it merely slid slightly to one side. "They knew Ah had come from America," Peter went on. "They wouldn't let me near him. And not one soul would tell me where he lived."

Julie scratched her forehead. She needed to get *something* more substantial out of this guy. Peter Pike was her only source so far.

"Tell me this," she said, flipping to the next page of her notebook. "Why do you think the Patmians are so protective of him?"

Peter shrugged. "Who knows? He shore didn't look like much."

"Okay then, tell me more about his appearance."

"Well, he was about my height, but not as heavy." Peter let out a grunt. "The poor guy dressed like a country bumpkin. I'll tell you what, if he's John the Apostle, then Ah'm Billy Graham."

He let out an irritating snicker that sent a heat wave through Julie. She took a sip of lemonade and tried to relax.

"You said in your telecast that you thought he might be John. If you're not certain, why did you say that?"

Peter cleared his throat and crossed one leg over the other. "Ya gotta understand, dahlin'. At that pahticulah meetin', Ah was speaking to a bunch o' church people who are convinced that John never died. They were dependin' on me to kinda stroke their ideology, so to speak. Ah never said Ah believed all that. 'Course, Ah never said Ah didn't neither. Ah think it's important to please mah followers. Ya know what I mean?"

He stared at Julie's tape recorder and frowned. "That's off the record, girl. Ah hope you don't print any o' that." He looked at his watch. "Well, miss, our little chat has been extremely entertaining, but Ah must be goin' now."

The interview couldn't be over. Julie's mind scrambled for anything that might prolong their visit.

"One more question, please," she said.

Peter acknowledged her request with a nod.

"If John were still alive, Reverend Pike, how might that affect your followers?"

Peter turned away from her. He stared out the wall of windows, past his big white boat, past the lake, and somewhere off into the clouds. Julie followed his gaze. What sort of mystical message did this guy expect to get from up there? When he faced her again, his eyes had a far-away look that had her eying him suspiciously. Did this preacher really communicate with a higher power? Julie doubted it.

"All Ah know is, if John is still alive, Ah'd have to invite him to appear on mah show." He burst out laughing then and spilled lemonade all over his rich Turkish carpet. Julie scowled and turned off her recorder. With a defeated sigh she rose to her feet and extended her hand. After thanking Peter for the interview, she gathered her belongings and left him sitting by the window, still snickering and wiping tears from his eyes.

Peter's wife was nowhere in sight, so Julie let herself out the front door, got in her car, and drove down the brick drive, shaking her head and wondering exactly how much useful information she might have gotten from that mess of an interview. From the moment she rang the doorbell until she left, her visit with Peter Pike had amounted to a measly half-hour, hardly enough time to get what she needed for her story. But she could have stayed all day and it wouldn't have mattered.

As she approached the end of the drive, the wrought iron gate opened and a white van plowed through, cutting her off. On its side in red and black letters was written WPIX TV NEWS. Jason Redding was in the passenger seat. He glared back at her.

The van careened toward the house. Julie's entire body tensed up. So, Andy was right. That snoop had gotten wind of the rumor and had started on the same trail.

There was no stopping Jason Redding. Somehow, Julie had to stay two steps ahead of him.

Dejected, she continued to watch, as the van pulled up to the circular drive. Jason tumbled out and scrambled up the steps to the front door, his over-laden photographer close at his heels. Peter had mentioned a boating date. An afternoon on the water would give Jason all the time he needed to get information out of the preacher. Even before Julie could get started, her story was doomed.

Then, a movement drew her attention to the lake. She couldn't believe her eyes. Peter's yacht was pulling away from the dock, leaving Jason pounding on the Pikes' front door. She allowed herself a smug grin, though it would be short-lived, for Jason wasn't the type to give up easily. In fact, she was going to have to look over her shoulder from now on.

6

JULIE

Wednesday morning came too fast for Julie. She put her clothes in a large suitcase to be checked, and she packed a smaller carry-on bag with her tape recorder, camera, reporter notebooks, pens, grooming items, plus a change of underwear, thanks to Lakisha.

"They could lose your luggage," her girlfriend had warned her. "Make sure you pack the essentials in a bag you can keep with you at all times. You know, a toothbrush, deodorant, clean undies. And don't forget makeup. That way, if you get stranded somewhere without your main luggage, you can still survive."

Julie's cab arrived and she headed for the airport. The closer she got to the sprawling airfield the more restless she became. Each whine of a jet engine and each roar of a takeoff caused her to tense up. She tried to swallow, but her throat had gone dry.

This was silly. She wasn't afraid to fly. She'd been on plenty of vacations. The problem went deeper than mere physical danger. She was experiencing the resurrection of a long-buried stirring of her heart.

I can do this, she told herself. *I can see Mark again and it won't make one bit of difference. I don't have to say anything to him. I don't even have to sit with him. I can request a different seat assignment. Or I can just sleep.*

But sleep for an entire flight? That didn't make sense. The regional hop to New York's JFK, combined with Turkish

Airlines' Atlantic crossing to Izmir amounted to about 20 hours of travel. Who could sleep for 20 hours? The truth was, she couldn't avoid Mark entirely. He was going to be her traveling companion for the next week, and somehow she was going to have to deal with it.

Julie had confirmed her flight on her cell phone the night before. This morning, all she had to do was check her suitcase at the terminal door, pass through security, grab a seat in the gate area, and board the flight. Simple enough.

But by the time she reached security, she was a bundle of nerves. First, she dropped her purse on the floor. When she bent over to pick it up, she collided with the large-bottomed woman standing in front of her. In her hurry to remove her sandals she managed to get one off and limped around on the other. Somehow, she dropped both shoes in the tray before it slipped away from her on the belt.

Everything went downhill when the TSA agent asked her to open her carry-on bag. She fumbled with the zipper and spilled the contents all over the table. Quickly, she gathered up her notebooks, camera, makeup bag, and—horrors—her underwear. Red-faced and with her hair a disheveled mess, she managed to pass through the scanner without further incident.

With both sandals in one hand and juggling her bag and purse with the other, Julie wove through a stream of passengers to the gate area. It wasn't difficult to spot Mark. There he was, leaning against a pole with his ankles crossed and his hands in his pockets, like he didn't have a care in the world. She limped past him without saying a word and grabbed a seat in the waiting area. She put on her sandals, rearranged her baggage, dug inside her purse for a comb, restyled her hair, then pulled out a novel she'd brought along. Busy, busy, busy—anything to keep from making eye contact with Mark.

By some miracle, he left her alone. By the time she boarded the plane, her nerves had settled down. She located their row and slid into the window seat. Mark settled in beside her and rested his elbow on *her* side of the armrest. She cast a disgusted look in his direction, then turned and stared out the window.

For a while she feigned interest in the baggage handlers as they tossed luggage in the bin. The last thing she needed was to get corralled into a conversation with Mark. Hopefully, he'd take the hint and not say a word.

"Are you ready for this?" he said.

She shut her eyes and breathed a sigh. So much for total silence. "Ready for what?" she mumbled without turning from the window.

"You know. The project."

She huffed. "What project? This contrived search for a 2,000-year-old man? Get real."

"You never know..."

Smirking, she turned and faced him. "As far as I'm concerned, we're wasting our time."

He raised his eyebrows and his sky-blue eyes sparkled with mirth. "Then why did you take the assignment?"

"I wouldn't be here at all, except—well—I really didn't have much choice." She lost the smirk and swallowed. "They're laying off at the paper, and I wanted to make sure I kept my job."

Mark nodded with understanding. "Good decision. You won't be sorry you came, Julie. Not only are you in for an amazing tour of ancient ruins, but you might come home with a terrific story to tell."

"I doubt it." She eyed him with skepticism and allowed

the smirk to ease back to her lips. "My main goal now is to discredit that rumor and maybe dig up enough evidence to prove the Bible is nothing but a bunch of fairytales. How do you like those apples, Mark?"

She expected a retort from the guy, but a sadness washed over his face. "That's quite a goal, Julie. You'll be the first person in history to destroy a treasured collection of literature that has become the backbone of the Christian faith. Great plan. But, what if you fail?"

She shrugged. "If I fail, I fail. It won't be the first time."

"Or the last," Mark said with a chuckle.

"So, what is *your* plan?" She said with a sneer. "What earth-shaking agenda brought *you* to this project?"

"Me?" The blue of his eyes darkened. She nearly crumbled under his powerful gaze. "I'll be gathering information for a PowerPoint presentation," he said. "And, I'll put together some classroom materials, plus historical and archaeological data that could help me acquire a sizeable grant for my department." He'd responded in such a formal, professional manner, she almost forgot how he could shrink a girl's heart to the size of an acorn.

She caught her breath and pulled herself together. "But what about the old man? Did you forget why we're doing this in the first place?"

"No, I haven't forgotten."

"Do you really think he exists?"

"Anything's possible," he said, bobbing his head. "I kind of hope he *does* exist. Can you imagine what that could mean? But even if he's a figment of someone's imagination, I'm excited about all the other stuff. How often does a college professor get an opportunity like this?"

Julie shook her head despondently. "This seems like an impossible quest to me."

"What do you mean?"

"Where do we even start? We don't have a name. Or a street address. We're supposed to find this guy on Patmos, but we're going to waste two days of our time stomping around Ephesus. On top of all that, I have to keep one step ahead of Jason Redding. Are you aware of the pressure I'm under?"

Mark's brow creased in that whimsical way that used to make her heart jump. She turned and looked out the window again. When she looked back, Mark was smiling at her.

"You can make fun of me if you want to, Mark, but this is serious. If that bulldog beats me to the story, I could lose my job."

He patted her hand. "I'm here, Julie," he said, his voice soft. "I'm going to do all I can to help you succeed. Even if we don't find the old guy, surely you'll be able to go home with *something*."

For a brief moment, she submitted to Mark's coddling. She'd forgotten how safe and secure he once made her feel. If she'd had a problem at work, he'd wrap his strong arms around her and murmur comforting words in her ear. It didn't matter to her if those words came out of the Bible. Her troubles were gone and she...

She shook off the memory. She didn't need Mark or his biblical spouting. Not anymore.

With a huff she pulled the itinerary out of the side pocket of her carry-on bag. One of the pamphlets had a full-color photo of the library in Ephesus.

"So, we'll be visiting the ruins tomorrow," she said.

"That's right." Mark leaned close and peered over her shoulder.

The scent of his aftershave took her back to their first kiss. She slid away from him, folded the pamphlet, and tucked everything back in her bag. Was this the kind of yo-yoing her heart was in for over the next seven days?

Unable to face him, she fastened her seatbelt and set her eyes on the seatback in front of her.

"If the old man was spotted in Patmos, why do we have to make this side trip?" she said. "Why don't we just go straight to the island and start looking for the guy?"

"Ephesus is an important part of my research," Mark said. He'd raised his voice over the whine of the engines starting up. "Actually, we *both* need background information. How can you write an article about the guy if you don't visit the places where he once walked?"

"What do you mean?"

"Well, according to tradition, John went to Ephesus with Mary, the mother of Jesus. It's said she spent her last days there. Then, of course, there's the old ruins where John is supposed to be buried."

"*Supposed* to be?"

Mark nodded. "Some years ago, an excavation uncovered his tomb in Ephesus. It was empty. The archaeologists assumed John's bones had been moved to another location—Rome maybe. However, none of his relics are in Rome. It seems John—living or dead—has completely disappeared. Meanwhile, the bones of most of the other apostles were divided up and are on display in cathedrals all over Europe. There's a lot to uncover on this trip. Once we land in Turkey, you're gonna have your work cut out for you, Julie. Think you can handle it?"

A flood of heat rushed to her face. She thrust her chin in the air. "You bet I can. With or without you. If you think I need a babysitter, you can guess again, Mark. I'm perfectly capable of finding my own way."

Mark let out a snicker that annoyed her. Then, as if putting an end to their little chat, he pulled an in-flight magazine out of the seat pocket and started flipping through its pages.

They spent the rest of the regional flight in awkward silence. When they landed at JFK, Mark took off. "Follow me," he called over his shoulder. "I know this airport well."

He hurried ahead of her along the maze of corridors. Julie trotted after him, grateful that she had worn slacks and comfortable sandals. Still, she had to do double-time to keep up with Mark's long strides.

Somehow, she managed to keep sight of his broad shoulders and his flock of honey-colored hair. The vision took her back to her best friend's wedding reception two years before. Mark had his back to her then too. She'd watched with amusement as several of Lakisha's single girlfriends gathered around him, their faces turned up like a row of daisies soaking up the sunshine.

Julie kept her distance from the revolting display of flirtation. Suddenly, Mark turned around and looked right at her. It was as if she'd called his name, though she hadn't. She stared into his cool blue eyes, and was unable to turn away. What he did next shocked her. He left the bevy of coquettes and walked toward her. Without a word, he took her hand and swept her onto the dance floor. She could still remember the song—Elvis' hit, "Can't Help Falling in Love." Nor could she ever forget the wonderful yet frightening feel of his arm around her, or the intoxicating scent of Aramis on his jaw, or the sensation that she was about to melt like S'mores over a campfire.

"Hurry up, Julie." Mark's shout jolted her back to the present.

He'd moved farther down the concourse, and she was about to lose him. She cursed the unexpected flood of memories, picked up her pace and caught up with Mark at the gate.

A half-hour later, they boarded a wide-body for the long haul across the Atlantic. The plane was only two-thirds full. To Julie's relief, she and Mark ended up in a three-seat row all to themselves, which meant she could keep an empty seat between them.

She grabbed a pillow and a blanket from the overhead compartment, a signal to Mark that she intended to sleep for at least part of the flight. She checked her watch. Ten a.m. Taking into account the time change, she could expect to arrive in Izmir at about 7 o'clock the next morning. If Julie didn't get some sleep, she'd have to start the day touring Ephesus exhausted and unable to concentrate.

Soon after takeoff, the cabin crew served lunch. Julie took a few bites of a chef's salad, then shoved the plate aside. She wasn't concerned that her weight had dropped to a mere 110 pounds. She was healthy. Flu season came and went and she didn't get sick. In fact, she rarely even caught a cold. What's more, she had enough energy to complete a two-mile jog with Lakisha nearly every morning, followed by a full day at work.

She glanced at Mark in the aisle seat. He was taking huge bites from a ham-and-cheese sandwich. He tore open a bag of potato chips, finished them off, and followed with a long swig of Coke. Julie stifled a chuckle. She had forgotten how that man could put away a large meal yet somehow manage to remain toned and trim.

From the corner of her eye, she continued to watch him

with fascination. Mark pulled the call bell. An exotic, dark-haired flight attendant appeared, like a genie from a bottle. The girl had pulled her hair back in a tight knot, and she wore dark eyeliner, further accentuating the winged slant of her eyes. She leaned close to Mark.

Julie's face grew hot. She clenched her teeth and tried to swallow the green monster that had erupted inside her. One sobering thought ran through her head. *He is not my boyfriend. Not anymore.*

She reached up and turned on her air vent. The stream of air failed to cool the flush in her cheeks.

"Could I get a decaf?" Mark asked the smiling brunette. "With lots of cream and sugar?"

"Of course, whatever you want," the girl said, her accent thick and inviting.

Disgusted, Julie pulled her novel out of her bag. She didn't open it, but gripped it so firmly her fingernails nearly tore a hole in the cover.

Mark had his coffee in less than two minutes. The flight attendant also brought him a huge piece of chocolate cake. She slid it in front of him.

"From first class," she breathed.

Mark smiled and thanked the girl. From where Julie sat, it looked like the two of them were about to become intimately involved. The flight attendant hung around, her dark, beckoning eyes fastened on Mark. To Julie's surprise, he appeared to be more interested in the piece of cake. Without another glance at the flight attendant, he dumped cream and sugar in his coffee, then picked up his fork and dug in. The girl continued to stand beside his seat, like she was waiting for some sort of encouragement. To Julie's delight, it never came.

She looked up the girl, and their eyes met in a silent confrontation. She didn't back down, and the exotic beauty finally stuck her nose in the air and strutted off down the aisle. Though Julie experienced a ripple of satisfaction, she didn't know why. She made up her mind to forget about Mark and that little flirt.

"I like redheads," he said without looking up from his cake.

Fuming, Julie opened her book. She read the same paragraph three times but had no idea what it said.

Mark finished his coffee, and, heaving a long sigh, he reclined his seat and shut his eyes. Julie couldn't tell if he was asleep or merely faking. He had ignored her through the whole meal and now he was taking a nap. Her blood began to boil. *She* was the one who had planned to sleep so she could avoid *him*. He'd cut off their conversation twice, and now he sat there, like he didn't have a care in the world.

She jammed her book in the seat pocket and reclined her own seat. Still seething, she turned her back on Mark, pulled down the window shade, plumped her pillow, and snuggled beneath her blanket.

She must have drifted off, because the next thing, she awakened to the sound of Mark's laughter. He had donned a headset and was watching an in-flight movie, a Will Farrell farce. *Great!*

She tossed off her blanket. "I need to stretch my legs. Let me get out," she said, and she squeezed past Mark into the aisle. She smoothed the wrinkles out of her slacks, tucked in her blouse, and walked toward the front of the coach section. Aside from a couple with two extremely active children and a few businessmen who were scrolling through data on their laptop computers, most of the passengers were watching a movie or had fallen asleep.

She reached the bulkhead and was about to turn around when she noticed a distinguished looking gentleman sitting alone in the center of a three-seat row. His suit jacket lay on the window seat, and he'd loosened his tie. Patches of graying hair grew from his temples. He wore wire-rimmed glasses, and he held an open book. Julie stooped to read the title, *Heaven is for Real.* She suppressed a snicker. The man made eye contact, smiled, and nodded toward the vacant aisle seat.

"Will you join me?" he said.

Julie looked back down the aisle toward the rear of the plane. Most of the passengers had settled down and were turning off their reading lights. Shades had been drawn. Except for the hum of the plane's engines, there wasn't a hint of activity. Even the children had settled down.

The clink of glassware drew Julie's attention to a nearby galley. A male flight attendant was wiping down the counter and latching cupboard doors shut. Then he settled onto the jump seat with a magazine. As long as he remained there, she felt safe. She turned and searched the older man's face. Once again, he smiled and gestured toward the empty seat.

"It's gonna be a long flight," he said. "We can at least have a chat."

Maybe it was the kindness in his eyes. Or the reassuring tone in his voice. Or perhaps it was her own need to talk to someone, anyone except Mark, even a complete stranger. She hesitated for only a second.

7

MARK

When the in-flight movie ended, Mark removed his headset and poked his head in the aisle. Julie had vanished. He shrugged. *Oh well. Where can she go at 35,000 feet?*

He grabbed Julie's pillow and blanket and made himself as comfortable as he could in the cramped airline seat. But, he couldn't sleep and he knew why.

He hadn't seen Julie for an entire year. Seeing her at the airport that morning had sent him into a tailspin. The truth was, he hadn't gotten over her. He let out a chuckle. She looked as if she'd been dragged into the terminal by a cat with distemper. She limped barefooted into the gate area, her arms loaded down with half-open bags that were regurgitating some of her personal items. Her hair was in disarray, and her green eyes flashed with such fury, he didn't dare approach her.

Despite her bedraggled appearance, seeing her again had caused his heart to swell. He'd expected the trip might help him decide once and for all if he could move on. Now he knew. He couldn't. Part of him still wanted to reconnect with Julie. But so far, she'd given him no encouragement. In fact, she was as cold as an icicle in Siberia.

Suddenly, a pretty blonde entered his thoughts and he winced. He hadn't been fair to Katie. He shouldn't have let her believe they could be more than friends. Sure, in the beginning she filled the void Julie had left open—or at least tried to fill it. But, that empty place was shaped like a five-foot, five-inch redhead. At five-foot, two, Katie didn't fit the mold. But it wasn't only about size and shape. What Katie lacked most of all was the fiery independence he saw in Julie. She had a self-sufficient, unyielding attitude that could ignite a blaze in him. In comparison, Katie never challenged him. She'd make a fine wife for a politician or a business executive who merely needed a beautiful woman to host his cocktail parties. Mark needed more than that in a mate. He needed Julie.

He could thank Melanie Stevens for arranging this collaboration. His boss was fully aware of Mark's heartache. When he and Julie split up, Melanie helped him refocus by giving him extra work at the college. She even allowed him to spill his pain over lunch one day.

What a shame if he didn't at least try to win Julie's heart again. After all, Melanie could have sent any one of her professors on this trip. And calling Andy at the paper? That was genius. Mark could see from the get-go what his boss was trying to do. She was playing matchmaker. He didn't resent her for it. On the contrary, he adored her.

If only he could relive the last couple of years. That day at Greg and Lakisha's wedding, though he could have had his pick of Lakisha's friends, he'd only had eyes for Julie. Unlike the others, she'd kept her distance. She didn't pursue him. He pursued her. *He* asked her to dance. *He* invited her out to dinner. *He* made the phone calls.

His father had drummed it in his head from the day he turned 15. "The man does the chasing. The girl does the catching," he'd said with a laugh.

At the time, such advice sounded old-fashioned, but when

Mark became inundated with phone calls from hopeful debutants, the thrill of being pursued wore off fast. He'd turned away from the beauties who flocked around him at the wedding and he chased after the only girl who appeared to have no interest in him at all.

Perhaps that was the reason Mark was drawn to Julie. But, it had to be more than that, for he soon learned they were equals intellectually and she could give him as good an argument as anyone on his college debate team.

He loved the way she approached new ideas by first digging for the truth, a throwback, he assumed, from her training as an investigative reporter. He admired her tenacity, the way she persisted whenever she faced a challenge. She even debated at length with his father when he came up from Florida to visit them. Mark sat nervously by as they bantered back-and-forth about the demise of the Everglades, with Julie taking the view of progress and his father vying on the side of ecology. When his dad left, the old man gave Julie a bear hug and invited her to continue their discussion on his own turf. Then, he winked at Mark, a sign he approved of his choice.

The trip to Florida never happened. Two weeks later, Julie broke off the relationship. Looking back, he would do a lot of things differently if he had another chance. Mainly, he wouldn't press Julie to attend church with him like he did before. She came up with a different excuse every time. Hopefully, he'd learned enough common sense from his evangelistic classes to be able to reach someone like her.

Don't get in someone's face. Don't back people in a corner. Earn their trust first. Tell them what God has done for you. Then invite them to church. But don't keep pushing. Most people will run when they see you coming.

Isn't that what Julie had done? In her own way, she ran from him every time he asked her to pray with him, every time he pushed her to go to church. Until, finally, she shut the door on their relationship and refused to open it again. The breakup happened only a few days after he introduced Julie to his favorite spot, a country retreat on a hillside, 20 minutes out of town.

He had discovered the little slice of heaven years before when he went there as a Boy Scout leader chaperoning young kids on an overnight campout. He'd stood on the edge of the hill and looked out over a brilliant rolling tapestry. Rivers and lakes dotted the landscape, their diverse shapes like pieces of glass reflecting the early morning sunlight. At the time, the setting was too romantic for his reason for being there with a bunch of rowdy boys. But he made a silent vow to go back there one day with someone special.

That day finally came when he took Julie there one morning at the break of dawn. During the drive, his heart throbbed with joy as he anticipated sharing his favorite spot with her. Like a knight in shining armor, he leaped from the imaginary saddle and trotted around the front of his Nissan steed to open her door. He extended his hand and didn't let go until they stood side-by-side at the edge of the rise. He couldn't have painted a better scene. The early morning sun cast golden beams on a blanket of wildflowers tumbling down the hillside. A mosaic of grassy patches and swaths of moss stretched out at the bottom. In the distance a crystalline mist rose from the lake and river. Julie sighed with delight.

Mark had already decided the magical setting would be the perfect spot for a marriage proposal. Perhaps a picnic with a basket of fried chicken, fresh fruit, and a bottle of wine. A tiny velvet box in his shirt pocket. And Julie. Only Julie.

One thing was certain, he had never taken any other girl there and he never intended to. Not even Katie.

He could have proposed to Julie that morning. He even had the ring in his pocket. Intuitively, he held off. Even as they stood looking out at his Shangri-La, she stiffened, as if she knew what he was about to ask. She spent a few minutes by his side, then she yanked her hand away and hurried back to the car. The slam of the car door told Mark all he needed to know.

He shouldn't have been surprised. Julie had been pulling away from him for weeks. In fact, as he looked back over their year together, it was obvious to him that she'd never made a commitment to the relationship. He was the one who had envisioned a future for them. She'd never mentioned it.

The truth was, she knew everything about him, and he knew almost nothing about her. Except for a few times when she talked about her sister Rita, she refused to share anything about her home life. Her parents were alive. That much he knew. But, aside from where they lived, she never mentioned them. Her conversations pretty much centered around work and plans that didn't include having a man in her life. Though Mark admired her strong sense of independence, he longed for her to reach out to him for comfort and security. It never happened.

Their relationship died the night he pressed her to open up about her faith. She admitted she'd been raised in the church and had left six years ago, adding that she had no interest in going back.

"I used to believe like you do, Mark, but now I know better," she'd said, like she was talking to a teenager. "Why don't you find a nice Christian girl, someone who can share your passion for such things? I don't think I ever can—in fact, I'm certain of it."

Pastor Joe had warned him not to be unequally yoked with an unbeliever. Yet, she'd once believed, and he'd hoped that maybe, at some point, he might be able to draw her back to her faith again, if given half the chance.

The final blow came on a Saturday night while they were leaving a movie theater. Mark pressed Julie to talk about her past. Something had nearly destroyed her, and he was determined to help.

"You can tell me anything," he said. "I won't judge you, Julie. Please, won't you let me in?"

"I've told you before, Mark. There's nothing to tell."

"We've been dating for over a year. You know everything about *me*, but I don't know anything about your past."

"Oh, really?" She placed her hands on her hips and lifted her chin. "Like what?"

"Like, why did you leave your hometown? Why have you never gone back? Most of all, who hurt you, Julie? Who chased you away from God?"

She shook her head with a violence he'd never seen in her before. Tears flew from her eyes.

"I don't want to talk about it, Mark. I want to forget the past. What's more, I don't need your God, and I don't need your religion. If you can't handle that, then maybe I'm not the girl for you."

They stood facing each other in a bitter impasse outside the theater. It started to rain. Mark pulled his car keys out of his pocket.

"Come on, I'll take you home," he said softly. He reached for her arm.

She jerked back from him and hailed an approaching cab.

As the cab pulled up to the curb, she spun around and faced him, her cheeks were flushed and streaked with a mix of rain and tears.

"Leave—me—alone." She was sobbing audibly. "Don't call me, ever again."

Without looking back she stepped inside the cab and rode away.

Stunned, Mark stood on the curb and stared after the yellow vehicle until it disappeared in a veil of rain. The downpour soaked him through. He reached up and felt his cheek. The moisture on his face wasn't only from the rain. It had come from his own eyes.

Such memories should have discouraged him. Now he was traveling to a far-off land with the only woman he'd ever loved—a woman who wanted nothing to do with him.

But, Mark didn't know the meaning of the word "quit." Ideas raced through his mind. Of the two of them, he was the only one who had a knowledge of that distant land and the history behind the apostle. He was in charge. He could call the shots, but he'd have to do so carefully. This could be his last chance to win Julie. Whatever transpired over the next seven days would decide their future, whether they might be together again or separated forever.

With such thoughts tumbling around in his head, Mark rolled to his other side, punched Julie's pillow, and lay his head against its crumpled form. Still, no sleep came. He sensed Julie was hovering nearby—in the aisle—waiting to get into her seat. He opened his eyes wider. It wasn't Julie at all. It was the flight attendant. She looked different. The girl had let her hair down. It fell in curvy, dark folds around her face.

She was smiling at him. "What's the matter, sleepy-head? Having a rough night?" Her voice was thick and seductive.

He sat upright and shed the blanket. A surge of warmth flowed to his face. He wasn't used to waking up to a beautiful girl standing so close he could feel her breath on his cheek. His co-worker Jimmy sometimes bragged about his conquests. But Mark had tried diligently to remain true to his faith.

"It must be the time change," he said. "Back home, it's still only..." He glanced at his watch. "four o'clock in the afternoon."

A ripple of laughter escaped from her lips. They were painted a bright red. "I know the feeling," she said, softly. "These overseas flights really do me in. By the time I get home to my apartment, my inner clock has turned upside-down. I'm tired, but I can't sleep. And so, I either pace the floor or I crash on the sofa with an old movie. All by myself."

He recognized what she was doing. She was telling him she lived alone, that she didn't have a husband, maybe no boyfriend either, although that was hard to believe.

He ran a hand through his hair, embarrassed to find it a tangled mess. He smoothed the strands into place, his eyes on the exotic beauty hovering so close he could smell the floral scent on her neck.

"Mind if I join you?" she whispered.

He suddenly felt uncomfortable. It was a familiar sensation, one that surfaced whenever a woman came on too strong. He imagined a cat slinking toward him, low to the ground, ready to lunge on her unsuspecting prey.

"Uh—my friend should be back soon." He patted Julie's empty seat. "I think she went to the bathroom."

The beauty grinned and shook her head. "She won't be back for quite a while. She's sitting with a gentleman in the first row, and it seems they've struck up a pretty intense tête-à-tête."

Mark's heart collapsed in a heap. A swell of envy rose up within him. Julie, conversing with another man? Who was he? What was she doing? Was she trying to make him jealous? The temptation to fight fire with fire was overwhelming. He stared into the hopeful face of the flight attendant. He could easily scoot over to the middle seat and make room for her to sit on the aisle beside him.

But he didn't care for her greasy red lipstick or the heavy liner that framed her eyes. Not to mention her forwardness. How many men had succumbed to her advances? These were long flights across the Atlantic. Surely, he wasn't the first guy who caught her attention. Most of all, she wasn't Julie.

"Sorry," he said. "I'm gonna try to get some sleep."

Her smile faded. "Your loss," she said, raising an eyebrow.

Mark didn't wait for the girl to walk away. He turned his back on her and pulled the blanket over his shoulder. He gazed at Julie's empty seat. She was somewhere in the cabin, chatting with some faceless man. Jealousy roiled around inside his brain. How could he sleep? Then, he recalled a bedtime practice his mother had taught him when he was a little boy. It worked faster than counting sheep.

"Relax," his mom had told him. "Inhale deeply, then let it out slow, and let your whole body go limp, first your neck, then your arms, then your legs, right down to your itsy-bitsy toes."

He rehearsed her instructions now, in the darkened cabin, with the shade drawn and the brilliance of the afternoon sun shut out. He could melt into the seat, no longer a mere wedge of discomfort, suddenly transformed into the bed of a little boy.

His mother's words of advice came back, pulling him away from the world and into a place of peace and relaxation.

"Finally," she'd whispered. "Recite the verse of Scripture you learned in Sunday school last week. And then repeat some of the other verses you've committed to memory. You'll be asleep in no time."

The nightly recitations had worked, and they'd stayed with Mark over the years. Even now, at 35,000 feet above a vast body of water, he could draw on his favorite verses, not only as a pathway to sleep, but also as words of comfort for his troubled heart. His mother couldn't have known back then how valuable her advice would be more than two decades later.

8

JULIE

Julie accepted the aisle seat next to the stranger, but she perched on the edge, ready to bolt if necessary. She didn't want to go back to her own row, didn't want to spend any more time with Mark than she had to. Yet, she was hungry for someone to talk to.

She'd learned the man's name. Doctor Martin Balser. He told her he was a family counselor and that he was on his way to a symposium in Izmir.

"What about you? Are you on vacation?" he asked and raised his eyebrows in that quizzical manner people do when they expect a positive answer.

Julie shook her head. "I wish I were, but I'm not. My name is Julie Peters. I'm a newspaper reporter traveling on assignment."

"Ah, a reporter." The doctor smiled and nodded. "Let me see now." He tilted his head and eyed her with interest. "You're inquisitive, alert to your surroundings, and a perfectionist, maybe to the point of obsession. You ask many questions but offer few answers, unless provoked to do so. And you like to size people up before you begin your interview."

Julie smiled. With one quick analysis, the doctor had nailed both her profession and her personality. She slid back in her seat and began to relax. Then, curiosity got the best of her, and she nodded toward the book in his hand.

"You don't believe that stuff, do you?" She gave a little snicker. "That title, *Heaven is for Real*—are you serious?"

69

Balser lowered the book to his lap and turned off his reading light. "It's actually quite interesting," he said. "It's supposed to be a true account about a little boy who died and went to heaven. He came back with all kinds of amazing stories about people he'd met there—including his grandfather and his unborn sister."

Julie eyed him with disbelief. "I don't know. Sounds a little incredible to me. You're an educated man. Why would you be interested in something so ridiculous?"

Balser chuckled. "It's not so ridiculous. I've been reading a pile of books on the subject, including *Life After Death* and *90 Minutes in Heaven*, plus a whole slew of writings by Elisabeth Kubler-Ross."

Julie grunted. "I've heard of her. She died several years ago, didn't she? Tell me, did *she* ever come back to life?"

"Not to my knowledge," he said, chuckling.

Julie tilted her head. "I've never known anyone who came back from the dead, have you?"

"No, I'm afraid I haven't."

"Well, I need proof." She gazed into his hazel eyes that darkened whenever he laughed.

"You need proof?" He laughed again, and his eyes turned almost gray. "There's that reporter again. Just the facts, right?"

Julie ignored the comment. "Let me get this straight." She turned her body slightly toward him and narrowed her eyes. "You're going to this symposium, and you'll probably take one side of a debate. You'll contend that people can come back from death and talk about heaven and their departed loved ones. And some of your colleagues will argue a different view. What will that accomplish?"

"Not much, I'm afraid," he said, his tone serious. He

70

removed his glasses. "I'm actually looking at both sides of the issue. In addition to those books I just mentioned, I've read quite a few contradictory materials, as well. There's the Buddhist view of nirvana—that final state that's supposed to bring freedom from suffering. Then, there's the Hindu belief in reincarnation. And, of course, we have the atheistic argument—no God, no heaven, no salvation at all—only the end of existence. And let's not forget the agnostic person who needs proof."

She looked him in the eye. "Can anyone *really* prove there's a God or a heaven?"

The man shrugged. "That's one of the topics we'll be discussing at the symposium. I doubt we'll come up with a definite answer, but it'll be fun tossing theories around."

"And which theory will *you* push on your audience?"

He gave her a platonic smile. "I'll let my audience make up their own minds. This symposium is drawing some of the greatest theological minds in the world. They work in many different fields of medicine and science, and they come from a vast diversity of religious backgrounds. I admit, I'm one of the least of them. But, we'll learn from each other. Perhaps, depending on what is shared, we'll come away with a greater understanding of what happens to the dying."

"What does all that have to do with psychiatry? Don't you have enough to do trying to fix the living?"

Doctor Balser smiled. "To be honest, dying has everything to do with the living. Think about it, Julie. The way people view death influences the way they live their lives. And, in an interesting reversal, the way people view life often shapes the way they approach death. So you see, there exists a strong bond between the two—life and death."

71

Julie grunted. "I suppose I'm one of those agnostic people. Like you said, I need proof."

Balser's expression turned to curiosity. "That's a sad place to be, Julie. Like a true agnostic, you'll seek answers you're not willing to receive. You'll always come up with some sort of argument."

She shrugged. "I used to believe in God and Jesus and even life after death. I read my Bible and said prayers every night, and I enjoyed going to church and interacting with people of faith. I've changed."

He frowned. "What caused you to run from your faith?"

Julie shook her head. She hadn't opened up to anyone in years. So why should she now? But this man was a stranger. She'd never see him again. And he was a family counselor. He'd been trained to deal with such tough issues. Hopefully, he'd be better at it than the one her parents had sent her to.

She took a deep, shuddering breath. "I didn't run away. I was *chased* away," she said. "By a bunch of pious hypocrites."

He raised his eyebrows. "Go on."

She looked down at her hands, clasped tightly on her lap. The trauma from the past came back with full force and drove a flood of tears to her eyes.

"It's okay, Julie," The doctor said, his voice tender.

Julie glanced at the flight attendant, still on the jump seat. His nose was buried in the magazine.

"Something happened to me six years ago," she said, keeping her voice low. "A man in my church assaulted me. He was one of the deacons." She looked into Balser's eyes. "I was 17."

His eyebrows came together and he breathed a troubled sigh. "My Lord, child, did you report the incident?"

Julie nodded. "I did, but no one believed me. Why should

they? He was a pillar in the community, a married man with a teenage son, and I was a rebellious teenager."

Doctor Balser bristled. "He should have been punished. And you—you should have received support from your family, and your church. Did no one come to your defense?"

Tears ran down Julie's face. Balser grabbed his suit jacket from the seat by the window, pulled a handkerchief from the breast pocket, and handed it to her. She took a moment to mop her face.

"Except for my sister Rita, no one believed me," she continued. "Least of all my parents. That man was a friend of the family, a business associate of my father's. His wife served on committees with my mother. The whole church rallied behind him."

"So, you were shunned and they allowed a letch to run free."

She nodded. "Two years ago, Rita phoned me and said my attacker had been caught with another girl. She sent me the newspaper clippings. It was almost an identical scenario. There'd been a youth breakfast. The creep had stayed behind to clean up. A teenage girl was helping him. The report said the pastor had returned to the church to retrieve a notebook he'd left behind, and he found the two of them in the back of the fellowship hall. Of course, he immediately called the police, and that monster was arrested."

Julie wiped away more tears. "During his trial, several more girls came forward with similar stories. One of them was only 13."

She blew her nose. "He's been in prison ever since, and I hope they threw away the key."

"What about *you*, Julie? Did you go to the trial? Did you speak up and vindicate yourself?"

"No, I did not. When I left that place I made up my mind to never go back. At least the truth was out and he finally had to pay. As for me, I simply moved on. I have a career. I can take care of myself. If I learned anything from that experience it's that I don't need anyone."

Balser stroked his chin as though deep in thought. "That's a sad place to be," he said at last. "Are you traveling alone?"

She let out a sarcastic laugh. "No, I'm traveling with a man who's been a thorn in my side."

The doctor's face lit up with interest. "Tell me about him."

"We have different views about religion. He's one of those dyed-in-the-wool Christians."

"I see. And, this difference has created a rift between you?"

Julie smirked. "We dated for a while some time ago. He kept trying to push his faith on me. I wanted him to stop. He didn't, so I broke up with him."

Balser's face twisted with amusement. "And, you're back to dating again?"

"No, no, no," she scowled. "Somehow, we ended up on the same assignment. Mark's a college professor. His school is paying for the trip, and I was assigned to accompany him. It was a big coincidence, that's all."

"So, you had nothing to do with arranging this collaboration?"

"No. Believe me, Doctor Balser, this is temporary. I merely have to get through the next seven days and I'll be rid of him again. Like I said, it's a coincidence that we've been thrown back together."

"You know, Julie, I don't believe in coincidences. You being 'thrown back together,' as you put it, may not be a coincidence at all. It could be fate. Or God."

Julie forced a laugh. "Right."

Balser tapped the book in his hand. "When I read stories like this one, I can't help but wonder if maybe a stronger power is working on behalf of us all, opening and shutting doors, planting opportunities, solving problems that we're too ignorant or too stubborn to solve ourselves. Wouldn't you agree that coincidences sometimes have a master planner behind them?"

A retort lodged in Julie's throat but she said nothing.

He eyed her with curiosity. "What is this special assignment the two of you are on?"

She cast an embarrassed sideways glance at him. "Don't laugh," she said.

"I won't," he promised, though his eyes already were crinkling at the corners.

She blurted out what she herself considered to be absurd. "The two of us are going to Ephesus and Patmos to search for John the Apostle."

He leaned back. "You mean his grave, don't you?"

"No. I mean John."

Balser had an amused twinkle in his eye. "You're serious?"

Julie nodded. "I'm afraid so. Listen, this wasn't my idea." She tilted her head. "*Now* what do you think about people coming back from death—or maybe never dying at all?"

Balser shrugged. "I have lived long enough to know a person can't declare anything unequivocally. With God, all things are possible. I certainly will want to know the outcome of your search."

Julie glanced out the window. The sky had turned gray. Doctor Balser's face was shrouded in darkness. He grabbed his suit jacket, pulled a business card from the breast pocket, and pressed it in her hand.

She read the card. "Wait a minute. This says *Pastor* Martin Balser. You said you were a family counselor."

"I am. I didn't lie to you. In addition to running a counseling center I serve as an associate pastor at a non-denominational church."

Julie sat up straight. "Are you telling me I've been spilling my guts to a *minister?*"

"No. You simply shared your deepest pain with someone who cared to listen."

She looked again at his business card. "Your address—it's only a half-hour away from where I live."

"That's terrific. Listen, Julie. I'd be happy to counsel you further, if you want me to."

She shook her head. "I don't know..."

"Look, hang onto my card. You might change your mind."

She rose to leave, his business card still in her hand. Doctor Balser put on his glasses and turned on his reading light. Without another word, he returned to his book.

Julie retreated to the back of the cabin where she found Mark asleep under *her* blanket. Scowling, she opened the overhead compartment and pulled out another blanket and a pillow. Then she slipped past Mark and settled in her seat by the window. After tucking Doctor Balser's card in the side pocket of her carry-on bag, she lay back and drew the blanket up to her chin. Sleep didn't come. Her conversation with Doctor Balser was roiling around in her head.

She thought about what the man had said about there being no coincidences. Could it be that she really *was* meant to be with Mark? She couldn't deny the feelings she had for him. What if she gave him another chance? If things didn't work out, she could always walk away again.

$\mathcal{9}$

EPHESUS

J ulie woke to a flurry of window shades being raised, a
brightening of the cabin, and an announcement that breakfast service was about to begin.

She ate a scrambled egg and half of a bagel, plus a small
cup of orange juice. No surprise, Mark cleaned his plate and
then asked if he could have her bacon and the other half of
her bagel. A male flight attendant brought his coffee. There
was no sign of the exotic female, which perplexed Julie. The
girl had shown a definite interest in Mark earlier in the flight.
Now she had disappeared.

Julie didn't feel like getting into a conversation with Mark.
He kept eying her, like he wanted to say something, but he
didn't open his mouth except to stuff food into it. She avoided
his gaze. To pass the time, she pulled her novel out of the seat
pocket and this time she actually read a couple of chapters.

About an hour later, the captain announced they'd be
landing in 20 minutes. His Turkish accent had a musical,
staccato sound. "It's a nice morning in Izmir. Temperature
is 82 degrees. The area is well past the rainy season, so you
should have pleasant weather during your stay."

Mark left his seat. Julie grabbed her grooming pouch,
stepped out in the aisle, and headed for the bathroom. A
half-dozen people had already formed a line there. She hoped
she'd have enough time to freshen up before they landed.

When she got back to her seat, Mark was already seated

there, looking wide awake and refreshed, his blue eyes reflecting the exact color of his shirt. Julie tried to ignore the flutter in her chest. She slid into the window seat and gazed out the window.

The azure sea passed beneath the plane. Then came a scattering of islands, and up ahead, the Turkish coastline and the Bay of Izmir with its string of sandy beaches and whitewashed hotels. The only thing Julie knew about Izmir was what she had pulled up on the internet. She'd read that it was one of the oldest cities in the Mediterranean area and was once known as Smyrna, one of the seven churches John addressed in the book of Revelation.

They flew over a tapestry of greenery and dusty terrain. Ahead was the Izmir Adnan Menderes International Airport. Their plane banked for the final approach, then swept in for a smooth landing. Some of the passengers broke into applause.

A surge of excitement rippled through Julie. She was about to visit an unfamiliar, exotic land, far from home and certainly far from anything she had ever imagined.

When they arrived at the gate, she gathered her belongings and followed Mark into the aisle. Craning her neck, she caught sight of Doctor Balser juggling his briefcase while assisting an elderly woman with her bag. She was right about the guy. He really did care about others. After their little chat, a huge weight had been lifted from her shoulders. She considered his business card, tucked away in her bag. Perhaps she should call him later, and make an appointment.

"We'll play it by ear," Mark said, as they deplaned. Like before, he'd already assumed leadership. It didn't matter. She could always head off on her own if she needed to.

They passed through customs without a problem. Mark

exchanged a wallet full of U.S. dollars for Turkish liras, then the two of them caught a cab and headed to the bus station. An hour later, they arrived in the town of Selcuk, about two miles northeast of Ephesus. It was ten o'clock when they stepped out of the cab at the Hotel Bella, a magnificent three-story structure. A blanket of greenery covered its outer wall and sprays of purple hung from the upper balconies.

A fresh, tropical breeze wafting off the sea and the beat of the sun on Julie's back had her feeling more like a tourist on vacation than a reporter trying to save her job. She wished she could take a day just to relax on the beach or stroll through the marketplace. Here she was, thousands of miles away from her desk in that dingy office. No editors to prod her for copy. No deadlines. No sources to track down. And no Mary Beth Simmons.

She took a deep breath and headed for the hotel entrance. Mark was close on her heels. "I'm starving," he said.

Julie shook her head and giggled. "Why am I not surprised?"

"What do ya mean by that? I'm a growing boy. I need fuel for the day."

"Barely two hours ago you ate a huge breakfast on the plane, plus half of mine. How much fuel does a growing boy need?"

He didn't answer, but he had a silly smile on his face as he trotted ahead of her to the front desk.

They spent several minutes trying to convince the clerk they were not a married couple.

"We need individual rooms," Mark insisted.

The girl's smile faded and she gave them two rooms on the second floor. After unlocking the door to her room, Julie paused in the doorway for a couple of minutes and caught her breath. The Ottoman-style furnishings gave her compact quarters the flavor of a Turkish art museum. A red-and-gold tapestry graced one wall, and pictures of Selcuk hung on two other walls. There was a full-size bed with a hand-carved ebony headboard, a matching wardrobe, and two end tables with antique-looking lamps. Perched on top of the striped bedding was a pair of elephants someone had formed out of white bath towels.

She stepped gingerly inside, and breathed in the scent of mint and dried herbs. After lowering her bags to the floor she went to check out her private bathroom. It was a painfully small compartment with barely room for a shower stall, a pedestal sink, and an American-style commode.

"It's big enough for me," Julie said with a nod.

She quickly unpacked her things, and with her hair clipped in a ball on top of her head, she stood in the shower under a hot spray for several minutes. After drying off with one of the elephant towels, she donned a yellow knit top, a flowered skirt that hung to her ankles, and a pair of Clarks walking sandals. She paused for a quick primp in front of the mirror—she wasn't trying to impress anyone, but the long flight had left her looking a little frazzled.

At that moment, there was a tap on the hall door. She opened it and found Mark standing there with a big grin on his face.

"I have elephants on my bed." He giggled like a kid at a carnival. "Somebody formed two elephants out of my bath towels. I almost didn't shower. I didn't want to pull them apart. But, oh well, I'm afraid one of my elephants has met his demise."

Julie couldn't help but laugh at the image. "I found the same thing in here," she said, gesturing toward the lone pachyderm on her bed. Then, feeling uneasy to have a man standing in her bedroom doorway, she lost her smile. "Well, time to go," she said, her voice curt. She grabbed her purse and joined Mark in the hallway.

"Did you get a look at the view from your window?" Mark asked as they headed for the stairs. "We're practically in the front yard of St. John's Basilica."

"I haven't opened my curtain yet. After that long flight, I needed to get under a nice, hot shower."

Mark pointed toward the roof. "How about we get something to eat on the terrace? The manager told me they're getting ready to serve lunch up there."

Julie nodded. She could care less where they ate or what they had for lunch. In her purse was a notebook and a few pens. Now that she'd gotten over the tourist-on-vacation mood, she was ready to get to work.

They settled at a table for two beside the balcony railing. Several shops lined the street below. Beyond the commercial district, hundreds of whitewashed homes fanned upward on the hillside, their facades glistening in the midday sun. The remnants of the basilica protruded from the hillside, and above it, the castle of Ayasuluk loomed larger and more daunting than any of the buildings below it.

Mark let out a sigh. "I've been waiting all my life to see this. The entire hillside is steeped in history."

Julie eyed the scene with indifference, but as an afterthought, she took out her camera and shot a few photos.

While they waited for their server to bring lunch, Mark leafed with enthusiasm through a couple of pamphlets he'd brought along. He kept pointing at the notations and murmuring, "Yes, yes, yes."

They shared a platter of pita bread, bleu cheese, a variety of fruits, plus grilled sesame-crusted bananas and two tins of sardines. Mark mumbled a quick blessing. Though unimpressed, Julie waited until he finished, but stared straight ahead.

Except for an occasional smacking of Mark's lips and his sighs of approval, they ate their meal in silence. As usual, Julie picked at the food on her plate and Mark devoured everything, leaving behind only the empty sardine tins and the rind from a wedge of cheese. Though Mark had eyed Julie's nit-picking of her meal with a look of concern, she appreciated that he didn't say anything. She didn't need someone to remind her that she ate like a sparrow. She already knew it, and she didn't care.

About the time they finished eating, Mark's cell phone rang. Frowning, he pulled it out of his pocket. "It has to be six in the morning, back there," he said, and hit the ignore button. "So, Julie, are you ready for a day of adventure in Ephesus?"

"I'm ready," she said. "But, I honestly don't know where to start."

"Don't worry. You have your own personal guide today." Mark cleared his throat and squared his shoulders. "Madam, for only a few small coins," he said, his voice suddenly nasal and high-pitched. "I will bring those ancient ruins to life for you."

Julie couldn't help but laugh. Mark had a gift for changing his persona at the drop of a hat. He should have been a comedian instead of a Bible school professor. But then, maybe he entertained his students in much the same way.

"Our tour will include *The Great Theatre*," he said with a flare.

Then, aware he'd drawn attention from other diners, he

lowered his voice. "We'll also visit the Library of Celsus and a few other surprises, including the royal bathhouses. But don't assume those outdoor latrines are there for your use. That will make the gods very angry."

Julie's giggles seemed to stoke a fire under Mark. He leaned toward her, like he was about to tell her a secret. "Make sure you spend some of your hard-earned money in the agora, my friend. You simply *must* take home a few souvenirs. Perhaps a Turkish carpet, or one of our miniature goddesses—for luck."

Julie had forgotten how quickly Mark could lighten the mood. His little monologue had eased the tension between them, and for the time being, she let her resistance slip, but only a little.

"Okay, Mr. Tour Guide," she said. "Let's go."

Mark paid the bill and they squeezed into a crowded shuttle in front of the hotel. A suntanned little man named Nikos climbed into the driver's seat. He wore blue jeans and a short-sleeved shirt, plus a black uniform vest and matching beret. He pulled away from the curb and immediately began to extol the virtues of the ancient ruins they were about to visit. Julie suppressed a chuckle. Their driver's high-pitched, sing-song voice sounded an awful lot like Mark's impression of a tour guide.

As they followed the winding uphill road, Nikos continued his spiel. "Did you know that Ephesus is one of the Seven Wonders of the Ancient World?" he said in near perfect English. "As you walk through the ruins today, stop and listen to them. They speak of ancient civilizations far superior to the world we know today. I suggest you sit for a while in the Great Theatre. Close your eyes and imagine what it was like 2,000 years ago when people came to listen to Paul the Apostle."

"Visit the old library," Nikos went on. "The ancient scrolls are gone now, but four statues guard the entrance as symbols of the four aspects of the human spirit—wisdom, virtue, judgment, and authority. Finally, don't forget to stop in the marketplace and purchase a remembrance of this wonderful place."

Julie nudged Mark and giggled. "Didn't you already say all that in the restaurant?" she whispered. He returned her smile. The look of adoration in his eyes stirred an emotion she thought was long dead. She quickly turned away and looked out the window.

It was a short jaunt to the ruins less than two miles from the hotel. Nikos left his passengers at the East Gate with a promise to pick them up at the north end in four hours. Julie donned a pair of sunglasses, thankful that she'd remembered what the brochure had recommended. She'd also brought along a bottle of water, which she kept in the side pocket of her purse. Prepared for a few hours in the blazing sun, Julie slipped from the van and walked with the group to the entrance of Ephesus, where Mark paid their admission fees.

From the moment she stepped inside the gate, she felt as though she'd entered another time period. Mired in dull browns and grays, the ruins of Ephesus looked like one of those faded antique oil paintings often seen hanging in museums. If not for the patches of greenery and a proliferation of bright red poppies on the hill, the landscape would have been dull and lifeless. Julie paused at the top of a descending street and took in the scene. A broad mosaic of broken and cracked pieces of marble stretched before her. On either side were crumbling statues of gods and goddesses—some of them headless, some without arms. They spoke of lost battles and fallen kingdoms. The vision tapered off in the distance where everything grew smaller and fainter.

The perspective, along with its stream of tourists, offered Julie an opportunity to get some outstanding photos. She took out her camera and shot several pictures, then she pulled the strap around her neck so she'd be ready for more.

Mark came up beside her, his eyes hidden behind a pair of aviator glasses that made him look like a movie star incognito.

"Shall we?" he said.

He took her arm and guided her onto the descending thoroughfare. Julie didn't resist, but allowed Mark to hold onto her as she maneuvered around the cracks and fissures in the slabs of marble.

"They've been rebuilding this place for years," Mark said. "They still have a long way to go. Over the centuries there were lots of wars and earthquakes. But, they persist in the reconstruction, even though all their hard work can crumble at any moment from the slightest tremor."

Julie tried to imagine what Ephesus might have looked like 2,000 years before, when the walls stood firm and the statues hadn't lost body parts. Perhaps she would have liked that simpler life, before shopping malls, cell phones, and automobiles came into existence. She wouldn't have to put up with people like Jason Redding and Mary Beth Simmons. But then, maybe she would have met a different kind of adversary.

They paused on the path beside a wall of arches that ran along a grassy mound to their right. It had crumbled to almost non-existence. Julie started taking pictures.

Mark glanced at the brochure. "This pile of rubble was once a magnificent structure," he said. "It was built as a tribute to Titus Augustus in the first century. Titus was the leader who destroyed the temple in Jerusalem in AD 70. He also completed the building of the Coliseum in Rome. The brochure says this memorial was later dedicated to Domitian and it has remained in his honor to this day."

The name Domitian triggered a memory from a Sunday school lesson Julie had read as a kid. "Wasn't he the emperor who banished John to Patmos?" she said.

Mark's eyebrows went up. "I'm impressed, Julie. It's not in the Bible, but that's exactly what tradition says. Also, during Domitian's rule, John was supposedly boiled in oil, but it's been said that he survived without a mark on him."

"Sounds horrible." Julie frowned with disgust.

"If it's any comfort, Domitian met a terrible end himself. One of his servants stabbed him in the groin while he was sleeping. Then a bunch of other people rushed in and hacked him to pieces."

Julie winced. "That must have been some wakeup call. Whatever became of hanging someone? Or poison? Or anything more humane than hacking a man to death?"

"You have to understand," Mark said. "That was the kind of mentality back then. Anyone who held power fell prey to extreme paranoia. Somebody was always trying to kill them. So, it was either kill or be killed."

"If Domitian was so hated, why did the Romans dedicate a monument in his honor? Such an act of respect seems inconceivable."

Mark shrugged. "Like I said, it was a different world back then. You had to have lived in that day to understand their culture, or at least tolerate it."

Julie shot a few pictures, stepped back and tried to capture the entire monument. Without intending to, she caught Mark in two of her photos. When she finished shooting, she scrolled through her collection, nearly deleted the two with Mark in them, but she decided to leave them alone for the time being.

"Let's move on," Mark said, and they continued downward along what the brochure designated as the Street of Curetes. Julie imagined how an obsessive-compulsive person might try to navigate the uneven slabs of broken marble. She giggled, then made a game of it, stepping from one stone to the next, avoiding the cracks much like she and her sister Rita had done as kids, fearing they might break their mother's back. She caught Mark smiling at her and blushed.

At that moment, Mark passed through a stone archway. Julie followed him into a large, open-air enclosure with walls that towered at least 30 feet above their heads. It was the community bathhouse, complete with washbasins and latrines. A couple dozen openings ran along the top of a stone ledge. Julie's hand flew to her mouth and she gasped. "I can't believe people used those things in public," she said, widening her eyes.

Mark laughed and patted her on the back. "Yep, there you have them. Community toilets. Picture it, Julie, prominent government officials sat there defecating while making political decisions that could affect the entire population of Ephesus."

Julie wrinkled her nose and walked away in a huff. She ignored Mark's snicker that followed her. "Men," she mumbled below her breath.

10

MORE OF EPHESUS

Julie was relieved to get out of the bathhouse and back on the main drag. She didn't need anymore of Mark's jokes. Directly ahead was the Library of Celsus. The honey-colored, two-story structure loomed like a fractured mausoleum, with only half of its bones still standing. She counted 16 huge columns, three main entrances, and eight broad steps that rose to the first level.

She took a ton of photos, while Mark cited information from the guidebook.

"At one time this library stood three stories high," Mark said, a hint of astonishment in his voice. "It's one of several libraries that were built in the first century. The ancients loved their libraries, Julie. Not only did the buildings store thousands of scrolls and treasures of all kinds, many of them also housed colleges where wise men came from all over the world to teach virtually every imaginable subject—science, art, literature, philosophy, medicine, astrology." His voice rang with excitement.

That was the man Julie liked to remember. There were times when Mark barged into her condo fired up about some new archaeological discovery. He'd spend the entire evening raving about it. As long as he stayed off the subject of religion, they got along just fine.

Now he opened the guidebook in front of her. "Look at this, Julie."

She lowered her camera and peered over his arm at the diagram of the library. A wave of heat rushed to her face and she caught her breath. Mark was wearing Aramis. She knew the scent well. Here, in the hot sun, the fragrance seemed to evaporate off his face.

She hadn't allowed Mark to get this close for more than a year. Though she tried to deny it, the chemistry was still there. She stepped away from him.

Oblivious to Julie's sudden emotional upheaval, Mark continued to babble about the library. "See those columns, Julie?" He pointed. "They were constructed in what is called Corinthian style—like tapering candles. Notice how they placed the shorter ones on the outside and the taller ones in the center, creating an optical illusion that makes the construction appear even larger than it is." Mark laughed and shook his head. "Like they needed to use any tricks-of-the-eye for *that* mammoth construction."

He flipped the page, and Julie took another step back.

"It says here, this particular library was the brainchild of a Roman senator, Celsus Pelemeanus, hence the name Library of Celsus. The guy loved books. Get this, Julie. He's supposed to be buried directly under the floor."

She was still trying to collect her thoughts. She had to stay focused; had to keep from thinking of this place as romantic and magical. She had a job to do and it didn't include falling in love.

"Let's go in," Mark said, nudging her arm.

She hurried ahead of him across the plaza and up the wide stone steps to the platform. Larger than life statues greeted them from giant niches between the doorways.

"What did Nikos say about those statues? Do you remember?"

She nodded. "He called them wisdom, virtue, judgment, and..."

"Authority," Mark interjected.

Setting her camera on video, Julie pivoted slowly and captured a 360-degree panorama of the area. Tourists crossed in front of her view. It didn't matter. They didn't obstruct the picture. In fact, they put life into an otherwise funereal setting.

She moved away from Mark and strolled around the upper level, drew close to one of the pillars, and ran her fingers over the ridges. The outside was warmed by the sun, the shaded side remained cool and moist. She enjoyed the moment. There was something other-worldly to be able to touch a part of history most people never get to see.

"C'mon, Julie." Mark gestured with enthusiasm toward the center entrance. She followed him through the archway. They spent the better part of an hour wandering around the ruins. Julie grabbed her camera and shot the debris—huge chunks of marble, stone walls, pillars, carvings of angels, plus birds and other forms of wildlife. She wasn't sure how the scenes would fit into the story on John, but they were fascinating enough to make her want to record them. Though she was eager to move on to Patmos and start looking for the old man, she could see why the library was the highlight of Ephesus. In fact, this antiquated, broken place had stirred her imagination more than anything had in a long time.

A short time later, they left the library behind them and turned onto Marble Street. The walk was riddled with deep grooves and crevices. Julie looked at Mark and raised her eyebrows.

It was as if he could read her mind. "Carriages," he explained. "Horse-drawn carriages, wagons, and the coaches of the rich made those ruts centuries ago. Fascinating, isn't it, how the marks of the past can still be witnessed today?" He spoke with such reverence, Julie wondered if he was about to break down. She was certain he had tears in his eyes.

For the first time since Julie met Mark, she was seeing him as more than a Bible teacher. When they were dating, he often talked about the classes he taught, and he showed her maps and photographs of historical sites he wanted to visit one day. She assumed he was planning a vacation. But he really cared about all this antiquity. It wasn't until Julie came to this place that she was able to see another side of Mark. His professorship wasn't merely a job to him. It was his life.

They arrived at the Great Theatre and merged with a group of tourists filing through a portico into a massive open-air arena. At that point, everyone scattered. Mark and Julie climbed half-way up the tiered stadium and sat on a hard, stone slab. Mark leaned back, rested his shoulders against the ledge of the next row, and crossed his arms in front of him. Despite the hard rock behind his back, he looked comfortable.

"The Romans started building this arena during the reign of Claudius," he told her. "Do you believe the size of this place?" He waved his hand toward the top of the arena, then to the side, and finally, toward the bottom. "This arena can seat 25,000 people. Of course, the best seating is down front—marble pews reserved for the officials and the rich people. The commoners sat higher up on this hard stone, right about where we're sitting now."

"I guess we're commoners, then," Julie said, snickering.

"Maybe you are," he quipped. "Since I'm a teacher I'd be entitled to a front seat. Teachers were respected in those days." He gave her a sideways glance. "You, on the other hand, would have had to marry well to sit down there."

Julie made a face at him. "Oh no. I would never have

allowed it. I would have stayed home and watched television or something."

He laughed and the twinkle in his sky-blue eyes caught Julie off guard. Once again, she found herself drawn to Mark.

"Okay, consider this," he said. "Can you imagine somebody like Billy Graham putting on a crusade in this place? He could have filled this arena. And who knows? Maybe Paul drew an equally large audience. After all, by the time Paul visited Ephesus, he was quite popular."

Mark pointed toward the center of the arena, a large flat area where the people looked like tiny stick figures walking around.

"I imagine Paul stood in that very spot," Mark said. "Picture it, Julie. Almost 2,000 years ago, a silversmith named Demetrius riled up the crowd of merchants against Paul for turning the people away from their false idols. He was ruining their business." Mark grunted. "In the end, they lost. Chasing Paul out of the city didn't stop the spread of Christianity. The people of Ephesus clung to their newfound faith. Aquila and Priscilla ministered to the Ephesians. Then, Timothy took over the church here. And, John became an elder in Ephesus. So you see, Julie, long after Paul left this place, the church of Christ stood strong."

Julie bristled. She should have known Mark would turn the conversation to issues of faith.

"So, where is all the religion now?" she snapped. "The entire city lies in ruins. It's nothing more than a commercialized tourist trap. Remember the statues of gods and goddesses along the entry road? There are plenty of false idols, but no sign of God in this place."

Mark shrugged. "Okay, I admit it *is* a tourist attraction.

I'd like to say it's a Christian memorial, but the truth is, this place has fallen prey to a synchronization of religions. When we get to the marketplace you'll see statues of Jesus mixed with icons of Artemis, the ancient Greek goddess. Sadly, Ephesus may well be a sign of things to come."

He put his hands behind his head, and shut his eyes, ending their conversation. Julie stared at his face, now bathed in gold from the sun. For a moment, with his sandy hair and his chiseled features, he could have been a model for any one of the Greek and Roman gods standing guard along the walkway.

She squeezed her eyelids shut and tried to block out Mark's image, but the outline of his head remained, like the negative of a photo.

A cloud moved across the sun and a chill swept over her. She opened her eyes. Mark was looking at his watch. "We'd better get going if we're gonna meet our driver at four," he said. "We have only a half-hour to get to the gate."

With a groan, he stood to his feet, then turned toward Julie and offered his hand. She allowed him to help her stand up, then she yanked her hand away and sprinted down the tiers ahead of him.

They headed north toward the exit, but when they approached the ruins of the Church of the Virgin Mary, Mark wanted to take a look. Julie had no interest in that church or any other. She headed toward the souvenir stalls near the exit. As Mark had predicted, merchants were selling tiny crucifixes and little statues of Jesus at one table and images of Artemis at another. More tables spilled over with various icons. The merchants also sold silver platters, glass bowls, and, of all things, "genuine fake watches." Julie laughed and shook her head.

Then a display of glass jewelry caught her eye. An elderly woman in a flowered skirt and blouse stood behind the table. Her dark eyes followed Julie and brightened when she lifted a pair of earrings with effervescent blue beads dangling like tiny prisms.

"Ten euros," the woman called out in a raspy voice.

Julie calculated the exchange at about $15 in American money. *Not a bad price.* She pulled out her wallet.

"You're supposed to bargain," Mark had come up behind her. His sudden presence startled her.

"They expect it," he said. "Go on, tell her you'll pay five."

Julie stared into the merchant's dark brown eyes. She was entranced by the aura of peace that lay within their depths. She ignored Mark and handed ten euros to the grinning saleswoman.

"Go with God." The woman said, her gravely voice softening. Smile lines formed at the corners of her eyes, which now appeared like two ripe olives. Julie held her gaze for a minute, then she mumbled a soft "Thank you," and turned onto the path leading away from Ephesus. With each step, the antiquities of the past fell away, and she reentered the real world, the one she knew well, the one she clung to for protection, but sometimes resented.

As he had promised, Nikos was waiting by the van. Julie and Mark piled in with the other tourists.

On the way to Selcuk, Nikos made a slight detour. "We now go to the House of the Virgin Mary," he said. "You will have a wonderful experience there."

He parked at the side of the road, and Julie and Mark joined the others on a long trek to a yellowish stone dwelling nestled among cedar trees on the side of a hill. Visitors were lining up single-file to enter the arched doorway of the boxlike structure. As she entered the tiny house, a wave of claustrophobia overcame her.

"The mother of Jesus spent her final days in this place," Nikos whispered amidst the murmured conversations. A noticeable hush had fallen over the crowd. "There is much to see and appreciate. Come. Move quickly."

The sanctuary was ornately decorated. An altar stood at the far end. Above it was a life-size statue of Mary, framed inside a stone niche. A solitary candle set off an ethereal glow. Goose bumps appeared on Julie's arms. It didn't help that Mark was standing close enough to brush his arm against hers. She stepped away from him. More tourists filtered into the room. The press of bodies and suffocating body odors mixed with cheap perfumes nearly had her gasping for air.

"I need to leave," she said. She backed away from the others and stumbled toward the exit. Once outside, she took a deep breath and was immediately distracted by a high stone wall with strips of fabric and bits of paper stuck to it in a giant collage of color. People lingered there and attached more remnants to the already saturated wall. They bowed their heads and moved their lips in mumbled prayer. Fascinated, Julie couldn't take her eyes off of them.

Nikos emerged from the shrine. "It's called *the wishing wall*," he said. "Go ahead. Make a wish."

Julie stared at the little man. He smiled and nodded his encouragement. She hesitated. He reached in his vest pocket and withdrew a clump of ribbons from which he selected a red one.

"Here," he said. "Tie it to the wall and make your wish."

Julie shook her head. She hadn't wished on stars, or birthday candles, or crossed fingers, since her childhood.

Nikos shrugged. "It's simply a tradition, but who knows?"

Not wanting to hurt his feelings, Julie accepted the ribbon and stepped toward the wall. *Make a wish?* She had no idea what to wish for. But, as she drew closer to the profusion of colored remnants, the old woman at the jewelry table came to her mind. A noticeable peace had emanated from those dark eyes, a peace that had eluded Julie in recent years. At that moment, she knew exactly what she wanted to wish for.

She attached her ribbon to another scrap of cloth that dangled there, and she bowed her head. Here she was, standing before the wishing wall, and she'd erected a wall of her own. Now she began to wonder, had her personal wall kept danger out, or had it blocked her in? Was it a shelter? Or a prison?

She didn't try to stop the flow of tears that came. "I know what I need," she whispered. "I need what that woman in the marketplace has. I need what Mark has. And my friend Lakisha. And Doctor Balser, the man on the plane. There's supposed to be a peace that passes all understanding. If you're real, God, and if you're hearing me, give me that peace."

11

MARK

The drive back to Selcuk passed through a rural area that appeared to be frozen in time. For Mark, a student of ancient history, nothing could compare with what he was experiencing in this strange and distant land. He sat back and enjoyed the scenery as it floated by his window. Their van sped around a curve. Its growling gears sent a flock of chickens scurrying behind a stone house. They passed a herd of sheep grazing in a field perilously close to the road. Undaunted by the van's noisy engine, the animals turned their wooly backs to the highway and huddled together as they yanked at tufts of grass. On both sides of the road stretched massive orange groves, fig trees, and healthy garden plots.

Around the next bend, they passed an old man who sat hunched on a wooden seat in a horse-drawn cart, its rusted metal wheels scraping against the pavement. Burqa-shrouded women walked along the side of the road with thick bundles balanced on their heads. A young boy jogged in the opposite direction behind a wheelbarrow loaded with watermelons. Stray dogs and cats roamed freely about the streets.

As they turned onto the main street of town, Mark noticed two middle-aged men who were wearing identical brown jackets and matching berets. They could have been twins sitting there at an outdoor table tipping demitasse cups and waving their hands in animated conversation. A teenage boy walked by carrying a platter of flatbread on his head. And two olive-skinned women in gaudy floral outfits stood behind a makeshift stand selling fresh produce.

Another turn brought their van into the 21st century as it came to a halt behind a black BMW in front of their hotel. A trio of teenagers in blue jeans strolled by, their arms linked, their voices joined in song. As Mark followed the others out of the van, a man in a business suit emerged from the BMW and strode ahead of them into the hotel. His right hand pulled a large suitcase on wheels, his left gripped a copy of the Wall Street Journal.

Mark shook his head in wonder over the fascinating time-travel journey he'd just taken. He slipped a few bills to Nikos. "I have a question," Mark said.

The little man straightened. "At your service." He looked about to give a salute, but instead, he simply remained at attention, his beady little eyes fastened on Mark's face.

"Nikos, this isn't merely a vacation for me and Julie. We're on a mission to find someone."

Nikos' eyebrows went up with interest.

"I don't suppose you've seen an elderly man who possibly lives here or visits occasionally? He'd be someone who stands out in a crowd, an eccentric fellow who maybe wanders around town helping people."

Nikos stroked his chin like he was pondering an answer. He shook his head. "In Selcuk we have many people who match your description." He shrugged. "Who knows? You could be speaking about anyone."

Mark persisted. "The man I'm looking for may not even live here. In fact, he may live on Patmos and possibly visits Ephesus often. He may spend time at the shrine where Mary once lived, or he might go to the basilica. He might preach on street corners or talk to people in the marketplace. He would be someone you may have noticed during your trips to the different sites."

Nikos' eyes sparkled and he slapped his forehead like he'd suddenly remembered something important. "How brainless I am. There is a fellow—an elderly man, bless his soul—who used to come here from Patmos, but I haven't seen him in quite a while. For all I know, he may have died."

Mark nodded with enthusiasm. "Did you catch a name?"

Nikos shook his head sadly. "So sorry. I did not."

They would have to wait until they got to Patmos to continue the search.

"Thanks, Nikos. You've been extremely helpful."

Mark caught up with Julie inside the hotel. "Dinner?" he said, raising his eyebrows.

She stared back at him. Her hesitation sent a wave of discomfort through him.

"There's a restaurant I'd like to try," he said. "It's only a few blocks away. It might be nice to take a stroll through town."

Her green eyes were so intense they could have looked right into his heart. With a sigh, he started to turn away. "See ya' lat—"

"Dinner sounds good," she said, stopping him. "Give me a few minutes to freshen up."

On his way to his room, Mark smiled with anticipation of an evening out with Julie. But when he pulled out his cell phone to check his messages, his smile faded. There was one text from his boss, but multiple voicemails from Katie. No sooner did he enter his room when his phone vibrated again. Katie's image came up.

Mark scrunched his lips in indecision and almost hit the

"ignore" button. He wasn't in the mood for the third-degree. But, he'd have to face the truth at some point. He exhaled loudly and answered the call.

"Hi there," he said, trying to sound like he was glad to hear from her.

"I've been calling you all day," Katie whined.

Mark cringed. This wasn't going to be easy.

"Is everything okay?" she said. "You didn't return any of my calls."

"Sorry, Katie. I was on a tour of Ephesus. I had to turn my phone off for a while. I didn't want to disturb the tourists in our group. Plus, I was working. You know that's why I came here."

Before Katie could launch into one of her meaningless accusations, Mark plunged into a long monologue about the sites he had visited. He purposely avoided mentioning Julie. The diversion didn't work. When he ran out of things to say, he fell silent, and Katie asked the question he'd been dreading.

"Was Julie with you?"

He sighed. "Uh-huh."

"The whole time?"

Another sigh. It was like getting caught with his hand in the cookie jar. But he wanted to be honest with her. "Yeah, we were together the whole time."

There was a moment of discomfort while Mark considered a myriad of explanations. They all fell flat.

"We hardly spoke, Katie." At least that was partially true. "Julie has her job to do and I have mine. Even though we'll be searching for the old man, in the meantime we're on different missions. I'm focusing on whatever I can put together for my classes. Julie has her own agenda. As I said, we hardly spoke."

Mark thought he heard a little sob.

"Is she—is she as pretty as she was when you dated?"

Mark could have kicked himself for leaving Julie's photograph on his desk at home. He didn't think it mattered. But, apparently it did. Katie had gone ballistic. Now he wished he had tucked it away somewhere, maybe in his underwear drawer. That little blonde would never have looked in there.

Mark pressed his lips together, his frustration mounting. Julie, pretty? Yes, darn pretty. But he certainly couldn't tell Katie that. He was at a loss for words.

"You don't have to answer," Katie whimpered. "I guess I should go now, Mark. I won't bother you again."

Before he could respond, their connection went dead. Mark set down his phone, walked over to the window, and stared at the purple mountains in the distance. He hadn't expected to become entwined in such a conflict of emotions. After seeing Julie again, he knew the truth. He still cared for her. Now, he had hurt someone who had done him no wrong, and he hated himself for letting things get so far.

He continued to berate himself while he freshened up in the bathroom. By the time he emerged, he'd made up his mind. When he returned from this trip, he had to set things straight with Katie. Whether things worked out with Julie or not, he was certain Katie was not the girl for him. He'd have to let her go so she could find happiness with someone else.

He knew he was slitting his own throat. He had no guarantee Julie would ever give him so much as the time of day. He could end up completely alone. No Julie, and no Katie, either.

Before leaving his room, he quickly checked his boss's text. Melanie was merely asking for an update. He flipped open his laptop computer and sent her a quick rundown of his day in Ephesus. Then he signed off, purposely left his cell phone on the bureau, and went downstairs to meet Julie.

By the time Mark entered the lobby, all thoughts of Katie had gone out of his head. Julie was already there looking fabulous in a light blue sleeveless dress that hung to her ankles. She'd let her hair down, and the blue glass earrings she had purchased in Ephesus bobbed from between her fiery red waves. As Mark took in the vision, an uncontrollable flutter erupted in his chest.

Mark swallowed the golf ball in his throat. "You look nice," he said, as casually as he could. But, his voice cracked and he had to force himself to look away. As they went out the door, he offered Julie his arm and was pleasantly surprised when she took it.

During the walk to the restaurant, they hashed over their observations of the visit to Ephesus, then they became interested in the shops and the people they passed on the street. The aroma of grilled meat sailed from a nightclub where locals and tourists sat at small tables on an outdoor patio, drinking beer and wine, their voices mingled with loud chatter and outbursts of laughter.

As the sun settled behind the hills and the sky took on a violet hue, they arrived at the Agora Restaurant, which Mark assumed was one of the finer dining places in town. They sat at an outdoor table near two older men who were puffing on thin, brown cigarettes and ogling the young women who walked by. One of them winked at Julie. She shrank behind Mark, a move that boosted his ego, if only for the moment.

Mark was surprised when Julie agreed to share a carafe of red wine. He ordered an appetizer platter of goat's cheese, grapes, and mixed nuts for the two of them. For dinner, Julie chose roast vegetables and rice pilaf. Mark opted for a full meal of grilled lamb on a skewer, curried rice, green beans with slivered almonds, and a salad.

For probably the first time in his life, Mark was tongue-tied. The flickering candle on their table and soft music in the background made their casual night out feel an awful lot like a romantic dinner date. Perhaps he should have chosen one of the less formal eateries they'd passed along the way.

Julie looked absolutely gorgeous under the subdued lighting, with her crimson hair framing her suntanned face, her soft green eyes glistening in the light of the candle, and the hint of a smile on her lips. He'd felt more at ease as her pseudo-tour guide that afternoon. But sitting here, lovesick and desperately hoping to win back his former girlfriend, he didn't know what to say without sounding like an idiot. Julie toyed with her silverware as though unable or unwilling to look him in the eye. All he could do was feign interest in the people walking by the restaurant.

To Mark's relief, their sizzling platters arrived sooner than he'd expected, and for the time being, he could lose himself in his dinner. Ravenous from the day's walk through Ephesus, he dug into his salad with gusto. In between bites, he glanced up at Julie's plate, relieved to see her roasted veggies disappearing. She even mopped up the juices with a slice of bread, and then she accepted a cup of lemon ice offered by their waiter.

Mark grinned. Perhaps their trip had had a positive affect on this waif of a girl. She'd lost several pounds since the last time he saw her. Even back then, he'd had some concerns about her weight, but the medical experts said not to force people to eat when they don't want to. The pressure would only push them in the opposite direction.

When dinner ended, Mark suggested they take a walk by some of the shops.

"This isn't like small town America," he said. "Back home, the streets fold up by 9 o'clock at night, except, of course, in big cities like New York and Chicago. But, in this part of the world, the locals eat their biggest meal at around one in the afternoon, then they close up shop for a siesta. The streets come alive after 8 p.m. The evening is a time for fun. It's a whole other culture, Julie."

"Well, I find the laid back atmosphere refreshing. Maybe we Americans can learn a few things from these people."

They strolled along the cobbled street past lighted stores that spilled their wares onto the sidewalks. From the alleys spewed the aroma of freshly brewed espresso, sizzling sausages, and loaves of bread coming out of an oven. Strains of lyres and flutes and the rhythmic patter of tambourines and bells poured from bars and nightclubs. Muted lamps bathed one side of the road in a soft blue glow, while dazzling white lights illuminated store entrances on the other side.

"Did you want to do some shopping?" Mark offered. "We passed a couple of dress shops near our hotel."

Julie stopped walking and stared at him in astonishment. He could have guessed what she was thinking. Like most men, Mark couldn't care less about dress shops. He just wanted to be with Julie, and if that meant he'd have to go inside a ladies' store, so be it.

Her smile encouraged him. "I've been wanting to buy a Turkish-style blouse," she said. "The kind with full sleeves and some needlework. Do you know what I mean?"

He shrugged. "I'm afraid I *don't* know, but let's check anyway. I'll help you look."

They headed in the direction of the hotel and located a string of clothing stores amidst the souvenir shops and carpet emporiums. Julie was drawn to one particular shop that displayed an entire rack of Turkish blouses. She selected several and disappeared behind a curtain to try them on. She ended up purchasing two—a mint green top with lace around the hem, and a bright yellow one with embroidered flowers down the front.

As soon as they hit the street, Julie said the words he'd been dreading all evening. "I'm tired, Mark. I'm going back to the hotel."

He would have loved to prolong their time together, but there was nothing he could do. He tried to cover his disappointment with a smile. "Okay, Julie. Get a good night's rest. Tomorrow, we'll hit the basilica. Let's say we meet at 8 a.m. for breakfast on the terrace."

Julie headed for the hotel. Mark followed at a distance and waited until she disappeared inside the lobby. Then, he turned around in search of a quiet bistro where he could sip a little espresso and collect his thoughts. He was about to make a life-changing decision that could affect two women in his life. Hopefully, no one would get hurt.

12

JULIE

Before climbing into bed, Julie turned on her laptop and checked her emails. Her editor had sent a message with one word, *"Urgent,"* in the subject line. She opened his email.

You need to keep your eyes open, Julie. I just learned that your "friend" from WPIX is getting ready to leave for Patmos with a photographer. This concerns me. Do you remember how Redding handled the exposé on that local pastor? The poor guy was innocent, but Jason tore him to pieces. Don't let him get ahead of you, Julie. If he gets to the old man first, you won't have a prayer of getting an interview. You'll need to move fast on this one. Let me know how things are progressing. Andy.

Great. Her boss's message killed her chances for a good night's sleep. Throughout the night, she woke to Andy's words echoing in her brain. She even got out of bed once to read his email over again.

The next morning, she tumbled out of bed, feeling like she'd been dragged through the streets of Selcuk by a pack of angry dogs. She managed to get through her grooming ritual, but wore no makeup this time, not even lipstick. With her hair pulled into a ponytail and wearing the blue glass earrings, she donned a denim skirt and pale blue blouse. She made it to the rooftop restaurant ahead of Mark and grabbed a table near the balcony.

Mark lumbered into the restaurant with dark circles under his eyes and five-o'clock shadow on his chin. His hair stuck out on one side. He didn't say a word until he finished eating.

"Let's go," he mumbled. He tucked in his shirt and ambled toward the exit.

The basilica was so close to the hotel they could almost reach out and touch it. Mark suggested they walk. Julie had no problem with that. She'd put on her running shoes that morning, and she'd been missing her early morning jogs with Lakisha. A little exercise would be better than nothing. Plus, a dose of fresh air could get her brain in gear.

Within a half-hour, they stood inside the entrance to a giant architectural skeleton. While Julie had little interest in the bones of an ancient church, Mark came to life in an amazing transformation. The sleepy-eyed, bedraggled tourist was now her wide-awake tour guide.

"This cathedral goes back to the sixth century," he said, as they strolled among the ruins. They approached a glass case that contained a model of what the basilica must have looked like in its glory days.

"Notice that it was constructed in the traditional cruciform style," Mark said, pointing. "Most of the early cathedrals used the shape of a cross out of reverence for God. This entire structure was constructed out of stone and brick, an unusual combination for that day and age. And, it was huge."

The massive size became more evident as Julie wove through a maze of walls that seemed to lead nowhere. The entire landscape was riddled with rocks, pebbles, cobblestone paths, and pillars that towered overhead. There were numerous niches and crannies that had no discernable purpose. And there was no roof. Only a vast blue sky stretched overhead. To Julie, the brokenness spoke only of death and destruction.

"What happened to this place?" She couldn't deny the

depression that came over her. It was like visiting someone's grave.

"An earthquake destroyed this church in the 14th century," Mark told her. "The church leaders made mediocre attempts to renovate, but it didn't work out. This is all that has remained for centuries. Several years ago, archaeologists uncovered a baptistery and a chapel with frescoes of saints painted on the walls. They sent the most valuable items to museums throughout Europe."

A warm breeze tickled Julie's hair and tugged at the hem of her skirt, but it failed to soothe the discomfort that roiled within her. She had a strong desire to run. Instead, she followed Mark into what appeared to be the main courtyard. In the center was a large slab of stone framed with four pillars, one in each corner. At the front was a marker written in both Turkish and English, *St. Jean in Mezari, The Tomb of St. John.*

Mark leaned close. "You're standing on holy ground, Julie. This cathedral was built over John's burial site." He lowered his voice, like he was about to tell her a secret. "But, John's not there," he said. "The last excavation uncovered an empty tomb. No bones. No relics of any kind. The religious leaders insist John's remains were taken somewhere else. Rome maybe. But, they believe the tomb is sacred. Just the thought that John's bones may have lain beneath these ruins is enough to draw believers from all over the world. Christians have come here to worship for centuries."

"Seems futile," she said, frowning. "They have no proof John was ever buried here." She snickered. "Before we left on this trip I had time to do a little research of my own. I read that John died in his sleep at around the age of 90. He could be buried somewhere else. Sounds to me like people need a place to worship so badly they'll turn anything into a shrine."

Mark's blue eyes darkened but he didn't dispute what she had said. "I suppose that's true for some," he acknowledged. "Many people believe that whether in body or spirit, John is still living beneath this monument and that every breath he takes disturbs the dust on the surface, giving it a healing quality. They scoop up particles and take them home with them, hoping to cure an ailment in a loved one or even in themselves."

"Isn't there a law against stealing stones and dirt from sacred places?"

Mark shrugged. "My guess is the authorities are glad they do it." He chuckled. "At least, they're keeping the floor swept clean."

As though confirming what Mark had just said, two veiled women approached the memorial and dropped to their knees. They rocked back-and-forth and murmured what must have been a prayer to the apostle. One of them reached down and gathered some grains of sand off the ground. She stuffed them inside a handkerchief, kissed the bundle, and slipped it inside a knit bag.

"That's pathetic," Julie whispered.

"Not to these people. That little bit of sand could be that woman's last hope to help a loved one who may be sick at home. Imagine how she must have panicked when all other attempts at healing failed. Nothing worked. Doctors, medicines, maybe even surgery. People like her travel miles, often on foot, to seek John's help. Then they go home with a teaspoonful of sand and they pray for a miracle."

Julie wrestled with a sudden rise of tears. At first sight, the women had appeared to be hopeless fanatics. Now Mark had opened a window to their lives. They were someone's wife, someone's mother, or someone's grandmother. They had a loved one waiting at home hoping for a cure, and they had come here in a desperate plea for help.

She chewed her bottom lip to stop it from trembling. Mark was staring at her, adding to her discomfort. He was standing so close, she couldn't breathe. She blinked back the tears, but they continued to surface.

She'd come here with no expectations except to fulfill her assignment and go home. But stepping into these ancient sites had drawn her into another realm—one of mystery and romance and spiritual implications. The sense of awe was overwhelming.

"Are we done here?" she said, struggling to keep her voice steady. She couldn't let Mark know she'd nearly crumbled like the walls of this broken monument. "I'd like to leave."

"First, I want to show you something." He took her hand and led her to the highest spot, and pointed. "Look down there and tell me what you see."

The descending hillside was riddled with tufts of scrub grass and patches of rust colored soil. She huffed out a sigh. "I see an ideal hiding place for snakes and rats and whatever other vermin might lurk in these hills."

"What else?"

She peered farther out. "I see something that looks like a pillar of stone, and a pile of rocks, and the remnants of another pillar."

"Do you know what you're looking at?"

"No. Why don't you tell me." She didn't try to keep the irritation out of her voice.

He smiled like he wasn't the least bit intimidated by her

sharp tone. "You are looking at the ruins of the temple of Artemis, the Greek goddess of fertility."

"So?"

"So, those broken stones represent the false idol Paul preached against when he came here. You can read the whole story in the book of Acts. When Paul came here, he found the area steeped in idol worship. He spoke against it and nearly got himself killed. But in the end, the idol worshipers lost. That bit of rubble is all that's left of their false religion. The same thing is going to happen to all false religions, in the end. Even the religion of atheists and agnostics—"

"Atheists have no religion." Julie snapped. "Neither do agnostics."

"Ah, but they do, Julie. They follow the religion of disbelief. They have their own gods—pride and self-sufficiency."

Julie crossed her arms. "I suppose you'd rather follow a religion that breeds clones who are told what to believe and how to live, with no regard for independent thought."

"All I'm saying is, all the options are out there, and you've gotta make a choice at some point."

"What if I don't want to choose? What if I just want to be left alone?"

"Listen, Julie. Ultimately, everyone will have to choose. You can be part of something temporary, like the cult of Artemis, or atheism—or agnosticism. Or you can belong to something greater, something that can restore hope where there is none."

Julie tensed up. He was doing it again. Only a year ago she walked—no *ran* away from him after a similar argument. She refused to be trapped in the same discussion all over again. "Stop it, Mark. Stop pushing me."

He stood firm. "You're pathetic, Julie. Here you are, working on an assignment you don't believe in, looking for a man you don't think exists, accompanied by another man you wouldn't give the time of day. When are you going to come out of that shell and start living again?"

"You have no right to judge me. I never—"

"Look, I don't know what else to say to you. It's obvious there's a war going on inside you. I've been walking on egg shells, trying to keep from saying the wrong thing. You insist you don't want anything to do with spiritual issues, then I catch you shedding tears over a couple of strangers kneeling at John's tomb. What am I supposed to do with that?"

"You can leave me alone, that's what you can do. We've been getting along fine until now. Why don't we both just do the job we came here for and then go our separate ways?"

He gazed at her with pity in his eyes. "Okay, Julie. Take your pictures and fill your notebook with whatever you think is important to your story. Write an article you think will please your editor. Ignore the spiritual significance of these places. Whether or not you come away with the truth doesn't matter."

With trembling hands Julie reached inside her purse for a tissue. Embarrassed, she turned away from Mark and blotted the tears from her face.

When she turned around she discovered he'd walked away. She searched the stream of visitors. Then she spotted him walking outside the memorial toward the citadel on top of the hill. She started after him, slowly at first, but once she got on the path, she picked up her pace.

Ahead of her loomed the castle with its bright red Turkish flags and a larger banner depicting the founder of the Turkish republic. She kept moving up the hill and caught up with

Mark, who had stopped walking. He turned to face her. The troubled lines on his forehead dissolved and his blue eyes darkened with concern.

"I'm sorry, Julie," he said. "I didn't mean to rile you back there. It's just that—"

"It's okay," she mumbled. "I'm all right. Let's just get this over with."

"C'mon," he beckoned. "We're almost at the citadel."

They ascended together, but came to a barricade with a "Do Not Pass" sign several yards below the fortress.

"It looks like the castle is closed for reconstruction," Mark said, pointing at the smaller text. "If you want to take pictures, you'll have to do it from here."

Julie began to snap her photos, but could get only a few good shots from where they stood. She edged away from Mark. If she focused on her work, perhaps he'd leave her alone.

He stepped away from her, as though allowing her room to breathe. Then, out of the blue, he cleared his throat and began another one of his spiels of information.

"You might be interested to know, this fortress dates back to the sixth century," he said, as though teaching a college class. Surprisingly, his voice contained no signs of the emotional upheaval he'd experienced only moments before. What drove the man? He could be down one minute and up the next.

She stared at him standing there, gesturing, flipping through a guidebook, delivering a talk on ancient landmarks. He was the image of self-confidence.

"Do you see those huge stones around the outside?" Mark continued, unaware that he was being evaluated for another rejection. "They came from some old Roman ruins and were brought here by ship." He paused, then pointed at the massive building. It spanned the crest of the hill, like a huge fortress, impenetrable and unnerving with its brown-gray facade and its daunting parapets.

"Fifteen towers were strategically placed around the perimeter so sentries could stand at the top and observe the entire hillside all the way down to the sea. From that vantage point, they could see if any pirates were approaching the castle. They had the ultimate defense system for that day."

There was a rustling behind her. She turned and caught her breath. About a dozen tourists had followed them from the basilica and had formed a half circle. Julie pressed her lips together and smothered a giggle. Their eyes were trained on Mark.

He didn't falter. He scanned the small crowd, and, raising his voice so those in the back could hear, he talked about the construction on the hill and gave details about the internal reservoirs and the fortifications. He spoke for another ten minutes, without interruption.

"To this day, the castle still stands as a symbol of strength, protecting the people of Selcuk and the surrounding area," Mark concluded. "It's believed that John the Apostle sat on this very hillside while writing his gospel and possibly his three epistles, as well."

Murmurs rose from the crowd. A few people applauded. Then they dispersed and wandered back down the hill. One man approached Mark and tried to hand him a couple of liras.

Mark held up his hand. "No. No thank you," he said, laughing. "I'm a tourist, like yourself."

The man shrugged, stuffed the bills back in his pocket and walked off, a confused expression on his face. After he'd moved out of their hearing, Mark and Julie burst into hysterics. The moment of levity melted the block of ice Julie had constructed between them. She looked at him now and a sharp regret stabbed her heart. Mark meant well, she was certain of it. Why had she reacted with so much emotion? Wasn't he entitled to his religious beliefs?

He extended his arm. She slipped her hand in the crook of his elbow and walked beside him to the bottom of the hill. Once again a blatant silence settled between them. Perhaps tomorrow the ice would melt a little more and they might find common ground. She didn't want to go home with more regrets.

13

PATMOS

J ulie spent the next hour in her room packing for her trip to Patmos and pondering the emotional highs and lows of the day. She'd had a feeling Mark might start to pressure her again. Their confrontation, though brief, had left her drained. Her only goal was to get through the week and go home.

Late that afternoon they hopped a mini-bus bound for the seaport city of Kusadasi. Though Julie would have liked to tour the popular resort, they were on a tight schedule. They caught a cab and went straight to the docks where they boarded a private ferryboat Mark had chartered. He had spent a good chunk of the college board's money for that charter, but Mark had told her they could make the 40-mile trip across the Aegean Sea in record time, without having to switch to another ferry boat at Rhodes or Samos.

Julie found herself on what might have been a romantic crossing had she not closed her heart to a relationship with Mark. As they pulled away from the dock, she placed her elbows on the railing and looked back at the retreating shore. It grew smaller and smaller, and the expanse of water began to engulf their boat. With the approaching darkness, the azure sea turned gray, then black. A rising moon cast silver streaks across the choppy water. She was relishing the moment of tranquility, when Mark came up beside her. She could feel his eyes on her and trembled.

"You cold?" he said.

She shook her head.

"When we get to Patmos tonight, we'll just relax at the hotel." He'd raised his voice over the rumble of the boat's engine. "Tomorrow, we'll get an early start. We'll walk in the places where John once walked. Today, it's one of the most popular tourist attractions in this part of the world. Back then, it was a desolate pile of rocks and dirt, sparsely inhabited except for those who had been banished there. As a person in exile, John probably labored in the rock quarries and endured other types of menial punishments."

Julie nodded but didn't say anything. She'd entered a classroom of sorts, and Mark was going to be her teacher, like it or not. The truth was, she could use some advance information for her story, especially with Jason Redding breathing down her neck. From what Andy had written, her nemesis might already be in Patmos.

"Tell me everything you know about John," she said, and she shifted her gaze from the sea to his face. The full moon planted a sparkle in his eyes. Julie caught her breath and turned back toward the water, its steady slapping against the boat a welcome diversion.

Mark leaned against the rail next to her and together they looked out to sea. A breath of wind stirred Julie's locks. She breathed in the salty air.

"Let's see," Mark said, as though pondering an answer. "Most of what I know about John comes from the Scriptures. For example, Jesus called John and James 'Sons of Thunder.' Nobody knows for sure why he said that, but it could have referred to an aggressive nature. In another passage of Scripture, the two brothers wanted to call down fire from heaven on the Samaritans. And they may have been a little self-serving, because later on, they asked to sit beside Jesus in the kingdom of heaven. That must have riled the others, don't you think?"

Julie shrugged but continued to stare out at the water. "They sound like they were real people who had real impulses and real flaws. Nothing unusual about them."

"Absolutely. They were no different from you or me. But then, John's no-nonsense attitude shows up in his three epistles. For example, he warned his followers to beware of false prophets. He challenged people to examine themselves spiritually. He dared them to choose light over darkness, truth over lies, love over everything else."

Julie nodded. "Go on."

"If people claimed they had no sin, he called them liars. In all of his writings, John spoke about the importance of truth, love, light, and faith. He warned about the danger of loving the world, insisted that it keeps people from a relationship with the Father. And he exposed by name those who had turned against the faith."

Julie turned and leaned her back against the rail. She dared to look at Mark, though his moon-bathed face sent a ripple into her heart. "Sounds like he must have been a tough guy," she said. "Who could possibly live up to all those rules? It seems to me, John's idea of Christianity created too difficult a path for anyone to follow."

"Not really," Mark said, turning his entire body toward her. She took a step away from him but remained glued to the rail.

"John wrote all of those things with kindness and sensitivity," Mark went on. "He referred to his readers as 'little children' and encouraged them to love one another. Even during his personal life, apart from a few explosive incidents, he had a sweet and gentle side. After all, didn't he rest his head on Jesus' breast during the last supper? And, wasn't he the apostle who referred to himself as *the one Jesus loved?*"

"Oh, yes, *the beloved*, right?"

"Right. To this day, he's known as the beloved apostle."

A fresh argument rose up in Julie. It was time to unleash the reporter within her. *Stop being a tourist and start thinking like you're on the job.*

"So," she said, her tone emphatic, "if John is still alive, then the man we're looking for will be living up to his own rules, won't he?"

Mark nodded. "Probably."

"And, he'll have the same godly wisdom he had 2,000 years ago, maybe even the mind of Christ himself, right?"

"Yeah, but what are you driving at, Julie?"

She faced him then without feeling intimidated by his overwhelming presence. "If we find such a man, isn't he going to see right through us? Won't he know what we're up to and why we're there?"

"Absolutely," he said, an amused smile on his lips. "Which is why we shouldn't try to deceive him. If we're fortunate enough to find this man, we need to be up front with him. We need to tell him who we are and what we're trying to accomplish. We're after the truth, Julie, so we have to be truthful in return."

A sudden breeze kicked up. Julie felt a chill. She walked to a bench where she had left her carry-on bag, and pulled out a sweater. Mark was right behind her. He put out his hand to assist her, but she quickly slipped her arms into the sleeves without his help. Exhausted from trying to keep her

119

balance from the rocking of the boat, she dropped onto the bench, leaned back, and shut her eyes.

She remained there and may have drifted off. The next thing she knew, the sound of a fog horn drew her from the bench and back to the rail. Mark was standing there, his eyes fastened to the sea ahead. She peered beyond the bow of the ship. A slim shadow stretched across the horizon. It grew larger as their ferry drew closer to the ancient port of Skala. A lonely lighthouse scattered its welcoming beam across the sea. The amber glow of streetlamps lit up the dock area, and white lights poured from a string of shops and cafes along the shore. Higher up the hillside, like a sentry watching over the settlement of Hora, stood the imposing Monastery of St. John the Theologian, its spotlights illuminating the houses on the hillside below.

In her research, Julie had seen photos and descriptions of the island setting. Now she was seeing it in person. Even in the semi-darkness, she could make out the hourglass curve of the coastline with its jagged rocks and tiered landscape. Growing ever larger, the harbor came into full view with a mix of sailboats and fishing boats docked there and a gigantic cruise ship moored for the night. Eager to get ashore, Julie hurried off the boat as soon as it docked. Once again, she depended on Mark to lead the way. She tackled the five-minute walk, pulling her suitcase and juggling her purse and overnight bag, and she finally passed through the arched entrance to the Skala Hotel, a white-washed, three-story building shrouded in bright pink bougainvillea.

The front desk was manned by a dark-haired clerk who welcomed them with a toothy smile.

"Let's see, you're Mr. and Mrs...?"

"Not again," Julie snapped. "We are *not* married." She immediately regretted her outburst. "Sorry," she said, softening her tone. "We're on a business trip and we need separate rooms, please."

The clerk nodded and slid another sheet onto the counter in front of Julie. She and Mark completed their check-in and headed for the third floor.

To Julie's dismay, there was an adjoining door between their rooms. She was about to go down to the front desk and ask to change her room, when she glanced out the balcony window and noticed she had a magnificent view. Her corner location looked out on both the dock and the monastery. She lingered there and was soaking up the scene when there was a knock on the adjoining door.

Reluctantly, she plodded over to it and opened it a crack.

"There's some activity down by the pool," Mark said, a hopeful lilt in his voice. "Do you want to go down and grab a bite to eat?"

Julie shook her head. "I'm tired," she said. "I'm gonna take a hot shower and jump into bed."

As she shut the door in Mark's face, a part of her wanted to fling it open again and rush into his arms. But another part of her added a layer of stone to the imaginary wall she'd erected between them, and she headed straight for the shower instead.

Mark stifled his disappointment and went down to the pool deck, alone. He ordered a beer at the kiosk bar and grabbed a bag of peanuts to munch on. For the first time during their trip, he'd lost his appetite. Maybe later, in an hour or so, he could get something in the restaurant, if it was still open.

He selected a comfortable deck chair, popped a few nuts in his mouth, and considered calling Katie. With the time difference, she'd be leaving her job at the elementary school about now. But he wasn't in the mood for a confrontation. He'd wait and talk with her in another day or two. Best to leave things alone, at least until he could get his head on straight.

He'd made a huge mistake by forcing Julie into a corner that afternoon. He'd vowed he wouldn't press her, but he'd broken his own rule. And what happened? Like before, she'd pushed him away. He should have learned last year that she wasn't the kind of girl who succumbed to high pressure. He'd come on this trip determined to hold back and give her space. The mess he'd made wasn't going to be easy to fix.

He sipped his beer, closed his eyes, and let the sounds of nature take over. From somewhere at the edge of the property crickets squeaked like tiny violins tuning up for a concert. A rustle in a nearby flower bed alerted him that something had slithered past. He opened his eyes and peered around the deck. A group of young men had swarmed around the poolside bar and were laughing and toasting each other. Mark caught snippets of their chatter, something about a new project, a few promotions, and bonuses.

He finished his snack, heaved a sigh, and went inside to the restaurant, where he ordered a grilled steak and mashed potatoes. Still engrossed with thoughts about Julie, he was surprised to find his plate had been mopped clean, and he couldn't remember eating a single bite. He would have liked to know what the thing tasted like.

Around 10 p.m. Mark trudged up to his room. Though exhausted, he flailed about on his bed for the next hour, fighting off visions of Julie on the ferry boat, her crimson locks undulating with the breeze off the sea, her emerald eyes glistening in the moonlight. There was no doubt in his mind, he'd fallen hard for that strong-willed, outspoken girl. In fact, like an idiot, he'd unashamedly bared his feelings before her, like a turkey with his head on the chopping block, waiting for her to lower the axe.

Moonlight streamed through his window and struck the adjoining door between their rooms. Julie was probably sleeping soundly on the other side of that blasted door. He flopped over on his other side and flung the covers over his head. Though he squeezed his eyes shut, sleep didn't come. He gazed again at the adjoining door, suppressed the urge to break it down, and sent a prayer through the window, over the rooftops, and beyond the hills of Patmos. Surely, his anguished plea would reach the ears of God, for without divine intervention, there was no hope for his aching heart.

14

MARK

Mark awoke the next morning bleary-eyed and with a stuffy nose. He managed a haphazard shave and a quick comb of his hair. Blindly, he grabbed some clothing from his suitcase, then he stumbled down to the hotel restaurant and poured himself a cup of black coffee at the buffet. He scraped together a couple of boiled eggs, two slices of toast, and some fresh fruit and cheese.

He found Julie at a table across the room. She appeared wide awake and refreshed. He figured she'd slept like a baby while he tossed and turned for most of the night.

She gave him a once-over. An amused twinkle came to her eye. "You mixed a plaid shirt with striped shorts?" She let out a laugh. "Who's your fashion consultant? Steven Tyler?"

Mark glanced down at his outfit and shrugged. "It's the latest thing—cacophony of colors," he said and plunked into the chair across from her.

She laughed again and went back to eating her breakfast.

Mark eyed her miserable bowl of muesli. "Wha-ja do, pull the stuffing out of your mattress and pour milk on it?" he retorted.

Julie smirked at him and, widening her eyes, she scooped up another mouthful of cereal. "Yum!"

In between bites of his own breakfast, Mark eyed Julie with interest. She wore a tan skirt and the yellow blouse she'd bought at the little shop in Selcuk. She looked like a teenager with her hair pulled back in a pony tail and the blue glass earrings dangling in full view. So appealing and yet so unreachable.

As a distraction, he spread several brochures on the table. He tapped the cover of one pamphlet that showed an aerial shot of the island. "This is a terrific guide book," he said. "It gives a lot of information about our little paradise."

Julie scraped up the last of her cereal, drained a glass of orange juice, and peered across the table at the brochure. "What does it say?"

"Well, it says the population here is less than 3,000 people. This area where we're staying is the main commercial port, but other settlements fan out along the beaches and in the farming district. The majority of the people live right here in Skala and in the capital city of Hora, where all the ancient sites are located. In a few weeks this place will be inundated with European tourists, so we've come at a good time. We should be able to travel around unhampered by crowds."

"The weather seems perfect too," Julie said with a sigh. "It's not too cold or too hot."

"Yeah, like a tropical paradise." He took the last bite of his toast, finished off his coffee, and opened the brochure to an inside map. "It's a small island, about seven miles long by three miles wide. Our main interests lie in this area right here." He ran his finger in a circle over the middle of the map. He glanced at Julie. She stared at the map, but said nothing. "We can probably walk to most of those places," he said. "The citadel is about a 30-minute walk from our hotel." He paused and surveyed her reaction. She didn't flinch. "We could always take public transportation." Still no response. "You know, buses, cabs, whatever."

Julie gave him a half-smile. "What? No donkey rides?"

Mark chuckled. "I could try to find us one, if you insist. Or how about a camel?"

She wrinkled her nose. "No thanks. I wore my walking shoes." She lifted her foot from beneath the table, showed off her Reeboks and smiled with satisfaction.

Mark should have known she'd have no reservations about a trek up the hillside. Hadn't she spent several hours walking around Ephesus without uttering a single complaint? The girl's love of the outdoors matched his own, as did their mutual affinity for exercise. Julie went jogging nearly every morning with Lakisha. He hit the trails by himself. As for Katie, a good workout meant a trip to the nearest shopping mall. She would drag him from store to store until he made a quick escape to find a coffee shop.

Mark looked at the girl across the table from him. She was his perfect soulmate and she didn't even know it.

Even now, she was sorting through the brochures on the table, oblivious to his admiring gaze. He loved her interest in the unfamiliar and the way she tackled each project with enthusiasm.

She lifted a brochure with the Monastery of St. John on the cover. "It's magnificent," she said, wistfully. "I can't wait to see it up close."

"According to the map, we'll have to walk through a residential area to get there," Mark said. "Be sure and take your sunglasses along. In these communities, nearly every house has been whitewashed to a blazing shine. When the sun hits them, it can be blinding."

"Thanks for the warning."

Mark gathered up the brochures and rose to his feet. "First

thing, we'll need to exchange our Turkish liras for euros. The front desk should be able to help us with that. We'll spend at least an hour at the Monastery of St. John. Then, we'll head along the hillside to the old nunnery that houses the Cave of the Apocalypse. I figure, we can hit the shopping area around one o'clock and stop for lunch while the sun is at its peak."

Julie signaled her approval with a nod. She hadn't griped one time over the hectic schedule he'd devised. There was no silent pouting, no frustrated sighs, none of the stuttering excuses he'd have gotten if he'd brought Katie along.

Katie. At some point, he was going to have to call her. For now, he'd have to keep his mind on their itinerary. He and Julie had three days left to gather the information each of them needed before they headed home. And there was that all-important quest for the old man.

"This afternoon, we should talk to some of the locals," Mark said. "We can try to find out where John's double might be living."

She agreed, but added no ideas of her own. He eyed her with concern. Julie would follow for just so long, but once she set her mind on a path that didn't include him, she'd be off and running.

Before leaving the hotel, they stopped at the front desk. The clerk gave them directions to the monastery, which involved a trek along the main road and a turn upward into the hills. The higher they went, the narrower the street became. They trudged around sharp turns between continuous exterior walls with doorways to the individual houses. None of the homes were stand-alone. Everything was strung together in one long, whitewashed blur of residences. The monastery loomed ahead. Its imposing gray-brown facade contrasted with the spread of chalk white structures on the hill below.

Long shadows fell across their path. Tamarisk trees sprang from patches of open land, and, now and then, the pavement disintegrated into crumbling slabs and crude, sloping stairways.

Mark moved ahead of Julie and led the way. Near the top, he turned his head and smiled. She was right on his heels. He quietly enjoyed her dependence on him, though he knew it would be short-lived for this outrageously self-sufficient woman. Moments later, she proved him right by lunging ahead of him. She made it to the top of the hill first.

Undaunted, Mark took a moment to check out the view from the base of the monastery. He turned and looked out over the rooftops. He inhaled deeply, whispered a prayer to the Creator of all he could see, and then he joined Julie closer to the castle.

"It's huge," Julie breathed, her face turned toward the upper parapets. "From a distance it appeared much smaller. Now it makes me feel small."

"Me too," said Mark. He gazed up at the top and pointed toward the pinnacle directly overhead. "Do you see that opening high above the entry?"

Julie craned her neck. "Yes, I think so."

"They once called that *the killer*."

Julie grinned at him. "The killer, huh?"

"Yeah. When the enemy came close, the people who were holed up inside doused them with hot oil, boiling water, molten lead, or whatever caustic liquid they had on hand."

He leaped backward. "Watch out!" Julie jumped and let out a shriek. He laughed with delight.

Scowling she jabbed him in the arm. "Thanks a bunch,

Mark. Too bad it's the 21st century instead of several hundred years ago. *I'd* be up there dumping the hot oil, and *you'd* be standing down here directly in the line of my attack."

He flinched. "Ouch," he said, chuckling. On the surface he hoped he could keep their banter going. Deep inside he knew it would be short-lived. The best thing he could do for now was morph into his college professor-tour guide routine. It was like putting on a mask. He could hide behind it and not show his heart.

He took a breath, opened the brochure, and cleared his throat. Julie's steady gaze had him believing she was truly interested in what he was about to say.

"This monastery's construction began in 1088 under the leadership of a Byzantine monk named Ioannis Christodoulos. Get this, Julie. The guy's name means *John, slave of Christ.*"

"Fascinating," was all she said.

He'd expected a little more of a reaction. But that was okay. There was more to come that might pique her interest.

"What do you think?" he pressed. "Maybe the Apostle John kept coming back from the dead. Ioannis could have been one of his many identities over the centuries."

She tilted her head and her eyes flashed with skepticism.

"I'm serious," he said. "Why do you suppose the guy built a monastery so close to the exact location where John is said to have written his book of Revelation? This had to be a pretty special place for the apostle. After all, this is where he last met Christ."

She smiled and shook her head with a slight stirring of her ponytail. It was a cute response, but one that troubled Mark. He was never going to be able to break through that tough wall of hers.

"C'mon, Julie. What's happened to your imagination? Does everything have to be, 'Just the facts?' Set aside your reporter notebook for one minute and consider possibilities beyond the norm. You might surprise yourself."

She let out a giggle. "Sorry, Mark. I'll reserve judgment for now."

"Well," he said. "As for me, I'd like to learn more about this Christodoulos." He lifted the brochure. "I've read some fascinating things about him already. For example, they've stored a ton of his writings and a whole slew of his artifacts in this monastery. I hope we might get a look at some of them. Apparently, the people of Patmos highly esteem this guy, like he's some kind of saint. Twice a year, they hold nightly vigils in his honor."

He tucked the brochure in his pocket. "Let's go inside and check things out. You might find something of interest for your—um—article." He purposely said it with an air of boredom.

He thought he heard her say, "*I doubt it,*" but he wasn't sure. It didn't matter. His own excitement growing, he strode ahead of her.

15

THE MONASTARY OF SAINT JOHN

Admission to the monastery was free, but a donation basket stood by the entry. Mark dropped a couple of euros in. The attendant gave them a nod. With Julie close at his side, Mark passed through the main door into an open-air courtyard. Streams of sunlight fell upon the pebbled floor that stretched like inviting fingers toward mysterious doorways. Strategically placed pillars created arches to walk under. Large white panels broke up the classic gray and brown architecture. Potted plants gave a profusion of red and green to the muted stonework. High overhead on the roof, two sets of bell towers, stirred by a breeze, sent a subtle tolling into the air. The entire area was bathed in an ethereal glow that had Mark catching his breath.

"Awesome," he whispered. The setting would be a dream come true for any archaeology professor. No longer was Mark standing in a classroom merely talking about such an experience. He was living it.

When he finally emerged from his reverie, he discovered Julie had moved away from him. She was in the center of the courtyard and was running her hand over what appeared to be a stone cistern. Mark walked over to her and rested his hand on the concrete lid.

"At one time, they probably used this as a storage tank for water or wine." He said. "Imagine the monks coming here every morning with their urns, collecting their daily supply."

Julie smiled but said nothing. Either she wasn't impressed or she was doing a good job of hiding her interest. Unless she was trying to make a point, she tended to keep her thoughts to herself. No wonder it took him almost a year to find out she resented his talking about his faith. If he could have gotten her to open up sooner, perhaps their relationship might have taken a different path.

Mark set aside his regrets and moved on. He wanted to make the best use of the time he had in this place of antiquity. The feel of the aged structure fascinated him. It even smelled old.

They strolled with other tourists through the maze of corridors, courtyards, and side rooms reserved for various purposes, including a fully stocked library and a restoration facility where lay workers were using modern technological tools to restore decaying books and icons.

The monastery had ten chapels, each of them adorned with ornate frescos in deep browns and bright reds, and all of them were trimmed in pure gold.

At the end of their tour, they returned to the main courtyard where Mark spotted a monk talking to a couple of tourists. He grabbed Julie's hand.

"C'mon," he said. "That guy was speaking in English. Let's have a chat with him."

They hurried across the cobbled pavement toward the monk. As the other couple departed, Mark called out to him. "Sir, could we have a few words with you?"

As the monk turned around, his long black cassock swirled about his ankles. He was a mature individual, probably in his mid-50s, had a full, dark beard, and his hair was bound in back into a ponytail. He wore black sandals and a headpiece that resembled Abe Lincoln's familiar stovepipe hat. From his studies in Greek Orthodoxy, Mark conjured up the word. *Kalimavkion.* He suppressed a laugh. It sounded like a type of pastry instead of a hat.

The man extended his right hand toward Mark and smiled. "Welcome," he said. "I'm Brother Agapios, but everyone calls me Brother Pio. And you are..."

Mark introduced Julie and himself and explained the purpose of their trip, that Julie was doing an article for a newspaper and he was gathering information for his work at the Bible college.

"We could use a little help with our research," Mark admitted. "Do you have time to talk with us and maybe show us a few things we might have missed?"

"Of course. That's why I'm here," Agapios said, with only the hint of an accent. "In fact, for a small fee, I'll be happy to guide you through some areas most tourists never see."

"That's wonderful," Mark told him. He was surprised that Julie had stood quietly by his side. She'd clammed up for some reason. He glanced in her direction. She was a blank wall.

"It's too bad you missed our celebration of Pentecost a week ago," Agapios said. "The festivities are always memorable, you understand. There's a procession, the lighting of candles, special recitations, and here at the monastery, we give out samples of the traditional bread reserved for that observance."

"Sounds terrific," Mark said. Julie remained silent. He'd expected her, a reporter, to plunge right in with a few questions, but she had frozen up like a statue. He cast another glance at her. She was unreadable. He shook his head and returned his attention to the monk.

"Brother Agapios—I mean, Brother Pio—you speak excellent

English. Are the monks here trained in other languages?"

Pio released a chuckle. "I studied for the ministry in your country, at Princeton. I thoroughly enjoyed my time there, but when my schooling ended, I returned to my homeland. I first served as a priest at a cathedral in Athens, but now I have become a monk. Priest. Monk. It makes little difference to me. I still serve the same God and I minister to people with equal enthusiasm in either post. At this point in my life, I have chosen a celibate communal existence with my spiritual brothers."

"So, what might we see of significance in this place?" Mark asked.

"Our visitors roam freely through the different chapels and hallways. But, for a nominal fee of six euros each, you may enter our museum of antiquities where we keep some of our most treasured artifacts. We currently have on display a parchment from the Gospel of Saint Mark. We also have on loan the skull of Saint Thomas."

Mark perked up. To be able to see, up close, such relics of religious significance sent goose bumps along his arms. "I'll pay the fee," he said. "It's well worth it."

Julie trailed behind Mark and Pio as they walked to another part of the monastery.

"I'm curious about the man behind all this grandeur," Mark said, gesturing toward the arches and icons. "What sort of person was Ioannis Christodoulos?"

"You pronounce his name well," Pio said, his tone one of amazement. "Most people hardly get past Ioannis."

They laughed together and Mark began to relax.

"Christodoulos," Pio said. "*The Servant of Christ*—or so the name implies. From the traditions handed down over the years, he was an intriguing man, yet he was a contradiction in many ways. Though he lived an ascetic life and shunned close relationships, he begged the authorities to establish this monastery, and then he helped populate it with a host of monks from his order. Though he shunned formal education, he read voraciously and created a huge library here. Though he accepted responsibility over every aspect of this place, he never sought recognition for himself."

"Impressive," Mark said. "Apparently, he set an example for the other—"

"Mark thinks John the Apostle and this Christodoulos might have been one and the same." Julie had broken her silence by interrupting Mark.

Her sarcastic remark caught him off-guard. Up till this time, she'd been quietly following. Now she stood there with a mischievous twinkle in her eye. She finally had something to say, and she'd made fun of him. He didn't know if he should laugh it off or defend himself.

Agapios burst out laughing and took the edge off. "Young man, you're not the first to wonder if there might be a connection between the two."

Mark smiled sheepishly at the monk. "I was only kidding. The man's name made me a little suspicious, that's all."

Pio gave a nod. "Let me simply say this. The Patmians are an idealistic people, you understand. They look beyond the tangible evidence and they cling to the romantic legends of this place. The truth is, Ioannis was a man, nothing more. Believe me when I say, he was not John resurrected from the dead. Christodoulos lived, and he died."

With a swirl of his cassock, Pio turned away and gestured with one arm. "Come. Let's go into the museum."

135

As he entered the sacred place, Mark went speechless. Floor-to-ceiling murals depicted the apostles of Jesus, and one prominent painting showed John perched on a seaside cliff while writing his account of the Revelation. Different cases held jeweled crowns, silver and gold crosses, and writings that dated back several centuries. The entire room was bathed in a soft glow. A border of embossed gold trailed around the upper walls, and two six-foot brass candlesticks stood like palace guards in front of the central icons.

Pio pointed toward a wooden chest, its sides trimmed in gold and silver.

"Saint Christodoulos' bones rest inside," the monk said, a hint of reverence in his tone. "He died in 1093 and his remains came to this monastery a few years later."

Julie stepped closer to the vault. She pulled out her camera, but Pio put up his hand. "Sorry, no photos."

She tucked her camera in her purse and faced the monk. "So, you say those are Christodoulos' bones in there. How do you know that?"

Mark winced. She'd finally started talking and she was challenging the guy. He tried to signal her, but she either didn't see him or was purposely ignoring him. *Stubborn girl.* Though he usually admired her spunk, sometimes it surfaced at the wrong times.

Pio raised an eyebrow and smiled platonically. "You have doubts?" he said, his eyes on Julie.

She shrugged and raised a defiant chin. "I merely question the validity of things people tell me. I like proof." She gestured toward the sarcophagus. "A bunch of people make a memorial to a man who died—what?—a thousand years ago? Must everyone believe those are his bones in that box?

Isn't it possible they came from someone else or even an animal that died?"

Mark wiped the perspiration from his forehead. The girl was completely out of his control.

"Whether people believe or don't believe is of no consequence," the monk replied in an even tone. "God knows what is the truth, and that's good enough for me. If we are in error, we will learn from it. If we are correct, people like *you* will learn."

Pio took a step closer to Julie and focused entirely on her. Mark stood aside and became a mere observer at this point.

"Miss Peters," Pio said. "No one in this place intends to force a particular belief on those who visit. Monks are not despots who demand that you agree with everything they say. We believe God has given people free will and we honor that. You can believe whatever you want, but it doesn't make the truth any less accurate."

Mark had been watching Julie. He was surprised when she didn't back down. "So, what do *you* believe, Brother Agapios?" she challenged him, narrowing her eyes.

Julie hadn't used the monk's nickname, maybe out of defiance. She certainly hadn't shown the man any respect. Mark's shoulders sagged and he bowed his head. *God help her.*

To his surprise, Pio responded with a chuckle. "Well, I could recite the Apostle's Creed for you. That might tell you what I believe—what *all* of us who serve here believe."

"No, I mean, how do you know there *is* a God?"

Mark perked up. Perhaps the monk might be able to convince Julie what he'd been trying to tell her from the beginning—that God was real and that He cared about her.

Pio didn't disappoint him. "God has made himself real to

me every day of my life. One needs only to seek Him, you understand. It was God who drew me to this work and God who sustains me in it."

As Mark should have expected, Julie didn't back down. "How do you know your life's work has not been in vain, that you haven't spent all these years locked up in this prison when you could have enjoyed a more gratifying lifestyle?"

Pio didn't appear the least bit flustered. "First of all, I don't think of this place as a prison. I know without a doubt that I'm in the right place. Since the day I responded to God's call I have never regretted my decision. A gratifying lifestyle? I can't imagine anything more gratifying than to serve God where He has called me."

"How did you know for certain that God called you here? Did He speak audibly to you? Did you have a vision? What proof did you have that God was calling you? Couldn't it have been self-motivation?"

"Miss Peters, doors shut and windows open. I simply stopped whenever a door shut and I moved ahead when a window opened."

Julie tilted her head, her mouth twisted in a mock smile. "Doors? Windows? What if the door slams shut and the window never opens? What if you're trapped in a place you can't leave? *Ever.*" Her bitterness came through with the last word.

Mark stared in amazement. Julie's interrogation of the monk had turned into an admission of her own personal struggle. He backed away, hoping Pio might be able to tear down the wall he himself had failed to demolish.

From Julie's first question, Mark had been eliminated from the repartee. Now he stood on the sidelines and tried to glean whatever might help him understand this complex woman he adored.

"Are you telling me you never experienced the will of God in your life?" Pio also seemed to have picked up on the root of Julie's cross-examination. "Haven't you sensed God working, directing your steps, carrying you through the rough places, even allowing bad things to happen, but blessing you along the way?" he asked with astounding wisdom.

Mark kept his eyes on Julie. She fidgeted with her purse strap. The smirk left her face and was replaced by a nervous tremor. His heart went out to her.

"I—I used to believe, but now I know better." She was crumbling. Mark had a sudden urge to run to her rescue, but he restrained himself.

"Child," the monk said, his eyes clouding with compassion. "Don't give up on God. He loves you. Though it's hard for you to see that right now, He's never abandoned you. Even during your darkest days, He's been standing in the shadows. Though you weren't physically aware of His presence, believe me, He never left your side."

The man's intuition astounded Mark. Somehow, he had looked inside Julie's heart and had seen what it took Mark months to notice, that she was a frightened little girl trapped inside a woman's body. She looked like she was about to cry. It was time to rescue her. Not from Brother Pio, but from herself.

"Pio," Mark said, drawing the monk's attention. "I can see why Julie asks such probing questions. After all, she's a reporter. She's trained do that. Sometimes, people find it intimidating, but she means well."

He glanced at Julie. She glared at him, and he expected

her to tell him she could speak for herself. But she stiffened her jaw and remained silent. He wanted Julie to trust him, not to resent him.

He cleared his throat. "Tell me, Pio. On another topic, what do you know about John? Are there any local legends regarding the apostle?"

Pio chuckled, and he shook his head. His eyebrows came together in amusement.

"I know of a couple stories that serve no other purpose than to add a little sensationalism to our island. Some might think such tales make good newspaper coverage." He glanced at Julie, then turned back toward Mark. "The people of Patmos insist there were miracles. Whether they are true or not, I can't say. For example, John was supposed to have miraculously saved several individuals from drowning in the sea. And there's an ongoing tale that he protected the island by fighting off a mythological monster. Others say John had healing powers. Of course, that's entirely possible. After all, didn't Jesus' apostles come away with such gifts of the Spirit?"

Pio shrugged. "But, listen, you two. Don't dwell on the mystical and the theoretical. Why don't you enjoy the *historical* significance of the legacy John left us? Study the real man who served God right to the end. I suggest you visit the Cave of the Apocalypse when you leave here. Simply walk down the hill a ways on the designated route most pilgrims take when they visit Patmos."

"We will," Mark said, then he risked one more question. "We've heard talk—a rumor—and I know this will sound ridiculous—but is it true that the Apostle John still lives on this island?"

Pio let out a hearty laugh. His eyes sparkled with moisture.

"I know that sounds juvenile, Pio," Mark explained. "But hear me out. Patmos had to be special to John. Though he must have suffered while he was exiled here, how could he not develop a passion for the place where he had come face-to-face with his resurrected Lord? It's been said that after John's release, he traveled the world. Doesn't it make sense that he would want to come back and live out the rest of his life here? What if, as Jesus said in the Bible, John would remain until the Lord's return? Jesus hasn't come back yet. John could still be waiting."

Brother Agapios didn't flinch. "I'm familiar with the verse," he said, nodding, "and I know the rumor. But my son, why do you trouble yourself with fables? They have no place in your college project." He turned toward Julie. "Nor will they add any credibility to your newspaper report, Miss Peters. In fact, such an inclusion might even discredit your publication and embarrass you at the same time."

Mark wasn't satisfied. "Okay, then let's talk facts. Many written records tell how the other apostles died. Matthew was beheaded. Bartholomew and Peter were crucified head down. Andrew faced martyrdom on an X-shaped cross. Philip and Simon the Zealot also suffered crucifixion. Thomas was pierced with a lance and was burned to death. James the Less was stoned, Judas Thaddeus died from a cruel beating, and Matthias was either run through with a lance or hacked with an axe while also being crucified. There exists no such evidence about John, no written documents, not even from his followers. The early church leaders were students of John, yet not one document exists saying when or how he died, and no bones have been found."

Pio's eyebrows went up. "I see you've done your homework,

Mark. But, that doesn't mean John is still alive. As for his bones, isn't there a tomb in Ephesus?"

Mark pressed on. "You know as well as I do, John's bones are not in the tomb at Ephesus. No one knows where they are. It seems to me that something that precious should have received better care."

Pio folded his arms and took a firm stance. "So, you're saying lack of evidence of John's death means he could still be alive?"

"No, not only lack of evidence. An early church practice involved the fragmentation and distribution of the bones of the saints to cathedrals in Rome and other holy shrines. I've been to St. Peter's Basilica and the Church of the Holy Apostles. I've seen such treasures. So why aren't any of John's bones included in those sarcophagi?"

Mark glanced at Julie. She was scribbling in her notebook.

He swallowed and went on. "Pio, let me get to the point. There's supposed to be an old sage living somewhere in the hills of Patmos. Apparently, some believe he might be John, either resurrected from the grave or possibly never died. Julie and I have come here to look into that rumor. Do you know of this guy?"

Pio nodded. "Of course I do. You speak of Yanno," he said, a smile crossing his lips.

Mark tried to hide the excitement that arose within him, but he'd never been one to mask his feelings.

Pio's eyes had misted over. There was no doubt this Yanno was special.

"I'm not sure what the two of you expected to find in Patmos," the monk said. "Perhaps you, Mark, hoped to add a little mystical slant to your teachings. And, Miss Peters, maybe you hoped to leave with a sensational newspaper article about a man who never died or possibly came back from the grave. Have either of you considered how such wild tales could destroy your credibility in that logical, punctilious world you live in? After all, aren't college professors and reporters supposed to deal with *provable* facts, not assumptions or myths?"

Mark opened his mouth to reply, but Julie cut him off. "Oh, I agree with you, Brother Agapios," she said. "To me, this whole idea has sounded ludicrous from the very beginning. But, I'm on an assignment to prove or disprove the credibility of that rumor, and I'm determined to fulfill my duty, no matter what I find out." She huffed. "As a non-believer, I doubt whether John ever existed at all, but even if he *did* walk this earth, I believe his ministry ended 2,000 years ago. Like your Iannis Christodoulos, he lived and he died. *That's* the report I intend to take back with me."

Pio let out a sigh and turned to Mark. "I'm afraid you're going to be disappointed if you think John is still alive. If you want to prove otherwise, then do what you will. I'll satisfy your curiosity with this. The man you are seeking is Yanno Theologos. He's a harmless recluse who lives in the hills of Hora. He bothers no one, you understand, but the locals flock to his home bearing gifts. In return, they ask him for prayer, for words of advice, and for the healing concoctions he makes from herbs that grow in his garden. Those foolish Patmians would make a saint of him, if we allowed it."

"I'd like to see him for myself and talk with him," Mark said. "Maybe then we can put to rest the curiosity that has arisen about him back home. Do you know where he lives?"

The monk's brows arched with impatience. "I don't advise a

visit," he said. "The people guard that man like a rare treasure. They don't appreciate outsiders, and they *definitely* don't want their island paradise turned into a media circus."

"You said his door is open to visitors," Mark persisted.

"Yes, it's open to the *locals*. But, someone from the outside?" He shook his head. "I don't know."

"Have *you* met him?"

"No. And I have no desire to meet him. Don't ask me where he lives. I don't know the exact location, and I wouldn't tell you if I did."

Pio gestured toward the far end of the court. "I must return to my duties," he said, his voice firm. "Keep in mind that the monastery closes between one-thirty and four o'clock." He smiled. "For our midday nap," he said. Then with a wave of his hand, "Goodbye, my friends. Enjoy your time in Patmos."

Before Mark could say anything else, Pio spun away and strode off, his sandals striking the pavement in a clipped rhythm, his black robe beating the air behind him. He disappeared around a corner.

Mark looked at Julie. She had a smug expression that disturbed him. The frightened little girl had returned to her place of hiding. The inveterate reporter was back. But the chat with Pio had unveiled another side of Julie, one that Mark hoped to resurrect at some point during their trip. After all, God sometimes opens a window.

16

THE CAVE OF THE APOCALYPSE

The feverish exchange of words in the monastery had left Julie feeling drained and bitter. What right did that priest—or monk, or whatever he was—have to badger her the way he did? He'd backed her into a corner, but she had surfaced unscathed—hadn't she?

As Mark headed down the uneven stairway to the Cave of the Apocalypse, she purposely lagged behind him. She was still getting over her exchange with that monk, and she didn't need Mark to pick up where Agapios had left off. In fact, Mark seemed quite content with the way things ended back there. The jerk was actually whistling.

The walk took fifteen minutes. The cave lay at the end of a well-worn donkey path, a mere two-lane walkway that twisted and turned down the hill. To Julie, the outside looked more like a grouping of white boxes than a shrine. Except for a mosaic over the entrance and a solitary cross on the top, nothing about the outside had any religious significance.

She drew up beside Mark and pointed at the work of art above the door. "What's that supposed to be?"

"It's a depiction of John and his amanuensis."

"Amanu—what?"

"Amanuensis. A scribe. John supposedly dictated the final book of the Bible to a servant named Prochoros."

"So this is the location where John is supposed to have received visions for the book of Revelation? You're kidding, right?" Julie didn't try to keep the sarcasm out of her voice. "Look at this place. Does this look like holy ground to you?"

"I'm not going to justify that with an answer," Mark said. He cast a disgusted half-grin in her direction, then he quickly moved ahead and paid the fee for both of them. A *Welcome* sign, written in both Greek and English, had a couple of warnings. *"No shorts"* and *"No photos or videos."* Julie let out a frustrated sigh. How was she going to get anything meaningful if she couldn't take any pictures in these places?

She'd already made up her mind to keep her visit brief. She'd come to Patmos determined not to let the sites influence her preconceived ideas about whether or not there was a higher power. She had a job to do and it didn't include falling into some sort of religious stupor.

Yet, when she passed through the main door, an eerie prickle ran along the back of her neck and down her arms. She removed her sunglasses and paused to allow her eyes to adjust to the semi-darkness. The inside was exceptionally small and claustrophobic. With a steady stream of tourists coming in behind her, Julie moved toward a simply adorned chapel.

A few randomly placed icons greeted her at the entry. A rack of votive candles created an other-worldly atmosphere, and the sharp smell of incense grew stronger as Julie passed with the crowd from one area to the next.

A young priest was speaking in Greek to a small group of visitors. She hurried by them and passed an altar where worshipers sat on benches with their heads bowed. Their lips moved in quiet prayer. The devout scene reminded her of the desperate women she had seen at John's tomb in Ephesus. *Desperation.* That was the word that came to mind. What did

146

these people think they might accomplish praying to statues and sending prayers up to a God who never answered a plea for help? *Fools,* was the other word that came to mind.

She scanned the area and tried to commit the scene to memory. Silver incense globes hung from the ceiling. A huge tapestry depicted John lying on the ground near the feet of Jesus with a half-dozen angels hovering in a circle above them. The portrait drew Julie back to her youth and a set of images in a children's picture Bible. She'd once flipped eagerly through the colorful pages and even imagined herself growing up in biblical days. That was when her heart was young and innocent. She knew better now.

Shaking off the fantasy, she found Mark under a thick slab of stone that stretched overhead like a half-open cocoon. The rock ceiling hung so low, some of the people reached up and ran their hands along its surface. She drew close to Mark, partly to get away from the press of bodies, but also because she depended on him to feed her information. If nothing else, Mark was better than hiring a tour guide.

He pointed to a large fissure that split the upper rock in three places. "What do you think caused *that,* Julie?"

"I don't know. Was there an earthquake or something? These foreign cities are supposed to be prone to tremors."

Mark's eyes creased at the corners. She got the feeling he was laughing at her.

"Okay, smarty," she said, scowling. "What do *you* say happened?"

"It's not what *I* say. Tradition says those splits in the rock could have been caused by the blast of a trumpet. Or even by the voice of God."

"Do you agree?" she challenged him.

He shrugged. "Anything's possible."

She turned away from him and walked over to a fenced off area at the far end. She paused there and stared at the jag of stone that protruded from the wall.

"That was where John lay his head when he slept." The accent was definitely American. Startled, Julie looked over her right shoulder. A young man had quietly slipped up beside her. He couldn't have been more than 17. He had spiked red hair, a tuft of fuzz on his chin, and pimples. He wore blue jeans and a "Jesus is King" T-shirt, and a camera hung from a strap around his neck.

"I wish I could shoot some pictures," the youth said.

Julie nodded. "Me too. Looks like I brought my camera for nothing."

"It's okay. I'm just happy to be able to see all this. I waited three years to make this trip. I worked a part-time job, saved up my money, and now I'm here. At last."

Julie eyed him with amazement. He had tears in his eyes. They sparkled in the soft glow of nearby candles. He looked at her and blushed. "I love the Apostle John," he said, brushing a drop from his cheek. "He's my hero."

Julie eyed the youth with interest. He had so much passion for one so young. What could that possibly feel like, to blindly believe in something you can't see?

"I'm going to enter the monastery next year," the boy said with conviction. "If they'll have me."

"You—you want to be a *monk*?" Julie thought about Brother Agapios. He'd said he was contented with his choice. But this was a mere child. "Are you telling me you want to give up your life in America for such a subservient commitment?" She didn't attempt to keep the sarcasm out of her voice.

"Yes, Ma'am," he said, never faltering. "But, I hadn't thought of my decision as giving anything up. I see it as *finding* something. I want to serve my Lord who died for me. I can't think of a better place than right here on Patmos—where John lived."

He stared into Julie's eyes, his own eyes aflame. "Isn't there *something* you dream of doing that would give purpose to your life?"

His question caught Julie off guard. "I—I don't know. I never really thought about it. I mean, I believe I've already discovered what I want to do."

"Well, don't let too much time pass by before you make sure," the boy challenged her. He lowered his voice. "Do you want me to pray for you?"

A sudden discomfort swept over Julie. She glanced about the cave, now packed with visitors. "Sure, but not now. Remember me in your prayers. That should be enough."

She turned away. The crowd had closed in on them, blocking her path to the exit. The candles emitted a suffocating aroma. The warmth of bodies enveloped her. She couldn't breathe, couldn't stop trembling.

She didn't bother to search for Mark but wove through the maze of tourists and headed for the exit. Then, she burst from the shadows into the bright sunshine. She fumbled in her purse for her sunglasses and sought out a ledge under a tree, where she could sit and recover from the harrowing experience. She withdrew a water bottle from her purse and gulped its contents.

While waiting for Mark, Julie sat on the rock ledge and pondered her encounter with the young man inside the cave. He had to be six or seven years her junior, yet he possessed a maturity far beyond that of any teenager she'd ever known. He knew exactly what he wanted to do with the rest of his life. When Julie was a kid, she also had made plans, but they had nothing to do with serving God and a whole lot to do with her own personal interests.

When she was that boy's age, her whole life came to a shattering end. Plan a future? She didn't know if she could survive the past.

Until coming on this trip, she thought she'd put all the trauma behind her. Then she'd met Doctor Balser on the plane. And Brother Agapios. Now the teenage boy had broken through her wall of protection. How could she ignore their words of hope and restoration?

She choked up like she was about to cry, but tears didn't come. There was only one way to fight off the memories. The same way she always did. By hardening her heart until it was as cold as the stones that were used to build these monuments. The wall she had erected had worked fine for the past six years. Why was it crumbling now? In this place?

She stood up and paced back and forth in front of the shrine, relieved when Mark finally emerged. Now she could get as far away from these ruins as possible.

He walked up to her, but he didn't say a word. Instead, he held her hand and quietly guided her down the hill toward Hora. Had he witnessed her interaction with the boy? Had he watched her flee from that enclosure? His silence told her he knew a lot more than he was letting on.

Weakened by the experience in the shrine, Julie was grateful when Mark selected a quaint cafe where they could sit for a while. They settled in wicker chairs at an outdoor table. The sunlight filtered through a thriving eucalyptus tree and sent striped shadows across the terrace. Lulled by the tranquil setting, Julie sat back and didn't object when Mark ordered two glasses of the house wine. As she sipped the tangy liquid, the gnawing upheaval gradually left her.

Still, she didn't say a word. Nor did she look at the menu. Or at Mark. He suggested seared salmon and spinach risotto. She nodded her approval.

When the food arrived, Mark said a quick blessing, and they dined in silence. Julie picked at her food, then she set down her fork.

Mark ate like a starving refugee. He glanced at Julie's half-eaten meal. "You gonna finish that?" he asked, raising his eyebrows.

Julie snickered and shook her head as he scraped up the remnants on her plate. There were times when she wished she had never met him, and there were times when she wished she hadn't pushed him away—times when she trusted in his strong shoulder, his godly wisdom, his genuine interest in whatever concerned her, and times when she blocked out everything he said and did.

Mark wiped his mouth with a napkin and gazed at her. She smiled. He smiled back. Thankfully, he didn't say anything.

After paying the bill, Mark suggested a stroll through town. Julie welcomed the diversion.

"If nothing else, this has proven to be an interesting vacation," she said in an effort to sound light-hearted. The last thing she wanted was for him to ask her if anything was wrong.

"The weather has been great," she rambled on. "Look at that blue sky. There isn't a cloud in sight. The monastery was quite fascinating. I enjoyed talking to Brother Agapios, didn't you? And how about that cave? My goodness, someone must have spent an awful lot of money putting that thing together."

She suspected from the frown on Mark's forehead that he was perplexed about her behavior. She had to admit, her irrational chatter was out of character for her. But, it was the only way she knew to keep him from prying.

"I have enough material to get started on my PowerPoint presentation," Mark said. "I hope you'll share your photos with me."

"Sure. No problem." She snickered. "All I have so far were from Ephesus. I didn't get a single shot in the cave, thanks to their rules."

"Well," he said. "I guess the only thing left to do now is for us to find Yanno."

"That monk wasn't much help," Julie said with a smirk. "He had a lot of knowledge about the monastery, but let's face it, Mark, he avoided talking about the old man in the village. You can't tell me he doesn't know where the guy lives. He didn't want *us* to know. But we're going to find out. From my experience, if you want to get to the root of something, you go straight to the people. That's where you get the *real* story. If we want to find the old man, we need to ask the villagers who visit him."

"You're right, Julie. I was thinking the same thing. Let's go to the marketplace and talk with some of the merchants. We'll look for folks who've lived here for a long time." He raised his eyebrows and leaned toward her, a look of anticipation on his face. "But take it easy on them, Miss Reporter. Don't bombard them with tough questions, like you did with Brother Pio. We have to win their confidence first."

"Listen, Mark. I've done this before. When I'm interviewing

a tough subject, I know how to wait for the right moment. Trust me. I won't spoil our chances."

"Good. I don't want to put these folks on the defensive before we get the opportunity to ask them how to find this guy. Pio said the villagers protect him like some kind of treasure. If we don't handle this right, we may never find him."

Julie was already feeling the pressure. She wasn't the only reporter on a hunt for the old man. Jason Redding was on his way to Patmos and might already be there. A flame ignited within her. She was primed for battle. *Bring it on, Jason,* she thought.

"We can't let anyone know I'm a reporter," she said aloud. "People shy away from the press. We have to let everyone think we're tourists, at least until we find this Yanno fellow."

Mark let out a long sigh. "I don't know, Julie. I don't like to start off with a lie."

"It won't be a lie. We'll simply be omitting the truth."

He shook his head. "The Bible talks about a sin of omission. We should—"

"Look," she said, her face heating up. "Until now, you've been in charge, and I haven't given you a hard time. It's my turn now."

He puffed out another breath. "All right. I'll go along with your plan for the time being, but as soon as I think the lie has gone too far, I'm gonna have to speak up."

"Don't worry. I've got this whole thing under control. Trust me, Mark. I know what I'm doing."

17

THE SEARCH BEGINS

Downtown Skala was a pleasant surprise. It was a quiet, peaceful setting, with little traffic, except for compact cars and motor scooters. The main mode of transportation along the paved downtown streets appeared to be one's own feet. That was okay by Julie. Walking gave her more freedom to roam about as she pleased.

Besides a multitudes of alleyways that led to obscurity, the main drag held a string of two- and three-story buildings with open-air shops and cafes on the lower floor. Upstairs were what looked to be apartments.

This time it was Mark who lagged behind, and Julie led the way past the stores, the *tavernas*, and the cafes, their inviting aromas of fresh baked bread, roast lamb, and ground coffee pouring onto the street.

"Hungry?" Mark said.

She laughed. "You're kidding, right?"

Mark nodded. "Just wanted to see if you were paying attention."

"If we want to save time and cover a lot of ground, I think we should split up," she said.

Mark looked disappointed. "Are you sure?"

"Yes, I'm sure. We can hit more stores that way, maybe get some of the shop owners to talk. They won't feel intimidated if they only have to deal with one person instead of two."

Mark conceded with a nod, but he didn't look happy about splitting up.

"Remember to win their trust first," Julie went on. She was enjoying the role of leader, though she knew it was temporary. For now, she'd have to call upon her experience as a reporter. Mark may have been a college professor, and he may have a ton of knowledge about the sites, but she had learned how to get a source to open up.

"You can't plunge right in and expect to get someone to tell you anything," she told him. "If the people are protecting this guy from outsiders, like Brother Agapios said, they're not going to tell us anything until they're certain it's safe. Winning someone's confidence takes time, Mark."

"We don't *have* a lot of time."

"All the more reason to take it slow and get what we need. Otherwise, we'll be spinning our wheels."

"I'm gonna get started," she said, pulling away from him. She left him standing there with his mouth open.

Propelled by her newfound surge of confidence, she hit store after store, chatted briefly with each proprietor, and then moved on. Her sixth sense told her she hadn't found the right source yet.

A variety of shops held everything from household goods to electronics, plus colorful clothing, handbags, and jewelry. She strolled into one store and pretended to be shopping. A suntanned woman in a flowered sundress smiled at her from behind a counter. Julie searched through a pile of colorful scarves and pulled out a couple she liked.

She looked toward the counter. Though other tourists drifted past, the woman hadn't taken her eyes off of Julie.

She lifted a scarf with a red-and-purple pattern. It would make a perfect gift for her friend Lakisha. She raised her eyebrows. "How much?"

"Three euros."

Julie pulled out her wallet. What was it Mark had whispered in her ear at the stall in Ephesus? *"You're supposed to bargain,"* he'd said. *"They expect it."*

If she wanted to look like a real tourist, she'd have to play the part. "Will you take one euro?"

The woman shook her head. "Two."

"Okay." After completing the purchase, Julie lingered by the counter.

"Have you lived on Patmos long?" she asked.

The woman nodded. "Long time. All my life."

"It's a fabulous island," Julie said. "I'm having a wonderful time here. And the people are so friendly."

The woman pulled some blouses out of a box and began to hang them on a rack. Julie followed her.

"I'm still learning my way around. Can you recommend a good restaurant?"

"They are all good."

This wasn't going well. She was about to move on to another shop, but chose to give it one more try. "Do you happen to know of a man named Yanno Theologos?"

The woman stared bullets at her for a moment, then she raised her chin and stared down at Julie, like she was evaluating her. A second later, she appeared to relax.

"Yanno, a good man," she said, nodding. "He save my daughter."

"Saved her? How?"

The woman shrugged. "She sick. He make better." She hung another blouse.

"Why, that's wonderful. So, Yanno can heal the sick?"

The woman bobbed her head.

Julie's mind raced. "I've been getting these bad headaches." She patted her temple. "Do you think he could help me?"

More nodding, but not a single word of information.

"How can I find this Yanno? Do you know where he lives?"

The woman's eyes clouded over. She turned away from Julie and began to fuss with a pile of purses.

An imaginary wall had gone up between them. Julie knew the signs. It was time to move on. She hit several more stores, talked to their owners, and came away with the same disappointment.

Back on the street, she spotted Mark coming out of another store.

"I tried," she told him.

"I did too. Not a single soul would tell me a thing. Pio warned us that we'd get that kind of reaction."

Julie released a sigh and pulled out the scarf she had purchased. "This is all I have to show for my efforts. A souvenir for Lakisha."

"Hey, lighten up," Mark said and he opened the bag in his hand. "All I got were two belts. I don't need them, but—oh well, it's for a cause."

For the first time that afternoon, Julie laughed. She was ready to hand the reins over to Mark. "What should we do next? It's your call."

"Let's stay together," he said. "People keep thinking we're on our honeymoon. Maybe if we let these store owners believe that, they'll be more receptive."

The thought both troubled and excited Julie. It had been a long time since she dreamed of a wedding day and an intimate vacation with the man of her dreams. But, they were play acting with a purpose. This wasn't a real honeymoon. It

157

was a farce, wasn't it? When they return home, they will go their separate ways and never see each other again.

"All right, let's do it," she said, and she surveyed the shops ahead. "Let's try that little grocery store sitting all alone out there. Do you see it? Away from the other shops? It looks like something the locals probably use."

The tiny shop was constructed of makeshift boards. It had an awning and a row of potted plants on a shelf outside the wall. Inside, the shelves were loaded with jars of jelly, honey, and olives. Central counters bore boxes of pasta, packages of beans and rice, and an assortment of bottled condiments.

An older man in a pair of blue jeans and a plaid shirt was leaning over one side of a table, pricing packages of peppermint candies. The smell of cinnamon drew Julie's attention to a simmering infusion pot on the counter. Behind the register stood a woman, probably the guy's wife. Her welcoming smile put Julie at ease.

"I'll take a few of those peppermints," Mark said to the man.

The merchant stepped back and signaled for him to choose from the pile. Mark grabbed a couple of packages, paid the man, and slipped the peppermints in his sack with the belts.

"Do you speak English?" he said.

"A leettle," the man replied with a long "a" and "e."

Mark nodded toward Julie. "We're visiting from America. So far, we've been to the monastery and the Cave of the Apocalypse. Perhaps you can suggest some other sites."

The man pulled up a wooden stool, sat down and faced Mark and Julie. The woman, still smiling, stepped out from behind the counter. No one else was in the shop.

The woman rested a hand on her husband's shoulder. Julie guessed they were probably in their 70s, however, in this part of the world, the nearly constant sunshine had turned their faces to leather. The man had a grizzled chin and his eyes appeared like two black beads above several folds of skin. Webs of crow's feet fanned out to his temples. Julie restrained a chuckle at the sight of the Cincinnati Reds baseball cap on his head.

The woman had the typical Patmian cheekbones, broad and high on her face. She'd pulled her salt-and-pepper hair into a bun at the base of her neck. She'd bound an apron over a house dress that hung down to her calves, and she wore men's shoes over a pair of black socks.

"Do you mind if I take your picture?" Julie said, lifting her camera.

The couple glanced at each other. A silent message traveled between them. Then they giggled and adjusted their clothing. The woman brushed back a stray lock of hair, and the man pushed the baseball cap back from his forehead.

She shot a series of pictures of the couple and their tiny shop.

In the meantime, Mark told them their names and explained that he and Julie had only three days remaining for their vacation.

The old man responded eagerly. "My name Damien Petra, and this my wife, Sofia. Welcome to our humble island."

"No, not humble," Mark said. "It's an enchanting island, full of so many wonderful surprises."

Damien nodded, a big smile accentuating the fine lines on his face.

"How should we fill our remaining days?" Mark said.

"There be many walking paths from the village," Damien said. "But you won't get lost."

"Yes," Sofia added, her head bobbing with enthusiasm. "You go up, then come down, always come to main road, no matter where you start. Keep going down, down, down, and you find your home." Sofia's hand traced an imaginary stairway. She ended with a laugh at her own island humor.

"You two seem to have a great knowledge of the island," Mark said. "I'd like to know more about Patmos. Perhaps you might like to join us for dinner tonight."

Julie let out a sigh. What was Mark doing? They needed information and he was inviting them for dinner?

Damien and Sofia looked at each other again. Then, Sofia smiled and nodded.

"It'll be *my* treat, of course," Mark said.

"Treat?" Damien looked perplexed.

"It means, I'll pay. You pick the restaurant, and I'll buy your dinner."

Damien didn't hesitate. "Vangelis," he said with a grin. "It be a fine place."

"We'll find it," said Mark. "Seven o'clock?"

Damien nodded. "Seven. It's good."

18

CONFRONTATIONS

With time to kill before dinner, Mark suggested they take a stroll along the harbor. Julie liked the idea. They still didn't know where this Yanno person lived, but she trusted Mark had a plan.

"Why did you ask that couple to join us for dinner?" she asked.

"I was simply doing what you suggested, winning their trust. What better way than over a nice, relaxing meal with new friends?"

"We're running out of time, Mark."

"Maybe. But we weren't getting anywhere with the other shop people. This could be an ice-breaker."

"I sure hope so. I don't want to head back home without having accomplished anything except a tour of old ruins."

As they approached the dock area, Julie began to relax. The sea had a calming effect. The tranquil water stretched out to the horizon, and rarely stirred beyond a ripple, except for an occasional splashing from the passing of a boat.

Behind Julie stretched the rocky shoreline. A never-ending wall zigzagged up the hill. Well-spaced doorways led to family dwellings. There were no stand-alone houses, merely an unbroken string of residences climbing higher and higher up the terraced hillside. The midday sun blazed hot against the whitewashed structures. Julie removed her sunglasses, shut her eyes against the glare, and turned her face toward the sun. For the moment, she had escaped into that other place where no one else could enter.

When she opened her eyes, she caught Mark staring at her. A tenderness had returned to his eyes, and she knew his feelings hadn't changed. The man was still in love with her. Flustered, she backed away from him and hid behind her sunglasses.

A ferryboat pulled up to the dock and was about to shed a fresh batch of tourists onto the island.

"It's going to get really crowded here in about two seconds," she said.

Mark pointed toward the hillside. "Let's take a walk. We can enjoy the view from up there, away from the crowd."

Julie nodded. They strolled past the shops and took a side street into a maze of stairways and ascending paths. Higher up, they passed several extremely small country churches.

"I'm amazed by the charming simplicity of this island," Mark said. "I haven't been this relaxed in a long time."

Julie had to agree. "These people seem to live an uncomplicated lifestyle. They have their flowers, their fresh produce, their handmade clothing, their whitewashed homes—all of which look alike, by the way. I wonder what it might be like to leave all my cares behind and start over in a place like this."

"It's a nice idea, except people rarely leave their cares behind," Mark said with a grunt. "They take their troubles with them wherever they go. Eventually, the weight pulls them down and they're right back where they started from. Only the scenery is different."

Julie couldn't help but wonder if his comment was directed at her. She'd been carrying a huge weight for the last six years. Had she brought it with her from Fairview to Springfield and now to Patmos?

They reached a level spot on the hillside, turned and looked out over the rooftops, the tamarisk trees, and the flat-roofed buildings below. Julie took in the scene like it was a magnificent painting. Clusters of rocks fanned away from the shore. From where she stood the sea took on a transparency that exposed a sandy bottom and a scattering of more stones and rocks below the surface. The turquoise water stretched as far as the eye could see, with no observable demarcation line between water and sky.

Julie raised her camera and took a series of pictures. Out of the corner of her eye she caught Mark staring at her. She tried to ignore the tightening in her chest and the steady throb that pulsed in her neck. With that man standing so close, in this exotic setting, her resistance started to slip away. What girl didn't welcome a little romance in her life? What girl didn't want to feel admired and appreciated?

Frantically, she snapped picture after picture. She turned her back to Mark and kept moving her camera from one captivating scene to another.

He set his shopping bag on a rock and stepped closer. Julie dared not look into his eyes. He placed a hand on her camera and stopped her from shooting. Despite the heat of the day, she began to tremble. He grabbed her shoulders.

"Julie," he whispered.

She looked away. "Stop it, Mark."

"Julie," he repeated. "You know I still care for you, don't you?"

"Please, let me go."

"Listen," he said, and she gazed into pleading eyes. "I want to help you. Whatever it is that you've been struggling with, I want to help."

"I'm fine, Mark. I don't *need* any help."

"I think you do."

"I can take care of myself. I told you that before. Why don't you listen?"

"Because, I know you well enough to see beyond your excuses. We dated for a year, Julie. There was obviously more going on inside that head of yours than you ever let out. Why don't you trust me? I'm not the enemy."

She shook her head. She couldn't let him tear down the wall she'd erected. There was danger on the other side of that wall. All she ever wanted was to remain safe in her own little world.

"I'm fine, Mark. Please, let's go back down the hill. I have enough photos."

Mark still gripped her shoulders, but his touch was gentle, not forceful at all. He leaned close, but she didn't feel the least bit threatened. In fact, his nearness comforted her.

She lifted her head and met his gaze. "I know you're not the enemy. You've always treated me with kindness. But I like my life the way it is. I *need* to be alone."

He shook his head. "I don't accept that. I can help you, Julie. And, believe it or not, God has a plan for your life. He can free you from this self-imposed prison you're in."

That did it. Why did he always have to mention God? She shook her head and pushed him away.

"Do you know what, Mark? I've been just fine without your God—and without you. I don't need anybody."

"Yes, you do, Julie. Everybody needs someone. Someday, you're going to admit that."

"Leave—me—alone. I'm not interested in a romantic relationship."

She didn't give him time to respond, but spun away from him and started down the hillside. Tears blurred her vision.

She stumbled over the uneven path, tripped over ruts and stones, entered the housing district with its claustrophobic walls, its cobbled walkway, its broken steps. She kept going, determined not to stop until she reached her hotel. She flew through the lobby, past halted conversations and quizzical stares. She charged into her room and locked the door behind her. Then, she fell sobbing on her bed and poured out her pain until she thought her heart was going to burst.

Though Mark had wanted to stop Julie from running off, he merely stared after her until she disappeared from view. She left him in confusion. Hadn't she looked into his eyes? Hadn't he seen a plea for help in those dark green pools? Once again, he'd misread her signals. Once again, he'd acted on impulse. And, once again, she'd pushed him away.

And why not? She did the same thing a year ago, and what did he do then? He let her go, then he grieved for days.

His friend Greg introduced him to one girl after another. With half-hearted interest, he sat at restaurant tables across from complete strangers. He never called them again. He avoided parties and dinner invitations, stayed clear of singles clubs and college functions. He became a hermit of sorts.

His work at the college became his new girlfriend. He plunged in with fervor. Within a few months he moved from associate status to a full professorship. Yet, in spite of all he'd accomplished, he hadn't survived losing Julie, and he'd begun to think there really was such a thing as a soulmate.

Then he'd met Katie and she'd served as a distraction for a while. But something was missing from their relationship, and he couldn't figure out what it was. Now he knew the difference. His former feelings had come back, and he didn't think he could survive losing Julie a second time.

He stood on the hill for several minutes and searched the blue expanse overhead. *Please, Father in heaven. I can't continue pining away over this girl. Either move Julie's heart or help me get over her.*

He needed to talk with someone. Pastor Joe was too far away. A counseling session over the phone didn't cut it for him. Brother Pio came to mind. In the brief time they'd had together, Mark had connected with the guy. Plus, the monk had figured out Julie within mere minutes.

Instead of heading back to the hotel along the route Julie had taken, he traversed the slope and took a couple of side trails back to the monastery.

He walked into the monastery's main courtyard and searched for Brother Pio. The monk was talking with a group of tourists. Mark waited until their conversation ended. Then he hurried forward. Pio smiled in recognition, but as Mark drew closer, his smile quickly faded.

"What's wrong, my friend?"

"I need to talk," Mark whispered. "Please. Is there somewhere—"

Pio put a hand on Mark's shoulder. "Come," he said and guided him to a secluded area of the courtyard, away from the steady flow of tourists.

They stood facing each other. The monk tilted his head, his brow crinkled with concern. "What's troubling you, my son?"

Mark looked at the floor and shook his head. "I don't know where to start."

Brother Pio remained silent.

"Your name," Mark said, raising his head. "Agapios. It means *love*, doesn't it?"

Pio nodded.

Mark let out a nervous laugh. How could he describe the flood of emotions that had come over him to a man who lived a celibate life?

"My problem, Brother Pio, is love." He stumbled over the words. "Unrequited love."

He must have sounded like a schoolboy, yet the monk offered a sympathetic smile. "Is this about the young lady who accompanied you here today? Miss Peters?"

Mark sheepishly nodded.

"Of course," the monk said. A twinkle came to his eye. "I caught your interest almost immediately. In your eyes. In your patience with the girl. In the protective way you hovered beside her."

"Was I *that* obvious?"

Pio snickered. "Yes, my friend. But I also saw something in *her* eyes."

"You did? What did you see?"

"I saw pain in Miss Peter's eyes. Despite her feisty pretenses, a terrible pain has taken residence inside that girl. It probably invaded her heart many years ago. I'm guessing it's something so bad, it even destroyed her faith in God." His eyes clouded over with compassion. "Mark, your friend is a broken vessel. You need to handle her with care."

"You're right," he acknowledged with a nod. "From the first day we met two years ago, Julie appeared to be so fragile I feared I might actually break her. She had her own defense system. She erected a wall between us. Even so, I developed such strong feelings for her, I ignored those initial signs. We dated for a year, but I still hadn't broken down that wall. I suppose it was a superficial relationship. I was more

167

committed than she was. Yet I believed we had a future. In fact, I was about to propose marriage when she ended it. No explanation. No chance to fix whatever went wrong. She just walked away."

"Too bad," Pio said with surprising tenderness. "But now, somehow, you're together again."

"Only by accident. Our bosses arranged this assignment. I had nothing to do with the planning of it. Really, I had thought I'd gotten over her, but when Julie walked into that airport rotunda, those old feelings hit me like an avalanche, and I knew I was still in love with her."

Mark tried to keep his emotions in check as he relived the ups and downs of their relationship. Agapios listened with folded hands and an occasional nod.

"Julie told me she once had been a practicing Christian," Mark said. "For some reason, she walked away from the church. She never explained why. She resented any mention of spiritual significance and didn't like it when I brought up my faith. I shouldn't have been surprised when she came into this holy place and behaved like a heathen. She couldn't help herself." His shoulders sagged with a sudden realization of the truth. "Brother Pio, I love her, and she hates everything I stand for."

"So, you accepted this assignment, and you hoped you might be the one person who can help her. Am I wrong?"

Mark offered a weak smile. "You're absolutely right. Now that I'm spending time with her again, it's like getting a second chance." He breathed a shaky sigh. "So, what can I do, Brother Pio? I've tried patience. I've tried kindness. I've tried restraint. But a half-hour ago, while we were hiking in the hills, I confessed my feelings for her. I looked into those icy, green eyes, and for a moment I was certain a plea for help was there. But I was wrong. She shouted at me to leave her alone, and she ran off."

Agapios let out a chuckle, like a parent might release when comforting a troubled child. Mark bowed his head in hopelessness.

"The answer is simple," the monk said, his voice turning serious. "The first thing you need to do is get your eyes off of Julie and onto God. You told me earlier that you and Julie will be in Patmos for several days. Okay, then. Forget about the incident on the hill. You can be sure that's what Julie wants to do."

Mark raised his head and listened with the intensity of a drowning man who had found a lifeline.

"God is a God of second chances," Pio said. "And third chances and fourth and fifth, and way beyond the thousands. Every hour offers a fresh start. Why don't you simply commit the rest of your time here to God? Your friend may or may not have feelings for you, Mark, but if you don't wait on the Lord—if you don't trust him—you'll never find out. You'll drive that girl away from you and that will be the end of it."

Mark ran a hand through his hair. "I know you're right. But knowing and doing are two different things. When I'm around her, I—" Tears spilled from his eyes. He felt no shame for crying in front of this man of God. So much compassion radiated from the monk's face, Mark had no problem baring his soul to him.

Pio smiled and patted Mark's back. "I know your pain, my friend."

Surprised by the comment, Mark looked into Pio's eyes. "What do you mean?"

Pio laughed. "Do you think a monk who spends his days overseeing religious artifacts has never had a personal life? That none of us know what it's like to love and to lose?"

"Well, no—I mean, I had no idea."

"If that's what you think, then you're wrong."

Mark found himself blushing. "I suppose you might have been in love at some time in your life. Anything's possible."

"Not only possible, but a reality." Pio nudged Mark. "Come. Walk with me, and I'll tell you *my* love story."

Perplexed, Mark stepped up beside the monk and the two of them strolled side-by-side through the monastery. Mark kept pace with the monk's easy lope.

"I grew up in a little village outside of Athens," Pio said. "My father was a wealthy olive farmer. As a teenager, I attended a private school in the big city. After graduation, I left for America and applied at Princeton with the intention of pursuing ordination as a Greek Orthodox priest. Before returning to my homeland, I married an American girl from a devout Greek family."

Mark was stunned. "You're *married?*"

"You're surprised?" Pio laughed.

"I thought—"

"I once was married to a wonderful woman. Unlike my Roman Catholic counterparts who make a vow of celibacy, as a Greek Orthodox priest I was able to marry and even have children."

Mark stopped walking and stared at the monk. "You have children?"

Pio raised a hand. "Wait," he said. "Allow me to tell my story."

Mark nodded and they resumed walking again.

"I served in a church in Athens for three decades," Pio

went on. "My wife Onna faithfully served beside me. Sadly, we had no children. But, we had our ministry, and we had each other, you understand. Then, ten years ago, my Onna died. I endured a lengthy period of mourning. Apart from my commitment to God, she was my whole life. It was difficult for me to remain in Athens without her. So, I gave up the pastorate, came to this monastery, and became a monk in residence."

Mark shook his head in sympathy. To think the man had found his true love and lost her. "Oh, Pio, I'm so sorry."

"No more sorry than I am. My heart still breaks for my Onna. Every day."

Mark expected to see tears, but Pio brushed his hands together, like he was wiping away the memory. "I keep busy with my work. I pray. I cook for my brothers. And I serve the people who visit this place. I guess you might say the monastery is my wife now."

The monk stopped walking and gestured toward the walls and the arches and the hidden doorways. "I love this place, Mark. Its historic treasures fill my life with joy. Anyway, what other human could ever replace my Onna? So, you see, my son, I'm not so different from you. I know what it means to love one woman. And I know what it means to lose her."

Mark stared at Agapios. He was no longer a monk without a life of his own. He was a man who had loved and lost, a fragile human being, who, much like himself, had a heart that could be broken—and was.

"Take my advice," Agapios said. "If you move too fast, you will lose your Julie forever. It's time you *let go and let God*, as they say." He placed a hand on Mark's shoulder, and a fatherly expression came over his face. "Now. Stop being so

171

melodramatic. Enjoy your time on Patmos. Take in the sights, the food, the people. Forget about the old man. Make this a pleasurable visit—for both of you."

They had completed the circuit of the monastery and had arrived back in the main courtyard. Mark extended his right hand. "Thank you, Brother Pio. I'll try to follow your advice regarding Julie. But, forget the old man? I can't ignore my assignment. I have a responsibility to the college that sent me here. You, of all people, know the importance of fulfilling a commitment."

Instead of taking Mark's hand, Pio drew close and the two men embraced with a traditional old-world kiss on both cheeks. As he was about to pass through the exit, Mark looked back at where he and Pio had been standing. Other people were treading on the very spot where he had shed his pain. They were oblivious to the invisible heartache he had scattered on the pavement. Now, maybe he could follow Brother Pio's advice and forget about it too.

Outside, he stood on the hill and surveyed the spread of flat, white roofs below. People lived in those houses. Some of them had probably met Yanno. Mark had a job to do and he was going to do it. Brother Pio was right. He had to entrust Julie to God, and then wait and see what happens. But, somewhere out there was an old man of tremendous interest, and he was determined to find him.

He took a deep breath of fresh mountain air. A familiar hymn came to mind. He began to whistle, "Go Tell It on the Mountain." Then he shoved his hands in his pockets and, matching his step to the tempo of the song, he started down the path toward the hotel.

19

THE PETRAS

Julie had meant to shut her eyes for only a few minutes, but when she awoke, the afternoon sun had begun to descend. She sat upright and checked her watch. It was six o'clock. The Petras had agreed to meet her and Mark at seven. Groaning, she dragged herself into the bathroom, looked in the mirror, and gasped in shock. Her eyes were as puffy as two poached eggs.

"I can't go out looking like *this*."

She rushed to the telephone, dialed room service, and ordered a carafe of hot water and two tea bags. She paced the floor until her order arrived ten minutes later. She dampened the tea bags with the hot water, lay back against the pillow, and waited for the tiny pouches to cool enough to press them against the swelling beneath her eyes. She'd read about that trick in a women's magazine. She hoped it would work now—and fast.

As she lay there, she mulled over the afternoon's fiasco with Mark. *What was I thinking? Instead of running off like a frustrated schoolgirl, I should have stayed and defended myself. For goodness' sake. We're on a business trip. I'm not supposed to get emotional.*

She was still berating herself, when a knock on her door jolted her upright.

"Julie?" Mark's voice called from the hallway. "It's 6:30."

"All right, Mark. Give me ten minutes." She tried to keep

her tone light, so he wouldn't suspect how badly their clash on the hill nearly destroyed her.

"I'll wait downstairs."

To her relief, Mark's voice also sounded casual, as though unaffected by the afternoon's disaster. Perhaps Julie had made more of their little spat than it deserved. She hurried into the bathroom, checked her eyes and was relieved to find that the tea bags had done their job. A little makeup also helped. She went to the closet and pulled out a bright red dress, then completed her look with black sandals, plus a pair of gold hoop earrings and a matching bracelet, the only valuable pieces of jewelry she owned. After a quick brush of her hair, she was ready to go.

When Julie arrived in the lobby, Mark was waiting by the door. His eyes swept over her and sent a thrill down her spine.

"Wow," he said.

"Wow, back," Julie said, with a lilt in her voice. But, inside she was swooning over the suntanned Adonis in a white sport coat, jeans, and a sky blue polo shirt that matched his eyes. One thing was certain, Julie was attracted to Mark on a physical level. Too bad he was so hooked on God.

She didn't resist when Mark took her arm and ushered her out the door of the hotel and down the street toward the restaurant. Along the way, he chattered with excitement about meeting the Petras.

"This could be the break we needed to help us find the old man," Mark said. "But, let's not overwhelm this couple with a lot of questions, at least not at the start. I don't want to scare them off."

Julie nodded. Mark made sense. Take it slow. Gain their confidence, then hit them with the tough questions. Like

Barbara Walters always did when she interviewed a tough source. In the end, she always got the truth.

They arrived at Vangelis Taverna right on time, seven o'clock, and found the Petras already waiting there. Sofia looked like a typical country housewife in a handmade floral dress and a crocheted shawl draped around her shoulders. Damien stood there in a limp tan suit, dingy white shirt, and threadbare tie. Julie's heart went out to the impoverished couple. Their out-of-the-way market was probably their only source of income. Whether or not she and Mark got any information out of the Petras, at least they could treat them to a free meal tonight.

After a perfunctory greeting, Sofia tilted her head and smiled at Julie. "Aaah, lovely," she whispered as she reached out with arthritic fingers and caressed one of Julie's gold earrings.

Julie smiled back at her and uttered a soft, "Thank you," then she followed Mark into the restaurant. They sat in the outdoor garden at a table with a green-and-white checked tablecloth and a candle in the middle. Overhead, individual lanterns hung from a fern-draped awning and illuminated the area. Strains of Greek guitars and flutes poured from inside the restaurant. Julie took a deep breath and lifted the menu. She swallowed hard. *Wait till Mark gets the bill for this one.*

Surprised that her appetite had returned with full force, she selected moussaka, which the menu described as a beef and eggplant casserole, and a small salad. Damien and his wife decided to share a platter of grilled lamb and rice pilaf, and Mark ran wild with stuffed grape leaves, grilled salmon with tzatziki, roasted vegetables, and a glass of ouzo for himself and one for Damien. Julie and Sofia both decided to abstain.

175

"And for dessert bring us four orders of baklava and some strong coffee," he told their waiter.

Though Julie had grown accustomed to Mark's enormous appetite, the Petras stared wide-eyed as he completed the order.

"What?" he said, his eyes darting back-and-forth from one to the other.

Julie shook her head and giggled, and the Petras burst out laughing.

"You thin for a man who eats so much," Damien said. "What be your secret?"

Mark blushed and shrugged his shoulders. "Right living, I guess."

Damien laughed again and tapped the table. "That make sense. I try it someday."

Sofia's eyes sparkled with delight. Julie leaned toward her. "So, how did your sales go today?"

"Good, good," the older woman replied. "You bring us luck. After you go, many tourists come, talk with us, buy lots of vegetables, peppermints, lots of good things."

"Clean us out," Damien said with another burst of laughter.

Mark was beaming. "That's wonderful," he said. "Business was good."

Mark never failed to astound her. A man of his position, yet he was at home with monks and villagers and college professors. It didn't matter what their status was. He could strike up a conversation with anyone.

"Do you grow your own produce?" he asked the Petras.

Damien nodded. "Most items, like oranges and apples. For others, we go to farms and pick for small price."

"Tell us about yourselves," Mark said. "Do you live in town?"

"Oh no. In town very expensive." He'd lost his smile. "Country better for us. Little distance, but not too far."

"Is it only the two of you?" Julie said. "Do you have children? Grandchildren?"

Sofia didn't answer, though Julie had directed the question at her. The sparkle left Sofia's eyes and she bowed her head.

"No children," Damien said, patting his wife's hand. "She lose before they born. Bad, bad time for Sofia."

A flicker of guilt struck Julie's heart. They were a sweet couple, likeable, and so unhampered by the modern world. They would have fared better in another time period, before modern technology passed them by. They probably didn't even own a cell phone.

"How do you spend your days when you're not working?" she asked. "Do you have a hobby or an activity you enjoy together?"

"We travel," Damien said. A proud smile took over his face. "We travel on Patmos and sometime we go to other islands. I take pictures. My Sofia, she keep a scrapbook. Many memories."

"Sounds wonderful," Julie said. "I'd love to see your collection of photos. I've been taking pictures myself of your island. I've gotten some fascinating shots, including one of a very amazing couple who own a grocery store." She leaned toward Sofia and patted her wrist.

"Someday, we visit your country—America," Damien said. "That our dream. But it far off. Maybe never get there. Who knows?"

"Sounds like a good plan though," Mark said. "I would be happy to show you around."

"What bring you to our island?" Damien looked from Mark to Julie. "A honeymoon?" He gave them a toothy grin.

Julie's cheeks burned and she shook her head. Mark merely chuckled. "No, we're not married," he said. "It seems a lot of people *think* we are."

Julie quietly fumed. He liked the idea. She needed to speak up. "Mark is a college professor and I'm helping him with a project," she blurted out. She didn't mention that she was a reporter. That was part of the plan, wasn't it? "This stop in Patmos is part of Mark's work," she went on. "We're only here for a few days, then it's back to America again."

Sofia's smile faded. "No honeymoon?" she said, her voice weak. The poor woman had presumed they were newlyweds. Julie looked at Mark, sitting there, engrossed in the plate of food in front of him. What if they *had* been married? Would that be such a bad idea? She caught herself then and shook off the image. A marriage to Mark would never work. They had equally strong personalities. Why, they'd be at each other's throat.

To Julie's relief, Damien picked up the conversation. "Your work? Have you had profit?"

Mark answered between bites of salmon. "We've seen a lot of interesting sites," he said. "And Julie's taken some wonderful pictures." Then, uttering expressions of euphoria between mouthfuls, he talked about their time in Ephesus, the boat ride to the island, and their visits to the citadel and the cave. Julie listened along with the Petras, amazed that Mark recalled details she'd already forgotten. While she had relied on her pad and pen, he'd recorded everything in his brain. He'd told her at one time that he had an IQ of 130 and a photographic memory. Now, she believed it.

At the end of the meal, Mark drained the last of his coffee, then he lifted his glass of ouzo in a toast. Damien did the same.

"To new friends," said Mark.

"*Yia Mas!*" Damien exclaimed. "To your health!"

The clink of their glasses signaled the moment Julie had been waiting for. It was time to ask the Petras about Yanno. A flush of shame washed over her. Though Mark's suggestion of a friendship with this couple had been sincere, once they got the information they came for, they'd say good-night and probably would never see the Petras again. She knew the truth. They had tricked this sweet couple with a free meal for one purpose—to find the old man.

Mark set down his glass and turned to Damien. "I wonder if you can help us clear up a rumor that seems—well—preposterous, but perhaps it's true."

The Petras smiled with innocence. Another wave of guilt pierced Julie's heart. She tried to shake it off, but it returned with full force.

"It's been said there's a man living on the island who is quite old," Mark went on. "They say he's filled with wisdom and that he takes care of the people here."

A knowing look crossed between Damien and Sofia, but they said nothing.

"I need to meet the man and speak with him," Mark pressed.

Damien's smile disappeared. Sofia looked down at her lap. She toyed with the fringe of her shawl.

"It's a curious thing," Julie said, breaking the silence. "Such a man is a mystery to us. We come from a country where he would receive honors."

"No mystery," Sofia said, raising her head. "You speak of Yanno." Her face beamed with delight.

Damien elbowed his wife. She'd said too much. She responded with a scowl. The couple looked like players in a

179

silent film. Words could never speak the messages that passed between them. Damien, in his own way, had told his wife to shut up. And, in her own way, she had resented it. They weren't so different from American couples, after all.

The waiter returned with the bill. Mark took one look at it but barely flinched. He passed a credit card to the waiter, then turned back to Damien. "Yes, yes. The man we heard about is named Yanno."

Damien dabbed his lips with the napkin, folded the square of cloth into a neat triangle and placed it beside his plate. "My friend," he said, his eyes on Mark, "You do not know what you ask."

"What do you mean?"

"Yanno special to the people of Patmos. He help us. He teach us. My people no want outsiders come here and take Yanno away. You leave Yanno alone. Go back to America without him."

Mark let out a laugh. "We're not going to take him away, Damien. We'd like to meet him, that's all."

"But, you will leave. You will go back to America, tell people about our Yanno. Then what happen? To him? To our island?"

Julie thought about her assignment. The publicity that would evolve from this one article could pose a threat to Yanno and the people who lived on Patmos. Though she wanted to write this story, if the wrong people got a hold of it—Jason Redding for example—it could turn this peaceful island into a media circus. She suddenly felt torn. She and Mark had come too far to fail. But, she was having second thoughts. If she dropped the story now, what would she tell Andy? Yet, how could she look this couple in the eye, knowing she was about to destroy their world with one sweep of the pen?

She reached out and touched Sofia's hand, hoping the

gesture might comfort the older woman. Sofia looked back at her and smiled that same innocent smile she'd had from the moment they met.

Mark appeared unaware of the indecision that had swamped Julie. He continued to press Damien for answers. "We need to find out where this Yanno lives," he said. " I can pay money for that information." He leaned across the table toward the older man. "Perhaps a hundred euros in return for an address?"

Damien's eyes widened with interest. Julie did a quick mental calculation. That amount probably equaled a week's income. She thought about Jason Redding, hot on the same trail. If she didn't write the story, that monster of a TV reporter would certainly do it. She was tired of being scooped by him. Her heart began to pound. Somehow, she needed to get the old man's address.

Mark persisted. "Tell us, Damien, do you know where he lives?"

Damien nodded, but a sadness filled his eyes, as though he were about to betray a friend.

"I know," Damien admitted. "But, I cannot say." He slowly shook his head.

"Why not, Damien?" Mark shrugged. "What harm would it do to tell *us*?"

"My friends, it be unwritten law with the people of Patmos." Damien struck the table with his knuckles in a rhythm that accompanied his next words. "We—-must—protect—Yanno."

Mark leaned closer. "Two hundred euros."

He counted out a few bills. Julie trembled with anticipation.

"Here," she said. On an impulse she removed her gold earrings and bracelet. "A gift for Sofia."

The woman's eyes lit up.

Damien looked at his wife, then at the jewelry, and lastly, at the wad of bills on the table. Slowly, he reached out and picked up the money. Sofia removed her cheap earrings and slipped Julie's gold hoops into the holes in her ears, then she slid the bracelet on her wrist. She peered back at Julie with a happy grin that revealed two missing teeth.

Julie eyed her with concern. How long would it be before the old woman had to sell the jewelry to pay for more important necessities? But, that didn't matter now. The main thing was, Sofia had accepted the gift. And so had Damien.

Mark was smiling. "Does Yanno speak English?" he asked. "Do you need to go along with us and interpret?"

"No need," Damien said, though he was unable to shed the sadness in his voice. "Yanno speak many languages. Also English."

Mark nodded. "Of course."

"One more thing," Damien cautioned with a wink. "It custom in my country, you visit, you bring gift. Food, or nice item for his home."

"We will do that," Mark promised.

They left the restaurant with Sofia carrying a package of leftovers and Mark holding a slip of notepaper bearing Damien's scribbled directions to Yanno's house. They parted in the plaza, mouthing promises to meet on another day. But Julie couldn't envision that ever happening now that they'd gotten what they came for.

A shadow hung over Julie. She hung her head as she walked alongside Mark to the hotel. His shoulders had dropped slightly and he avoided her gaze.

"I feel terrible," he said. "We deceived that wonderful couple."

"I know. I can't explain it, Mark, but I feel awful too." She sighed and tried to regroup. "Well, there's nothing we can do about it now. We have the old guy's address. We came here to do a job, and we can't let guilt keep us from doing it."

"Yeah, but that doesn't help me feel any better," Mark said, a tense despondency in his voice. "There was something about that old couple that made me want to pick up and leave the island and forget about this whole deal."

"I had the same thought, but it lasted for only a minute. I came all this way for a purpose, Mark, and to tell you the truth, I'm kind of curious about this Yanno. He sounds like quite a character."

Mark straightened his shoulders and picked up his pace. "Yeah. I couldn't return home without at least meeting the guy. He's probably a sweet old man who happens to help people. On the other hand, what if he's more than that? What if—"

Julie shook her head. *There he goes again, off in some dreamland.*

"Get real, Mark. If nothing else, I'll get a nice human interest story. Hopefully, Yanno will clear things up and discredit those loudmouthed Christians who are trying to turn him into a saint."

Mark stopped walking. Lines of disbelief gathered on his forehead.

"So, is that what am I to you? A loudmouthed Christian?"

"I didn't mean you, Mark. But, some people go off the deep end with all the spiritual nonsense."

"Maybe," Mark said, his voice hard. "I'm wondering how you might handle the information you get tomorrow. You and I both know about the power of the pen. Some journalists misuse it. I hope you won't be one of them."

"I'm not."

"So you say. But some reporters choose exactly the right quotes to make their subject look bad while completely ignoring those that make him look good. And what about the photo journalists who print unflattering photos of a political candidate yawning or a movie star picking his nose? You can't tell me you people leave out your personal opinions."

Julie's defenses shot up. "I try not to do that."

"What are you saying? That you can keep your own feelings out of a story, especially this one—a piece that could turn your opinion of religion on its head?"

"That's right. I try to remain unbiased in my reporting."

"Oh really? You just mentioned loudmouthed Christians. That sounds pretty biased to me."

Julie shrugged and kept walking. "Don't read anything negative into it, Mark. Let's go. I want to organize my notes and get a good night's sleep before we visit Yanno in the morning."

They walked on in silence. With their final clash of wits, Julie had thwarted Mark's interest in her once and for all. He'd leave her alone now, she was sure of it. She'd accomplished pretty much all of what she'd set out to do this evening. She was going to complete her assignment, and she had erected a permanent wall between her and Mark.

A smug smile crept across her lips. At the same time, a nagging uncertainty rose up within her, and she wondered if she'd unknowingly driven a dagger straight into her own heart.

20

YANNO

During a quick breakfast of scrambled eggs, fresh fruit, and cheese, Mark looked over Damien's directions to Yanno's house. Julie sat quietly at the table and munched on her usual bowl of "mattress stuffing," the label Mark had given to her daily cereal.

As they were leaving the restaurant, Julie purchased a slice of traditional Patmian cheese pie.

"I see you took Damien's suggestion seriously," Mark said, eyeing the colorful box in Julie's hand. "A visitor's gift for Yanno? That should help break the ice."

Julie tilted her head to one side. "I'm a reporter, Mark. I pay attention."

Mark paid the bill and hurried out to the street to hail a cab. With their trip quickly drawing to a close, he didn't want to waste a minute of their time.

They followed a winding, uphill drive to a small piece of land a stone's throw from the Cave of the Apocalypse. To Mark's amazement, the dry and rocky landscape had opened up to a lush gentleman's farm. He exited the cab and took in the scene before him. On his left stood several gnarled olive trees and a thriving grape arbor. Farther up the hill, a vegetable patch stood ready for harvest with rows of plump cabbages, tomato plants, and beans dripping from vines on poles. Beyond, a herd of goats grazed on a grassy knoll. A few sheep huddled nearby, and chickens rooted around inside a wire enclosure. Apart from the acrid odor of animal droppings, the pastoral setting created a sense of peace and awe.

On Mark's right, dapples of sunshine penetrated the feathery branches of a group of tamarisk trees and struck the flagstone path with bullets of light. In the center of a clearing stood a traditional Greek dwelling, whitewashed to a glare. A proliferation of greenery hugged the left side of the house, and on the right a vine-draped stairway wound upward to the flat roof.

Mark paused and sucked in his breath. "It reminds me of a Thomas Kincade print that's hanging in my office. You ought to shoot it, Julie."

She handed Mark the to-go box and took out her camera. "Don't you dare eat that," she said, nodding toward the little box in his hand.

"Who? Me?"

Julie knotted her eyebrows and raised her camera. Mark quickly stepped aside and dodged the rapid fire of Julie's shooting. Then she turned her camera on him. He made a face the instant she hit the shutter.

"Okay, let's go," he said. He shoved the pie in Julie's free hand, and started up the flagstone path to the house.

Though the scene had created a moment of tranquility for Mark, his head cleared when he passed beyond the tree line and caught sight of a carport with a cherry red Vespa LX motor scooter parked underneath it. A vision came to his mind of an aging centenarian skidding around mountain curves on that bike. He laughed out loud. "There's no way," he said.

Julie came up beside him. "Do you think that's his?"

He shrugged. A part of him wanted to believe it was. Then he shook his head and proceeded to the house.

On the front stoop stood two wicker chairs and a matching cafe table bearing a long-stemmed pipe, a leather pouch, and a book of matches. A stone window ledge jutted out from the wall. On its top, a variety of herbs spilled over the rims of a half-dozen clay pots. Mark recognized basil and parsley, but none of the others. He stepped up to the front door, a crude construction of boards and nails. He raised his hand to knock, then hesitated and looked at Julie.

"This could be John," he whispered.

"Or not." Julie raised her eyebrows smugly.

"So, you've already made up your mind?"

"Maybe," she said. "But, it seems so have you."

"Let's say I'm open to whatever comes. Do you realize what this could mean? For the college? For your newspaper? For our careers?"

"Come on, Mark. I admit, I *am* curious, but my goal is different from yours. Like I told you last night, I'm more intent on proving this whole thing is a farce."

Mark opened his mouth to fire back but thought better of it. He didn't want to repeat the argument from the night before. It was the same kind of verbal sparring that tore them apart almost a year ago. He turned away from Julie and rapped on the door.

From inside the house came the barking of dogs. Their barks grew louder. So did the clickety, click of doggie nails closer and closer to the door.

With a sigh, Mark knocked a second time, and a third. There was the scraping of shoes, a man's cough, and the clank of a latch. The door opened a crack and a pair of dark eyes peered at them through the aperture. The dogs continued to bark.

"Alpha! Omega! *Isihaste!* Settle down, I tell you."

The barking stopped and the clicking of their nails faded to a distant part of the house.

"Poios einai ekei?" The voice sounded gruff and bore a hint of impatience.

"I'm sorry," Mark said. "I don't speak your language."

"Who's there?" the voice repeated in English.

"My—my name is Mark Bensen, and," he gestured toward Julie, "this is Julie Peters. We're from America. We're looking for Yanno Theologos."

The two eyes examined them through the narrow opening. The man didn't respond right away, which made Mark a little nervous.

"I am Yanno Theologos," the old guy finally said, his tone soft but firm. "My visiting hours start at ten o'clock. You'll have to come back."

The door began to close. Mark raised his hand and stopped it.

"Please. We've come a long way, Mr. Theologos." He checked his watch. "It's only 8:30. It's important that we speak to you. Alone. Won't you make an exception?"

The door opened a few more inches, exposing a bearded face, the color of buckskin, and lined from years of laboring in the sun.

"How can I be sure you're not here to rob me? Or to kill me?" The voice still sounded gruff, but the eyes twinkled.

"Look at us," Mark said, spreading his arms. "Do we look like robbers? Or killers?"

"I don't know. It's been a long time since I last experienced that kind of evil."

Mark offered a smile. "Believe me, we're here to talk.

Nothing more." He pointed at the to-go box in Julie's hand. "We have a gift," he said. "Patmian cheese pie."

Yanno's eyebrows went up. The door opened all the way revealing an elderly man with a stocky build. His straight back denied his years, as did the youthful glint in his eyes. Sunlight fell on a square-shaped face and set aglow his leathery complexion. The man's mop of hair, streaked with silver, was bound into a ponytail in back. He wore a linen shirt with billowing pirate sleeves, a brown leather vest, khaki slacks, and, of all things, a pair of Nikes on his feet.

"I see we have the same taste in shoes," Mark said, lifting his foot.

The older man smiled. "Come inside," he said, and he grabbed the to-go box before Julie made it across the threshold.

Mark extended his hand. "Mr. Theologos—"

"Please, call me Yanno. Everyone does."

"All right. Yanno. It's good to meet you," Mark said as he pumped the man's hand.

"Come. Sit," Yanno said, the same way he'd ordered his dogs.

He gestured toward a couple of wooden chairs oddly positioned in the middle of the room across from a rocking chair, as though the old man had been expecting visitors all along. He headed to the kitchen with the to-go box.

Julie settled in one the chairs, and Mark took the one to her left. With Yanno out of the room, he took the opportunity to scan his surroundings. It was a simple setting with meager furnishings, mostly handmade tables and chairs and a sofa covered by a threadbare throw. The wood floor had a worn path that stretched from the front door to the chairs where Mark and Julie sat, as though many feet had trod there. From where he sat, Mark could see a good part of the kitchen, which had a modest grouping of appliances, including a three-burner gas stove, a small refrigerator, and a microwave oven. He chuckled to himself at the thought of a 2,000-year-old man zapping his food. What did he make? Lean Cuisine? Hot tea? Popcorn?

Mark's eyes drifted to the dining room. A glass-fronted hutch stood against the far wall. Even from this distance, he could see its contents—unmatched pieces of china and a lopsided clay bowl that looked like it had been crafted by a five-year-old. There was an ebony dining table and four chairs that matched the two Mark and Julie were sitting on. A set of folding TV trays leaned against the side wall. Mark snickered. The guy was an intriguing mix of the old and the new.

Yanno came out of the kitchen and turned on a free-standing lamp, shedding more light on the living room. He headed down the hallway and disappeared into a side room. Water was running. Then, there was the rattle of a cabinet door being opened and shut.

Mark took the time to check out the rest of the room. Julie was doing the same, her head swiveling from one side to the other, her lips parted in awe.

A far wall of shelves swelled with books, ledgers, magazines, and several versions of the Bible. Mark's attention froze on a bunch of rolled parchments leaning against a wall in the corner. He raised his eyebrows and nudged Julie.

"What do you think those are? Blueprints? Ancient documents? Unless this guy builds high-rise apartments, they could prove to be interesting."

She shrugged and looked away. Mark followed her gaze.

Before them, stood a large rocker, like a throne the old man probably used during interaction with whoever sat in the two chairs. Next to the rocker was an end table and more clues to the complexity that already surrounded this guy.

There was an open Bible, a pair of Ben Franklin-style spectacles, and—what? A TV remote control? Mark turned around and looked at the wall behind him. Above a fireplace hung a flat-screen TV, and beside it, a cantilevered shelf held a DVD player and a modest collection of movies. Beneath that, another shelf held a combination radio/CD player and a stack of CDs. Mark couldn't imagine what kind of music this Yanno listened to. *Probably rap,* he thought with a chuckle.

Smiling, Mark leaned toward Julie. "This guy has really aroused my curiosity."

"Mine too," she said, her voice hushed. "Look at that." She raised her chin toward the front door. Above it hung the most unusual clock Mark had ever seen. Someone had braided barbed twigs into a round frame that resembled, to his astonishment, a crown of thorns. In the center, twelve hand-carved wooden numbers encircled two metal spikes that indicated the time. Mark checked his watch, which he'd already set to Patmian time. The two timepieces agreed to the minute.

"What about all that?" Julie said, gesturing toward a desk on the other side of the room. Strewn across it were a laptop computer, a cell phone, stacks of paper, and several textbooks. On the wall over the desk hung several framed certificates.

"We're gonna have to get a closer look at all that before we leave," Mark said.

Yanno entered the room and temporarily interrupted their surveillance. He sat on the rocking chair and set it in motion, eliciting a rhythmic slapping against the wood floor.

The sound brought the two dogs running from the back of the house. The scruffy animals paced about the living room, sniffed the air, and eyed Mark and Julie from a distance.

"Alpha. Omega. *Katse kato.* Sit." Yanno commanded. The dogs danced in tiny circles, then, satisfied, they lay down on the floor at their master's feet.

"My companions," Yanno said with a smile and a shrug. "They were street dogs. Starved and emaciated. I took them in two years ago. Now look at them. They eat way too much."

"So you rescued them," Mark said, with appreciation.

Yanno nodded. "It's a common practice among my people. We care for the stray animals that roam our streets. It's how God wants us to treat all his creatures, with compassion and kindness."

Mark suspected Yanno's kindness probably extended to the villagers, as well. But to him, the two dogs looked like rejects at the pound, a mix of breeds that he couldn't identify. *Alpha and Omega,* he thought. *Interesting.*

"You have a lovely place," Julie said. "I especially like your garden. Do you care for it all by yourself?"

Yanno continued to rock. "I work the garden with the help of some neighborhood children, when they're not in school. Then I share my harvest with their families."

Mark was impressed. Yanno spoke flawless English. The old man paused and tilted his face toward Julie. "And you, child—you have beautiful red hair. It sets a dull room on fire." He stroked his beard. "It reminds me of someone I knew a long time ago."

Mark looked at Julie. Her face had turned crimson. He had forgotten how easy it was to get her to blush, especially when someone paid her a compliment. She was one of the most beautiful girls he'd ever seen, yet she didn't know it, which was one of the reasons he was drawn to her.

"I'm certain you didn't come here to talk about my garden." Yanno surprised Mark with his honest perception. "Tell me, what can I do for you?"

Something about Yanno's demeanor told Mark the old man couldn't be fooled. He didn't want to make the same mistake he'd made with the Petras. It still bothered him that he had misled the sweet couple. No, this guy was going to get the truth from the start.

"Yanno, I'm a professor at a Bible college. I teach biblical history and archaeology, and I'm gathering information for a classroom project. Julie's a newspaper reporter. We're following up on a rumor that's been circulating among some Christian groups, a rumor that you may be John the Apostle."

There. Right to the point.

Yanno let out a laugh, but said nothing.

"The whole thing sounds ludicrous, but we had to follow up."

Yanno laughed harder, then he started coughing and had to stop rocking. He took a deep breath, pulled a handkerchief from his vest pocket and wiped mirthful tears from his eyes.

"You'll have to forgive me, son. That rumor always tickles me."

"Always? You mean it's been around for sometime?" Mark said. "It *is* only a rumor, isn't it?" He raised his eyebrows and waited for an answer.

Yanno tucked his handkerchief away and resumed rocking.

"Let me say this, young man. There exists a fine line between truth and fiction, and a fine line between reality and rumor. The truth is real, no matter what anyone claims or denies. And a rumor is merely what you want it to be.

Either concept can build someone up. Either one can tear a person down. Of course, I prefer truth, but what exactly *is* truth? Whether a truthful saying is harmful or helpful is of no consequence. The main thing is that it *is* truth. Nothing can ever dispute it. A rumor, on the other hand, is more likely capable of destroying someone, so it's best to be careful when handling a rumor."

Mark scratched his head and looked at Julie. She stared back at him, a look of puzzlement on her face.

"Yanno," Julie said. "I've brought along a tape recorder. Do you mind if I use it?"

"Mind?" Yanno replied. "I don't mind. I'm always up for a challenge. Whatever I say here today I could say to the whole world. I have nothing to hide." He nodded. "Fire away," he said, a glint in his eyes.

Julie set the recorder on the end table between Yanno's Bible and his remote control and angled the microphone toward the old man.

Mark took immediate control of the interview. "Yanno," he said. "Your lifestyle fascinates me. The natural setting, your garden, the relaxing atmosphere—it's a virtual Garden of Eden. Inside your house," he gestured about the room, "you have the ancient and the modern, all rolled up in one package."

Yanno smiled. His rocking chair creaked and slapped the floor.

"I'm fascinated by your diversity of tastes," Mark continued.

Yanno chuckled. "My diversity of tastes, as you say, is no different from yours or anyone else's, Mark. Think about it. You told me you teach biblical history and archaeology. You exist in a modern world, yet you must have acquired a few artifacts over the years. Perhaps, as a budding archaeologist, you might have participated in a few digs."

Mark nodded. There *were* those fossils he collected from an excavation in Egypt. And what about the skull he unearthed at an ancient Sumerian site? And the silver coins he acquired during a tour of Israel?

Yanno continued with his evaluation. "You probably have textbooks and charts on ancient civilizations, but don't you also have a television set and a microwave oven?" He pointed at Mark's shoes. "You obviously enjoy physical exercise, but don't you also drive a car? And what about your clothes? Hasn't it been years since you updated your wardrobe? But didn't you go out and purchase new clothing for this trip?"

Mark frowned. He'd only met the man a few minutes ago. "How do you know all that?" he said, frustration rising within him.

"I know, because I know people," Yanno replied. "I look for telltale signs. Your books and artifacts were an easy guess. After all, you said you're a college professor and you have an interest in ancient history. You must have collected *something* of significance. Concerning your clothes—your shirt still has the crease-marks from store packaging, and your blue jeans have no stains and no tears. Such conclusions required no miraculous abilities. You are able to do the same, if you try."

Mark was always up for a challenge. "Okay. That motor scooter parked underneath the canopy outside... is it yours?"

Yanno smiled. "Does that seem odd to you, that an old man should enjoy a thrill on the highway now and then?"

"Well, no. I guess not. It's unusual, that's all."

Yanno leaned back in his chair and continued rocking.

Unsure of how to proceed from there, Mark sent Julie a "help me out here" look. She picked up his cue and pulled out a notebook and pen.

"I've prepared a list of questions," she said. "I hope that's all right. It will keep us on track."

Yanno tilted his head, an amused twinkle in his eye. "Use your reporter skills to your heart's content. I'm ready."

"Have you ever lived anywhere else besides Patmos?" she said, though her voice sounded a little shaky. "You know—the Holy Land? Rome? Ephesus?"

The old man nodded. "I have lived in many places, from one end of the earth to the other. Yes, I've lived in the Holy Land. It's a wonderful region, full of religious history and spiritual significance. I've lived in various cities in Europe. And Asia, a land of mystery and intrigue. I spent a lot of time near Ephesus, a captivating city of antiquity. And I've even visited your wonderful country. I've been to the Grand Canyon, to New York City, Chicago, Dallas, and to the beaches on both coasts. Once, I even went to Disney World. I've had the fortune of meeting people of many different cultures and in diverse lines of work. I learned a great deal from those interactions. Travel has been one of the most fulfilling and educating experiences of my life."

Julie was scribbling away. Mark also jotted some details in the little notebook he carried in his shirt pocket. But most of all, he wanted to observe the guy, watch for clues, maybe catch him making a mistake, and ultimately, prove whether or not he was John.

"Tell me this," Mark said. "What did you do for a living, and, how are you subsisting now?"

Yanno cocked his head in a whimsical manner. "In my younger days, my family owned a lucrative business," he said. "I left home to serve in missions. Then I went to school. I studied several languages, and now, in my later years, I am a translator of ancient documents, which helps to supplement my retirement benefits."

He paused and looked at Julie, then at Mark. "So, tell me something about yourselves," he said. "I sense that you have a friendship that goes beyond your work."

Mark hesitated. He'd come there to gather information. He hadn't expected to be *answering* questions. But if he wanted to keep the visit going, he supposed he'd better humor the guy.

Before he could open his mouth, Julie jumped in with an answer. "We were friends at one time," she said, her response matter-of-fact. "It was a long time ago and that friendship no longer exists. We are simply two professionals working on a project. When we finish, we'll go back to our own lives."

Mark's confidence waned. Until now, he hadn't considered their friendship over. For him, the relationship was merely placed on hold. But Julie's remark sounded so final. He looked at Yanno. The old man's eyes were on him, reading him, perhaps even evaluating his reaction.

Mark squirmed under Yanno's scrutiny. His mind raced with possible responses to what Julie had said, but he couldn't put a simple sentence together, so he just sat there in utter defeat.

Suddenly, Yanno glanced at the wall clock, sighed, and rose from his chair. "It's time for my mid-morning cup of tea," he said. "Will you join me?"

Mark shrugged. "Sure." He welcomed the diversion. A little tea party would give him time to rebound. Besides, he was always up for a food break.

Julie turned off her recorder. "Can I help?"

"No, I'll get it," the old man replied, just before he disappeared in the kitchen.

21

TEA WITH YANNO

With Yanno out of the room, Mark walked to the desk and checked out the certificates and degrees that hung on the wall. The framed accolades were embossed with logos of multiple colleges and universities from all over the world. Mark frowned and peered closer. He shook his head in awe of each accomplishment.

Bachelor's degree in English literature. Master's degree in business. Master's in religious studies. Doctor of Philosophy. Doctor of Psychology. Doctor of Anthropology. There was even a framed pilot's license. The dates had been obscured by a black marker. Puzzled, he tried to read beyond the dark smudges.

"Look at this," Mark whispered. Julie came up beside him and peered over his shoulder.

"This guy has studied everything from aeronautics to horticulture," Mark said. "He's undoubtedly the most educated person I've ever met."

"Amazing," Julie murmured. "How long do you think it takes someone to earn all of these degrees?"

"Years," he said. "Maybe even centuries, unless he studied multiple subjects at the same time."

"Is that even possible?"

"For someone like me; impossible. But for a man like Yanno..."

"Yes, I see what you mean. He's incredible."

"Unless other people earned these degrees and Yanno merely collected them?"

Julie shook her head. "I don't know. Did you notice the artful way he evaded our questions? This guy is nothing short of genius."

From the kitchen came a clattering of china, the opening and closing of cupboard doors, and the whistle of a tea kettle.

Mark took a quick look at the stack of textbooks. They were difficult subjects. Physics, cosmology, calculus, and numerology.

"So." Yanno entered the room. "How do you like your tea?" The old man was carrying a tray with three steaming cups, plus cream, and tiny bowls of sugar and lemons. Mark spotted a plate of Oreos. He rushed over to Yanno. "Here, let me carry that for you."

"It's okay. I've got it," Yanno said. "Just grab one of those folding tables in the dining room."

Mark set up a TV tray in the middle of the floor, positioning it within easy reach of their three chairs. Yanno placed the tray on the table and reached for his cup, an antiquated silver goblet that had no handles. A hairline crack ran down one side, but not one drop of tea had seeped out.

"That's an interesting cup," Mark observed.

Yanno took a careful sip of the hot liquid. "Yes," he said. "It was given to me by a dear friend. It does an excellent job of keeping my tea piping hot and my lemonade ice cold."

Mark picked up one of the other teacups, an uninteresting piece of china compared to Yanno's tumbler. He doctored his tea with lemon and sugar and gathered up a handful of the Oreos. Julie sipped at her own tea and ignored the cookies.

When Mark had finished the last of the cookies, he dusted the crumbs from his shirt and took a final sip of tea. He breathed a troubled sigh. So far, their interview had gone nowhere. He glanced at the discolored parchments in the corner. They'd been calling out to him since he'd walked in the door.

He nodded in their direction. "Can I ask what those scrolls are?"

Yanno eyed them. "They're merely a lot of mediocre scratchings. It's a translation project I've been working on, when I have time."

"They appear to be very old. I'd be interested in taking a look at them."

Yanno shook his head. "Sorry, Mark. I can't show them to anyone until I've finished with the translation. I'm afraid you'll already have left Patmos by that time. It could take years, in fact."

Mark knew then that he could do nothing short of getting a search warrant. He released a frustrated sigh. He and Julie had two more days to visit with Yanno and so far they hadn't gotten anything of significance. He didn't want to get pushy, didn't want to offend the old guy and ruin their chances of being welcomed back.

He gestured toward the wall of degrees. "You have quite a collection of accolades, Yanno. If you could accomplish anything else, what would it be?"

"That's easy," he said without a blink of the eye. "I'd pursue more education." He chuckled and set his chair in motion. "I'm afraid I'm an eternal student. I love to learn and I love to share what I've learned. The world is filled with opportunities for mental growth. But I didn't just attend college. I traveled. I talked to people. I went to the school of hard knocks, as they say." He paused, then looked Mark squarely in the eyes. "So, what about you, Mark? You're an educated man. Are you one of those dull professors who find their satisfaction in textbooks and lesson plans? Do you pass worthless tidbits to your bored students and come away thinking you've done them a great service? Or do you give them the gift of your personal experiences? If nothing else, it could make you more interesting to those eager babes as they get ready to step out into the world. They're trusting you to get them started on the right path."

Mark had to admit at times he'd seen boredom written all over his students' faces.

Yanno leaned toward him. "I'd like to challenge you, Mark, to never stop learning. Never stop reaching for the prize. You won't be disappointed and neither will your students. You have been given a great responsibility. Send them out of your classroom with a desire to learn more. From life."

Without waiting for a response from Mark, Yanno turned toward Julie. "And what about you, young lady? What is your educational experience?"

She appeared startled by the question. "Of course, I earned a degree in journalism," she said. "And, now—now, I'm always learning *something*. That's the life of a reporter. Every assignment presents a crash course on a new topic. Before I ever interview a single source, before I write one word, I have to do tons of research. Like this trip. I spent a couple days researching the material. I feel like I'm in school every day of my life."

"But, what about the school of *experience*?" Yanno insisted. "What, exactly, have you learned from *life*?"

Julie seemed a bit unglued. "Well, I—um—I guess the most important thing I've learned is not to trust anybody but myself."

Yanno frowned and raised his forefinger to his lips. "That's sad," was all he said.

Mark scowled. *He* should be asking the questions. Not Yanno. Somehow, this guy had switched roles with them.

Then a thought struck him like a thunderbolt. *Isn't that what Jesus did when the Pharisees confronted Him? Didn't He answer their questions with questions of His own? Didn't he turn the tables and put them on the defensive?* Mark suppressed a smile. *It was as if the old guy had learned from the greatest master of debate that ever lived.*

Before Yanno could ask another question, Mark jumped in and took charge again. "Aside from your educational accomplishments, what have been some of your personal goals?"

Yanno smiled. "Only one," he said. "Love. I want to love and to be loved. To that end, I help people who are in trouble. I like seeing the look of relief on their faces when their problems are solved. I'm not talking about simple everyday problems. I'm talking about deep troubles that cause people to lose hope. In some cases, they have strayed far from God." The old man glanced at Julie. She lowered her gaze to her notebook. "Many times, they merely need a nudge to get them moving in the right direction," Yanno added.

"*I* have a question," Julie said, raising her chin. "It's obvious you live alone. Have you ever been married? Do you have children? Or grandchildren?"

Mark eyed the old man and wanted to add, *How about great-grandchildren?* but he thought better of it and said nothing.

Yanno appeared to be pondering Julie's question. His eyes clouded over and his smile faded. "I had only one true love," he said, his voice carrying a touch of sadness. "She died many years ago. There has been no other. As for children? We didn't have any. We had each other, and that was enough."

"I'm sorry," Julie murmured. Mark thought she was about to cry. Instead, she plunged in with another question.

"Do you ever get angry about anything, Yanno? Do you

ever shake your fist at people? At circumstances? At *God*?"

Yanno stroked his beard. Mark expected him to react with passion. But the old man's voice was calm. "Angry?" he said. "The Bible tells us to be angry but not to sin. So, yes, I guess I *have* been angry on occasion, but hopefully without sinning. I've been angry at injustices in the world, though such things are beyond my control. I become angry when a loved one dies, and like so many humans do, I ask 'Why?' even though no answer comes, and that makes me angry too. I fix the problems I'm able to fix, and I leave the impossibilities to God."

"That's commendable," Mark said. "But we're living in a fallen world. What do you think about all the evil around us?"

"First, you must consider what is at the root of evil." Yanno said, sounding much like a seasoned preacher leading up to a sermon. "The Bible tells us sin comes from three sources—the lust of the flesh, the lust of the eyes, and the pride of life."

Mark knew exactly where that verse was in the Bible. And it was written by John.

"Think about it," Yanno went on. "The lust of the flesh leads to pornography, infidelity, and adultery. The lust of the eyes incites coveting, robbery, even murder in order to get what one wants. The pride of life is seen in self-aggrandizement, gossip, conceit, and ignorance of other's needs." Yanno shook his index finger at them. "Though evil began in the Garden of Eden, every heart contains its seeds. Such evils can be overcome only through the power of a loving, all-powerful God."

The atmosphere dissolved in silence. That old sage had just expounded on John's first epistle. Mark mulled over Yanno's message. He glanced at Julie. Her pinched lips said a lot about the way those words had affected her. Perhaps she was under conviction.

Mark was about to pose another question, when Yanno looked at his wall clock for the second time during their visit. "My visitors will be arriving soon."

"Visitors?" Mark said.

"Every morning at ten o'clock, they come to my door— some for counsel, some for healing, and some merely for a few words of comfort. Then, precisely at 12 o'clock noon, I shut the door. They know this, and they accept it. They also know that during those two hours, I belong only to them. I listen to their problems, I seek God's guidance, and I tell them what the Lord impresses on my heart."

Julie turned off her recorder. Before Yanno could protest, she gathered up the remnants of their morning tea and carried the tray to the kitchen.

"Do you mind if we stay?" Mark asked, then quickly added, "We won't interfere. I promise."

Yanno stroked the sides of his mouth, as though contemplating Mark's request. "I've never had anyone stay during this time." He took another full minute, then conceded with a nod. "I see no harm in your remaining. The villagers won't be speaking your language, so their conversations will be private enough." Then he pointed toward the dining room. "You can observe from in there. Quietly. There will be no talking while I minister to my people."

Footsteps scraped along the front walk. Muted conversations rose from outside the door. Alpha and Omega leaped to their feet and began their incessant barking. Yanno gave his dogs a stern *"Fyge!* Go Away!" The two animals disappeared into a back bedroom. Mark and Julie retreated to the dining room, and the parade of visitors began.

22

YANNO'S MINISTRY

Julie tucked away her tape recorder, but she held onto her
notebook and pen. From her chair amidst the shadows in
the dining room, she had full view of the people who came
through Yanno's front door. Perhaps the old man's interactions with the villagers might reveal some truths about him.
She could only hope.

Precisely at ten o'clock, an elderly woman came through
the door, thrust a loaf of bread into Yanno's hands, then went
straight for the chair where Julie had previously sat. Yanno
took the bread to the kitchen and returned to the living room.
He positioned his rocker directly in front of the old woman
and leaned close to her. In turn, she hunched toward Yanno,
said something in Greek, and to Julie's surprise, the poor
woman immediately burst into tears. Her unguarded show
of emotion revived a memory of the two worshipers at John's
tomb in Ephesus. Julie shook her head in disbelief. Did all
of these people react like grieving widows? What kind of
force moved them to such an emotional state?

She watched with interest as Yanno placed a hand on the
woman's shoulder and whispered something in her ear. They
fell into muted conversation for several minutes. Yanno kept
bobbing his head, listening and uttering sounds of comfort.
In the end, the woman wiped away tears and smiled. She
headed for the door and kept repeating the words, *"Efcharisto.
Efcharisto."*

Julie leaned toward Mark. "What does that mean?" she whispered.

He shrugged.

"You studied Greek, didn't you?"

"Yeah, *biblical* Greek," he whispered back. "I translated a few passages of scripture, that's all. What these people are speaking is *conversational* Greek. I'm guessing she said, 'Thank you.' That makes sense anyway."

Julie spelled out the words phonetically on her notepad with the intention of searching for the translation later. She turned her attention back to Yanno and the procession still coming through his door.

No sooner did the elderly woman leave than a young couple came in with a little boy of about three years old. His arms were thin as broom handles. He clung to his mother, and his head lolled on her shoulder. Beneath the woman's red-rimmed eyes, dark circles spoke of sleepless nights.

The couple settled before Yanno on the two chairs. The child groaned and flopped onto his mother's lap. Julie let out a soft gasp, but no one heard, except for Mark, who patted her hand, and whispered a comforting, "It's okay."

The little guy wore frayed pants and a stained dress shirt that looked to be two sizes too large for him. His parents' clothes were equally shabby, like someone else's castoffs.

A tear rose to Julie's eye. "I've seen this kind of thing before," she murmured to Mark. "Last year, I took an assignment to interview homeless people. They were dressed like this family, and they had that same look of desperation in their eyes."

"It happens all over," Mark said. "Even here."

At that moment, Yanno rose from his chair and went into the kitchen. Julie leaned to one side to catch sight of him through a side door. He filled a paper sack with produce that probably came from his garden. Julie's mouth dropped open. Yanno had pulled her Patmian cheese pie out of the refrigerator and was placing it inside another bag along with the old woman's loaf of bread. Then, he returned to the living room and handed both sacks to the little boy's father.

The man accepted the bags and nodded. *"Efcharisto,"* he said. There it was again. That strange response.

The young mother pulled her son to her breast and smiled at Yanno. Tears streamed down her cheeks and fell onto the boy's shirt. When they departed, Yanno took out a handkerchief and mopped his own face.

Julie glanced at Mark. He was staring after the departing couple and their boy. His eyes were moist and he appeared lost in thought.

"I've been so consumed with my job at the college, I had forgotten that such situations exist outside my door," he mumbled. "We have folks back home in Springfield who suffer this way." He sighed and shook his head. "If nothing else, this experience has given me a whole new perspective on what really matters."

Julie silently agreed, though she buried the thought along with a growing pile of emotions that had been generated on this trip.

So it went over the next two hours. People brought gifts that ended up in other people's hands. Some stumbled into the room, their backs bent under an unseen weight. When they departed, their backs were straight, their steps lighter. Through some unspoken agreement, each visitor kept an eye on Yanno's wall clock. At the end of ten minutes, no matter where they were in their conversation, they bid farewell to the old man and left the house.

Julie jotted the numbers on her notepad. By keeping that schedule for two solid hours, Yanno ministered to at least a dozen families. She did the calculations. In one month's time, more than 300 visitors passed through that door, and in the course of a year, the number amounted to several thousand. She scratched her head. The old man ministered to all of these people without having stepped one foot outside his door.

What astounded Julie most of all was Yanno's genuine interest in every visitor. He gave each one his undivided attention. Perhaps the man really did have a gift for healing, whether emotional or physical, it didn't matter. Each visitor went away healed, at least for the day.

At one point, a woman came through the door carrying a limp toddler. Yanno rushed toward them, lifted the boy's shirt and lowered his ear to the tiny heaving chest. He pressed his palm against the child's cheek and his forehead. With wrinkled brow, Yanno went into the kitchen and pulled a small bottle of brown liquid from the refrigerator, handed it to the mother and spoke what Julie surmised were words of instruction. With her free hand, the woman gave Yanno a hug. She blubbered into his shoulder for a minute, then, kissing her child, she slipped out the door, the vial clutched to her breast.

At that point, Julie succumbed to the press of tears she'd been restraining. Now, while Yanno continued to minister to his string of visitors, she let them flow.

"Are you okay?" Mark said.

She blotted her eyes with a tissue. "I've never seen any-thing so—so—"

"Humbling?" he interjected.

She nodded and wept into the tissue.

"Kind of breaks your heart doesn't it?" he said, his voice soft.

Embarrassed, she turned her face away from him and tried to regain her composure. When she turned back, Mark was writing in his notebook. She relaxed, grateful that he didn't press the issue.

At the end of two hours, Yanno latched the front door and limped back to his chair, without acknowledging Mark or Julie. He sat down with a heavy sigh and immediately fell asleep.

Julie looked at Mark. "What now?"

Mark raised his eyebrows and shrugged. "I guess we wait."

"Wait? For how long?"

"I don't know. Let's see what happens."

Julie flipped back through her notes. "By the way, did you see that cup Yanno used for his tea? It looked pretty old, didn't it?"

"From the bowels of antiquity," Mark said with a nod.

"You don't suppose..."

"Suppose what?"

Julie suppressed a grin. "Wasn't there something called a Holy Grail? And wasn't it missing?"

Mark chuckled softly. "I think Indiana Jones went looking for it."

Julie jabbed his arm. "Right," she said with a snicker.

At that moment, Yanno let out a noisy yawn and stretched his arms. He turned toward the dining room.

"So sorry," he said. "I don't like to fall asleep when people are depending on me. I've done that before, with tragic consequences, I'm afraid."

"No problem," Julie said, as she entered the living room. "You received visitors for two hours. Such a schedule would tire anyone."

He smiled and pointed at the unusual wall clock. "Perhaps we should have some lunch before we continue."

"Why don't you let me fix something?" Julie offered.

"We'll do it together," Yanno said, his face beaming.

He took Julie's hand and led her into the kitchen. Mark trailed behind them. Inside the refrigerator Julie found some eggs, a sweet pepper, and some cheese.

"Omelets," she announced.

They went to work like a well-oiled machine. While Yanno made coffee and Mark browned and buttered the toast, Julie prepared the eggs. Within minutes, they were seated at the dining room table, consuming their lunch and chattering about the day's events. When they finished, Julie realized with chagrin that she had cleaned her plate. *It must be the country air,* she reasoned.

With lunch over, they returned to the kitchen. Julie pushed up her sleeves and plunged her hands in soapy water. Mark grabbed a dish towel, and Yanno paced back and forth, putting the dishes away. The whole scenario brought a tightening to Julie's chest. It seemed like only yesterday, her family had gathered in the kitchen to clean up after supper. Her mom had done the washing, her dad the drying, and Julie and Rita had put the dishes back in the cupboard.

Without warning, Yanno placed a hand on her shoulder. "You can get it all back," he said. "It's never too late."

Get it all back? Puzzled, she kept her back to him. Unexpectedly, her eyes filled with moisture. Then her tears dropped into the soapy water, like the beginning of a gentle rain. *How does he know so much?* she thought with annoyance.

"Take it one step at a time, child," Yanno whispered. "It all begins with believing."

Mark stopped drying the dishes. He set down the towel and tiptoed from the room, leaving Julie alone with the old man. She turned around and looked into Yanno's eyes. "I don't know what you mean," she said.

"It's all right." He stroked Julie's hair. His touch had a soothing effect, as did his words that followed. "You'll know when the time is right."

Julie lowered her sleeves and straightened her shoulders. "I'm fine, Yanno. Can we get on with the interview now?"

"Yes, we can, child."

The conversation during the rest of the afternoon progressed much like it had in the morning, with Mark and Julie asking questions and Yanno nodding, smiling, and asking questions of his own, subtly refusing to give them a direct answer, and glibly taking over the flow of dialogue. Several times, Julie switched tapes in her recorder. At one point, she took out her camera and asked Yanno if she could photograph him, but the old man raised his hand and shook his head.

"No camera has ever survived a battle with me," he laughed.

Julie didn't insist. *Maybe later,* she thought. *When I've earned his trust.*

Mark continued to pose questions, but to no avail. The clever man took complete control of the meeting. Mark had passed all his college courses with flying colors. He was brilliant, but Yanno was ten times smarter. She doubted either one of them could stump the old guy.

She gestured toward Yanno's desk. "You fascinate me, Yanno," she said. "It's obvious you live a simple life, but you haven't ignored the trends in technology. You have a computer and a cell phone, plus a TV set and all the latest media equipment. It seems to me, you've adapted quite well."

"Ah, technology," Yanno mused aloud. "Sadly, those contraptions have taken the place of intimate conversations and face-to-face interactions. I have to admit, I've fallen into the texting trap. How else can one stay in touch with people these days? It saddens me that our society has been relegated to such an impersonal form of communication, yet, I go along with it. If I don't, I will be left in the dust of cyberspace."

"So, progress has swept you along?" Julie tilted her head, coyly.

"Like a tidal wave," he said with a chuckle. "I personally like how Thor Heyerdahl said it. 'Progress is man's ability to complicate simplicity.' That man knew what true adventure was all about. He stepped into uncharted lands and made a name for himself, without the help of modern technology."

"What about your *own* adventures?" Mark jumped in. "What has been your greatest adventure?"

"That's easy," Yanno replied, without taking time to think it through. "My greatest adventure happens every day when I communicate with my Savior."

Julie perked up. "And exactly how do you communicate with Him?" She'd set the trap.

But Yanno appeared undaunted. "Nothing compares with spending time in God's word and praying," he said. "Those two daily activities give me what I need to minister to my people. I fall to my knees, and I come away refreshed and ready to serve."

Another evasive answer. Frustration mounted inside Julie. She struggled to curb it. "You say you get answers. How do you know for sure what God's telling you?"

"Well, we don't text each other." Yanno said with a giggle that annoyed Julie. Had he just made fun of her?

Then the lines on his face grew deeper. "Every time I pick up my Bible, every time I kneel in prayer, I am communicating with my Savior, and He's communicating with me," he said. "Throughout the day, he puts situations before me. You observed a brief sample of it this morning. People come to my door; I don't go to them. Except for chance encounters when I'm in town, I don't go out looking for people to help. I'm no one special, Julie. I'm a mere instrument through which Jesus cares for others and nothing more."

Mark shifted in his chair, like he was about to speak. "Lots of people go to church and pray and read their Bibles—including myself—but we don't have a ministry like yours, Yanno. What you do here is really special."

The old man eyed Mark with interest. "You're wrong, son. What I do here is no more special than what you do in the classroom." He faced Julie. "Or what you write about people you encounter." He spread his hands like he was about to preach a sermon. "We all have a job to do. Whatever we work at, we should do it heartily, as to the Lord. Some people think that when they put on their Sunday best and go to church they are worshiping God. But we don't have to wait for Sunday to worship. We can worship him every day of our lives, and we do it best when we're helping others. Think about it, Mark. You too, Julie. What happened here today was me worshiping God. And aren't we worshiping him right now? You came here with a need. I am trying to satisfy that need to the best of my ability. There's no doubt in my mind that, as the Lord promised, he is sitting right here in this room, sharing this time with us."

A tingling sensation ran up Julie's arms, as if an electric current had passed through her. She stared into Yanno's eyes, so filled with wisdom that she felt small and insignificant. Was this man John? Or was he simply a good imitation?

"Tell me," Mark said, leaning toward Yanno. "One day your work will be finished. How do you plan to face death?"

213

Julie held her breath, her eyes on Yanno. He stopped rocking and looked from one to the other. "Dying will bring a welcome release from a life of aches and pains," he groaned. "I have worked long and hard. Unlike Paul, who said he had finished his race, I'm still finishing mine. You saw what happens in this place." He nodded toward the front door. "I doubt the Almighty will allow me to depart this earth until I have fulfilled all that He has called me to do."

"What does that mean, Yanno? Are you waiting for Jesus' return?" Mark said. He wasn't wasting time anymore.

"Aren't we all?" Yanno replied with a wink.

Once again, before either one of them could ask another question, Yanno glanced at the clock on the wall. "The sun will be setting soon," he said. "You should start back to town, so you won't get lost in the dark."

"How could we get lost, when the floodlights from the monastery light up the entire hillside?" Mark said, with a laugh. "If I forget to close the curtain in my hotel room, I won't be able to get to sleep."

"True," said Yanno, smiling. "But I have work to do. Scrolls to translate, manuscripts to transcribe. Perhaps, you'd like to return tomorrow?"

Julie breathed a sigh of relief. Until that moment, there was no guarantee the old man would welcome them a second time.

"We'd like to come back," she said. "If you don't mind."

Yanno stood to his feet. "What more can an old man ask but to have another visit from such an intriguing couple?" He danced a little jig, another sign his aging body still had a lot more life in it.

Julie reluctantly gathered up her belongings and joined Mark in the center of the room. "Tomorrow then," Mark said.

23

JULIE FACES HER PAIN

Mark suggested they walk back to their hotel instead of calling a cab. Julie agreed. The sun hadn't set yet, and the evening air felt cool and inviting.

Mark slipped his hands in his pockets and set a pace that was easy for Julie to keep. Her mind was flooded with remnants of the day's events. Yanno was an intriguing man, there was no doubt about it.

"What do you make of what we experienced today?" Julie said. "Do you think we're getting anywhere with this guy?"

Mark grimaced. "If he isn't John the Apostle, he sure is an incredible facsimile," he said. "Did you notice how he took charge of the conversation and turned everything around in his favor? I'm telling you, that guy would have destroyed my entire college debate team."

Julie laughed softly. "He was one of the most challenging people I've ever had to interview." She looked at Mark. "What makes you think we'll do any better tomorrow? Won't he give us more of the same?"

"All I know is, we can't give up. The man is definitely not a con artist. He sincerely helped people today. None of what we saw could have been staged."

"I know. Those people..." she shook her head. "They were so pathetic. And, Yanno? There's something mysterious about him. He scares me a little. I was certain he looked right inside my brain—like he knew what I was thinking."

"He certainly nailed me, didn't he? All that stuff about my clothes and my job. How could he possibly know those things unless he had some type of spiritual discernment?"

"Well, don't forget, he *is* old," Julie said. "A person can't live several decades on the earth and not know *something* about life. But it's more than that; he made me care about him. I wanted to protect him, maybe even join the villagers' effort to keep him a secret. Is that weird or what?"

"You can't go there, Julie. We have to keep our focus on the reason we came to this island in the first place. Tomorrow, we'll look for an opening, another chance to ask him if he's the apostle. And we can't let him weasel out of it this time."

"There's something else we can do," Julie said. She'd been thinking about a solution for the last couple of hours.

"I'm all ears," Mark said.

"Do you remember how Yanno dropped off to sleep after all the visitors left?"

Mark nodded. "So?"

"Well, if that happens again tomorrow—and I'm guessing it will—I'd like to pluck a couple of hairs from his head."

Mark's sudden stop stirred up gravel on the path. He let out a laugh. "What? You're kidding, right?"

"Now hear me out, Mark. We can take those hairs to a forensics scientist or some other expert who's able to determine how old that man is. It's worth a try, isn't it?"

Mark started walking again. "I guess taking a hair sample makes sense. But, I'm not sure a forensics scientist is the person you want. I mean, they can do that kind of study on cadaver bones and such, but someone's hair? I don't know."

Julie huffed out her disappointment.

"Listen," he said. "There may be another way. A few months

ago I attended a conference in Atlanta. They brought in scientists and college professors from across the nation. A molecular geneticist from UCLA gave a lecture on some cutting-edge technology called epigenetic modification. Though it's still in the testing stage, it seems that by examining chemical changes in a person's DNA, they may be able to determine the chronological age using tissue taken from any part of the human body—bones, skin, blood—even hair follicles."

Julie felt a surge of excitement. "Did you get the man's name?"

Mark nodded. "I have his contact information back home in a pile of notes from the conference. I'll try to find his number. He may laugh at us, but like you said, it's worth a try."

For the first time that day, Julie was encouraged. Aside from her notes and tape recordings, a bit of Yanno's hair could be the single most important piece of evidence they could acquire.

Though Julie had left Yanno's house with fresh hope, by the time she reached her hotel room, she'd fallen back into a slump. Something the old man had said kept running around in her brain. *"You can get it all back. It's not too late. One step at a time. It begins with believing."*

Though he'd spoken those words with kindness, nevertheless they tormented her, and she spent a restless night. More than once, she turned over in bed, trying to shake off Yanno's voice. He was right. She had lost it all, or at least she felt like she had. It had taken only one moment in time for her to lose everything. Her family. Her home. Her innocence. Her self-respect.

She lay in bed, staring at the ceiling. Her mind drifted back six years to a rainy afternoon in the church fellowship hall. She was 17 years old and had signed up to help clean up after a Saturday morning youth breakfast. She was trying to do something worthwhile so she could prove to her parents and everyone else that she wasn't the loser they thought she was.

Lightning flickered outside the hall windows. Julie began to count the seconds. As expected, the thunder followed. The storm was about five miles away.

She was alone in the hall with Mr. McAndrews, one of the deacons in the church and a guide to the youth programs. All the other kids had departed with excuses about housework, or babysitting jobs, or anything else they could come up with.

Julie tossed soiled paper plates in the trash. McAndrews swept the floor. She rearranged the chairs. He picked up debris. They were on opposite sides of the room. He started a conversation, asked about school and sports. She gave him short answers. After all, how does a teenager talk to a man his age?

Lightning flashed. *One, one-thousand. Two, one-thousand. Three, one-thousand.* Boom!

McAndrews mentioned the business deal he'd made with her father, like she cared. It was just casual talk. Totally boring.

Then, something changed in his demeanor. He walked toward her, with a strange look on his face, like he'd gotten a piece of dust in his eye.

"So, do you have a boyfriend, Julie?"

A flash, followed seconds later by a thud.

She shook her head and took a step back from him.

"No boyfriend? Has a boy ever held your hand, or kissed you?"

The memory tormented Julie as she continued to toss on her hotel bed. Like before, McAndrews' face came before her. His eyes—filled with evil. Even now, she could almost smell the stale coffee on his breath, could almost feel his hands restraining her. She gasped for air and rolled to her other side. The image remained. She had tried to push him away, but he'd overpowered her. She'd even screamed. No one came to her aid. Not even God.

Another loud crack. The storm was upon them.

A cry lodged in Julie's throat. She sat up in bed, flung the covers off, and ran to the bathroom. She splashed cold water on her face. Then, she caught her image in the mirror. The confident, aggressive newspaper reporter was gone. Looking back at her was the face of a frightened little girl—a mere teenager who'd been raped and humiliated.

Her entire body shaking, Julie returned to the bedroom and sat on the edge of the bed. Tears ran down her cheeks. Her thoughts turned to Mark. Poor Mark. She never gave him a chance, never trusted him. He had confessed his feelings for her and she'd rejected him. Again.

Then there was Yanno, that loveable old sage who had stirred up all the garbage from her past. She was doing fine until those two came into her life. Mark, whose promise of love had her wondering if she could be truly happy with him. And Yanno, whose insightful piercing of her soul threatened to revive her long-buried faith in God.

Exhausted, Julie leaned back against her pillow. Her protective wall was crumbling. Mark had pulled away one of the stones. Yanno had chiseled out a large chunk of it. How could she go back to that house again? Did the old man know he was about to break away the rest of her protective shield? Deep down, she longed to be free. She wanted to find God waiting for her on the other side of that wall.

She pulled the covers up to her chin, gazed at the blank expanse of her ceiling, and whispered a simple prayer. *"Dear God, if you're real and can hear me, help me."*

24

DAY TWO WITH YANNO

The next day's visit with Yanno echoed what had occurred the day before. Once again, Yanno's two barking dogs, Alpha and Omega, welcomed Mark and Julie in a flurry of excitement. And like before, Yanno shooed them to a back room and welcomed the two of them inside his home.

Mark smiled at the old man's getup—a lemon yellow shirt, blue jeans, and a pair of sandals. Yanno had pulled his salt-and-pepper hair back into a pony tail and he'd wrapped a yellow and green bandana around his forehead. He looked like he was on his way to Woodstock.

"Come in, come in," he said, his eyes shining. "I've been looking forward to our visit." Then he disappeared down the hall.

Julie grabbed the chair she'd used the day before, like the creature of habit she was. Mark settled into the chair beside her. He was surprised when Yanno returned carrying a basin of soapy water and with a towel draped over his arm. The old man went down on one knee before Julie.

"Yanno, you don't have to—" Mark objected.

"Yes, I do." he said.

Julie gasped as he removed her shoes and plunged her foot into the frothy liquid. The scent of rose petals filled the air. With gentle strokes of the towel, Yanno wiped her foot dry and then did the same with her other foot. Mark locked eyes with Julie. She gawked at him but didn't—or couldn't—speak, though her lips were parted in a silent protest.

Then, Yanno slid the pan in front of Mark and began to unlace his shoes. Though flustered, Mark submitted to Yanno's act of service. In a way, he understood. An image crossed his mind of another cleansing of feet, one that took place more than 2,000 years before.

When the ritual ended, Yanno rose from the floor with a groan and shuffled off with the pan of water.

Mark replaced his socks and shoes. "What did you think about that?" he whispered.

Julie responded with a shrug. "I don't know. It was... humbling, to say the least."

Yanno returned to the room and raised one hand. "Not another word about this," he said, his voice firm. "I did it more for myself than for you. Whenever I am able to perform such a service, I feel closer to my Savior." He sat in his rocker, a contented look on his face, and set the chair in motion.

Mark considered what had just happened. Was it a clue? Or a coincidence? He didn't know anymore.

"So, let's get down to business," Yanno said, matter-of-factly.

Mark grinned. The guy was a total enigma.

During the next half-hour, Mark peppered Yanno with questions. At one point, he began to peel a scar from his own heart.

"If God is a God of love," he said, "why are there wars, famine, disease, and other forms of suffering in the world?"

"That shouldn't surprise a Bible scholar like yourself, Mark. It all started in the Garden of Eden. The Good Book tells us such things will continue until Jesus returns. As you well know, God may not cause the tragedies, but He doesn't stop them from happening. He's letting the world do its own thing, until He chooses to act in His own good time."

"His own good time?"

"That's right, Mark. I'm sure you know the passage from Ecclesiastes that talks about a time for everything. Well, we're in a particular season now, but the day is coming when He will bring judgment on the earth, followed by restoration of the creation the way He intended it to be from the beginning, before man came along and ruined it."

"But, Yanno, why doesn't He stop bad things from happening now?" Mark didn't try to hide his frustration. "At least for those who belong to Him. For example, why do believers suffer, and become ill and die? Why are children left without parents and parents left without children?"

He had held his pain inside through most of his young life. Even when his father took him to counselors, he'd refused to ask the questions he'd been holding inside, afraid that he might not like the answers he got. Until now, it had been much easier to simply leave them buried. Somehow, being in this house in a foreign land, with this old man and Julie, he'd let down his defenses and had finally asked the questions that had been plaguing him for more than a decade.

Yanno stopped rocking and appeared to be moved to tears. "Oh Mark, you sad young man. You should know that God never promised us freedom from trials. He only promised to be *with us* while we're going through them." His eyes locked with Mark's. "You have suffered a great loss. Someone close to you, right?"

Mark nodded. "My mother. When I was 12." His eyes began to sting, and he regretted having broached the subject at all. He gazed back at Yanno through a blur.

"Your mother." Yanno shook his head. "Such a loss is a terrible thing for a youngster. Tell me, son, who raised you?"

"My father."

"It appears he did a fine job."

Mark smiled. "My father was a pillar of strength. He kept us both going after Mom died. I don't know what I would have done if I'd lost him too."

"And how did the two of you deal with such a loss?"

Mark glanced at Julie. She had turned her eyes away. Strange. Though he'd shared nearly everything about his life with her, he'd never opened up about his deepest pain. If he had, she might have trusted him with her own secrets, too. Now, with Yanno egging him on, he spilled out the trauma of the past.

"For weeks after Mom died, we followed the same routine," Mark said in response to Yanno's question. "I'd come home from school and I'd find my dad had quit work early. Then, we'd sit together on the sofa. He'd wrap an arm around me and I'd lean my head on his chest. Then we'd cry. Both of us. And we'd pray, and we'd cry some more. After a while, we'd go into the kitchen and make dinner. Together."

Mark sighed and brushed away a tear. "If not for my father, I would not have survived."

"And, how did you feel about God when that happened?"

Mark lifted his head. "I never faltered. Let me clarify that and say that I *would* have faltered except for one thing. My mother left me a note telling me I should never blame God for her illness. She said she knew where she was going, and she was contented with that. She also said she'd wait for me and my dad to join her one day. At the end, she quoted a verse from the Psalms."

"*Precious in the sight of the Lord is the death of his saints.*" Yanno said.

223

"How did you know she chose that one?"

"It's one of my favorite verses, and it's used quite often at funerals."

"That one verse told me my mother is with God, and she isn't suffering anymore."

The old man left his chair and approached Mark. He bent close, reached for Mark's hands and held them fast. "Now do you understand what I said about seasons? Your mother was ready to leave. She said as much in her note to you."

Yanno stared into Mark's eyes, then content that he'd gotten through to him, he went back to his chair. The three of them sat in silence. Mark had no idea what was running through Julie's head at that moment, but she looked like she was about to cry. A comforting relief washed over him. It was like he'd been to a counseling session and had dumped his worst hurt on the counselor.

Mark felt drained and unable to continue with the interview. He checked his watch. Yanno's tea time was coming up fast.

"Julie, do you have any questions for Yanno?" he said, almost out of desperation.

Julie nodded and flipped through her notes. She asked several casual questions, but they hardly moved things along. He was beginning to doubt the reporter in her would ever surface. Then she struck.

"What about the matter of sin, Yanno? You do a lot of good deeds. The people who come here depend on you, and you help them. But, can you look back on your life and say you've never sinned?"

Yanno chuckled, then he immediately grew serious. "My child," he said, his eyes trained on Julie. "It is sin that drives me to the foot of the cross every single day. In fact, before I shut my eyes at night, I go over the day's events and I consider my actions and my reactions. Did I insult someone? Did I have an unkind thought? Did I neglect to help a person in need? By the time sleep overtakes me, I feel as if I've cleansed my soul. Then I fall into our Father's arms and I get a good night's rest. But without that cleansing, I can expect to toss and turn all night long."

Julie sat back and glared at the man. Yanno had obviously struck a chord with her. Maybe he'd opened a door Mark hadn't been able to unlock. If anyone could do it, he believed Yanno could.

But instead of continuing the conversation, Yanno sprang to his feet and headed for the kitchen. Heaving a sigh, Mark figured more tea and crumpets were coming. As he suspected, minutes later, Yanno reappeared, balancing a tray.

Even as he sipped his tea and downed a few cookies, Mark decided not to waste another minute. He plunged ahead and got Julie rifling through her notes.

"As we told you yesterday, Yanno," he said. "Julie and I have been trying to uncover the rumor that John the Apostle is still alive."

Had Yanno chuckled? Was that an amused grin on his lips?

Mark continued. "We've been to Ephesus. The grave is empty. So, what became of John's bones? It looks like he simply disappeared."

He searched Yanno's face for some kind of response. The guy was a blank wall.

"Church records describe the deaths of most of the other apostles," Mark went on. "But nothing has been recorded about John. There are no documents, no relics, no bones, no John. It seems he simply vanished. So, where did he go?"

Yanno took a bite out of a cookie, then he slurped his tea from his favorite goblet, the one with the crack down the side. He wasn't going to answer until he was good and ready. He finished off the cookie, took another sip of tea, then set down his cup and cleared his throat. Mark suppressed an impulse to get up and shake the guy. When was this old sage going to give him an answer he could use?

Finally, Yanno set his rocker moving. A pensive look came to his face, and he began to talk.

"John lived a long time, well into the first century," Yanno began. "Perhaps God had more work for him to do than was expected of the others. Perhaps God's plan included exile to this little island where they could commune without interruption. But, where is John now? All I know for certain is that God's thoughts are far beyond our thoughts. If God wanted to keep John's death and burial a secret, you can be sure He had a good reason."

How frustrating. Yanno had once again avoided giving a direct answer. Yet, the old man made sense. As always, he'd supported his response with Scripture, which made it impossible to oppose him. Mark shook his head and grinned. The man was a genius at tactical evasion. The U.S. military could use him as a foreign diplomat. After all, didn't Damien Petra say Yanno could speak several languages? And what about all those degrees on the wall? Why on earth had Mark presumed he could win in a battle of wits with the guy?

The minutes had ticked away and before Mark knew it, it was ten o'clock, time for another stream of visitors. He signaled to Julie, and they reluctantly retreated to their hiding place in the dining room. Seconds later, the traffic started.

The first to enter was the young woman who'd come in the

day before with a sick child. This time, the little one had wrapped one arm around his mother's neck. He gazed about the room, wide-eyed and smiling. Apparently, the medicine had worked.

The woman went down on one knee before Yanno and blubbered her gratitude. The old man lifted her to her feet, shaking his head and murmuring something in her ear.

She dropped a few coins in Yanno's hand. He tried to give them back, but she turned away. Hugging her little boy to her chest, she hurried out of the house. Not long after, her coins ended up in the pocket of an elderly man who shuffled through the door, his back bent, his tattered shoes scraping against the wood floor.

And so the day went, like before, with people bringing gifts, and Yanno transferring them into the hands of someone else. The room's atmosphere was filled with audible sobs, cries of grief, muffled conversations, and now and then an eruption of laughter. Each petitioner faithfully stuck to the ten-minute limit, and Yanno concluded each visit with a bow of his head and a prayer.

Near the end of the visiting period, Mark cast a glance out the dining room window, which offered a wide view of the front walk. The line of people had dwindled to a few stragglers. Then, a sudden chill went through him. Near the end of the path by the street stood two lone figures, dressed in black. They looked out of place compared to Yanno's other guests. One of them was holding a camera with a huge zoom lens. The other was scribbling in a notebook.

Mark elbowed Julie. "What do you make of those two?"

She leaned close to him and peered through the window. "Oh, no." Though she kept her voice to a whisper, it carried a flash of panic.

227

"That's Jason Redding and his flunky cameraman," she said. "What are we going to do, Mark? We have to keep them away from Yanno."

"Right. But how?"

"I don't know," she mumbled. She backed away from the window. "Think of something, Mark. Fast."

He settled back in his chair and scratched his head. "We could warn Yanno about him."

"Do you honestly think that will make a difference?" She'd raised her eyebrows in disbelief. "Yanno couldn't possibly know anything about Redding and his malicious tactics. If Jason can delude all the government officials in Springfield, how can an old man escape? Yanno will fall right into his trap, and we'll be out in the cold."

Mark shook his head. "I think he's smarter than that. But, you're right, Julie, we need to do something."

Seconds later, the problem of Jason Redding was far less significant when a familiar voice drew Mark's attention to the living room. Damien and Sofia had come through the door. Their eyes were on Mark and Julie, and an angry frown had crossed Damien's forehead. Mark shifted uncomfortably. He looked at Julie. She'd frozen like a statue, her eyes on the Petras.

The older couple continued to glare at them. Yanno was saying something in their language. The Petras conversed briefly with him, then, scowling, they left in a huff.

His heart pounding, Mark looked at his watch. They'd have to wait another ten minutes for 12 o'clock. He peered again out the window. The Petras were walking right past Jason Redding and his cameraman. Jason said something to the old man. Damien ignored him, grabbed his wife's hand, and kept walking.

Jason nudged his cameraman and together they headed along the path toward the house. Mark held his breath.

The last visitor departed, the wall clock struck noon. Jason approached the front stoop. And Yanno shut the front door and hit the lock. The persistent knocking didn't deter him. He turned away from the pounding and returned to the living room.

Mark turned to Julie. "Whew! That was a close one."

Together they returned to the window in time to see Jason and his photographer climb into a compact car at the end of the walk. The two of them sat there and stared at the house. Then they peeled out, kicking up gravel on the country road.

Mark returned to the issue at hand. The Petras. He was about to get up and ask Yanno what Damien had said to him, when the old man retreated to his rocker and immediately dropped off to sleep.

With a sigh, Mark signaled Julie. "We'd better move fast if you want to get a piece of his hair," he said. "And make sure you get the root. It may be necessary for the test."

Julie pulled a plastic bag from her purse. The two of them tiptoed over to Yanno. His chin had dropped onto his chest. Julie reached behind his head and yanked out a couple strands of hair.

Mark stepped close and plucked a couple of hairs from Yanno's beard.

Julie tucked the follicles into the plastic bag and returned it to her purse. Then, without making another sound, they slipped into their seats across from the old man just as he began to stir. He looked from one to the other. "Did you get what you needed?" Yanno asked.

For an uncomfortable moment, Mark stared blankly at him. Did he know what they'd done?

Without waiting for Mark to answer, Yanno stood up, stretched, and announced, "Lunchtime."

Mark didn't feel like having another omelet. "How about letting us take you out to lunch?" he offered.

Yanno grinned like a schoolboy and hurried toward the hall. "All right," he called over his shoulder. "First, let me freshen up."

Minutes later, Yanno emerged wearing a green polo shirt, khaki pants, and a black beret, cocked to one side. He could have walked off the streets of *Old Paree*. The old man also had traded his sandals for his Nikes.

"For walking," he explained.

While Yanno took his dogs outside for a potty break, Julie freshened up in the bathroom, followed by Mark. Then they joined Yanno on the front stoop.

"I can call a cab," Mark suggested.

"No, no. Let's walk down," Yanno said, grinning. "It's a beautiful day. Going downhill will be easy. We can take a cab when we return home."

25

LUNCH WITH YANNO

As she strolled along the country road with Yanno and Mark, Julie was fascinated by her surroundings. She'd left small-town America with its cloned houses lined up in neat suburban rows, and she had found herself in a slice of Eden, tucked away in the hills of an island called Patmos. As they walked away from Yanno's tiny paradise, they left behind his lush gardens, fruit trees, greenery, and farm animals, and fell captive to the dry and barren stretches of land on either side of the road. Even in the midst of a literal wilderness, a soft breeze brought Julie a sense of freedom she hadn't experienced in a long time.

For the moment, she carefully tucked away the Jason Redding sighting and the unusual reaction of the Petras, which could be addressed at a later time.

As they progressed downhill, they entered a more populated area, where towering white walls closed in on them. A lace curtain billowed from an open window. On the sill stood a vase of brilliant red flowers.

The image conjured up a long-forgotten child's bedroom with its floral wallpaper, lacy curtain, and canopy bed. There had been times when Julie yearned for that haven of safety, but the desire had faded over the last couple of years, and she no longer considered going home. Until now.

While Julie was mentally traveling into the past, Mark and Yanno had moved ahead on the trail. They were engrossed in a conversation about sheep and goats. She dropped back a little and allowed their voices to fade. She wasn't yet ready to leave the house where she grew up or the people who lived there. She envisioned her mother setting Sunday dinner on the table, her sister Rita taking the chair next to hers, and her Dad at the head of the table, bowing his head for the blessing.

Awakening from the trip to the past, she shook off the ache of nostalgia and quickened her step to catch up to the other two.

They turned into a small hillside *taverna* with a broad deck that jutted out toward the sea. A row of cedar trees stood like soldiers beside the patio, and a vine-covered canopy presented a suitable protection from the blazing midday sun. Julie settled into a high-backed wicker chair and gazed out over patches of cacti tumbling down the hillside toward a jagged, rocky coastline. A tranquil sea stretched into the distance like stained glass reflecting the azure sky and its puffs of white clouds.

A waiter slid a menu in front of her. She ordered the soup of the day, a spicy minestrone. Yanno selected seared fish and vegetables. And—no surprise—Mark ordered an appetizer platter of fried shrimp, crab, and calamari, a Greek salad, and a main course of braised lamb with herbed orzo. Julie grinned and shook her head. Yanno raised his eyebrows but didn't comment.

During lunch, Mark mentioned the nice weather and the spectacular view. He went into detail about their time in Ephesus, then he talked about their visit to the monastery and the Cave of St. John. Julie wanted to say something about the Petras. She was about to speak up, when Mark mentioned their downtown stroll and their meeting with the old couple. She immediately jumped in.

"They came to your home this morning," she said. "You don't have to tell us anything personal, Yanno, but did they have a special reason for being there?"

Yanno set down his fork and stared into Julie's eyes. His serious demeanor troubled her.

"I—I don't mean to pry, but—" Julie stammered.

"They came about you," Yanno said, his voice hard.

"About me?" Julie's throat tightened. Her cheeks began to burn.

Yanno nodded. "About both of you," he said.

Mark pushed back from the table. For the moment, he'd stopped eating. "What are you saying, Yanno?"

Yanno's face was void of emotion. There was no telling what he was thinking or what he might say next. "They had gotten word about this strange couple that was in my house, and they wanted to know what you two are up to," he said, glancing at one, then the other. "They told me you had paid them for directions to my house."

Julie's mouth dropped open. "Yanno, I—we ..."

"They said you pumped them for information," Yanno continued. "That you tricked them into thinking you were tourists. They talked with some of the other shopkeepers and discovered the truth."

Julie struggled to come up with an explanation. The truth was, she and Mark *had* deceived that couple. And now Yanno knew it too.

Shame washed over her. She was at fault. She had convinced Mark to omit the truth and to let the Petras think they were on a different kind of assignment. Now their lie had come back to haunt them.

But Mark didn't falter. Nor did he pass the blame to Julie, though he rightfully could.

"Yanno," he said with confidence. "We did nothing wrong."

We, he'd said. *We,* like he was sharing the responsibility.

"We asked several people where we might find you," Mark told the old man. "No one would tell us anything. You have to understand, we're on an assignment, and we don't have much time. We *had* to find you, to talk to you."

To Julie's amazement, the lines on Yanno's face softened and a sparkle returned to his eyes.

"Thank you for your honesty," he said. "Don't worry. The Petras are friends of mine. I told them you meant no harm. I asked them, 'How else is an outsider supposed to find me unless they get someone to speak up?' So, you *paid* them for my address." He chuckled. "How ingenious."

Then Yanno leaned toward Julie and patted her hand. "And you, dear child, you didn't tell the Petras you're a reporter. If they had known you were working on a story, they might not have given you directions to my house. But you knew that already, didn't you?"

Julie answered with an embarrassed shrug. Her face must have turned ten shades of red. "We didn't mean any harm, Yanno. It's just that, when people find out I'm a reporter, they clam up. Posing as a tourist had to be far less intimidating."

Yanno slid his hand away and picked up his fork. Julie relaxed and got back to her soup, aware that the old man could have come down a lot harder, but didn't.

Mark also had plunged back into his meal. But, he continued to press the old man. "Tell us, Yanno," he said. "Why all the secrecy? I mean, you're somebody who helps people. So, why do the villagers want to keep you to themselves? For all they knew, we could have needed help, too."

Yanno sat back. A half-smile tugged at the corner of his mouth. "Secrecy?"

"Yeah," Mark said, gravy dripping to his chin. He quickly mopped it up with a napkin. "And what about the Petras' behavior this morning? Were they angry with us?"

Yanno shrugged and shoveled a piece of fish in his mouth. "Why do you care what the Petras think?" He looked from Mark to Julie. "You've come to Patmos on an assignment. You didn't come here to make friends. Why not complete your work and leave the rest in God's hands?"

"That's it?" Mark said. "You think we're so heartless that we don't care what the Petras think of us?"

"No, I think you had a goal. You two are like those ships out there." Yanno nodded toward the sea. Two sailboats drifted past. "You charted a course with a specific destination in mind. You didn't concern yourselves with rocks or sandbars or any other navigational hazards." He gestured toward the lighthouse, a lone sentry on the rocky shore. "Do you see that landmark? During the day, its light is concealed by sunlight. Everything turns blue—the sky, the sea—they're the same color, and it's hard to tell where one ends and the other begins. Seamen can't see the light of the lighthouse during the daylight hours, but it's still there, nonetheless."

Yanno took a sip of his wine. "But at night," he said. "At night, when everything turns black, the beam of light comes to life. It casts a silver trail upon the water and provides a safe path to the island."

"And, the point is?" Mark asked.

"The point is, my children, sometimes you need to get your eyes off of your goal and simply enjoy the journey. God is like a lighthouse. He can guide you safely to shore. He can bring you to your goal. You only need to put down your personal compass and trust Him."

Julie stopped eating. What was he trying to tell her? That she'd been trying too hard, not only with this assignment, but with every aspect of her life? It seemed everything Yanno said had a double meaning.

"Yanno," Mark said, his tone serious. "What you say is true. Julie and I may have tried too hard to accomplish this goal. But you have to understand, we're working against the clock. We had less than a week to complete the entire project, and here we are, only two days from our departure. To be honest, I don't feel like we've accomplished our mission."

Yanno nodded. "Why do you feel that way?"

"I have too many unanswered questions," Mark said.

Yanno looked at Julie, his intense gaze urging her to speak.

"Mark's right, Yanno. I've been under pressure this whole time. I watched you from the shadows while you helped people with health issues and emotional problems and who knows what else? We came here with a purpose. Why don't you help us too?"

"All right," Yanno said, smiling. "I'll submit to your questioning. Let it never be said of old Yanno that he hindered the work of such a fine young couple."

As though motivated to resume the interview, Mark nodded toward the dock where a trio of fishermen were unloading their catch. "Have *you* ever been one of those sailors, Yanno? Have you spent a day on the sea and returned with a load of fish?"

Julie was smiling inside. She'd learned the Bible story when she was nine.

Yanno replied without hesitation. "Well, I've caught my

share of fish in my day. In fact, I had many a profitable time on the sea."

"And?" Mark probed.

"And, all I can do now is dream about getting out there once again. Unfortunately, I no longer have a boat, so I must depend on the generosity of friends who own one."

"Did you ever haul in more than you expected?" Mark pressed.

Yanno leaned back and put his fingertips together. His eyes began to glisten, like he was remembering.

"My experience had less to do with the catch of fish than it did with the journey and the people who went with me, people who meant a lot to me." He got a faraway look in his eyes. "You must know the difference, Mark. Julie. Even now, you've embarked on a fishing trip of sorts, and I guess I'm the big fish you're after." He let out a laugh, then he grew serious again. "I suspect you have not enjoyed this journey. You're like two shanghaied sailors, swabbing the deck, trimming the sails, and attending to other duties, without so much as a kind word passing between the two of you."

Julie blushed and cast a sheepish glance at Mark.

"That's right," Yanno said. "While you've been interviewing me, I've been watching you. What I've seen is a couple of nice people sitting side-by-side, yet there's a noticeable gap between you. You don't even *see* each other. Yet, I suspect that chasm did not exist at one time."

Julie leaned back in her chair and gazed into Yanno's eyes. He was right about them. There was a chasm, and she'd put it there. Now she wasn't sure she wanted it to remain.

"You're very perceptive, Yanno," Mark said. "Julie and I dated for about a year. It didn't work out between us."

Though Julie didn't like to air her laundry in public, she

was relieved to have the truth out. Now maybe they could get down to business.

But Yanno didn't let things rest. He shoved his plate away and leaned toward Julie. "My dear child, on the surface you are a self-assured young lady. But, when I look deeper, I see chains around your heart." He turned toward Mark. "And, I see thorns around yours," Yanno said. "They're pricking away at the surface and leaving painful holes."

Bristling, Julie drew back from him. "That's ridiculous, Yanno. Chains? Thorns? What on earth are you implying?"

The old man gave her a knowing smile. "I'll tell you what I'm implying. The chains are keeping you from living the life you were meant to live. You've allowed your past to bind your heart, and it's been keeping you prisoner ever since."

Julie snickered. "And Mark's thorns?"

"They prick his heart whenever he thinks of the losses in his life. Yet he endures the pang, and the next, always hoping it will be the last."

Julie pondered Yanno's analysis, irritated that he had gotten so close he could almost read her mind. How did he know so much? And what about Mark? She glanced at him. He was staring out at the sea, as if deep in thought.

Except for the flutter of bird wings and an occasional chirping in the trees, their lunch concluded in silence. Mark called for a cab to take the three of them back to Yanno's house. The old man knew way too much about them, but it didn't matter. They'd come to this place to learn about *him*, and Julie wasn't going to give up until she fulfilled her mission. Yanno had loosened up a bit. His stomach was full. He'd had a glass of wine. Surely, he could be broken down if she and Mark teamed up that afternoon.

But during the ten-minute drive to the house, Mark complained about an ache in the pit of his stomach. Julie eyed him with concern. By the time they reached Yanno's house, Mark was doubled over in pain. Though their cab was air-conditioned, beads of sweat had formed on his forehead.

Julie reached out and felt his cheek. "You're burning up."

Yanno emerged from the cab. Julie followed him out the door but she kept her eyes on Mark. With noticeable effort, he slid from the seat and stood hunched over with one hand gripping the vehicle's door handle.

"It must be something I ate," he said, his voice strained. "Julie, why don't you stay here with Yanno? I'll take this cab back to the hotel."

Julie tensed. "Wait a minute, Mark. We should take you to the hospital."

The cab driver leaned over the seat. "Hospital? No hospital," he said.

Yanno came up beside Julie. "There are no hospitals on the island, only a couple of clinics and a few independent doctors. They're all reliable professionals, of course, but for emergencies there's a big hospital on Rhodes. It serves all twelve of the Dodecanese islands. To get you there quickly, we'd have to call for a helicopter."

Yanno grabbed Mark's arm and tried to hold him upright. "My son, why don't you come inside the house? I can fix you something—"

"No, I'm okay," Mark mumbled. "I have antacids in my bag at the hotel. I'll take a couple and go to bed." He slipped back into the cab and dropped like a sack of potatoes on the back seat.

"I'll go with you," Julie offered. She took a step toward the cab.

"No, Julie. I want to be alone. You stay here and visit with Yanno. I'll be fine."

Reluctantly, she backed away. Yanno shut the car door and the cab drove away. Julie stood in the middle of the street and watched after it. Yanno stood by her side. She took one look at him and caught her breath. An aura of tranquility emanated from that whiskered face. He placed a hand on Julie's shoulder, and a flood of peace washed over her. She looked back down the street. Mark's cab turned the corner and disappeared from view. Somehow, she knew he'd be all right.

26

ALONE WITH YANNO

With halting steps, Julie walked beside Yanno along the path to his house. It wasn't that she feared for her physical safety—not with this man—but how could she continue the interview without Mark? The two men were more intellectually compatible. She felt like a dunce in a discussion with them.

She paused on the threshold. She was going to be alone with this wise sage for the rest of the day. He'd already unnerved her with his subtle probing. He'd invaded her personal space, had somehow gotten her to unearth her past.

She was about to suggest they call for another cab, when the old man took her by the arm and led her inside. To Julie's surprise, Alpha and Omega didn't bark this time. They circled around her, sniffing and wagging their tails, like a welcoming committee, letting her know she'd met their conditions for entry. She patted their heads and they ambled off to a quiet corner of the room.

She'd have to take control right from the start. Otherwise, Yanno would take charge, and who knows where their conversation would end up? She pulled out her tape recorder and her pad and pen.

"Down to business?" Yanno said with a twinkle in his eye.

"We're leaving the island tomorrow evening," she explained.

Yanno went into the kitchen and returned with two bottles of water. He handed one to Julie. She set it on the floor beside her chair. Yanno opened his bottle, sat back in his rocker, and took a noisy swallow.

"Okay, Barbara Walters, fire away," he said, smiling.

Julie released a nervous laugh. "I'm hardly Barbara Walters."

He cocked his head to one side and raised his eyebrows. "You underestimate yourself. Barbara Walters didn't start out at the top. I believe she was about your age when she was a backstage go-fer. That's right, Julie," he said, as though noticing her shocked expression. "Barbara Walters started out as a nobody, but in time she moved up the ranks, and she proved herself to be one of the most successful interviewers of television history. You can accomplish similar feats, if you don't give up."

"I doubt it," Julie said, blushing. She cleared her throat and flipped through her list of questions, hoping to accomplish what she and Mark had failed to do to this point.

"Okay, you want Barbara Walters?" she said, her eyes trained on the old man. "That woman could be brutal. She didn't hold back, and somehow she always got what she wanted."

Yanno nodded. "That's true. First, she set up her prey, won their trust, and then, when they weren't ready for it, she pounced. It was quite an effective technique, one that caught her sources off-guard and got her the dirt of the story."

"Is that what you think I'm after? The dirt?"

He chuckled. "In a way. Otherwise, you'll have failed your assignment. You want to go home with the most mind-boggling story you can put together. Didn't you say your editor gave you only a week to do it?" His forehead knitted together in amusement.

She raised a shoulder.

Yanno harrumphed. "Sounds to me he was setting you up for failure."

The thought hadn't struck Julie until now. But Yanno could be right. Had Andy sent her on a wild goose chase? She gritted her teeth. After losing a story to Jason Redding, this was very likely her last chance to prove herself.

She checked her list again. She couldn't waste anymore time. She had to hit the old man with a direct question.

"Yanno," she said, "have you ever been ill to the point of death?"

He got his rocker moving. "That depends," he said.

Julie frowned at her notebook. He was about to give her another vague answer. Dejected, she gazed into his eyes, hoping to find some flicker of truth there.

He stared back at her—no, through her—no, *inside* her. Then his demeanor softened. "Let's see. Have I ever been ill to the point of death? Well, I've had a multitude of sicknesses in my life, a couple of them *near* death. Or at least I felt like I was dying."

"And?"

"And," he said. "I'm as human as you are. I've had stomachaches and headaches and, yes, colds and the flu. Once I even had the measles. That was a horrible time in my life. But it happened a long, long time ago."

He took another long swig of water, then he let out a contented sigh and placed the bottle on the end table. Julie eyed him with suspicion. The clever man was about to lead her on another rabbit trail. She couldn't let that happen.

"Does death frighten you?"

Yanno shrugged. "I have a strong immune system. If I catch a cold, I blend together some herbs from my garden. I mix in a little hot water, and, though it's a disgusting concoction, I drink it all at once. Then, I go to bed for a week, drink lots of liquids, and what do you know? My cold is gone."

"But that's the normal progression of a cold. Doctors tell you to drink plenty of liquids and to get bed rest. The cold will be gone in a week."

"Aren't the doctors smart?" Yanno said with a giggle.

She glowered at him. He was playing games with her, having fun at her expense.

"You must know that someday you *will* die, like the rest of us," she said, her tone bitter. "What will you do when the time comes? Do you have family members who will need to be contacted? Have you decided how you want your remains to be handled? Do you prefer burial? Or cremation? Do you want your ashes placed in an urn or spread over some special place?"

"Hmm. A lot of questions. Let's start with my family. You've seen my family. They come to my door every day. Mothers, fathers, children, the old, the young. The people of Patmos are my family, Julie. If anything happens to me, they already know my wishes."

Julie nodded. "So, knowing death could come at any moment, how does that affect the way you live?"

"I find life and death are somewhat synonymous," Yanno said. "Anticipating death should make a person live a better life. Awareness of life should make a person strive for an end with no regrets." Yanno spread his hands. "By expecting death, I have chosen to live a life of value. That's why I help others. That's why I give. It's even why I receive. When I give without reservation, I am blessed. And when I accept gifts from others, I help to bless them." He folded his hands on his lap and pressed his lips together in a pensive smile. "Julie, I want to live in such a way that I leave this world a better place. So you see, life and death go hand-in-hand. You can't consider one without the other."

Once again, Yanno transformed Julie from reporter to student. At any moment she expected she'd be sitting at his feet. With a huff, she regrouped and tried to take back control of the interview.

"Okay," she said. "Say you die within the next year. What sort of legacy are you hoping to leave?"

He stopped rocking and thought for a minute, then he got his chair moving again and acknowledged her question with a nod. "I'd like to leave a legacy of many components," he said. "Of course, love has to be one of those components—possibly the *main* one. I want people to remember me as someone who loved them the way God loves—unconditionally." Yanno stopped his chair and leaned toward Julie, his eyes steady. "Another component is truth. It's important that my friends know I never lied to them." He sat back and pointed at his head. "The third component is self-evaluation. I need to take an honest look at myself, admit any failures I've committed, and try to correct whatever is in my power to correct. I hope by combining those three components, I can bring people closer to the only One who can save their souls."

Julie reached for her water bottle and fumbled with the cap. She sloshed a little water on the floor. A flush surged to her face, and she glanced nervously at him.

"I don't know what's wrong with me," she said. "I guess I'm worried about Mark."

"Mark will be fine," Yanno assured her. He rose from his chair, walked to the kitchen, and came back with a towel. He knelt beside her and mopped up the spill.

"Are you certain that's all that's bothering you, child?" His penetrating gaze unsettled her.

"I'm okay," she said. "Shouldn't I be concerned about Mark?"

"Of course." He eyed her with curiosity. "But I think there's something more going on with you."

She held her breath. The man had closed in on her. His face was inches away. Then, as though aware of her discomfort, he returned to his chair. Julie exhaled. Never before had she experienced such difficulty during a simple interview. She'd talked to politicians, entertainers, even the governor of her state. This man was unlike any other person she'd ever met.

Flustered, she looked at her notebook. It had become a blur. She looked up at Yanno. His image swam before her. Why did Mark have to go and get sick? She needed him. Needed his help with this fiasco of an interview. Needed him to draw Yanno's attention away from her. She squirmed under the old man's steady gaze.

"Julie, you probably have many more questions for me, but aren't there some things you'd like to settle for yourself? Things I might be able to resolve for you?"

His tone had softened. "I want you to know, child, that God is holy, but He's not inaccessible. He's not out there— somewhere," Yanno waved his hand the way Julie had done in Andy's office only a week before. "He truly does care about you."

More tears filled her eyes. Though she blinked hard, she couldn't stop the flow.

"God *is* real, and He *does* care," Yanno said. "Trust me, Julie. He understands your pain." He pulled a handkerchief from his pocket and held it out to her.

She accepted it and dabbed at her tears.

"There's a story in the Bible that tells about Jesus' power to bring a friend back to life," Yanno said. "But he delayed. By the time he got to Lazarus's gravesite, he stood there and grieved. The Bible says, 'Jesus wept.' Two words. Isn't it amazing that the shortest verse in the Bible speaks volumes about the heart of our Savior?"

Julie's shoulders sagged and she twisted Yanno's handkerchief into a knot.

"Julie," Yanno went on, "no one knows for certain why Jesus wept. Perhaps He was grieving for his friend. Or maybe he cared deeply about the mourners that had gathered there. Or perhaps he was saddened by their disbelief. In any case, while they were wailing and mourning aloud, he wept softly."

Julie looked into Yanno's face, the interview forgotten now. She had a strong desire to crawl onto his lap and rest her head on his chest, like a little girl seeking the comforting arms of a kind, old grandfather.

"It's the same with us," Yanno went on. "Though God doesn't keep bad things from happening to us, you can be sure He is with us through it all. He promised to do that, and it is during our most difficult times—when we feel utterly alone—that He's closer than you think."

He paused and gazed into her eyes. "I sense you've been carrying a burden far too long," Yanno said. "It's time to open your heart, Julie. Stop trying to live without God. Tell Him you need His help."

She choked back a sob. Tears flowed freely down her face.

Yanno pressed further. "Do you know what God is saying right now? He's saying, 'Don't cry, my child. I'm here.'"

Julie put her face in her hands. Sobs erupted from deep inside. Yanno's approaching footsteps told her he was right beside her. His arm went around her shoulder. She didn't resist. His beard brushed against her forehead, and she succumbed to his comforting touch.

"Go on, child. Release your burden," Yanno whispered. "I'm here."

Julie rocked back and forth under the soothing caress of Yanno's hand on her back. His voice, tender and sympathetic, showered her with a love she'd never experienced before. She'd been reduced to one of those villagers who had come there for help. Only this time, she wasn't watching from the dining room. She was experiencing what they had experienced, the love of God shed upon her through a simple man.

"What we mortals see as coincidence may be the work of a loving, yet powerful God," Yanno murmured. "You may think your trip to Patmos had to do with an assignment, but I think God had a bigger plan. I think He brought you here, to this island, and to my home, so He could free you from that wall you've built around yourself."

Julie leaned back and looked into the old man's face, shocked to see tears in his eyes.

"Yanno," she said. "How do you know these things?"

"You told me," he said. "With your eyes. With your heart. With every unspoken word."

He left her again and returned to his rocker. Several minutes passed. Neither spoke. The clock on the wall ticked louder in the pronounced silence. Had God really coordinated the assignment—even Mark's illness—so she could be alone with Yanno and perhaps release the burden she'd been carrying for so long? While she would welcome such a release, she also feared she might become that vulnerable little girl again, subject to the control of others, unable to defend herself, with no one to rescue her.

"I'm not sure I can trust God to protect me," she said. "All these years, I've made a safe place for myself. Now I'm afraid to leave it." She shook her head and raised the wall again. "Yanno, I've been fine. My life has been fine."

"Fine? Do you remember how I said during lunch that you were trapped in chains? Tell me, why do you cling to those chains so adamantly? Don't you know they are strangling you?"

As she had done on the plane with Doctor Balser, she let down her defenses once again. Like a dam that had broken, Julie released the trauma she'd experienced at the hands of McAndrews. She poured out her anguish, told Yanno about her parents' distrust, the rejection by the church members, Dina McAndrews' angry accusations, and her own guilt over what had happened. When she finished, she collapsed once again in a heap of remorse and regret.

"You know, Julie, you've been dragging all this around with you for way too long," Yanno said. "It's time you stopped torturing yourself." He exhaled a long breath. "Listen to me. You were a teenager. You did what teenagers do. They rebel. They make mistakes. They put themselves in danger. And then, hopefully, they grow up. Now stop this nonsense. Stop looking back at the confused teenager you once were. See, instead, the fantastic woman you've become."

Julie shook her head. "I don't know how."

"I must ask you, child. Have you ever belonged to Jesus? Or, more importantly, has *He* ever belonged to you?"

Julie nodded. "When I was 11, I gave my heart to Jesus. I wanted to be a missionary. Then, I fell away from my faith, and after the attack, I began to wonder if I'd ever belonged to God at all. So I chose another path, one that didn't include God or anyone else. I depended only on myself."

"And now, do you see how that self-sufficiency has put you in bondage?"

She nodded.

Yanno stood to his feet and spread his arms. "Then, release those chains."

Julie pushed off her chair and fell against him. His arms enfolded her. Her trembling ceased and a flood of relief washed over her.

"I don't want to live this way anymore," she murmured into Yanno's shirt. "I'm so tired of trying to do everything on my own. I need to have God in my life again. I don't want to be alone."

Her face streaked with tears, Julie looked up into the old man's face. Tender eyes smiled down at her. "You're not alone, child. You have just let God back into your life."

"Just like that? I don't have to *do* anything?"

Yanno shook his head. "Not a thing. Reaching out to God is the only action that is required. You said you already received Jesus as a child. Now you have renewed your faith." He paused. "But there may be one thing that could keep you bound in chains."

She searched his face. "What one thing?"

"Unforgiveness," he whispered.

"Unforgiveness?" She frowned at him.

Yanno nodded. "Unforgiveness," he repeated, louder. He straightened. "To be able to move ahead, you must forgive everyone that was involved in your trauma. Your parents. The people in your church. McAndrews and his wife—"

"No. Don't ask me to do *that*. I can never—"

Yanno raised his hand to silence her. "You must. By forgiving your parents, you can restore that broken relationship. You can be a family again. By forgiving the church people who spoke against you, you can rise above them. Otherwise, you allow them to keep on hurting you. By forgiving your attacker, he no longer has power over your life. That man has put a fear in you that keeps you from trusting other men. Isn't that what stopped you from having a full and happy life with someone who cares for you? Mark, perhaps?"

"So if McAndrews has kept me in bondage, why should I forgive him?"

"Because, it will free you from that bondage. The attack ended years ago, but that man is still controlling you. By forgiving him—*and* his wife—you can shake that dust off your feet and move on."

Julie shook her head. "I can't—"

"That's not all," Yanno said, his voice firm.

Julie's shoulders sagged. "There's more? I don't know if I can handle more."

Yanno smiled and a web of creases spread from the corners of his eyes. "You must also forgive yourself," he said, "and you must forgive God. Don't you realize He was the one person you needed most? Instead, you've been shaking your fist at Him. You've been trying to survive under your own power and you've gotten nowhere."

Julie felt drained. More tears surfaced. She allowed them to flow, unchecked. As a youth, she had learned those principles of her faith—trusting God, forgiving others, your enemies, yourself. But she hadn't done any of those things, or wanted to, until now.

"I can try," she said, her voice weak.

Yanno took her hands in his. "That's all you need to do, Julie. Be willing to try, and God will do the rest." He stepped away. "Now," he said, "you must be wondering how that young man of yours is doing. Shall we go see him? I'll take along a jar of my herbal remedy, and we can pray for the return of his health."

"Yes," Julie said, nodding. "Let's go." She put away her notebook and tape recorder. "Shall we call a cab?"

"*What?* Call a *cab?* Why do we need to call a taxi, when I already *have* transportation?"

Without another word, Yanno retreated to a back room and returned with two helmets. He thrust one into Julie's hands. She immediately was reminded of the red Vespa waiting inside Yanno's carport. Any question she might have had about who that thing belonged to was finally answered.

Smiling, she put the helmet on. Yanno went into the kitchen. There was a rattle of glass, the shutting of the refrigerator door, and he came out carrying a bottle of disgusting-looking brown liquid.

"For Mark," he said.

Julie scrunched her nose. "Do you honestly believe Mark will drink that?"

He raised the bottle toward the window where a ray of sunlight turned it to a golden hue. "He'd *better* drink it, if he wants to get well."

They left the house. After securing the front door, Yanno tucked the bottle in his vest pocket. He led Julie to the carport. With amazing agility, he swung his leg over the seat of his Vespa and motioned for Julie to climb on behind him. She wrapped her arms around Yanno's torso and pressed her cheek against his shoulder. Her crimson locks poked out from under her helmet and merged with Yanno's silver ponytail.

Yanno turned the key and with a sputter and a roar, they lunged out of the driveway. Julie shrieked with delight. Yanno gave the engine full throttle. The two of them leaned from side-to-side as one. The bike skidded around turns, bounced over ruts in the road, and zipped down the hill toward the heart of Skala.

Squealing and laughing, Julie clung to Yanno with all her might. The man had systematically dismantled her flawed belief system and had given her a fresh start. The chains were finally dropping away. Her heart was almost completely exposed.

Now she was racing toward Mark, and she couldn't wait to tell him about the miraculous change Yanno had wrought in her. She no longer feared that young man. No longer resented him. Instead, she wanted to be part of his world—if he'd still let her in.

27

HEALINGS

Yanno parked his bike in the Hotel Skala parking lot. Julie's heart raced in time with her hurried footsteps as they rushed up to Mark's room. She paused in front of the door and turned to Yanno for support.

"It's going to be all right," he said. Then he knocked.

A full minute later, the latch released and the door eased open, revealing Mark in a damp T-shirt and wrinkled boxer shorts, his hair splayed across his forehead and his eyelids were half shut. His face had turned the color of toothpaste and he looked about to fall over. Julie's heart ached at the sight of him.

Mark opened his eyes briefly, then he turned away and staggered to the bed. Groaning, he flopped down on the crumpled quilt. Julie ran to his side. Yanno was there in a second, feeling Mark's forehead.

"He still has a fever," he said, and he began to tug the T-shirt over Mark's head. Julie rushed over to Mark's suitcase and pulled out a fresh shirt. Yanno disappeared inside the bathroom and returned with a damp washcloth. He mopped Mark's face and neck. Then he helped Julie get him into the clean T-shirt.

"Thanks," Mark muttered, and he fell back against his pillow.

Feeling helpless to do any more, Julie backed away from the bed. "Should we ask the hotel clerk to call a doctor?" she said, aware of the tremor in her voice.

Yanno shook his head. "Let's try this first." He removed the bottle from his vest pocket. "Prop up his head a little."

She obeyed him, and Yanno dribbled the vile-smelling liquid into Mark's mouth. How could something so rank cure anyone? Mark would surely puke it out. But, after draining the bottle, he slumped back against the pillow and shut his eyes. Moments later, he was snoring away.

"Now, we wait," Yanno said. He settled into a chair on the far side of the room. Julie perched on the edge of the bed, her eyes on Mark.

The minutes ticked away. She kept checking her watch. Four o'clock. Five. Six. Mark sank into a deep sleep. She rose from the bed and stepped out on the balcony, rested her elbows on the railing, and looked out at the tiers of whitewashed homes, the sun-streaked walls of the monastery, and the rolling hills in the distance. A Psalm from her youth came to mind.

"I will lift up mine eyes unto the hills, from whence cometh my help. My help cometh from the Lord, which made heaven and earth..."

She closed her eyes and she prayed. But not for herself. This time she was praying for someone else, someone who had remained faithful to their friendship in spite of her harsh rejections, someone who had done her no harm but had tried to lead her back to her faith. Inside that hotel room, Mark lay helpless on a sickbed, in a foreign country, his only hope an old man with a homemade formula and a woman who had gotten so far from God she didn't know if He would hear her prayer.

"Please God, help Mark," she murmured. *"Yanno has convinced me that you are a God who cares. Please, don't let me down again.*

Show me that you can heal me spiritually and at the same time heal Mark physically."

She opened her eyes and let fresh tears spill out. Without shame, she wept for the man who lay helpless only a few feet away from her, a man she now admitted she loved.

She turned and caught sight of Yanno still sitting there with his head bowed and his hands clasped on top of his knees. Comforted by the sight of him, Julie returned to the railing and stared at the wisp of clouds that separated above the city, exposing a darkening sky.

Despite having turned her back on her faith, the ability to pray came back to her like a wave off the ocean. When she was a child, she'd talked to God regularly. Now she'd become that child again. With heartfelt innocence, she sent up another plea.

"Lord, what do I do with Yanno?" she whispered. *"I'm not sure what to make of that man. I came here to do a job, but I don't feel any peace about exposing him to the world. I'm torn between my responsibility to my employer and my growing affection for this man. He's had a profound effect on my life. I don't want to hurt him or the people who depend on him. The Petras. The woman with the sick child. The poor and needy and hurting who come to his door. Please, tell me what to do."*

From inside the room came a moan and a stirring on the bed. She hurried back inside, then slowed her pace and tiptoed closer to Mark. Yanno rose from his chair and stepped up beside her. They stood very still and watched Mark breathe. He wasn't snoring anymore. A mere whisper of breath escaped from his half-parted lips.

"I'm going to leave you now," Yanno said. "Mark is going to be all right." He turned toward Julie. "You should get some rest too."

256

"What if Mark should take a turn for the worse?" she whispered.

"Don't worry, child." He placed a hand on her shoulder. "If Mark doesn't improve by morning, you can have the hotel summon a doctor, but I don't think you'll have to do that."

Yanno started for the door. He turned to face her. "Trust God. He didn't bring you all this way to abandon you—or Mark. You have to believe He has a plan for your life. Now that you've renewed your faith, you can expect wonderful things to happen."

Julie forced a smile. "Okay, Yanno. I'll get some sleep, and I'll check on Mark in the morning."

Yanno hugged Julie, then he shuffled out the door. A few minutes later, his Vespa sputtered to a start and roared up the street. She went to the bed and took one last look at Mark. Then she planted a kiss on his forehead, grabbed his room card off the dresser, and walked out, easing the door shut behind her.

Julie's churning stomach reminded her she hadn't eaten since that bowl of soup at lunchtime. She went down to the hotel restaurant and ordered a full meal of chicken and potatoes and steamed vegetables. Once again, she wiped the plate clean, surprised at how her appetite had returned.

Back in her room, Julie dug inside her carry-on bag in search of the little New Testament Andy had given her. Then, she remembered, she'd left it at home. She searched the drawers in the room for a Bible. Finding none, she pulled out her reporter notebook and began to write verses from memory. She could hardly believe so many came tumbling back from her youth.

Several times during the night, Julie went out in the hall and listened at Mark's door. His steady breathing comforted her. After her third clandestine vigil, she went back to her own room, fell into bed, and slept like a baby until dawn.

A ray of sunlight spilled through Julie's balcony door and woke her. She sat up, aware that she had embarked on a new path for her life. Not only had Yanno helped her renew her faith in God, but she had a strong desire to restore broken relationships. Particularly with her parents. And with Mark.

She stretched her arms, sucked in a deep breath, and flung her legs over the side of the bed. After a quick shower, brushing her teeth, and a few flicks of a hairbrush, she dressed quickly and hurried out the door to Mark's room.

She knocked twice, but no one answered. She called out Mark's name and knocked again. Using his room card, she opened the door and poked her head in. Crumpled sheets lay on top of the bed. The curtains were opened wide. Mark wasn't there. The chair Yanno had sat in last night stood empty. No sound came from the bathroom. Julie peeked inside. Mark's grooming kit lay open. The mirror had a foggy coating, like someone had used the shower.

Confused, Julie stood frozen in the middle of the bedroom. Where in the world was Mark? Had he gotten worse during the night? Had someone taken him to the health clinic? Or worse, to the hospital in Rhodes? His suitcase was still in the corner. Where could he be?

Still pondering this, Julie turned away and started back toward her room. She was almost there when she noticed a slip of paper dangling from the door knob. She pulled it free, opened it and read, *In the restaurant. Come join me. Mark.*

Julie let out a laugh. Of course, the restaurant. Where else would Mark go when he recovered? She slipped inside her room, grabbed her purse, and danced down the stairs to the coffee shop.

Mark sat at a table close to the door and was shoveling scrambled eggs in his mouth like a hungry lion. He grinned when he saw her. She returned his smile and grabbed the chair across from him.

"You're better," she said.

"I don't know what Yanno gave me, but I got my appetite back this morning. Big time."

Julie let out a happy laugh.

He stared at her. "You seem different."

"We have a lot to talk about," Julie said, smiling. "Yanno didn't only help *you*, Mark. He worked a miracle on me, too."

Mark's eyes sparkled. "Why don't you grab something to eat and we'll talk about it?"

He slathered butter on a hot crescent roll, then he watched the golden drops as they spilled over the side. He took a huge bite, catching most of the butter before it dripped to his plate.

Julie shook her head. Mark was back and there was nothing wrong with him that a big meal couldn't cure. She sighed and walked to the buffet. Instead of her usual bowl of muesli, she loaded a plate with pancakes and sausage. While eating her breakfast, she kept glancing at Mark, still in awe at his quick recovery. She began to wonder if God had orchestrated the whole thing in order to give her time with Yanno, without Mark being present.

When breakfast ended, Mark suggested they take a walk. "It'll give us an opportunity to talk," he said.

As they strolled along the path, a soft breeze caught a lock of Julie's hair and swept it across her face. Mark brushed it back. This time, she didn't resist his touch. Mark was no longer a threat to her. In fact, she wanted him to hold her hand, to guide her up the hill, to repeat the words he'd said on the hillside only a couple of days ago. Her response would be quite different now, though there was no way he could know that.

Mark didn't reach out. He didn't speak. It was Julie, this time, who poured out her heart. Thankfully, he was a ready listener. She told about the assault and the opposition that followed. She left nothing out. He didn't speak, just shook his head and frowned. She ended by telling him about Dina McAndrews' devastating confrontation in front of the church. Then, she wept bitterly.

"Yanno wants me to go home and tell my parents I forgive them," she said. "I don't know if I can do that. I *do* want to see my little sister again and give her a long overdue hug. Rita stood by me when no one else did."

Mark stopped walking and turned to face her. "Julie, you're getting a fresh start. I can't tell you what to do, but you'd be wise to take Yanno's advice."

"Yeah. If not for him, I'd still be wallowing in self-pity and guilt." She met his gaze and didn't shrink back this time. "Tell me it's not too late, that we still have a chance."

She didn't have to explain. Mark grabbed her hand and raised her fingers to his lips. "Julie, I've never stopped caring for you. I think you already know that."

He pulled her close, planted a kiss on her forehead, then backed away and smiled at her tear-stained face. "More later," he said with a mischievous grin. "Now, I hate to change the subject, but we're running out of time. We have to take the red-eye out of Izmir tonight. I've chartered a helicopter to take us to the airport there. It'll be quicker than ferry boats and buses."

Julie began to panic. "We can't leave without saying good-bye to Yanno. Do we have time to visit him, one more time?"

"We do, if we hurry."

28

THE FINAL VISIT

As they neared Yanno's cottage, Mark's insides began to tremble. This was going to be the last time they'd see the old man. There was so much left unsaid, so much more to share.

To his delight, Julie allowed him to take her hand. He checked his watch. It was noon. The last visitor was leaving. He scanned the area. There was no sign of Jason Redding and his photographer.

They approached Yanno's door and Mark raised his hand to knock, but hesitated.

"This is the last time we'll enter this house," he whispered, his throat tightening. He blinked hard against a sting of tears. Then, he knocked.

As always, Alpha and Omega came charging at the door, followed by the scraping of feet and a gruff voice. "Visiting hours are over. Come back tomorrow."

"Yanno," Mark called out. "It's me, Mark. And Julie."

The latch moved, the door opened, and a smiling Yanno welcomed them inside.

"You look wonderful, Mark. My concoction must have worked."

"Yes, along with a little vomiting and a good night's sleep," Mark said, laughing.

Yanno beamed. "So, you have not had enough of this old man."

"Never," said Mark.

"I was about to make myself a sandwich. Can I offer you some lunch?"

"A sandwich sounds great," Mark said.

"Nothing too big," Julie interjected. "We had a huge breakfast this morning."

"Speak for yourself," Mark joked. "I can always stuff another bite of food in my mouth."

They followed Yanno into the kitchen. He laid out several slices of whole wheat bread, a jar of peanut butter, and a couple of bananas.

"I learned this recipe from Elvis," Yanno said, giggling.

Mark and Julie exchanged an amused glance.

"What? You don't believe me?" Yanno raised his eyebrows. "I spent an entire weekend at Graceland, in 1960, right after he was discharged from the Army." He shrugged. "It doesn't matter if you believe me or not. Get over here and give me a hand with this."

While Mark cut up the bananas, Julie slathered peanut butter on the bread. Yanno arranged the plates, setting aside a half sandwich for Julie, a whole one for himself, and one-and-a-half for Mark. He poured three glasses of milk and placed everything on a tray.

Mark eyed the tray. Something was missing. "Where's your special goblet? The one with the crack."

Yanno shrugged. "I had a visitor last night after I arrived home from your hotel. It was another reporter. Maybe you know him. Jason something."

"Redding," Julie sneered.

"Yes, that's it. Jason Redding. Polite fellow. But, I can't understand all this media interest. I had to shut down his photographer, of course. No photos. But I spent a little time with the two of them, just chatting, mind you, the way I do with you."

Mark was snickering inside. If Yanno conducted himself the way he did with him and Julie, Jason must have walked away completely frustrated. Hopefully, he gave up early.

Yanno frowned and puckered his lips, like he was annoyed about something. "One of them must have swiped my cup when I wasn't looking," he grumbled. "After they left, I couldn't find it anywhere." He whisked the tray off the counter. "C'mon. Let's eat in the dining room."

"Jason Redding." Julie's face had flushed a deep red. "Jason Redding."

"Why do you keep saying that?" Yanno asked her.

"That man is my worst adversary," she snarled. "What did *he* want, anyway?"

"I guess he wanted the same thing you did."

The old man set the tray on the table. He raised his eyebrows. "Don't worry. I didn't tell him anything of importance."

"That was wise," Mark said. "You can't trust that man. He's known as the king of fake news."

Mark kept his eyes on Julie. She went from scowling to huffing to clamping her mouth shut. He'd forgotten how animated she could become when provoked. It was one of the many things he admired about her.

Yanno grabbed the chair by the window. They sat across from him.

The old man said a blessing, and immediately followed with a hardy, knee-slapping laugh. He continued chortling for a full minute, then he held his side and drew in a deep breath. "You'll be happy to know, I sent that Jason fellow on a wild goose chase. He won't be coming back here anytime soon."

Julie was smiling now. "What did you tell him," she said.

"Well, I told him the man he's looking for may or may not be living in the monastery on the hill. I said he should ask for Brother Jonathan."

Julie started giggling. Mark nearly choked on his sandwich. He broke down laughing. "Brother Jonathan? Is there such a guy?"

Yanno shrugged. "Who knows? Maybe there is, maybe there isn't. The search should keep Mr. Redding busy."

Julie laughed hysterically. Then she started raving about her ride on Yanno's motor scooter. "That was some hair-raising adventure," she said, her emerald eyes glistening. Mark listened with fascination. His Julie had literally come alive. "Do you believe it?" she went on, still laughing. "When we got to the main road, Yanno cut off a taxicab. I looked back and the driver made some sort of hex sign at us. He yelled something out the window but, fortunately, I couldn't understand what he said."

Mark laughed at the image. "That was probably for the best."

Then Julie's smile faded and she turned pensive.

"Something else happened yesterday," she said, her voice soft, her eyes on Yanno. "My life changed."

The old man grinned like a kid with a popsicle. "The Lord works in mysterious ways, does He not?"

"Yes, he does," Julie said, bobbing her head. "I came here with one purpose, to get a story, but I'm going home with so much more."

"Ah, your story," Yanno said, leaning back in his chair.

"More than a story," Julie corrected him.

"So, is there anything else I can do for you two?" Yanno looked from one to the other.

Julie let out a heavy sigh. "I had a whole list of questions, Yanno, but now they seem insignificant."

He nodded. "And you, Mark?"

"I would welcome a chance to pick your brain one more time," Mark said. "If you don't mind."

"Ask, and you shall receive," Yanno said, and he took a big bite of his sandwich.

It was now or never. "Okay," Mark began. "Exactly how old are you, Yanno?"

The old man smiled. "Twenty-nine and holding."

"Come on," Mark said. He'd let a tone of impatience creep into his voice. "I've been thinking about this one question for three days. Give me *something*."

"To be honest," Yanno said, his eyes twinkling. "I am many ages. Sometimes, I am four years old again. I feel that way when I climb onto my Heavenly Father's lap, and when I tell him my problems, and when I cry out my pain. After all, doesn't the Bible say we should come to Him like little children?"

Julie nodded. Mark looked on, the frustration rising inside him. Once again, Yanno had found a way to evade the question.

"Sometimes, I'm a teenager," the old man continued. "At least, that's the way I feel when I'm riding my Vespa. If I don't look at myself in the rear-view mirror, I can imagine I'm young again. I can feel the wind in my face. I can tackle the sharp turns in the road. I can ignore the angry shouts from other drivers. I can act like I own the highway. After all, isn't that what teenagers do?"

Mark opened his mouth to speak, but Yanno plunged ahead.

"Sometimes," he said. "I am a young man, in love again with the red-haired beauty I told you about. When I look at Julie's fiery hair, I think of my own true love and my heart comes to life. But then, I have to remember I am no longer four years old. I'm no longer a teenager. I'm no longer a young man in love. I'm just a silly old coot trying to hang onto his past, one that's so fleeting, a day feels like a thousand years and a thousand years feels like a day."

Stunned, Mark looked at Julie. She sat there with a silly grin on her face. The guy could have said he was Superman and she would have accepted it.

"No, Yanno. That's not good enough. When were you born? Give me a date. And a year."

Yanno leaned toward him and lowered his voice. "I know what you want to hear, Mark. You want me to tell you I was born in AD 10 and now I'm 2,000-plus years old."

Mark fell back in his chair. "Are you?"

"If you want me to be."

"Come on." The words came out sharper than Mark had intended.

"Let's just say I'm older than the hills, and like everyone else, I will die one of these days. I'm not some supernatural figure, Mark. I'm simply a man."

He wasn't sure how to assimilate all that Yanno had said. He had mentioned a date—AD 10. Was he joking with him, like the Elvis thing? Perhaps a simpler question might give a clue.

"All right, Yanno," he said with a sigh. "During our conversations you occasionally quoted Scripture. When you consider the entire Bible, what is your favorite verse?"

"That's easy," Yanno replied quickly. "*Greater love hath no* man than this, that a man—"He turned his eyes on Julie. "Or a woman," he said. "*—should lay down his life for his friends.*"

Mark couldn't think of one time when he'd laid down his life for anyone. "I've heard about soldiers throwing themselves on grenades to protect the troops," he said. "Or how about a mother running into the path of a car to save a wayward child? And other acts of heroism. But, I've never been in a situation that required that *I* take such a risk. I'd like to believe I might do the heroic thing, but, to be honest, Yanno, I don't know for certain."

"My son, you're interpreting the verse only one way, to physically die so someone else might live. That kind of situation rarely happens." Yanno pushed aside his empty plate. "Perhaps what it *really* means is that we should give up our own dream so someone else can have his or hers." He leaned back in his chair. "That kind of sacrifice doesn't always end in life-and-death situations. It could be something simple. A person might give up something for the benefit of another, and the cost might be very great. That, my friend, is what laying down one's life is really about."

Mark shifted in his seat. He looked at Julie. He cared about her and he wanted her in his life. But now, considering Yanno's words, he knew he had to care enough to let her go, if that's what would make her happy. Perhaps, in a sense, he would be laying down his life for her. When his mother died, he had to let her go, but he had no control over that situation. This was different. This type of letting go was on purpose. It required a sacrifice he wasn't sure he could make.

The three of them sat in silence while Yanno's message sank in. Mark glanced at his watch. The minutes were ticking away too fast. He was at a loss for words.

As if sensing Mark's discomfort, Julie plunged in with a question of her own. "Tell us, Yanno, where else have you lived besides this island? I mean, it's definitely a paradise, and anyone should be happy living here. But you have all those degrees on your wall and you speak perfect English. Surely, you've been to other places that might draw you back."

Yanno turned around in his chair and stared out the window. When he spoke again, his voice was so soft Mark had to strain to hear him.

"There was a time when I didn't have the steady stream of visitors like those who came through here today. I left the island for a while and traveled to a number of different places in the world. I saw magnificent sights, and I met lots of interesting people." He looked back at them and a tear came to his eye. "But, I never forgot Patmos," he said. "It was here that I had my most intimate conversations with God. So, in my later years, I came back and settled here. Everything had changed. The population had grown. Farmers had planted trees and gardens. People had begun to take pride in their property. The government built up the dock and the downtown area. The island came alive with hotels and restaurants and shops. Tourists flocked here. I began to make friends, and the villagers started to visit me daily. Now, I have a fresh purpose for living. I want to help others as much as I possibly can."

Mark was mentally soaking up every word that poured from the old man's mouth. In a way, what he'd described probably took decades if not centuries. Encouraged, he plodded ahead.

"I was wondering, Yanno," he said. "What is your opinion of religious relics, like the bones of the apostles and the

Shroud of Turin? Are they real mementos of the faith or simply hoaxes?"

"I assume you're merely asking my opinion, not what is proven fact."

Mark nodded. Yanno crossed his arms. "Okay, then. In my opinion—and it's only my opinion, mind you—I think if something gives people hope and increases their faith, it doesn't matter if it's real or fake. It's what's in a person's heart that counts. People get encouragement from a lot of different sources. They have a meaningful dream. A preacher says something profound during a church service. A baby is born. That's a miracle in itself."

He bobbed his head. "Faith is like that, my children. It can grow simply because a person has *chosen* to believe in something. The relics make people feel closer to God. The Shroud of Turin? What harm can come from a piece of cloth? If it truly covered the face of Jesus, terrific. If it didn't, at least it has caused people to think about Him, and to worship Him."

Mark pondered what Yanno had said. It was time to get more personal. "Hypothetically speaking, Yanno, say you *did* walk with Jesus. What was the most important lesson you learned from Him?"

Yanno smiled, uncrossed his arms, and leaned across the table in an intimate merging of their minds.

"In all my walks and talks with the Lord, I learn the same lesson everyone else learns when they draw close to the Savior. The most important act in life is to love one another."

Julie straightened. "Love one another? Do you mean everyone?"

"Yes, including your enemies, Julie."

"I know I can love my parents. I never stopped, really. I

love my sister. But, what are you saying? That I should love McAndrews? And his wife?"

Mark eyed her with anticipation. Yanno had struck a chord with that girl.

"One day, you must love them both," the old man said, his eyes intense.

Julie shook her head. "I don't know if I can ever do that."

Yanno tugged at his beard. He looked Julie straight in the eye. "Tell me, child, why do you want to return to that dark place you left only yesterday? If you don't forgive those who harmed you, the past will hold you prisoner. You can count on it."

He reached across the table and took her hand. "Listen to me. You reached a wonderful plateau yesterday. Now you must move higher yet. Don't worry about tomorrow. God will make the opportunity when the time is right. You only have to be willing."

Julie bowed her head and slid her hand from his grasp. She didn't speak.

Mark took the opportunity to address the old man.

"Yanno, you have given us much to think about. I have to admit, you've been somewhat elusive, but I've been fascinated by your wit and your candor. I've observed your unselfish commitment to the people who come here. You've taught me lessons a person can't learn in a book." He took a breath, and continued. "Is it possible you learned such behavior from having walked with the Master Himself?"

Mark raised his eyebrows and looked into the depths of Yanno's eyes, hoping to find some truth there. The man was still a mystery.

Yanno looked down at his hands and came up smiling. "My son, we all have access to the Master."

"Be honest, Yanno. Honor me with at least one direct answer," Mark persisted. "Were you there? Did you walk the streets with Jesus? Did you rest your head on his breast at the last supper?" He raised his voice another decibel with every question. "Did you stand at the foot of the cross and receive Mary as your own mother? Are you, in fact, John?"

Yanno let an anxious few seconds pass. No one spoke or moved. Not Julie. Not Mark. Not Yanno. Not even the two dogs who lay quiet in a corner like a couple of stuffed animals.

"My children," Yanno said, at last, his voice soft. "You have been trying to find out the answer to that question from the moment you walked through my door three days ago. To be honest, yes, I walk with Jesus every day of my life. I rest my head on his breast when I am weary. I fall at the foot of the cross when I am troubled. And, I revere the virgin Mary as the mother of my Savior. But, am I John?" He paused, and his eyes strayed to Julie and back to Mark. "Very simply, God has put a little bit of John in all of us who believe. Anyone who has a relationship with the Lord also can be called 'the one Jesus loved,' because, you see, Jesus loves us with that same passion that He loved His favorite disciple. Aside from that, I am simply Yanno, a servant of the Lord, longing to be with Him in paradise."

Mark shook his head and checked his watch again. Three o'clock. They had to rush back to the hotel, pack their bags, and get to the helipad.

"We have to go," he said with resignation. "Yanno, will you call a cab for us?"

The old man pressed a hand to the small of his back and rose from the table with a moan. He left to make the call and Mark and Julie stared at each other

Julie shrugged. "Oh, well." She seemed to have lost her initial enthusiasm. Whatever had become of the inveterate newspaper reporter?

Mark released a sigh. "We'll go with what we have," he said.

"There were some clues," Julie said, as if she was trying to encourage him. Things that he said—"

"Yes, but are they enough?"

"We have those strands of hair."

Mark nodded. "The testing is new. I'm not sure—"

"Wait until I put something together," she said. "I have plenty of notes and tape recordings."

Yanno came back into the dining room.

"The cab will be here in ten minutes," he said.

They helped Yanno clear the table, then followed him into the living room.

Mark approached Yanno and gave him a big hug. "I'm going to miss you, my friend," he whispered.

"And I, you," Yanno replied.

Mark backed away and wiped his eyes. Yanno also had tears. Several droplets streamed down Julie's cheeks. She stepped forward and wrapped her arms around Yanno.

"I love you," she whispered, and the three of them clung together.

"Group hug!" Yanno announced, his voice breaking.

"I wish we could stay a few more days," Mark said. "There's so much I want to ask you, so much more to share."

"I'm sorry I wasn't more forthcoming with you. You have to understand, my privacy is important to me, and to my ministry here." Yanno stepped back and blinked away more tears. "Will you come back and see me one day?"

"We'll try," Mark said. He wasn't sure that would ever happen.

273

Yanno nodded. "You'll try? That's good enough for me. Please, keep me in your prayers—and in your hearts."

"We will," Julie said, rushing in for another hug.

"Will you consider a trip to America?" Mark suggested. "Perhaps visit *us?*"

"My son, I'm afraid I can't make such a trip. You see how it is." Yanno waved his arm toward the front door. "You've witnessed my interaction with these people. Though I miss my traveling days, my work here is not finished. If I take off, it's only for a few days, and then I have to come home again."

"It's—well, it's hard to say goodbye." Mark said.

"I know," Yanno murmured. "I have said far too many good-byes in my lifetime."

"We won't forget you," Julie whimpered.

"Forget me?" Yanno said with a laugh. "I'm guessing you will go home to your computer. You'll write a fantastic story about this old man you met on the island of Patmos. *What?* A man who may be 2,000 years old? The Apostle John still alive? Or did he die and now has come back to life in the form of this decrepit old man who lives a simple life helping people in much the same way he tends his garden. He makes peanut butter-and-banana sandwiches and rides a Vespa. Preposterous! Your story will hit the newspapers and it will go viral on the internet. Why, I may read it myself, all the way over here in Patmos. My friend Julie will be famous. And so will I." Yanno paused and turned his attention to Mark. "And my friend Mark? He will be a hit at his college. Who knows what wonderful stories he will tell his students now? He may even take his fantastic tales to colleges all over America."

The room went silent. Mark stood in shock. How did this

old man know their plans so well? They had never mentioned any of the details.

"That's very astute, Yanno," he said. "But how will such publicity affect your life here in Patmos?"

Yanno shrugged. "Let me worry about that. My God will look after me."

A car horn tooted. Mark peered out the window. An older model Ford sat idling in the street at the end of the walk. "Cab's here," he said, and his heart ached.

"Wait a minute," Yanno raised a hand and hurried to his desk. He scribbled something on a notepad. Then, he tore off the sheet and handed it to Mark.

"My phone number and my email address," he said, his eyes smiling. "I'm only a keystroke away."

Mark took another couple of seconds to memorize Yanno's face. The old man's forehead was lined with emotion.

"You will hear from me," Mark promised.

After another round of hugs, Mark and Julie left the dwelling. Julie slipped into the back seat of their taxi. Mark turned for one last look. A lump came to his throat. Yanno was standing on the path in front of his house. Alpha and Omega had come out. Now, they sat like front yard ornaments on either side of the old man. Yanno raised a handkerchief to his nose. With his other hand he managed a feeble wave.

Mark suppressed the urge to run back and give him another hug. He swallowed the knot in his throat, climbed in beside Julie, and shut the door. As they drove away, Mark looked out the back window and caught his breath. A chill went through him. He was certain a halo of light was bouncing off the silver strands on the top of Yanno's head.

29

LEAVING PATMOS

Except for Julie's uncontrollable sobbing, they rode back to the hotel in silence. Through a blur of tears, she looked at Mark. His face also was moist. Though he wrapped his arm around her, her heart ached over losing a friend she had only begun to know. She felt like she'd walked away too soon from a fountain of life, and she was starved for more of Yanno's godly wisdom. The farther they got from his home in the hills, the more intense the loss became.

As they entered their hotel, everything changed in an instant. Julie froze in the doorway at the sight of the Petras waiting in the lobby. Sofia's eyes looked red and puffy. Damien stood rigid, his face like stone. He withdrew a wad of euros from his pocket and tossed the bills to the floor at Mark's feet. Julie's stomach tightened. She glanced at Mark. He also appeared stunned.

"What's this?" Mark said. He picked up the bills and tried to hand them back to Damien. The man raised his hand in refusal.

"Blood money," Damien rasped between clenched teeth. "I cannot accept."

Sofia took a step toward Julie. "Here," she murmured. With trembling fingers she held out the gold earrings and bracelet Julie had given her at the restaurant.

"I no can keep," Sofia said. She pressed them in Julie's hand, then meekly bowed her head and slipped behind her husband.

Julie stared at the jewelry. "Please, Damien. Sofia. Why are you angry with us?"

"You lie. You no tourist. You *reporter*." Damien spit out the last word. "College professor and his companion, you say. Visit our Greek island. You feed us lies, and we swallow them."

"You're right, Damien." Mark told him. "I am a college professor working on a project. We didn't feel it was necessary to reveal Julie's occupation. Most people find her job a little intimidating."

In Damien's shadow, Sofia mopped tears from her face. Julie's heart went out to the old woman. She hadn't realized what pain she might inflict by withholding the truth.

"Please," Julie said. "We didn't mean any harm. You have to understand, we were desperate. Our time was running short, we had to find Yanno, and we'd gotten nowhere."

Damien shook his head. "No! You trick us. You call yourselves friends."

Mark moved closer to Damien. "We didn't lie to you. We *are* your friends."

"Lies make you no friend to me." Damien pierced Julie with his eyes. "Now, *xeni*, you go back to America. Write your news story. Tell the world about our Yanno. What do you think will happen?"

"I—I didn't intend..." Julie stammered. The truth was, since she'd met Yanno, she'd felt torn between fulfilling her job and protecting the old man.

"I tell you what happen," Damien went on. "More people come to Patmos. More news people. Paparazzi. Yanno no longer safe. He go away."

Julie shook her head. "Please, Damien. I can't say what I'm going to do. Yes, I came here with the intention of writing a story, but now I'm not sure I can do that."

He then narrowed his eyes at Mark. "You say, 'Oh, come

out with us. We buy dinner. Oh, here is money, you poor, miserable dog. This should buy your secret.'" His eyes darted back to Julie, "And, 'Sofia. You like my earrings? Here. I can lose them to get what I want.'"

Hot tears rushed to Julie's eyes. Her cheeks flamed. She peered at the old woman, still bowed behind her husband. She wanted to reach out to her, to apologize. Words lodged in her throat. None of them seemed able to heal the breach between them.

Damien continued with his tirade. "From my youth the people of Patmos protect Yanno. Now, who can protect him if you do this thing?"

A mortifying discontent settled on their corner of the lobby. Damien shook his head with disgust, then he grabbed his wife's arm and led her to the door. Before going through it, he turned around and faced Julie.

"I beg you. Don't do this evil thing. Bury what you learned here, and leave our island in peace. Tell no one about our Yanno."

"We love him," Sofia mumbled, as they went out the door.

"So do we," Julie whispered.

In a daze, Julie went through the motions of changing clothes and packing her bag. All the while, images of the encounter in the lobby tumbled around in her brain. She thought about Sofia's heartbreaking profession of love for the old man. Then there were Damien's angry accusations—well deserved, she conceded. His words echoed in her head. *I beg you. Don't do your evil.*

The struggle had already begun. Damien's plea only served to intensify the conflict raging inside her. The original plan was to go home and write a story about this old sage who lived in the hills of Patmos and ministered to the villagers. Whether he was John or not hadn't mattered to Julie. She had to write *something* if she wanted to keep her job.

Then, at some point over the last few days, everything had changed. She'd reached an unexpected crossroads. Though she didn't know for certain if the old man was John, there were clues. His knowledge of the Scriptures. His ability to control the interview. His profound insight into her life. His expressions of love—both spoken and unspoken.

The only tangible evidence Julie had was inside that little plastic bag. She withdrew it from her purse and held it up to the light. The strands of Yanno's hair glistened like silver threads.

Damien was right to believe more reporters might follow in her footsteps. That's the way the industry worked. What's more, Jason Redding had already been there. That snake could easily turn Yanno's life into a three-ring circus. Mercenaries of all sorts would attempt to make a fast buck off of this simple man. And Yanno's privacy would end. Like the Petras had feared, he might leave Patmos and seek refuge elsewhere. What would happen to all those hungry souls who came to his door for help, and of course, to Damien and Sofia?

Julie stepped out on the balcony and took a last look at the tiered landscape, the stark white boxes where the people of Patmos lived, the monastery on the hill. The scene blurred. She reached out and gripped the railing. Steadying herself, she looked up at the puffs of white separating, drifting, and exposing slices of blue sky.

"Please, God, tell me what to do."

She joined Mark in the lobby and together they left the hotel. As the miles slipped away behind their cab, Julie sank deeper into despair. She was leaving Yanno and the beautiful island, and she had no assurance she'd completed her mission. On the contrary, she believed she'd failed.

The helicopter ride provided a brief diversion. The pilot first took them on a quick tour of the island, maneuvering his craft over the monastery, then swooping down over the dock area, the string of rocks along the shoreline, and the beaches. Then they headed out over the Aegean, the helicopter's shadow rippling against the sparkling water below. They made the 40-mile flight in less than an hour and went to their connecting gate with plenty of time to check in.

After a brief stop at Istanbul, their flight continued on to New York City. A red-eye meant that after a late night snack, the whole cabin would go dark and most of the passengers would fall asleep. Julie had endured enough sleepless nights to know rest doesn't come to someone who has trouble running through her head.

While Mark flipped through an in-flight magazine, Julie continued to struggle with indecision. When answers didn't come, she turned to Mark. He'd already proven to be a rock of stability, a port in a storm for her.

"Can we talk?" she said.

"Sure." He turned off his reading light, rolled up the magazine and slid it into the seat pocket. "You have my full attention." He shifted his upper body in her direction.

Julie pressed her palms over her eyes and struggled to find the right words.

"I have an idea what's troubling you," Mark said. "You've gotta make a huge decision, don't you, Julie?"

She lowered her hands and nodded. "When I first agreed to this project, I wasn't excited about it. I think you knew that.

Skeptical is probably the right word. Initially, I refused to go. But Andy was giving me a chance to redeem myself, and Lakisha convinced me it was the best thing for my career. I made my plans, I did my research, and I became more and more passionate about it. After all, I was going to an exotic island. The trip would give me a break from my usual routine, a chance to do something out of the norm."

"I was excited about this trip from the very beginning," Mark said. "And the closer we got to departure, the more energized I became."

Julie smiled at him. "For you, it was a dream come true. But I needed to adjust to the whole thing. When we arrived in Ephesus I was taken back 2,000 years to a time and place that had been foreign to me. I could read about such places, but until I stepped foot in those ruins I had no idea how amazing they could be. And Patmos—that tiny island—the scenery, the hills, the monastery, and the people. Brother Pio. The Petras. And especially Yanno. This has all been so overwhelming."

Julie pulled a tissue from her purse and dabbed at her cheeks. "That man..." she whimpered. "You saw how he lives— that modest little cottage. He asked for nothing but he gave so much. Yanno got into my heart, Mark. He touched my soul." She raised her head and looked at him. "How do you think he knew so much about us?"

"I don't know, Julie. He was like no one *I've* ever met."

She shook her head in disbelief. "Somehow, Yanno knew I had a troubled past. In his own subtle way, he probed and pressed and prodded until I spilled it all out." She looked him in the eye. "Don't you see, Mark? Because of Yanno, I don't have to be afraid anymore. I can face my parents. I can forgive them. I can look those church people in the eye and not feel ashamed. And you, Mark. I feel differently about you too. I see the wonderful, patient, loving Christian man that you are, and I am no longer afraid of getting close to you."

He offered her a smile. By his silence, he encouraged her to go on.

"Now I'm facing the most important decision of my career. I mean, I could lose my job if I don't fulfill this assignment, but I don't want to destroy Yanno."

"Aha," Mark said. "To write or not to write? That is the question." He released a long sigh. "Well, let's evaluate your situation. You have those strands of hair. They might be able to prove our case one way or the other. If Yanno *isn't* John the Apostle, he sure makes a good facsimile, doesn't he? And, if he *is,* then, wow! We've got ourselves a real dilemma. We may never have an answer. In the end, the decision is going to fall on you, Julie. And on me."

She nodded and another wave of sadness swept over her. "What do *you* think, Mark? Do you believe Yanno has been living on this earth for 2,000 years? Could someone endure severe persecution, be boiled in oil, suffer a long, arduous exile, travel the world, and then return to Patmos to live out the rest of his life until Jesus returns? Do you know how ludicrous that sounds? Without the evidence from those hair samples, I don't think I could pull off writing a story like that. And, to be honest, I don't know if I *want* to."

"All you'd really have to do is tell the truth, Julie. Tell what you saw, and then leave it up to the reader to make a determination."

"I'm not sure I can do even that. Whatever I write, it's going to expose Yanno."

Mark shook his head. "This is a dilemma. When I was around that man, supernatural things didn't seem far-fetched anymore. Remember the scrolls in the corner? And how about that antique-looking cup he drank out of—the one Jason Redding ran off with? And all those degrees on the wall."

Julie smiled. "For the first time in my life, I encountered someone I couldn't break with my questions. He was so evasive."

"He sure made us work."

A giggle caught in Julie's throat. She looked at Mark. He seemed so strong, so confident. The problem was hers, not his, yet he remained supportive.

"I suppose you got what you needed for that PowerPoint presentation."

Mark nodded. "I did get lots of material from the archaeological sites we visited. I can put together a pretty decent college-level program, maybe work some of the information into a classroom lecture. And those photos you shot should work well in a PowerPoint slide show. I can dub in some Middle Eastern music and a taped narration by yours truly. Melanie stressed from the beginning, my main purpose is the grant for my department. Whether Yanno is a part of all that is insignificant. Unlike your assignment, mine doesn't depend on mentioning him at all. Melanie was merely humoring those two board members. She was more concerned about the grant. I can pursue it now, without any reference to Yanno. Those board members will simply have to swallow it."

"Okay, so you're all set. But what do I tell Andy? I'd be lying if I said I didn't want to write *something*. But, I had doubts when we left Yanno today. And the way Damien and Sofia tore into us showed me how much that man means to those people." She wiped away another tear. "They hate us," she moaned.

Mark rested his hand on her arm. His touch comforted her.

"Do you remember what Yanno told us before we left?" she said. "You know, about no greater love?"

Mark nodded. "His quote came from the Gospel of John. '*Greater love hath no man than this, that a man lay down his life for his friends.*' Yanno said it didn't always have to do with life and death situations, that it could be part of everyday decisions."

She swallowed. "I know what that means now," she said.

Julie went silent. Mark waited, in case she had more to say. But, when she shut her eyes, he knew their conversation was over, at least for the moment. He put his seat back and fell asleep, almost at once.

Sometime, in the middle of the night, Mark awakened. Julie had turned on her reading light. She was wearing a pair of ear buds and was playing her tape recorder. Tears poured down her cheeks.

Only God knew what was troubling her at that moment. Perhaps Yanno's voice had plucked at her emotions. Or maybe she was still struggling with a decision that could very well end her career. He suspected she needed to be alone, to listen to her tape recordings, to mull over the last few days in private.

When they landed in New York, it was dark. The nighttime had followed them across the ocean. The long-distance flight, coupled with the time changes, had drained him of energy. And the journey wasn't over yet. They still had another two hours to kill at JFK, before boarding their connecting flight home.

"Let's get something to eat," Mark said. "I'm starving."

Julie shot him a sardonic look. He shrugged and led the way to a Panini Express that had a few cafe tables and a display of pastries that got his mouth watering.

Suppressing a yawn, Mark pointed at a sausage quiche and a huge bear claw, then he asked for a tall cup of coffee. "With caffeine," he told the girl.

Julie settled for a blueberry scone and a cup of herbal tea. He stuck his hand in his pocket to get his wallet, and instead pulled out a clump of loose bills. His throat tightened. In his hand was the wrinkled bunch of euros Damien had thrown at him.

Despondent, he blinked back the memory and stuffed the wad back in his pocket. He'd make the exchange later, when he could handle seeing those bills again, though he doubted he'd ever get over the guilt or the despair of having offended that sweet couple.

Fortunately, he had enough American currency in his wallet to pay for their snack. Julie didn't say a word about the euros. Maybe she'd found it too painful to recall one of the most heartbreaking moments of their trip.

They gathered up their trays and chose a table in a far corner away from the other passengers.

Julie took a few bites of her scone. Mark dumped several creamers and two packs of sugar in his coffee. Julie stared at his cup with a smirk on her lips.

"What's the matter?" he said. "Haven't you ever seen someone doctor up a cup of coffee?"

She shrugged and her smirk broadened into a sparkle-eyed grin.

"This is how my mom allowed me to have coffee when I was

a little kid." He picked up a spoon and began to stir. "She'd pour me a cup of milk and flavor it with a dribble of coffee and some sugar." He shrugged. "I guess I never outgrew it."

Still smiling, Julie took a sip of her tea, and sat back in her chair.

"So," Mark said between bites. "Have you made up your mind what you're going to do?"

The smile faded from Julie's lips.

A thought struck him. "You're gonna can the story, aren't you?"

"I don't know, but I'm kind of leaning that way." She bit into her scone and frowned. "I can't get Yanno out of my mind. And I can't forget how disappointed Damien and Sofia were in us. I wish we could go back in time and make everything right."

"I'd like to do that too, but, the truth is, we can't go back, Julie. We can only go forward from here."

"I'm still undecided," Julie said, mopping her lips with a napkin. "By rights, I should fulfill my commitment to my employer. Doesn't the Bible say something like that?"

"Something," Mark conceded. "But you have to look at the context."

"Then I think about how an article about Yanno might affect innocent people," Julie went on, as though she hadn't heard him. "If I go ahead with the story, the Patmians will pay a terrible price. If I *don't* write the story, it could cost me my job. Or, at the very least, I'd suffer disgrace among my peers. Then there's Jason Redding. Who knows what kind of story he'll bring back? No matter what I do, somebody loses, and it's bound to be me."

Mark slurped his coffee and let out a sigh. He wanted to say, *"I'll support you, no matter what you decide."*

Instead, he came up with, "C'mon, Julie. There are plenty of writing jobs out there. You're a talented writer and you have a marketable skill. Besides, you don't know for sure Andy will fire you. The most that can happen is you'll receive one of his red-faced scoldings. Then, he'll toss another assignment your way."

Julie brushed crumbs from her hands and shook her head. "I'm not sure how Andy will react. He's unpredictable. One minute, he'll give you a pat on the back, and the next, he'll fly into a rage over some minor issue."

Mark bristled at the thought of the man screaming at Julie. He conjured up a mental image of himself on a white stallion, riding into Andy's office and sweeping his woman out of there. He reached out, patted Julie's hand, and gave her a sympathetic smile.

"Let me know what you decide and what happens afterward. I'll be there for you."

The offer was pathetically lame, a far cry from his white horse scenario, but it would have to do for the moment.

Anyway, Mark was facing his own challenge. Melanie needed some kind of report to give to the board of directors—particularly the two who had commissioned his trip in the first place. He'd have to come up with a detailed plan to make everyone happy. That was going to take time. He needed to wait another day to collect his thoughts. Perhaps, after a good night's sleep in his own bed, he'd be able to think more clearly. After all, why should a person do today what he can do tomorrow, but with much more perfection?

Mark gave a quick nod and a cocky smile to no one in particular. Yep. Tomorrow, things will fall into place a lot easier. For now, Melanie will just have to wait.

30

JULIE'S DECISION

Compared to the long haul over the Atlantic, the next flight ended almost as soon as it began. Julie knew exactly what she had to do. She gave Mark a hug in the baggage claim area, snatched her suitcase off the belt, and hurried outside to hail a cab. She didn't want to wait for him to get his car, didn't want to delay the inevitable one more minute.

At home, she dumped her luggage in the living room, grabbed her car keys, and went straight to her office.

"I've got to do this," Julie mumbled. "No matter what it costs me. It's the right thing to do."

She entered Andy's office and found her boss in the middle of a phone call. When he saw her come in, he uttered an apology to the other party and hung up the phone.

"Julie! Good to see you made it back. Pull up a chair. Tell me about your trip."

"The trip went well," she said, as she settled into the very chair where she'd sat when he first gave her the assignment. "I gathered a lot of information at some of the historic sites we visited, and I took plenty of great photos. With what I got I could put together a pretty decent travel piece for you."

"*Travel piece?!*" Andy's face turned three shades of red. "I didn't ask for a travel piece." He rose to his feet. "What's the matter with you, Julie? Don't you listen? I wanted an *investigative* story. You were supposed to find out who that flake really is—John the Apostle or a very cunning fraud. Did you even *find* the guy?"

Julie straightened. "Yes, we found him, and he wasn't a flake *or* a fraud." She raised a shoulder. "He was a nice old man. I thought you wanted proof, Andy. Did you want me to make something up?"

"Dang it, Julie. I never said I believed that hogwash. You were supposed to find the guy and write as much as you could about him." He sucked in a huge breath of air and dropped back in his chair. "So, what did you find out? Anything?"

Julie was surprised at herself. She'd been able to maintain control through all of Andy's tirade. His ranting had rattled the windows of his office, but it hadn't shaken her confidence. She breathed easy. She wasn't trembling. Her boss had flown off the handle, but she had remained calm. It was all she could do to keep from smiling.

"I'm sorry, Andy," she said, her voice steady. "I couldn't prove or disprove that rumor. At least, not at this time."

She'd measured her words carefully. She'd already learned her lesson about lying, and she didn't want to lie to her boss. A little plastic bag held the only tangible evidence she had. At some point, she had to have Yanno's hair tested, if only to satisfy her own curiosity. But, she didn't see any reason to tell Andy about it. At least, not now.

He scowled at her over the top of his wire-rimmed glasses. This man had intimidated her on numerous occasions. Oddly, he no longer had control over her. She'd handed control of her life to a much higher power. No matter what happened here today, she could walk out and never look back.

"Julie," he said, his voice strained like he was trying to control his temper. "I didn't send you to *the moon*. I sent

289

you to Ephesus. And to Patmos. Do you remember the assignment? Breaking news? The rumor? Jason Redding hot on your heels?"

A smugness came over her. "Come on, Andy, you knew this assignment was doomed from the start. Do you realize how ridiculous it sounds that John might still be alive?"

"Ridiculous or not, I sent you half-way around the world, and I assumed you would come home with *something*. Interviews. Photos of the guy. Now you're offering me a travel piece? There's a whole slew of them on the internet." Andy's voice had escalated. Julie laughed to herself. The guy was an emotional basket case, and she was watching from the wings.

With a surge of confidence, she looked him in the eye. "The man we found was a sweet old guy who lives alone and helps his neighbors. I couldn't come up with anything tangible. Maybe if you'd given us more time—"

"More time?" Andy's fist came down on his desk. Julie didn't flinch. "Are you kidding me?" he ranted. "It was bad enough I had to send you off on this wild goose chase." He paused and took a breath. "Okay, then. What did you get? Did you shoot any photos of the guy?"

"Sorry, he didn't allow it." She continued to keep her cool.

Andy eyed her with incredulity written all over his face. No one had ever stood up to Andy Jacobs the way she had, not even Benny Foster, the tough court reporter. Perhaps, she'd caught her boss off guard. It didn't matter. She was loving it.

"The man never admitted to being John," she said. "I'm sorry if you think I didn't do my job, Andy, but you were asking way too much. I can't give you such a fantastic story, at least not about him."

Andy fell back in his chair. His cheeks puffed up and he blew out a long breath.

"I can live without the bonus," she offered.

"I'm afraid this will cost you more than a bonus," he said, his voice hard. "I hate to say this, Julie, but it's gonna cost you your job. After you left town, a directive came down from the publisher. We've had a budget cut and it looks like one reporter has to go."

A flood of peace ran through Julie. She waited for the tears, but they didn't come.

"To be honest," Andy went on. "It was down to either you or Mary Beth Simmons. While you were away, Mary Beth dug up a breaking news story about a local official who embezzled community funds and ran off to Mexico with his girlfriend. Now, that's good stuff. Jason Redding was in Patmos, too far away to interfere with her interviews. Meanwhile, you had a simple assignment and you failed to produce anything."

Julie shook her head. "Sorry, Andy."

"I'm giving you two weeks' notice." It was as if he'd said, "Let's have lunch sometime." She wasn't troubled in the least.

Yanno's gospel verse came flying back at her. *Greater love hath no man than this, that a man lay down his life for his friends.* It occurred to Julie that she had done just that for Yanno. She smiled at the idea. She loved the old guy. He'd definitely become a friend, and she'd sacrificed her job to protect his identity. That was greater love.

She rose from her chair and was about to leave. "It was nice working for you, Andy."

"Well, wait—hold on a minute." He stood up and walked around his desk until he was face-to-face with her.

"You mentioned the possibility of a travel piece."

She nodded.

"Go ahead and submit something. If I like it, I'll run it in one of our Sunday travel sections."

"I can do that. But, do you mind if I send it from home? I don't want to spend another minute in that newsroom."

Andy managed a slight understanding smile.

"You've still got a week's vacation in the till, and you have some sick time. If you want to use it up, you don't have to come back to the office at all. I'll give you a nice little severance package too." His tone had softened considerably. "I don't like letting you go, Julie. You've been a good worker. All I ask is that you give me *something* from that trip. A travel piece will have to do. And listen, stay in touch with me. If by some miracle another position opens up, I'd like you to consider coming back."

"Thanks, Andy," she said, but she couldn't picture that ever happening.

She left Andy's office, headed straight for her desk, and started gathering up her personal belongings.

Mary Beth Simmons passed by clucking her tongue. "Ah'm so sorry ya'll got canned, Julie. We're gonna miss you."

Julie could almost see the honey dripping from the girl's mouth. It was hard to tell if Mary Beth spoke out of sincerity or if she was gloating. It didn't matter. Julie turned back to her desk and resumed packing. She let out a heavy sigh that drew Roger Cappella's eyes over the neighboring cubicle.

"Don't let Mary Beth bother you," he whispered. "*I'm* gonna miss you, Julie."

She gave him an appreciative smile and continued sorting through her desk drawers, taking care to leave behind whatever belonged to the company. The last thing she wanted was to be accused of stealing one of Andy's precious paperclips.

She crammed her stuff in her purse, tucked the box of tissues and Rita's photo under her arm, and said a hasty goodbye to Roger. Her head held high, she walked past the hushed keyboards, the stilled conversations, and the sympathetic stares. She made it to her car and to her condo without shedding a single tear.

In the quiet of her bedroom, Julie took a few minutes to unpack her luggage. She dumped her clothes in the hamper and put her grooming items in the bathroom. Last of all, she pulled out the bag of Yanno's hair clippings. With a dejected sigh, she started to throw the bag in the waste basket. What was the use of keeping the evidence now?

But, for some reason, she couldn't let go of that little bag. *This is all I have left of Yanno,* she thought. She dropped the bag inside the top drawer of her bedside table. Then, she locked the door of her condo and vowed not to emerge until she figured out what to do with the rest of her life.

31

MARK AND KATIE

Mark tried to call Julie several times that day. She must have turned off her phone. He wished he could have given her a few words of encouragement. She'd left the airport in such a flurry, and he'd stood there like a dummy, not knowing what to say. The decision had to be hers, of course, but he could have said something... *anything*.

He took a hot shower, unpacked his suitcase, and dumped his dirty clothes in a basket by the front door. He grabbed a Coke from the fridge, picked up the laundry basket and went downstairs to the apartment laundromat. He tossed the whites and colors together in one machine, inserted some quarters, and headed for the nearest McDonald's.

All through his lunch, he struggled with the impulse to go to Julie's condo and pound on her door. He tried phoning her two more times. His calls went straight to voicemail.

Something else was nagging him. No matter what happened between Julie and him, he had to end things with Katie. Of course, the polite thing would be to say it in person. He had to wait till school let out, which would give him a few more hours to gather his thoughts.

At 3:30, he phoned Katie and asked if she'd like to take a walk. She lived with her parents in a suburban development adjacent to a community park, the perfect setting for a heart-to-heart talk.

When Mark got to Katie's parents' house, she was sitting on the front steps waiting for him.

This time, he didn't take her hand, but walked quietly beside her. They headed down the street toward the playground. The plot of land was teeming with youngsters swinging, sliding, and climbing like monkeys on a jungle gym. Mark pointed to a bench a suitable distance away from the shouts and squeals.

He sat for a long time with Katie by his side. He watched the kids for a while, stared off down the street, looked up at the sky, mentally sent up a prayer for help.

She kept staring at him, probing him with her eyes, like she was trying to read his mind.

"So, how did your trip go?" she said, her voice weak.

"Fine. I got a lot of good material for my project."

More silence. More discomfort. More staring off at nothing in particular.

She suddenly started weeping.

"Katie," he murmured.

She broke into sobs.

"I haven't said anything yet. Why are you crying?"

"I know what you're going to say, Mark. You don't even have to say it out loud. You went back with Julie, didn't you?"

Mark groaned. He hadn't planned to let her down this way. He had a whole speech memorized, but now it was useless. He was always at a loss at times like this.

What did that character Henry Higgins say? *'Why can't a woman be more like a man?'* If a guy needs space, he doesn't worry about what to say or how to say it. Your buddies are okay. They'll find something to do until you get your act together. Men have an unspoken code that works, but it only works with other guys. Women? They just don't get it.

"I—I feel like we should step back for a while, Katie, that's all. We need to give each other some space."

"Sure. I know what *that* means." And she started blubbering again.

"You *don't* know," he said. It came out sharper than he'd intended. He softened his voice. "Katie, I think we should see other people. Not just me. You too."

Katie's sobbing increased and she started gasping. "I—I knew—this—was coming. I—I knew it."

He swung an arm across her shoulders and pulled her close. She wept into his shirt.

"Come on, Katie. Have you ever taken a good look at our relationship? We don't do much together except eat dinner. I go to the gym and you go shopping. We haven't discussed any kind of future. We're more like good friends, aren't we?"

Katie raised her head and looked into his face, her blue eyes so puffy they were nearly swollen shut. "Maybe *you* never said anything," she sputtered. "But, I thought we were heading in a more serious direction. My parents thought so too. Don't forget, we have one major thing in common. Our faith."

"That's true, and it's great. But, we don't have... chemistry."

"*Chemistry?*" She shrieked. "What does *chemistry* have to do with any of this?"

Mark looked toward the playground. The kids on the jungle gym had stopped climbing. They clung to the bars and stared in their direction. The boys playing ball had halted their game, and the girls on the swings had stopped pumping. It was like the whole world had frozen in mid-air.

He puffed out an exasperated sigh. "Katie, try to keep your voice down."

She slumped beside him and buried her face in her hands.

"Look," he said. "I have to admit, I *was* attracted to you in the beginning. But I don't think that can be called chemistry. I think chemistry is more than physical attraction. It goes way deeper."

"So... you have *chemistry* with Julie?" She hiccupped then, and it sounded so pathetic, he almost caved.

"You might say that," he conceded.

She collapsed in a heap. Mark was afraid she might fall off the bench with all that lurching and sobbing. He rubbed her back. "Shh, Katie, please."

"Take me home, Mark," she said, straightening. "I can't do this anymore."

More hiccups, more blubbering, more gasping for air.

Relieved to be able to leave the playground with all the little ears and eyes on them, he helped her to her feet. The walk back to the house seemed to take forever. When they climbed the stairs to the front porch, Katie was still weeping.

"You'll s-see, Mark. Julie's going to dump you again, like she did before, and this time, it'll be for good."

He sighed. "Maybe. But, I've got to give it a try."

He bent close to kiss her cheek, but she turned her back on him, and without another word went inside.

The rest of the evening went poorly for Mark. He tried to reach Julie several times, started to jump in his car to head for her place, but stopped and went back inside. *She needs time*, he told himself. *Don't rush her, or like Katie said, you may lose her for good this time.*

The next morning, Mark was in too much of a rush to spend time on the telephone. He'd have to call Julie later.

Everything had piled up on him, including the laundry he'd forgotten. By now, it was probably moldy, having sat in the washer all night. He made a stop in the laundromat, shoved everything in a dryer with a fabric sheet, and hurried out the door. He had to get to the college before Melanie got caught up in other business.

He met up with his boss in the parking lot as she was approaching the side entrance to the institute.

"Mark," she said, beaming. "It's good to see you. Come to my office. I have a few minutes before my meeting with the board of directors."

Right. The board of directors. Mark squashed the nervous jitter in his stomach. He'd have to stick with the story he'd concocted in his mind, give Melanie a recap of the trip, leave out the visits with Yanno, and stick with the main points.

They sat facing each other in two padded armchairs. Melanie crossed one leg over the other, her skirt swept to one side exposing a knee. She balanced one elbow on the arm of her chair and raised one hand to her chin. She could have been posing for the cover of a fashion magazine.

"Well?" she said, with a pronounced blink of her eyes.

"I'm afraid I can't give you John the Apostle." Mark chuckled, hoping his demeanor would ease the bad news. "But, the trip *did* provide enough material for an in-depth study *about* him," he said with optimism. "I'm already putting together a terrific syllabus for next semester's classes." He leaned toward her. "Our students will be able to trace John's footsteps from Galilee to Jerusalem to Ephesus and finally, to Patmos. While learning about the historical, spiritual, and archaeological significance of those places, they'll study the five books attributed to John. I'm weaving everything together chronologically. Combined with a PowerPoint presentation, the entire series will set us up for a nice grant."

Other than a nod and a blink of her eyes, Melanie didn't move. "Sounds interesting. Go on."

Mark moistened his lips, which had gone uncomfortably dry. "Julie took photos at all the locations we visited. I'll select the best ones for our presentation, do a narrative voice-over and dub in some appropriate music. When I'm finished, we can offer the program to colleges and universities across the nation. I wouldn't mind doing a little traveling, if necessary—to promote it, of course."

He sat back in his chair and waited for the praises. Melanie's hesitation sent a nervous flutter to Mark's chest. He swallowed.

"I like it," she said, at last. She uncrossed her legs and sat up straight, like a fire of enthusiasm had been lit underneath her. "I think your classes will be better than ever, Mark. And your PowerPoint idea?" She shook her head. "Awesome. I want you to present your ideas before the board. Aside from those two fanatics, the others will welcome your plan. I want you to call Susan in the administration office and get her started writing that grant for us."

Mark started to rise, but Melanie's piercing stare had him back in his seat.

"Tell me," she said. "And be honest. What became of the old man? I have to tell those two board members *something*. After all, they paid for your trip."

Mark ran his hand through his hair. He couldn't have evaded the question forever. He puffed out a long breath. "Well, we met an elderly man in Patmos," he admitted. "But, we couldn't get a straight answer from the guy." That was true anyway. "I don't believe he's John, only a nice old man who loves his neighbors, the way we all should."

"I accept your answer," Melanie said, rising. "To be honest, I was depending on you to squash that rumor. Can you imagine the embarrassment for this college if we promoted such a ridiculous idea? I'm truthfully relieved."

"If you felt that way, why did you send me in the first place?"

"Pressure. Those two board members wouldn't have let it rest. Now, I can go back and tell them you found nothing. I'm hoping that will placate them, especially when I tell them what you *did* accomplish."

The hard part was over. Now Mark could concentrate on putting together his program. It was nearing the end of June. He had the rest of summer to perfect it.

Melanie started to open her office door to let him out, but she stopped.

"What about that reporter?" she said.

"Julie?" He shrugged. "I don't know. She's dealing with her own issues."

"What's *her* plan, Mark? I hope she doesn't make fools of us."

"I've been trying to call her since we got home, but she's not answering."

"Well, let's hope she doesn't write something other than what you told me. If she claims the old man is John, you and I will both have to answer to those board members. And, believe me, it won't be pretty."

JULIE

Julie's phone rang incessantly. She checked the caller ID but refused to pick up. First Mark called. Then Lakisha. Then Mark again. The two of them alternated for the rest of the day.

The next morning, Lakisha pounded on her door. "Come on, Julie, open up. I know you're in there. Your car's in the parking lot."

"I need some time alone," she said through the locked door. "Please, Lakisha, give me a couple of days."

"All right then. I just wanted to make sure you're okay."

"I'm okay."

Julie's condo settled once again into blessed silence.

For the next two days she remained barricaded inside. She lived on Lean Cuisine, power bars, and herbal tea.

She felt like a failure. Andy had said she'd failed. Mary Beth probably had announced it to the entire newsroom. Her former feelings of worthlessness had come back like an avalanche. While she had tried to do the right thing—had convinced herself it *was* the right thing—she'd begun to wonder if she'd made a mistake after all. In protecting Yanno, she had sacrificed her career. Fortunately, something good had come out of their meeting. Like a surgeon in the operating room, Yanno had dug out the disease and had sewn her up with magic thread. She was free of the pain, free of the guilt, free of the overwhelming memories. Now, Yanno had left the most important decision of her career in her own hands. It was time to look ahead. Somewhere, there was that window Brother Pio had talked about.

She paced from the living room to the kitchen and back to her bedroom. She sat in a chair in the living room and stared out the window. What was she going to do with the rest of her life? She had no plan, no project, no more options. She thought of Mark and smiled. He'd given her a small ray of hope, but she wasn't ready to talk to him. She needed to stand on her own two feet before she could get involved in a relationship.

She paused for a second. Where had she put that New Testament Andy had given her? She hurried to her desk and found it on the floor next to the waste basket. Why hadn't she taken better care of the thing? Clutching it to her heart, she went back to her window chair and opened it to the Gospel of John. She read the entire gospel, stopping only to get something to eat or a bottle of water.

Several verses jumped out at her and grabbed her heart. One in particular addressed the obscure path she'd been on. She mulled over Jesus' words. *I am the light of the world: he that follows me shall not walk in darkness, but shall have the light of life.* She'd been walking in darkness for six years. Now she had a light. All she needed to do was follow God. But how? Which direction did He want her to take?

Something clicked inside her. She rose from her chair, went directly to her desk and opened her laptop. With fresh enthusiasm, she inserted her camera card and scrolled through the photos she'd taken in Ephesus and Patmos. She pulled out her notes and scanned through them, then paired them with the photos in a colorful display of art. She purposely ignored any mention of Yanno.

Gradually, the ruins of Ephesus came back to life. The Library of Celsus, the ancient baths, the descending street with its uneven pavement and its border of crumbling statues. There were several pictures of the Great Theater where she and Mark had sat in the noonday sun. There was the tomb of John the Apostle and those pathetic women who bowed there. Then images of Patmos flowed onto the screen. The boats in the harbor, the ethereal seascape, the whitewashed homes on the hill, the monastery, and the claustrophobic cave that had sent her fleeing to the exit.

Then she came across a shot of Damien and Sofia. It brought tears to her eyes. Their photo put a face on the humble people who lived on the island. With a sigh, she scrolled through the slide show again and selected several. In her mind she began to formulate a travel piece for Andy.

As an afterthought, Julie raced to her file cabinet and pulled out a journal she had taken with her on a vacation to Israel with her father when she was a freshman in high school. She had accumulated a wealth of photos and brochures on that trip.

She worked long into the night, stopping only for an occasional bathroom break or to fix herself another cup of tea. At three o'clock in the morning, she clicked *Save*, and stumbled to her bed. Sleep came quickly. For the first time in days, she slept restfully through the night and woke to a sunlit room at midday.

Julie stretched and lolled on top of her bed for several minutes. She discovered she was starving. She left her condo and headed for the grocery store, where she loaded up on fresh fruit, vegetables, and a filet of salmon. She went back to her condo and cooked up a gourmet meal, finished every bite, and, after slipping her plate in the dishwasher, she went back to her computer.

"Now, it's time for some self-editing," she said aloud. Leaving her phone on *silence*, she tackled her manuscript. It was far too long for a newspaper column. She needed to leave sufficient space for photos. Starting at the top, she checked every typo, every misspelled word. She moved entire paragraphs around and cut redundant text. When she finished, she read through the entire piece, then she did a word count—1,853 words. *Done.*

Next, Julie reworked her photos. She selected a dozen for her editor to choose from. Then, she packaged the project in a file labeled, *"In Search of the Beloved, In the footsteps of John the Apostle,"* and she emailed it to Andy.

Now, she reasoned, *it's time for a long overdue trip home.*

Julie was going to see her parents. She wanted to tell them face-to-face that she forgave them for not believing in her. She wanted to give them a chance to apologize. She needed that, and she figured they did too. What's more, she wanted to see her sister. And for her own sense of well-being, she wanted to walk into that little church and face those people who'd rejected her. Chances were the congregation had changed and grown since then, but some of the old gossips might still be there. Swallowing her bitterness, she determined to be as gracious as possible. Wasn't that the way Yanno would want her to handle it, with love and understanding? Funny how that man continued to influence her life, though they were thousands of miles apart.

Julie needed to catch up with Lakisha at some point and tell her about all the changes in her life. Most of all, her best friend would want to know about her time with Mark.

Lakisha had been trying to get them back together since the breakup. There was no doubt in Julie's mind, her friend would want to know everything that happened during the trip, and Julie was able to give her an earful.

But first, she had to contact Mark. So much had transpired between them, she couldn't run off to Fairview without first talking to him. She picked up her cell phone and dialed his number.

When Mark's phone rang, he leaped for it.

"Julie, where have you been? Why didn't you answer my calls?"

"Forgive me, Mark, I needed a little time to sort things out."

He breathed a sigh of resignation. "What's going on? I've been worried about you."

He listened intently as she ran through the details of the past few days—the decision about the story, the loss of her job, and finally, the travel piece.

"I feel really good about everything," she said.

"I know what you mean, Julie. I did something similar in my meeting with Melanie. I focused on my project for the school and played down the part about Yanno. She'll be glad to know you made the same decision."

"Believe me, I struggled with it, Mark. But, I couldn't expose Yanno. I kept seeing his face. Those twinkling dark eyes. His endearing smile. I relived all of those encounters he had with the people of his village. I felt so much love in that tiny cottage. How could I do anything that might hurt him?"

Mark breathed easier now. Without a word spoken between them, they had both protected Yanno. It was further proof that Julie was the right girl for him. When it came down to the really important issues, they thought alike.

"I'm sorry about your job, Julie, but you'll find something else."

"Thanks, Mark. I'm going to start an internet search tomorrow. I may have to move, but I'll face *that* problem when it happens."

Mark's heart did a flip. He hadn't considered Julie might have to leave Springfield. She'd have to go wherever the work called her. He doubted a long-distance relationship would work for them.

"Please, tell me you'll start your search locally," he pleaded.

"I will," she said. "But first, I have to do what Yanno recommended. I need to go home and make things right with my parents. I need to tell them I forgive them for doubting me. I can do that now, though it's only the beginning. It's gonna take a long time for us to restore our relationship to what it used to be."

"I'm proud of you, Julie. You're facing a long, tough road, but you'll do more than heal a relationship. You'll be healing yourself along the way."

"With God's help," she said, and he was comforted to hear her say that.

He wished he could pull her close to him and just hold her.

"Mark, there's something else," she said. "I'm going to need your help."

"Anything, Julie."

"I need to talk to a professional counselor. Not like before. This time I want someone who will believe what I tell him and help me deal with the most traumatic experience of my life."

"Of course. I know just the guy. You can talk to my minister—"

"Actually," she said, interrupting him. "I was thinking of someone else. While you were asleep on the plane, I struck up a conversation with a family counselor who was traveling to Izmir. In those few brief minutes, he won my trust. I think he can help me, Mark, and he's only a half-hour away."

A spark of jealousy ignited within him. That flight attendant had made sure he knew about the little chat Julie was having with some guy on the plane.

"Well," he said. "I guess you've made up your mind."

"I have. It's going to take several sessions. To be honest, I don't know if I can relate to any man in the church, except for you. Don't forget, a so-called 'servant of the Lord' assaulted me. The thing is, I don't want to be alone with him, Mark. I'd like you to go with me."

He relaxed. Julie had said she needed him. "Go ahead and make the appointment," he said.

33

HOME

The next morning, Julie packed an overnight bag, got in her car and began the five-hour drive to Fairview. She hadn't stepped foot in the little town in six years. The place probably had changed a lot since then. It was a lazy Saturday morning. Traffic was light. She turned on the radio. To her surprise, the deejay was playing Elvis's *"Can't Help Falling in Love."* It brought back a moment in time she had long since forgotten. Lakisha's wedding. Mark had swept her onto the dance floor. Julie smiled at the memory.

The long drive would give her time to think about the upcoming family reunion. Somehow, she was going to have to put aside the past hurts and give her parents a chance to apologize. She also had some regrets. Even after McAndrews' crimes were exposed, and her parents had tried to contact her, Julie had refused to speak to them.

She thought about the phone call she made last night. Margie Peters had squealed when she learned Julie was coming home for a few days.

"I'm sorry, honey, but I had to turn your old bedroom into a guest room," she'd apologized. "You know how it is. Your Aunt Ellie likes to visit us now and then, and of course there's Rita's friends from college."

Rita. The mere mention of her sister's name sent waves of nostalgia through Julie. Except through photographs and video calls, she hadn't seen Rita in six years.

When she left home, her little sister was still in middle school. Now she was in nursing college. Julie grinned as she recalled how no one ever believed they were sisters. Julie's bright red locks and green eyes made a stark contrast to Rita's ebony waves and brown eyes. It wasn't until their friends got a look at their parents at a science fair that they believed the two girls were related.

The kids from school gawked at the mismatched foursome. Her father, with his pitch black mop of hair and green eyes, had his arm around Julie's shoulder. Her mother, with her bright red curls framing her face, was holding Rita's hand.

Back then, her home life was filled with family traditions. Sunday mornings started with the aroma of roast chicken wafting from the kitchen, pulling Julie from her bed. Big band music poured from a radio on the counter, and her mother hopped from one foot to the other while cutting up vegetables at the kitchen sink. Without fail, her dad would be sitting at the kitchen table reading the newspaper, a cup of coffee in one hand. Rita would stumble down the stairs behind Julie, and they'd fly about the kitchen to see who could put together a bowl of cereal faster. The memory nearly tore her heart out of her chest.

The holidays were even better. Every Christmas Julie and Rita tumbled down the stairs before their parents got up and searched for their names on packages under the tree. Later that day, the house came to life with holiday smells—baked ham, apple cider, cinnamon, and chocolate chip cookies fresh out of the oven.

Summers included trips to the lake, hot dog roasts, drives in the country, and a stop at their favorite ice cream shop.

Julie chuckled as images flooded back. The Halloween

party when her parents dressed as Sonny and Cher, with her father totally out of character in a long black wig and flowing scarf, and Mom dressed in a furry vest, a fake mustache, and a short brown wig.

Then Ben McAndrews came to mind. Her smile faded. Not only had that man stolen her innocence. He'd also stolen her family. How could she think of the good times without also remembering the day her life was shattered?

The monster had been a business associate of her father's. They attended conferences together and took part in the Iron Man events at the church. Julie's mother and Dina McAndrews served on the church hostess committee. They planned covered-dish luncheons, bake sales, and anniversary parties.

They couldn't believe McAndrews was capable of such a horrible crime. Neither could their minister, or any of the other members of the church. Parents kept their kids away from her, as if she had leprosy. Except for Rita, Julie didn't have a single friend anymore.

From that moment on, she fell into a lonely, miserable routine—went to school, came home, went back to school. Weekends were spent at home, playing board games with Rita or watching TV. As soon as she graduated from high school, she was out of there.

As she drew closer to Fairview, all those memories came rushing back, the good and the bad. Was she capable of handling everything the way Yanno hoped she would?

It was almost noon when she pulled up in front of her parents' house. She didn't get out of the car right away, but sat there for a few minutes and stared with fascination at the two-story suburban home with its white siding, green shutters, and pitched roof.

There was the tire swing, still dangling from the old oak tree. Why hadn't her father taken it down? Were they hoping for grandchildren? She snickered.

The front yard appeared smaller than she remembered and the house looked as though it had moved closer to the street. In contrast, the azalea and hydrangea bushes had grown larger. Their prolific blossoms of bright pink and purple created a tranquil border along the forward edge of the porch. The front door still had that worn welcome sign hanging from it, and there was the creaky, old glider where she used to sit with a book and a glass of lemonade.

Julie released a long sigh. She'd come home. There was something warm and welcoming about the place. A lump came to her throat. Perhaps she could retrieve the good part, if she tried.

She stepped out of the car and pulled her overnight bag from the back seat. The walk to the front steps had a fatalistic feel. The prodigal daughter had come home.

She was about to climb the porch steps, when the front door burst open. Rita bounded down the stairs and flung her arms around Julie, almost knocking her over. She dropped her suitcase and grabbed Rita's shoulders with both hands.

"I missed you so much," Julie said.

"I missed you too." Rita's voice cracked with emotion.

When they backed away from each other, Julie had to blink away the moisture that had come to her eyes. She took a long look at her sister. Rita had outgrown her gangly arms and legs and her fly-away hair. The rumpled youth was gone, and in her place was a confident beauty with short-cropped black hair, penetrating brown eyes, and a slim physique that could have graced any fashion house runway.

"I can't believe you're really here," Rita said, her eyes flooding over.

The screen door squeaked open. Julie's parents paused on the front porch, as though waiting for her to make the first move.

"I've got your bag," Rita said, and she grabbed Julie's suitcase.

Hesitantly at first, Julie started up the front steps. Her parents came down and met her halfway. In that initial awkward moment, no one spoke. Julie's dad offered his hand. She took it and allowed him to guide her up the stairs and into the house. Once inside, her mother fell apart, spewing tears and blubbering something that sounded like a mix of regret and joyous relief.

Julie's bitterness began to melt away as a wave of compassion overcame her. She stared at her mother. More lines had taken over the woman's face. Margie Peters' beautiful red hair had faded to a dull beige. She took Julie's hand in hers and gazed at her with pleading eyes. She was still blubbering incoherently.

Her father showed more restraint as he wrapped one arm around his wife and the other around Julie. "We're glad you're home," he said.

Though his voice lacked emotion, his moist eyes told Julie he was happy to see her.

With the initial meeting over, Julie began to relax. Now that she'd seen her parents again, she felt like she really could restore their relationship. But so much pain had divided them, a reunion would have to come in stages. It wasn't something that could happen overnight.

"Come in the kitchen," Bill Peters said. "Your mom has fixed lunch. Margie, what are we having?"

"Sandwiches and macaroni salad," her mom said. She wiped

tears from her cheek, but smiled. "I made your favorite, Julie. Tuna salad and grapes on nutty grain bread, exactly the way you like it—toasted."

Julie hadn't had tuna-and-grape sandwiches since she'd left home. It had been her mother's idea to add the grapes, and though Julie had loved the tangy mixture and the crunch of the toasted bread, she'd left the recipe behind along with all the other reminders of her youth.

In the kitchen, she drew up a chair across from her dad at the round kitchen table. Rita assisted her mother by pulling plates of sandwiches and a bowl of macaroni salad from the fridge. Julie sat watching them. It had been a long time since she'd been a part of the meal-time rituals. Now, she didn't know how to help, or even if she should offer. She felt like a visitor in her own home.

She looked across the table at her dad. His hair had receded and crow's feet fanned out from the corners of his eyes. He was still handsome though.

After Rita and her mom took their seats, Julie's dad spread his arms. "Shall we pray?" he said, his voice characteristically formal. As a department manager everything he did or said had an official tone to it, even at home. Julie shrugged internally. That was her dad. Take him or leave him.

Her mom was a different story. She bowed to every word that came out of that man's mouth, like a true virtuous woman, yet with an air of subservience rather than willing service. Like she always did when Bill Peters was about to pray, or speak, or command, Margie bowed her head. Julie reached for Rita's hand on her left, then she accepted her mother's outstretched fingers on her right. A quiet sob emerged from Margie's throat, and Julie realized what intense emotional trauma her mother was experiencing with her return. Her heart went out to the woman, now a stranger, but somewhere inside that tearful face, a familiar person still resided.

"Lord," her father began. "Thank you for bringing our daughter home. Restore her to her rightful place in our family. Thank you for this food. Bless our conversation. In Christ's name, Amen."

Short and to the point. It was just like her father to speak to God like he was at a board meeting. His words sounded cold and unemotional.

Yanno had put so much more heart in his prayers. When he prayed, it was like the Holy Spirit was right in the room with them. True, Yanno's prayers weren't necessarily long and flowery. He, too, got right to the point, but he said so much more in a few words than her father did in his mono-toned benediction, like it was something he needed to get out of the way so he could eat.

Julie shifted her attention to her plate, and her mouth watered. She took her first bite of the sandwich and savored the long-forgotten sweet-and-sour taste of grapes and tuna blended together with a creamy mayo and cream cheese concoction her mother had created. She cleaned her plate and followed with a large glass of iced tea.

She looked around the table at the others. Her father had his sandwich in one hand and was flipping through the pages of his day planner with the other, now oblivious to the rest of the family. Her mother's face beamed with delight. Their eyes met and they exchanged a silent vow to try and make things work. Rita, too, had a look of contentment mixed with joy. Perhaps reconciliation wasn't going to be as difficult as Julie had thought.

Her father took one last bite of his sandwich, set aside his day planner, and turned his attention to Julie.

"We need to have a talk," Bill Peters said in his familiar, businesslike tone. Julie laughed to herself. There was hardly a time when the man shed his professional image and became just plain Dad. Even when he played with the girls on the beach, his movements had been stiff and mechanical, his shouts during a game of Frisbee sounding more like commands from upper management than a daddy having fun with his kids. Julie had a feeling this upcoming "talk" would involve her father monopolizing the conversation and the rest of the family relegated into members of an audience.

Her mother reached out and patted Julie's hand. "Dear, can you ever forgive—"

"Margie." Bill's sharp interjection sent a wave of color to her mother's cheeks.

"Let me handle this," he snapped.

Julie would have thought more of him if he'd groveled a little. How could she speak words of forgiveness to someone who behaved like a drill sergeant, ready to pounce on a helpless GI? A surge of defiance rushed through her. Without flinching, she stared bullets into her father's domineering eyes and conveyed an unspoken challenge. His shocked hesitation bolstered her confidence.

"No, father, let *me* handle this," she said with a boldness that astounded even her. "I have every right to be angry with the two of you. No matter how much I pleaded, no matter how many times I insisted I was telling the truth, you didn't believe me. Instead, you took the side of someone we hardly knew—over your own daughter. If you had trusted me, that monster might not have hurt the others."

315

There. She'd blurted out the hurt and anger of six long years. Finally, she'd unleashed the pain.

Her father appeared to crumble. "Julie, I—"

"You what, Father? You believed a lie instead of the truth? You didn't trust a helpless teenager?" She shook her head in disgust. "The one reason I'm sitting here with you right now is because someone—" She softened her voice. "A wise, old friend—convinced me this was the right thing to do. Believe me when I say, it isn't easy for me to forgive you and Mom. But, that's what I'm trying to do."

Her father appeared stunned. He blinked back at her, his mouth half open, like he was trying to say something but couldn't form the words.

"I only need to know why?" she said, bolstered with more courage. "Why didn't you believe me? Why did you allow me to suffer such shame? When I needed you most, why did you turn away from me?"

Margie sobbed into her napkin. Rita rose from the table, walked around to the other side and wrapped her arms around her mother's shoulders.

"My dear daughter," Bill said, and Julie was surprised to see his eyes brimming with tears. "You have to understand. I knew McAndrews—"

"You knew *me*, too."

"I never suspected he might be capable of such a horrible act." He leaned toward Julie and spread his hands. "Please, can't we put everything behind us and move on?"

It touched Julie's heart to see her father humble himself, it happened so rarely—in fact, hardly at all.

"I'm going to *try* to forgive you," she said, her tone milder. "I've arranged for some counseling when I go back to

Springfield. It wouldn't be a bad idea for you and Mom to get some too. Maybe, in time, we can get back to what we once had. For now, you'll have to settle for my willingness to try. You're my parents." She looked back and forth between them. "I love you both. I always have, and I always will. But I haven't *liked* you for a long, long time."

Margie reached for another napkin and blotted her damp face. "I have prayed for this very moment," she sobbed. "It's such a shame. To think, we could have resolved this long ago." She dabbed at her eyes. "I promise, Julie, we'll do whatever it takes to make things right again."

They sat in silence for a while. Rita had returned to her seat and was finishing her lunch. Margie continued to wipe tears from her face. Julie didn't know what else to say. Perhaps her outburst was all they needed to clear the air.

Her confidence was short-lived. Bill cleared his throat, a sure sign he was about to embark on a long-winded soliloquy. Julie wasn't mistaken. Her father leaned back in his chair and, as though nothing had been resolved, he dove into his monologue.

"I need to tell you, Julie, that when you said you were coming home, I immediately drafted a plan."

Julie glanced at her sister. Rita's eyebrows went up and she appeared to be fighting off a snicker. *Okay, so Bill Peters had come up with a plan. Great. After all, the man ran a huge company. He should be able to oversee a family of four*, she thought smugly.

Her father withdrew a slip of paper from his pocket. The "plan" had been there all along. It was there when she arrived at the house. It was there through the entire meal. It was there during Julie's tirade. She felt about to collapse in disgust.

317

"I like to call my program *the four steps to restoration*," Bill said, unaware that his words had resurrected the wall between himself and his daughter.

Julie looked away, unable to look at him without sending angry darts into his face.

"Now bear with me, Julie," he said, drawing her to attention. "Believe it or not, we've already passed through the first two steps. First was denial. We've acknowledged our problem, and we immediately moved on to the second step—acceptance and a willingness to find a solution."

"Like they do in AA meetings?" Rita blurted out.

Bill nodded at her, then he returned his attention to Julie. How she'd love to escape his domineering presence, maybe slide under the table or flee out the kitchen door. But there was no escape. Julie was a captive audience.

He lay the slip of paper on the table and pointed to Step 3. "We have now reached the level of discussion," he said, as if he hadn't heard a word Julie had said. "We need to air out any existing differences and resolve them." He leaned across the table toward her. "You see, Julie, you're not the only one who suffered. Your mother had a hard time when you left." Margie let out a sob. "We had no idea you'd gotten that scholarship," Bill went on. "If not for Rita relaying information to us, we never would have known where you were or what kind of work you were doing. You can't possibly know how painful that is for a parent."

He paused and checked his notes. "Anyway, we will concentrate on step three during your visit. Tonight, after supper, we will sit down and talk."

So far, Bill Peters' monologue was peppered with such words as "we need," "we never," "you can't," and "we will." Such demanding words bore holes in Julie's heart. She glanced at Rita. Her sister appeared anxious. Julie determined to stick it out, at least for the moment.

Bill was still talking, though she'd missed part of what he'd said. "...and so, each of us will have ten minutes to air our differences. Hopefully, at the end of our discussion, we will understand how the other parties feel. Then, and only then, can we move on to Step 4."

Julie was suddenly aware that her entire body had tensed up. She tried to relax, but a wave of claustrophobia swept over her. She wasn't even in an elevator or in a crowd of people, like she was when that feeling had come over her before. She was in a spacious kitchen with only three other people, and she felt like she couldn't breathe.

Step 4? What exactly was that?

Unaware of Julie's discomfort, Bill simply continued elaborating on his plan. "Step 4 will take more time," he said. "It involves a long-term process of restoring our family to the kind of relationship that existed before the separation. It may develop into an even better relationship, one that can function for a long, long time, with each member contributing toward a productive end."

Bill finished with that same self-satisfied smile Julie had come to resent over the years. He'd just concluded another business meeting and had put his own plan at the forefront. He wasn't open to anyone else's ideas. Julie wondered how an intelligent person could work under his authority for very long. Probably the turnover at his company was very rapid.

When she didn't say anything, he responded with what sounded like a dig.

"Why don't you ask your wise, old gentleman friend about it?" Bill sneered. "Get his opinion, if you like."

"I can't ask him, Father. He lives in another country. In fact, I may never see him again." The thought brought tears to Julie's eyes. The truth was, she may never again see Yanno, and it was even more heartbreaking than leaving her own father had been.

"Ever hear of the internet? Or the telephone?" Bill's mocking voice raised the hairs on the back of Julie's neck.

She strove to remain cool. "It's difficult. He's pretty busy."

"It doesn't matter. The main thing is, are you willing to practice the last two steps or not? With or without your guru's advice. Do you want to mend this rift between us? Or are you here simply because some old guy told you to come home?"

Julie wanted to be honest. "I suppose it's a little of both, Father. All I can say is, I'll try."

"Fine." Bill gave the table a tap with his knuckles. "It's settled then. Tonight, after dinner, we'll move into Step 3. We'll begin our discussions, no holds barred. You can go ahead and ask us anything you want. But remember, we're going to do the same with you. You can tell us what you've been going through these past six years, and we'll tell you how we've been trying to move on without our number one daughter."

"All right, Father." It was useless. His plan was set. He was winning again, although what was he winning? Unless they could come to terms, nobody was going to win. Not this time. Not ever.

She'd been calling him "Father" from the moment she'd arrived home. Somehow, the term, "Daddy," didn't exist for her anymore.

"Okay then," he said, breathing a sigh. "Let's take a break.

Why don't you two girls run off for a while? Take a tour of the town. You can see how it's grown and changed, Julie. Visit some of your old haunts. Your high school. The playground in the park. Grab a milkshake at the malt shop. Catch a movie at The Olde Cinema. Remember that place? You wouldn't recognize it now. They renovated the auditorium and put in stadium seating. They can't call it Olde anymore." He let out a laugh.

With every suggestion, Julie's throat had tightened up. Not only had he tried to plan her life from the time she was three, now he'd actually set a plan for her afternoon with Rita. Would it never stop?

She forced an amenable answer. "That sounds like a good plan," she said, directing her words more to Rita than to her father. "Let's help Mother clean up the kitchen first..."

"No, no," Margie said, rising. "You girls run along and have a good time. I can do these few dishes." She winked at her husband. "Your daddy will help me."

Rita leaped to her feet. "I'll get my purse. C'mon, Julie, let's blow this joint. I'll drive."

34

MEMORIES

Rita wove her little red Honda through the town. The place hadn't grown. It was still three miles square with a population of less than 5,000 people. Julie's old school still looked the same, a faded brick two-story structure with a flat roof, where the kids used to take breaks during lunchtime. They cruised around the corner, drove two blocks, and circled the property that surrounded the church. Julie started to boil as they passed the fellowship hall where McAndrews had overpowered her. Rita stopped in front of the sanctuary steps. A flame ignited within Julie. This was where Dina McAndrews had shouted accusations in her face, while other church-going "saints" had eyed her with disgust.

"Let's get out of here," she said, her voice cold.

"Sorry. I wasn't thinking."

Rita pulled out, went a few more blocks, and turned into a residential section past the homes of their former friends and classmates. It appeared that most of the town had remained stuck in the past, until they reached a part of the county that had burgeoned with huge mansions, country estates, and gentleman farms.

Julie raised her eyebrows. "There's some money here."

"Yeah," Rita said with a nod. "You wouldn't believe it. A couple of geeks started a computer business right after high school. Their business took off, they got rich, and now many of their top people live here."

Julie allowed a smirk to cross her lips. "Meanwhile, our parents remained in the same house they owned when they got married."

"That's Dad," Rita said. "He's probably invested most of his money in stocks or stashed it away in a bank. I don't know what he's saving up for. Retirement? A round-the-world cruise? How about grandchildren?"

"Or our inheritance?" Julie tossed in with a laugh.

"Shall we go to the Malt Shoppe?" Rita asked, a tone of anticipation in her voice. "You can get a milkshake, like Dad suggested."

"Okay, let's go. But, I won't get a milkshake. I don't have to do everything that man tells me to do. I think I'd like—um—how about a root beer float?"

"Sounds good to me." Rita maneuvered her car down a couple of side streets and onto the main drag.

The downtown area hadn't changed much. The same two dress shops stood across the street from each other, their competing sales pitches in their windows. There was the barber shop with it's iconic red-and-white striped pole. And the old firehouse that had a library on the second floor. Julie recalled how the siren blasted every day at noon. It didn't matter that a *Silence* placard stood in full view on the librarian's desk.

She basked in the sentiment of the moment. She'd forgotten how quaint and relaxing small-town life had been.

Then, there it was. The Malt Shoppe, a favorite hangout for teenagers, the window ads still offering the same shakes and fries, but with a few more dollars tacked onto the price. Julie entered through a glass-fronted door to the smell of hamburgers frying on the grill. She grabbed a red plastic stool at the counter, while Rita sauntered over to the juke box and inserted a couple of quarters. Within five seconds, the voice of Frank Sinatra came over singing, "Fly Me to the Moon."

Julie spun around on the stool and faced her sister, laughing. "That's a funny song for you to choose."

Rita raised a shoulder and gave her a half-grin. "Oh, well. I still like the old crooner."

They spent an hour at the Malt Shoppe, steeped in nostalgia over sweet root beer floats and crisp french fried potatoes. Several customers walked in, but Julie didn't recognize any of them, which came as a relief. She wasn't in the mood to see anyone from her past.

When they left, Rita suggested they take a drive down to the lake. "You're not going to recognize it," she warned.

Rita no sooner parked her car on the gravel lot than Julie slipped out of her sandals and swung her legs out the door. She tiptoed across the sun-stroked pavement and stepped onto the sandy beach with a contented sigh. The warm grains surged between her toes and gave her a sense of childlike freedom she hadn't experienced in a long time. Living and working in Springfield, she'd rarely taken time to go to the beach. Now she could soak up the odor of live fish and seaweed while splashing at the edge of the water. If she closed her eyes she could imagine herself on a tropical island off the coast of Florida. All her cares dissipated amidst the gentle breeze that wafted off the lake.

Rita came up beside her and poked her arm. "Wake up, girl. Enjoy the view."

Julie squinted against the glare of sunlight as it shot like millions of flaming daggers off the water. She brought her hand up to shade her eyes and scanned the opposite shore.

"Isn't that the property where they used to have carnival rides and a giant midway?"

Rita nodded. "Yeah, remember the fun we had over there? It's gone now. A couple of years ago, they tore it all down and put up a bunch of beach houses."

"That's sad." Julie sighed. "I used to love the rides. The hot dogs. The cotton candy." She giggled. "The boys."

Rita laughed with her. "Remember the time I wore your platform shoes so I could appear tall enough to get on the Fireball? I could barely walk in those things without falling, but the guy let me on the ride. He didn't so much as *glance* at my feet."

"And how about that old carny who tricked us out of a week's allowance over that stupid stuffed bear?" Julie said. "Then we went back the following Saturday with Dad, and he won it for us."

"You mean he paid big bucks for it. He must have tried that game a hundred times before he gave up and slipped the guy a twenty."

"He always had to win," Julie moaned. "He had to be right, had to be top dog." She turned toward Rita, whose eyes had widened in shock.

"That's sad," Rita told her. "You must still be struggling with all that's happened."

"It's okay." Julie assured her. "I'm dealing with it. I'm trying to figure out if I can *really* forgive him. Mom's easy, but Father? That's another story."

"You know, Julie, that incident tore up our whole family, not just you. Then you made it worse by withdrawing. You went to school every day with a sad face and you came home the same way. You disappeared inside your room and didn't come out until suppertime. Then we ate dinner like a bunch of zombies."

Rita let out a sigh. Her brown eyes flashed with pain. "You know what, Julie? I lost you long before you left home.

Then, I had to listen to Mom's whining and Dad's ranting, along with the bickering about whether they should have believed you and what they could have done differently. Dad stomped around trying to justify the stand he'd taken, and Mom sobbed in her room every night. As for me? I covered my head with my pillow and tried to get to sleep."

Julie was stunned. She hadn't considered how her personal tragedy had affected the entire family, but now, hearing it from her dear sister, a wave of guilt swept over her and a sudden rage stirred inside. She hated McAndrews even more.

"I'm so sorry you got caught in the middle of my problem," Julie said. "I didn't know how to cope with all the accusations. And that horrible counselor Mom hooked me up with. She made things worse. I needed to get out of there, Rita. Thank God, I had a scholarship. I buckled down and earned a four-year degree in three years. Immediately after graduation, I found a job. Things moved so fast I didn't have time to look back or even find out how everyone else had been affected."

Rita moved in front of Julie and faced her straight on. "Didn't you know that by isolating yourself, you also isolated me? We were so close before you left. Then I was all alone."

"Oh, Rita," Julie's eyes filled with tears. "I didn't mean to do that. I figured you had your friends. You'd keep busy. There was no reason for you to get involved in my problem."

"But I was involved, whether I wanted to be or not. I loved you."

"I loved you too. That's why my leaving was the best thing for both of us."

Rita scowled and put her hands on her hips. "I'm a lot stronger than you think, big sister. I *wanted* you to reach out to me, so *you* wouldn't feel all alone. Then, you were gone."

Rita's eyes swam in a puddle of tears. Julie wrapped her arms around her little sister and they cried together.

"You're the best sister a girl could ever have," Julie sobbed. "All I can say is, thank you for all the support you gave me over the years. Your letters. The newspaper clippings that proved I was telling the truth. Dear, dear Rita, promise me you'll stay as sweet as you are."

Rita stepped back and smiled. Her eyes sparkled, partially from the tears that remained, but also from what Julie could only imagine was a deep affection for her.

"Come on," Rita said, tugging on Julie's hand. "Let's splash in the surf... like we used to."

Arm-in-arm, they plunged barefoot into the rippling current. Together, they trudged along the length of beach, kicking up the froth as it bubbled under their feet. Julie savored the coolness of the fresh water. A soft breeze swept her hair across her face and she peered through the crimson strands at the scene before her. She released a chuckle.

"What's so funny?" Rita said, a quizzical expression on her face.

"Only a few days ago, I was trudging around Patmos, looking for a mysterious old man, and today I'm at the beach with my sister. Life is full of adventure, isn't it?

"Tell me about Patmos," Rita said, her voice soft. Then she fell silent.

As they continued swishing their feet at the edge of the water, Julie skimmed over the highlights of her trip. She even mentioned her roller coaster relationship with Mark.

They kept walking until they reached a rock wall with a sign restricting access to the private area beyond. Julie peered over the wall at the string of stilted bungalows, broad wooden decks, and fenced-in swimming pools.

She gawked at the flagrant display of wealth. "They've ruined this place."

Rita wrinkled her nose. "You can say that again. I liked the way it used to look. Simple. Barren. Over-run with teenagers. It was the most fantastic beach in the world. Now look at it."

Julie heaved a sigh. "Let's start back."

Rita didn't argue. She spun around and started in the direction of her car. So far, Julie had monopolized their conversation. She looked at her sister, the short crop of black hair tossed by the wind, her face a golden hue, tinged by the afternoon sun. Though Rita appeared untroubled, even euphoric, she had to have her own problems. Julie realized she'd been horribly selfish, thinking only of herself.

"We've been talking all afternoon about me and my problems," she said. "What about you? How's college?"

Rita snickered. "Tough. But, I'm determined to get my nursing degree. Anyway, Dad keeps reminding me how much money he's sunk into my education. I wasn't as smart as you. No scholarship. So now I have no choice but to finish."

"Rita, don't let him guilt you into doing anything you don't want to. You've got to make your own decisions. No matter what."

"I know. The truth is, I *want* to be a nurse. It's what I've always wanted."

"It's an honorable profession. It takes someone with a compassionate heart like yours to be a good one."

"Thanks, but I'm not always compassionate—or good."

"I can't imagine that," Julie said with a chuckle.

"Well, imagine it, because it's true. Do you remember that guy I wrote you about? Jeremy?"

"Yeah, you dated him for a few months last year."

"Well, I stole him right out from under a girlfriend of mine."

Julie widened her eyes in amazement. What had become of her *perfect* little sister?

"That's right," Rita confessed. "I moved in on my friend Donna's guy. I didn't stop to think about how it might hurt her. Now, I have so much regret. I lost a friend, and on top of that, my relationship with Jeremy didn't last."

Julie shook her head. "We sure learn a lot from our mistakes, don't we."

"That's for sure. I'll never allow myself to do *that* again. I don't care how charming the guy is. I'd much rather have my friend back."

Julie stepped away and looked her sister in the eye. "Don't forget, Rita, Jeremy had some responsibility in what happened, too. He must be fickle, moving from girl to girl, like he's trading baseball cards. So, where is he now?"

"Still moving from girl to girl," Rita said and she burst out with a hearty giggle.

Julie laughed along with her. "I love you, Rita."

"I love you too, Julie. Please, don't stay away anymore."

Julie took her sister by the arm and guided her away from the beach and back toward the parking lot. "You can relax," she said. "I'm not going to avoid my family any longer. This is a new beginning for all of us. I'll come back, Rita, but first I need to deal with some issues."

"Issues?"

Julie nodded. "I've arranged to meet with a family counselor. I've suffered with this mess for more than six years. It's going to take more than a simple, *I forgive you*, for me to move on."

Rita hesitated outside the car. Her serious expression told Julie there was something more.

"Okay, Rita. Open up. What is it?"

"Well," she said, then she paused. "Had you intended—I mean, did you ever think you might need to forgive Mr. McAndrews?"

"*McAndrews?!* That letch? Forgiving him would take a lot more counseling than there are years in my life."

But, hadn't Yanno suggested the same thing? Julie tried to shake off the memory, but the old man's warning kept coming to mind. She wouldn't be free until she could forgive everyone.

"I'm merely going to start by forgiving our parents," she said aloud. "Even *that* won't happen overnight. My coming home was only the first step."

"Like Dad's Four-Step Program?" Rita said with a snicker.

She gave her sister a sideways glance. "Not quite. I have my own agenda."

"I see." The sadness in Rita's voice troubled Julie.

"Rita. I have a long way to go. Sure, I'll talk things over with them tonight. But, I need to start those counseling sessions first. I've been praying for God's help. I want to get into the Bible again. I'll do whatever I can to get back to normal, whatever that means. So, don't rush me. And don't ask me to forgive that horrible man. *It ain't gonna happen.*"

Rita bowed her head. "I suppose you're right to feel as you do about McAndrews. He's in prison now and he's never gonna get out. He can't hurt another girl ever again. But, there's someone else."

Julie stepped back. "What do you mean? Who else?"

"*Mrs.* McAndrews. Dina. His wife."

Once again, Yanno's admonitions came back to haunt her. Had she taken him seriously, or not? Did she only intend to obey *part* of what he told her—or *all of it*?

Julie was about to get in the car, but froze when Rita said, "She gave Mom an envelope with your name on it."

"Who did?"

"Dina McAndrews."

"What? An envelope. Mom read my mail?"

"No. Settle down. She didn't *read* it. The envelope has never been opened. It was lying on top of Mom's dresser. I spotted it yesterday when I was helping her make their bed. I asked her about it, and she said Dina McAndrews dropped it off months ago."

"Why would that woman send me a letter?"

"It's very sad, Julie. After the truth came out about her husband, she and her son, Jimmy, stopped coming to church. Even when the other ladies tried to get her to come back, she isolated herself. The kids at school started taunting Jimmy about his dad, calling him a rapist's son and a 'chip off the old blockhead.' Dina pulled him out and put him in a home-school program. After Jimmy graduated, he enlisted in the Army. Dina has lived like a hermit ever since."

The truth hit Julie like an electric shock. Like Rita had said, she wasn't the only one who had suffered. Her parents. Her sister. McAndrews' other victims. His wife and son. That man's sin had destroyed so many lives.

For the first time, she imagined what life must have been like for Dina and her son. They, too, had experienced rejection, and shame, and the loss of fellowship. Their family also had been torn apart. Maybe it was some form of karma.

Then Julie recalled how that woman lashed out at her in front of the church with all those busybodies egging her on. The pain was unbearable.

Forgive Dina McAndrews? Not a chance.

"I don't need to see that letter," she said. "Tell Mom to tear it up."

35

RETURN TO SPRINGFIELD

After a grueling evening of warding off her father's insensitive remarks, coddling her sobbing mother, and trying to explain her own feelings, Julie went to bed exhausted. Rita wisely had avoided the entire Plan 3 session by disappearing in her bedroom with a book.

As far as Julie was concerned, their little "talk" went nowhere, but her mother seemed comforted, and that was good enough for Julie. Her mother actually brightened when she promised to return for the Fourth of July celebration. And, she was planning to bring a friend with her.

"A friend?" Margie said, beaming.

Julie nodded. "He's someone I want you to meet."

The next morning Julie awoke to sunlight streaming through half-open blinds and a melodic symphony pouring from the throat of a mockingbird outside her window. She glanced about her bedroom. Her mom had kept her furnishings—the white canopy bed and matching dresser with mirror, the single nightstand and the lamp with the frilly shade, the school desk in the corner. But, the rest of the decor had changed. Her sheer pink bedcovers and curtains had been swapped out for a striped blue-and-green bedspread and matching valance over the window. Gone was Julie's cork board with its photo collage of her friends at the beach.

In its place, a trio of framed floral prints added color to the white wall. Gone was Julie's collection of stuffed animals and "Missy," her favorite doll. Instead, a solitary basket of silk flowers stood on her dresser. And her desk, cleared of school books and colored pencils, was now home to a gooseneck lamp and a King James Bible. Julie's eyes stung. Her teenage retreat had been turned into a motel room for guests—and now, she was one of them.

There's no going back, she told herself. *Let go of the past and move ahead. You can do that now.*

She reached for her watch on the nightstand. Eight o'clock Sunday morning. The church service was in two hours. At last, she'd be able to walk into that sanctuary and hold her head up. By now, many of those people who had turned against her no longer lived in Springfield. From what Rita had written, some had died, and some had moved away. But the few that remained—and might remember the debacle—well, she could hardly wait to see their faces.

Familiar aromas wafted up the staircase to her bedroom. Toast. Coffee. Roast chicken. Her mom was chopping vegetables for her casserole. The blade struck the cutting board in a rhythmic cadence to Glenn Miller's "Pennsylvania 6-5000." Julie shut her eyes and allowed those scents and sounds to draw her back to happier days.

Today, as in the past, the family would gather at the kitchen table for a breakfast of cereal and toast. Then they'd pile into the car and head for church, after which they'd return home for dinner, with Mom using her best china and everyone seated in the formal dining room. That was the way they had done it for as long as Julie could remember.

Like clockwork, the morning went as it always had. The

family ate breakfast together, and while the women did the dishes, Dad pored over the Sunday newspaper. Then, he summoned everyone to the car. For Julie, the biggest rush would come the moment she stepped inside that little church and looked everyone in the eye. She had lived in defeat for so long, she figured she deserved to gloat a bit.

But as she prepared to face her antagonists, Yanno's face came before her. What might the old sage think of her plan of revenge? He'd probably cite that verse from Romans, the one that claimed vengeance belonged to the Lord. Funny how so many recitations from her youth had begun to come back to her, sometimes like a tsunami, other times like a trickle of rainwater off the roof.

As the family car pulled into the church parking lot, she pictured Yanno's eyes filled with disappointment in her, and an irrepressible wave of guilt swept over her. She recalled his plea to *love your enemies.* By the time Julie passed through those big oak doors and into the sanctuary, another burden had been lifted, one that had kept her chained to a life of bitterness.

Even when members of her mother's hostess committee flocked around her, cooing and expressing sickening sweet words of welcome, Julie swallowed her distaste for them, forced a smile, and listened to their accolades.

"Julie, you look wonderful. My, how you've grown into such a beautiful, young woman."

"I've been praying for you, Dear. And, I can see my prayers have been answered. You have such a glow about you."

"We are so proud of you, Julie. We hope you'll come home often."

More of her mother's friends showered her with

compliments until she thought she might drown in their good will. To her relief, the worship team began to sing, the women separated, and she went down the aisle to find a seat.

The service proceeded without another awkward moment, except for one time when the pastor singled her out with a flowery welcome. When Julie at last ducked into the shelter of her father's car, she scrunched down on the back seat and exhaled. Rita slid in beside her and sent her a sympathetic look.

"You did great," Rita said. "All those people—you handled yourself with such poise. I was proud of you.

Once they arrived home, the service was forgotten. Julie helped Rita lay out the feast her mother had prepared that morning. Comfort food had always been Margie's way of tearing down walls.

Bill launched into a boring monologue that was supposed to be grace. Julie winced. It sounded more like a canned pep talk he might give to his employees. With a grateful "Amen," she loaded her plate with a slice of chicken breast, a pile of her mom's vegetable casserole, and two homemade biscuits.

By the end of the meal, Julie had to loosen her belt. In the past two weeks, she'd put on five pounds, though it was not altogether a bad thing for someone who weighed far less than her height demanded. Now that her appetite had returned, she made a mental note to be careful not to overdo the eating from now on. Otherwise, she'd soon be shopping for a new wardrobe. It was one more miraculous change that had come about since her trip to Patmos.

The rest of the visit went well. Conversations remained light, and after dinner, the women gathered in the kitchen to do the dishes. It was as though nothing had changed for the Peters family. Julie washed, Rita dried, and Margie put the dishes away. The whole scenario resurrected a fleeting memory of a similar dishwashing event in Yanno's tiny kitchen. She released a sigh and wished she could relive such moments. They were like food to a starving refugee.

That afternoon, Julie packed her suitcase while Rita perched on the edge of the canopy bed, chattering away. After tearful goodbyes by the front curb, Julie gave a final wave and drove off.

During the ride back to Springfield, she made a mental plan of the next week. As soon as she got home, she'd need to begin a serious search for another writing job. The generous severance package Andy gave her would keep things going for a while, but she had to keep a roof over her head and put food on the table. The rest of the week held more obligations. First thing Monday morning, she'd have to call Doctor Balser's office for an appointment, and she'd have to make time for Lakisha and Mark.

She had to laugh at herself. She'd definitely inherited that organizational gene from her dad, but she hoped to temper it as much as possible. Maybe she was more like him than she wanted to admit. In any case, she didn't want to intimidate people the way he had.

The Fourth of July holiday was coming up. She'd promised to bring Mark home with her. A smile crossed her lips. She was going to introduce her family to her boyfriend. She wasn't alone anymore. She had someone who cared about her. And she cared about him.

She was about to turn on the radio, when her gaze strayed to her purse lying in the passenger seat. The corner of a white envelope protruded from a side pocket. Dina McAndrews' letter. Julie had grabbed it just as her mother was about to throw it away.

A tinge of bitterness resurfaced. Whatever could that woman say to her now? She pinched her lips together.

"I'll read it later," she said aloud. Then she shoved the envelope farther inside her purse, out of sight, and turned her attention to the open road.

36

A FRESH START

When Julie arrived home, the Sunday newspaper was lying on the mat in front of her door. Andy had promised to run her travel piece today. She fumbled with her keys, got the door open, and hurried inside. Then she slid the Daily Press out of its plastic sleeve and, holding her breath, she flipped to the *Travel* section.

The front centerpiece featured a color photo of Brother Agapios beneath the arches in the courtyard of the Monastery of St. John. A couple of smaller shots of the ruins in Ephesus bordered one side of the page. The text, along with Julie's byline, started beneath Brother Pio's photo. Turning to the jump page, Julie gasped in surprise. Her editor had given her story the entire page, from top to bottom, with no ads. Woven between several photos of Patmos and one of Galilee, the text ran down all five columns. Julie chewed on a hangnail and read through the story. Her editor had not cut a single word.

When she finished, she breathed deeply of this final labor of love. At least she wasn't going out a complete failure.

With her head still spinning, she unpacked her suitcase and separated her laundry for washing. Then she grabbed her cell phone and called Mark. His voice was upbeat, like he was thrilled to hear from her.

"How about dinner at seven?" he said. "I'll ask Greg and Lakisha to join us. You can tell us about your trip to Fairview. I'm in the middle of something right now, Julie, so I have to go, but I'll see ya later, okay? Oh, and by the way, nice story in today's paper."

Julie beamed with delight. He'd seen her article, and he wanted to know about her trip—more evidence that he truly cared about her.

With several hours to kill before Mark came for her, she got on her computer so she could conduct another search for a writing job. First, she checked her e-mails, surprised to find one from Andy.

"Julie, be sure and get a copy of Sunday's paper. You deserve kudos for your piece. Sorry we had to let you go. You know it had to do with budgeting and most valuable player at the time. This story proves you won't be idle for long. Don't forget, if we ever get to a place where we can open another slot, I hope you'll consider coming back. Meanwhile, I wish you well. Andy."

Another slice of bitterness left Julie's heart. In time, she might be able to look back at the whole scenario and find peace with it. She kept telling herself God may have other plans. He'd simply shut a door and opened a window, as Brother Pio had said. For now, she sent off a quick *"Thank You"* to Andy and began cruising the internet in search of a job.

Minutes passed. She came up with one disappointment after another. There was a sports writing job in an adjoining county. "Not my forte," she said, wrinkling her nose.

Several opportunities popped up in other states, but Julie didn't want to move away, not with Mark back in her life again. And then there was Lakisha. Her best friend would never stand for her moving.

Last of all, the Fairview Sun had put out a call for a features reporter, an ideal position for her, except... "There's no way I'm moving back home," she moaned.

Other openings involved grant writing, advertorials, and medical brochures, areas that hadn't interested her in the past and didn't now. No matter how long it took, Julie had to find another reporting job. She'd trained as a reporter, and she enjoyed the work. She couldn't imagine herself doing anything else.

After two hours of disappointing rabbit trails, she turned off her computer and headed to the bathroom for a soak in the tub. Feeling the need to gloat a bit, she took along her travel piece and a glass of iced tea. As she settled into the scented water, she breathed a long sigh, and reread her article. Mary Beth Simmons came to mind. How was that Southern bimbo getting along now that Julie was out of the picture?

A slight prick of guilt stabbed her heart. Mary Beth was a Christian, wasn't she? Now that Julie had returned to her faith, didn't that make them sisters—of a sort? Shouldn't she have only kind thoughts of someone who believed as she did? She frowned at the foaming water and tossed the newspaper on the floor. Then she lay her head back and closed her eyes. A prayer rose from deep inside her. *Please God, help me to live out my faith as I should, without animosity or prideful thoughts. Cleanse me from the bad habits I picked up over the last few years, and guide me into a more righteous walk with you.*

She remained there for a few more minutes, cleansing her mind along with her body. Then, rising from her bath, Julie turned her thoughts to the evening's dinner. She selected an aqua dress with cap sleeves and a pale yellow shawl. Using a blow dryer and a round brush, she styled her hair in front of a mirror, allowing her crimson waves to cascade to her shoulders. Then she applied a tinge of color to her cheeks.

Her heart pounded with anticipation. She hadn't been on

a real date in a long time. And she'd be with Mark. What if the magic of Patmos had worn off? What if he'd merely been caught up in the enchantment of an exotic island? He could have gotten back to his current lifestyle by now, involved in his college classes, maybe even resuming other relationships.

Her doubts were put to rest when Mark arrived punctually at seven. His eyes lit up and he blurted out an admiring, "Wow! You look great!"

He still had that same lovesick look he'd had on the hillside in Patmos. He hadn't faltered back then, and he wasn't trying to mask his feelings now. Julie smiled and grabbed her shawl.

They drove to People's Place, a popular eatery on the edge of town. Greg and Lakisha met them at the door. The restaurant was known for its grilled steaks and parmesan crusted tilapia. The guys went for the steaks, and Lakisha and Julie ordered the fish. Side dishes dotted the family style table setting. Bowls of boiled potatoes, garlic-buttered broccoli, and baked cinnamon-topped apples were positioned within reach of the four of them. They also shared a huge salad with house dressing and a basket of cheddar biscuits.

Their conversation immediately turned to Julie's trip home. She shared most, but not all, of the details, and gave them enough information so they'd know she'd accomplished much of what she had set out to do. She told them she'd communicated with her parents and had made an honest effort to forgive them.

Seeing her sister Rita had made the trip even more worthwhile. She talked about the town and all the changes that had occurred during her absence. She chose not to mention Dina McAndrews' note. It lay unopened on her dresser, and it was going to stay there until she was good and ready.

"So, what's next, Julie?" Greg asked. "Have you started a job search, yet?" He shoved a piece of steak in his mouth, but didn't take his eyes off her.

"I scanned the internet, but I didn't find anything of interest."

"Why not try something else?" Greg suggested. "Newspapers are going out of business anyway. People can get the news online these days. Why not look into writing for a publication's website instead? Or you could write copy for a TV news show. You have enough experience."

"What? Like for Jason Redding?" Julie crinkled her nose. "I wouldn't dream of going anywhere near that egomaniac." She dug her fork into the filet of fish, as if she wanted to make sure it was dead. She caught the others gaping at her, and she let out a nervous laugh. "It's not the same, Greg," she said, her voice more controlled. "Besides, I'm not sure small town newspapers are dead. Folks still like to read about their neighbors as they drink their morning coffee. You'd be surprised how many people still like to step out their front door in the morning and pick up their newspaper off the stoop. It's a difficult habit to break, especially for those in their senior years. They also look forward to the sales ads and the coupons."

She slid the piece of fish into her mouth.

"I'm with Julie," Lakisha said, giving her an encouraging wink. "Whenever I place a real estate ad in the online Multi-List catalogue, I also make sure I send one to the Daily Press. Many times, people come to my viewings with the newspaper ad in their hand."

Julie sent her friend an appreciative smile.

"How would you feel about getting into real estate?"

Julie frowned at her friend. "No thanks. I've seen how people run you ragged, my friend, calling at all hours of the day and night and not showing up for appointments. Besides, I love to write. It's like food to me."

Lakisha nodded and went back to her meal.

Julie glanced at Mark and laughed to herself. He was diving into his steak like a caveman who'd slain his first antelope. She had to wonder if she could still love him when he became fat and sloppy.

Love? The word surprised her, but her feelings toward Mark *had* grown. Or, maybe they'd been there all along, and she'd only now unearthed them.

Her attention strayed to Lakisha and Greg. They were reaching out with their forks and were sampling each other's entree. Greg whispered something in Lakisha's ear and she giggled. With a twinge of envy, Julie looked again at Mark. Her heart leaped, and she regretted having wasted so much time away from him.

That night, she lay in bed, staring at the ceiling and wondering what the next chapter of her life might be like. She had no job and no prospects. She had a boyfriend, but no promises. Could she really put the past behind her and move on?

She sure could use another word of advice from that kind old sage in Patmos.

She rolled to the left side of her bed, reached inside the top drawer of the end table and withdrew the tiny plastic bag that contained Yanno's hair clippings. She raised it above her head. From outside her window a beam from a streetlight caught the filaments and turned them to strands of silver. Smiling, she kissed the bag and slid it under her pillow, surprised at the comfort it gave her. Yanno may have been thousands of miles away, but he was closer than she'd ever imagined he could be.

37

MARK

Mark wasn't about to settle for a mere friendship with Julie—not this time. He couldn't risk losing her again. Her recent transformation amazed him. She had a fresh lightness in her step, a ready smile, and a sparkle in her eyes that hadn't been there before.

She'd even opened up to him about her first session with Doctor Balser. He'd sat in the waiting room, ready to run to her rescue if needed. Though he'd felt a twinge of jealousy when Julie first mentioned meeting the counselor on the plane, he'd come to appreciate and respect the man. Perhaps their meeting wasn't a coincidence. From his youth, Mark had believed that God sometimes orchestrated events for an even greater purpose. Maybe this was one of those times.

Best of all, he and Julie quickly settled into a trusting relationship. They got together nearly every evening after he left work, either went out to dinner, or she cooked up something in her condo.

It was that sort of evening when a most hilarious thing happened. While Julie was in the kitchen putting together a salad, Mark turned on the TV, dropped onto her sofa, and started flipping through channels. The aroma of broiled steaks stirred his stomach. Then Julie came into the living room and handed him a Coke.

"Dinner will be ready in ten minutes," she said. "Let's watch the six o'clock news and see what good ol' Jason Redding is up to."

Mark smirked. "Okay, but don't let it spoil your appetite."

He cued in the news channel and pulled her onto the sofa beside him. With one arm wrapped around Julie's shoulders, he made an honest effort to keep his attention on the TV, but having her that close made it difficult to concentrate on something as mundane as the news, especially with Jason Redding and his co-anchor Marcia Brooks going through their usual nightly banter. It was common knowledge that the two had been vying for the same top position on their network, so Mark expected more of the same old flack.

"Those two pit bulls have been at each other's throats for almost a year," Mark said.

Julie nodded. "Their bosses probably want to keep the battle going. Their silly antics keep the ratings up." She chuckled. "*Something* has to. They rarely give an honest news report."

Mark wasn't surprised to hear an air of bitterness in Julie's voice. Here she was, out of a job because she'd done something sacrificial, and that TV idiot kept his career intact by using underhanded methods.

"Oh my goodness. What is he doing?" Julie pointed at the screen.

Mark heard the word "Patmos," and a slide show immediately appeared behind Jason. Images of the island included a view of the dock area, various portions of the monastery, the entry of the Cave of the Apocalypse, and, to Mark's shock, the line of people on the walk in front of Yanno's cottage.

He released Julie and sat up straight. She leaned toward the screen, her mouth open, her eyes wide. Mark patted her arm. "Don't worry," he said, though a twinge of discomfort came over him.

Then Julie sprang to her feet. "Look!"

Jason was holding a sparkling silver chalice. Julie let out a shriek.

Mark stood up beside her. "Yanno's favorite cup! Jason really did steal it."

Mark had missed part of what Jason was saying. The idiot kept right on yammering away. " ... old guy *has* to be the one everyone's been talking about," he said, his voice strained, like one of those castrato characters in a Roman choir.

"Just look at this artifact." Jason lifted the cup higher, and the overhead lights glinted off its rim. "Check out this crack. I tested it under running water. It doesn't leak. Why, this cup has to be at least 2,000 years old. The Smithsonian will probably pay millions for this thing."

Marcia eyed the cup with skepticism. Frowning, she reached out to take it, but Jason quickly pulled it back. "Oh no. This thing is too precious to have a lot of people messing with it. You're gonna have to wait your turn, Marcia. I need to first get it to the authorities."

"Come on, Jason," Marcia coaxed. She grabbed the cup and leaned away from him, so he couldn't take it back. "Let me see..." she said, her tone chiding.

With an air of surrender, Jason puffed out a heavy breath, sat back, and crossed his arms. He looked like a pouty-faced kid who'd been told he couldn't have an ice cream cone.

"This is not good," Mark said. "That creep is going to expose Yanno, and there's no way we can stop him."

Julie plunked back down on the sofa. "If my boss is watching this—and he *never* misses the evening news—I'll be a gonner." She turned to face Mark. "The network could sue me for squashing such a big story. I'll be blackballed throughout the newspaper industry. No one will hire me after this."

Mark settled beside her. Jason Redding was about to break one of the biggest stories of his career, and it spelled disaster for Julie. She'd already lost her job. Now she stood to lose her reputation as well.

"Let's watch," he said, and mouthed a silent prayer.

Marcia was holding the cup at eye level. She turned it one way and then the other beneath the studio lights. A scintillation emanated from its sides. Anyone would presume it was an antique treasure. She ran a finger along the crack, then she turned it over and examined the bottom. A chuckle started in Marcia's throat. The chuckle grew into a ripple of laughter, which then evolved into a full belly-laugh. With the cup in one hand, Marcia continued chortling and holding her side with the other hand.

"What's the matter with you?" Jason snarled. He unfolded his arms and sat up straight. Scowling, he grabbed the cup from Marcia's grip.

She willingly released it, now free to pull a tissue from the box on her desk. She wiped tears of laughter from her eyes and from her cheeks. "Jason," she said, giggling and gasping for air. "Look at the bottom of the cup. Just look."

Jason slowly turned it over. His eyes grew wide and his face contorted in shock.

Still giggling, Marcia choked out the words. "It says, *Made in China.*" Then, she fell apart again.

Jason made a vain attempt to regain his composure. Then, the screen went black. Seconds later, a toothpaste jingle came on. Mark and Julie stared into each other's eyes for a moment, then they collapsed in hysterics.

"No wonder Yanno wasn't concerned about that cup," Mark sputtered. "It's worthless."

Julie caught her breath. "What a relief. I thought this was the end. And maybe it is—for Jason Redding."

They both dropped into another run of hysterics. Then, exhausted, Julie wiped away tears of laughter.

"Come on," she said, rising. "Turn off that idiot box and let's have supper."

Mark followed Julie into the kitchen and helped her get the food on the table. He settled before his plate, spoke a heartfelt message of thanks, then dug in. Even as he savored each bite of his steak, he occasionally locked eyes with Julie. An unspoken joke passed between them and they burst out laughing all over again. Jason Redding's public fiasco kept them entertained through the rest of the meal.

Julie used her napkin to mop away tears generated by their laughter. Mark did the same. His heart throbbed with love for the woman across the table from him. Unlike Katie or any of the other women he had casually dated, Julie shared the secrets of his heart. They could speak to each other with a look, a smile, a wink of the eye.

By the end of the meal, their laughter had died down. Julie set aside her fork and stared at Mark, her expression serious.

"What's the matter?" he asked, and he gave her his full attention.

An air of discomfort showed in her face.

"Come on," he pressed. "You can tell me anything. Don't you know that yet?"

She took a breath, and, with tears in her eyes, she began to speak.

"I've been struggling over some things Yanno told me I needed to do. He said I wouldn't have peace until I forgive Ben McAndrews of his horrible crime."

"That's right, Julie. But, I think you already knew that."

She gave a weak nod. "Maybe. I know he can't hurt me anymore. He's in jail and he's paying for his crimes. But, I can't shake the memory of that horrible day. That man ruined my life. And what about those other girls—especially the 13-year-old? That could have been my sister, Rita."

Mark eyed her with compassion, but he said nothing.

"The man was sick. I should be able to forgive him, shouldn't I?" Julie continued. "Doctor Balser said we should forgive others, as Christ forgave us. But whenever I begin to make progress in that direction, the memories get hold of me like a riptide on the ocean. It's like struggling toward the shore and then being pulled back out to sea."

Mark reached across the table and took her hands in his. "It's going to take time, Julie. You've carried this burden for six years. It's not gonna disappear overnight."

"There's more," she said, slipping her hands out of his grasp. "There's McAndrews' wife—Dina. I used to like that woman. But she said those awful things to me, and she turned the women of the church against me." Julie's voice turned sarcastic. "That woman couldn't believe her husband would do such a horrible thing. Not her Ben."

Mark eyed her with compassion. "What's it gonna take, Julie? You're gonna have to deal with this at some point."

"I don't know. She wrote me a letter. It's sitting on my dresser—unopened."

"Maybe it's time you read it." Mark gazed into her sad eyes. He wanted to gather her in his arms and protect her from all the pain, but there was more coming, and she was going to have to face it head-on.

"I know it's difficult," he said. "I experienced a similar

struggle when my mother died. I couldn't deal with it. I wanted to run away from the truth. She'd been ill for such a long time. She suffered, and she never got well. I wanted to lash out at everybody. The doctors who couldn't heal her. My father who didn't protect her like he should have. Even our minister who said her eulogy at the funeral. He said she was in a better place. What did he think *that* would mean to a 12-year-old? It took me a long time to forgive those people. And myself."

Julie's eyes had pooled with tears. "Yourself?" she said, as if shocked by the confession.

Mark nodded. "I was at school when she died. She was gone from my life forever, and she never said goodbye. She merely left me a note. My father gave it to me after her funeral. I'm ashamed to say, I put it in a drawer and I didn't read it until six months later. I wish I had read it right away. It could have saved me months of grief."

"That's sad, Mark. But this is different. You loved your mother. I—well, I guess I *hate* Dina McAndrews. She couldn't possibly say anything to me that would change how I feel about her."

"Not so different," Mark said, shaking his head. "It's not about the women who wrote to us as much as it is about what's inside the envelope. My mother's note brought healing. Maybe Dina's letter will do that for you."

Julie stared at him for several seconds, like she was pondering what to do. He didn't want to let the moment pass without giving her another word of encouragement.

"Why don't you read it now? While I'm here to give you moral support."

He raised his eyebrows. "It could be therapeutic."

"Or, it could destroy me," she said, frowning.

"You'll never know until you open that envelope. I'm here, Julie. You don't have to go through this alone." He leaned across the table toward her. "Do you want *me* to read it?"

Julie's shoulders sagged in surrender. Slowly, she rose from the table and disappeared inside her bedroom. She returned with the envelope in her hand and stood there, staring at it.

"C'mon," Mark urged. "Either open that thing or put it back on your dresser until you're ready."

He figured she had to be at least a little curious about Dina's message. He was about to utter another word of support, when Julie slid a fingernail under the flap and opened the envelope. She pulled out a folded page of light blue note paper.

She pressed the note in his hand. "Read it," she said. "Out loud."

Mark unfolded the note. Julie settled into her chair, her eyebrows arched in anticipation. He sent her a sympathetic smile, and then he began to read.

"My dearest Julie—"

Julie nearly lurched out of her seat. "*What?* My *dearest* Julie?"

Mark raised a hand to quiet her. "Patience, my dear. Just listen."

Julie settled down, but the scowl remained on her face.

Mark breathed a sigh, and continued to read.

"Words cannot express the sorrow I experienced when I learned the truth about my husband. For several months after his trial, I struggled with shame that my Ben had done that awful thing to you."

Julie leaped to her feet and began to pace. "Awful thing? *Awful thing?* Why doesn't she call it what it was? Her husband attacked me!"

Mark held his tongue. He needed to give Julie space. Needed to let her vent, if it would help.

She came up in front of him, her arms crossed, her lips pinched together, her eyes glaring at the note in his hand. Mark waited for the moment of discomfort to pass.

"She goes on to say..." He glanced at the note, then at Julie, as though seeking her approval to go on. She didn't budge.

Raising the note, Mark continued. "*I regret having treated you so terribly. You must have felt so alone. In your innocence, you needed someone to believe in you and support you, but no one did. I, least of all. It was wrong of me to lash out at you. While I was trying to be a dutiful wife and supportive of my husband, I was blind to the truth. I only hope you'll forgive me.*"

Mark looked up at Julie, expecting a response. When none came, he went on.

"*I have one more request of you, Julie, that you also find it in your heart to forgive my husband.*" Before Julie could lash out, Mark raised his hand to calm her. Then, he read on.

Please understand, Julie, Ben is a sick man. His behavior was not normal. Now, he's suffering the consequences for his actions. Prison is not an easy place for someone who's been convicted of such a crime. The other prisoners don't take kindly to a man who abuses a little girl, or in Ben's case, several girls. Believe me when I say he is a broken man."

Here, the words were smudged, as though someone's tears had fallen on the page. Mark squinted, skipped over them, and went on reading.

"*My dear Julie, my own sin against you troubles me every day of my life. I will never have peace until I hear you say you forgive me. This may not be something you can do right now. But if you ever come to a place where you can sincerely tell me you have forgiven me, I will welcome you with open arms.*

Trust me, Julie, the healing will be yours as much as mine. Do this one act of kindness, and you will free both of us from a lifetime of regrets.

Sincerely,

Dina McAndrews"

When Mark looked up again, Julie had tears running down her face. She picked up her napkin and dabbed the moisture from her cheeks.

He ventured to ask the question that had been resting on the tip of his tongue. "What do you think, Julie?"

"What do I think?" she said between sobs. She looked into his eyes, her own eyes filling with tears again. "I think I'll be going home for July Fourth weekend, and while I'm there, I'll need to stop and see Dina McAndrews."

Mark gave her an encouraging nod.

Julie breathed a long jagged sigh. "What do you think Yanno would say about all this?"

Mark stroked his chin and pondered an answer for a second, then he brightened. "I think Yanno would remind us that it's easy to love our friends and those who are kind to us, but the real test comes when we're challenged to love those who have hurt us. That kind of love can't happen without God's help."

She frowned, as though deep in thought. Then, her lips parted in a weak smile.

"I could never see Ben McAndrews again and say I love him, but I believe I can allow God to love him and not be bitter about it. And I can try to understand why Dina behaved as she did. I can visit her and maybe *try* to forgive her."

"Then go see her," Mark said. "It's as simple as that."

"Will you go with me? For moral support?"

"Of course, I will." He rose from his chair and gathered her into his arms, certain that his heart had just doubled in size. This independent, stubborn woman had just told him he was her protector, her rock of support, her knight on a white horse. It couldn't get much better than that.

38

RELEASING THE CHAINS

Friday, July 3rd, rolled around faster than Julie wanted it to. She still needed time to think over her decision to visit Dina McAndrews. She'd read Dina's letter multiple times until she almost had it memorized.

Mark had agreed to leave work early, so they could get on the road while it was still daylight. She picked him up at his apartment at three o'clock. She expected the roads to be packed with travelers. Tomorrow was Independence Day, and it was a Saturday to boot.

Julie's parents had planned a relaxing day at the lake with a picnic and fireworks. Rita was planning to come home, too.

Mark was going to meet her family. A few jitters ran through her, but she was not as nervous as she was about the prospect of facing Dina McAndrews again. How idiotic. Julie had done nothing wrong, yet she was afraid the meeting might not go well. She didn't want a confrontation to spoil the weekend for her and Mark.

They arrived in Fairview as the last rays of sunshine sent a streak of red across the sky. Julie pulled up in front of her parents' house. A final hint of gold caressed the front porch railing and set aglow the flowering shrubs below it. An American flag hung from a wall brace, and the family's cat lay curled up on the front porch swing.

"How charming," Mark said. "It looks like something Norman Rockwell would have painted."

Julie looked at him out of the corner of her eye and smiled. "Come on, Mr. Nostalgia," she said with a patronizing tone. "Let's go."

Mark grabbed their bags and followed Julie up the porch steps. They entered the house to the aroma of a tangy sauce that stirred Julie's appetite. As could be expected, the family was already seated around the dining room table. Rita quickly introduced her boyfriend, Danny Blakenship, a Joe-college type with spiked black hair, wire-rimmed glasses, and an athletic build.

Julie's father rose from his chair and greeted Mark with a warm handshake. "Thanks for bringing our little girl home for the holiday," he said, and Julie cringed with embarrassment. Will that man ever treat her like an adult?

Her mom was equally overbearing. Margie rushed around the side of the table, gave Julie a hug and held onto her hand, as she gushed over her. "So good to have you home again, dear. We have a wonderful weekend planned."

Julie smiled into her mother's face. She didn't want to spoil Margie's dream of having her family together and everybody getting along.

"Well, come on and sit down," Margie said, releasing her grip on Julie. "We've already started to eat."

Margie lifted the lid off a tureen in the center of the table and the aroma of herb-flavored beef wafted into the air. Spread across the table were bowls of honeyed sweet potatoes, buttered green beans, homemade rolls, and fresh salad.

Julie glanced at Mark. Was his mouth watering, or was it her imagination?

During dinner, casual chatter erupted around the table. Julie's father expressed a genuine interest in Mark's career.

And when the subject turned to sports, the two young men hit it off with a shared affinity for the Atlanta Braves.

For the weekend stay, the guys were relegated to Julie's old bedroom. She laughed internally at the image of two athletic guys huddled together in a canopy bed.

As for Julie, she would bunk with Rita, and that was okay with her. It might be her only opportunity to have a private chat with her sister.

They no sooner settled under the covers when Rita opened the conversation with a topic Julie had been avoiding till now.

"So you're gonna see Dina McAndrews tomorrow?"

"Yeah," Julie groaned. "I'm not looking forward to it, but I have to do it."

"I understand. It's like facing your greatest fear."

"Well, maybe not my *greatest* fear, but certainly one of them." Julie released a sigh. "Her letter broke my heart. I experienced the worst trauma of my life, but I ended up caring about someone else."

"So, you've forgiven them?"

"Not *them*. Only Dina. It's going to take me a long time to forgive that horrible husband of hers. Maybe never."

"And—yourself?" Rita said with a slight hesitation. "Have you forgiven yourself?"

Julie was forever amazed at her little sister's insight. She sighed with resignation. "You're right, Rita. I ruined my own life. I was a dumb teenager. I was rebellious, impulsive, and incredibly stupid."

"Okay, you've just described a couple million other teenagers." Rita's voice carried a touch of sarcasm.

"Not you though," Julie said, her tone softening. "You were... an angel."

Rita sat upright. "What? Don't kid yourself, Julie. What happened to you could have happened to me or to anyone else. And remember, it *did* happen to those other girls." She flopped back on her pillow.

Julie chuckled. "But, *you* never did the things I did. You didn't sneak out of the house with short-shorts under your skirt. You didn't hang out with the fast crowd. I'll bet you never even smoked *pot*."

Rita laughed aloud.

"Shh," Julie cautioned her. "Someone might hear us."

Rita toned her laugh to a giggle. "I didn't have the chance to act out. By the time I got into high school, Mom and Dad had put the clamps on me. After what happened to you, they became my personal wardens. I couldn't make a move without their permission."

Julie's heart softened with love for her little sister. Tears came to her eyes. Because of her own stubbornness, she'd missed a lifetime of joy by not being there to watch Rita grow up.

"You must have had a tough time of it," Julie said.

"Not really. I saw how everyone treated you and how you struggled to keep going. I was afraid to test Dad's boundaries, afraid the same thing might happen to *me*."

"So, one good thing came out of it," Julie said, her voice soft. "My kid sister was safe."

They settled into a moment of silence. Julie stared at the ceiling. Dots of light from the window created a constellation of stars above her head.

"What's Mark like?" Rita said out of the blue, and Julie felt her heart skip.

"He's fabulous. He's been so patient with me, and so kind.

I think I'm falling in love with him." The admission struck her to the core. Until that moment she hadn't expressed those feelings aloud. "What about you and Danny?" she quickly added.

"Danny's great. He's willing to wait until I finish college and get a nursing job before we talk about marriage."

"Marriage? Wow. I'm happy for you, little sister."

Rita sighed. "I'm so thrilled we can spend the Fourth of July with our boyfriends here and the whole family together."

"Yeah. Once I get through that visit with Dina McAndrews tomorrow morning, I finally might be able to relax."

"Hang onto her note, Julie. You said it had a positive effect on you."

"It did, but seeing her in person is going to be a whole different experience."

As Julie had requested, Mark went with her to the McAndrews home the following morning.

Dina greeted them at the door. Julie tried to hide her shock. The years had not been kind to the woman. Her hair was streaked with gray, and her usual rosy color had been drained from her face. Worry lines etched across her forehead and around her mouth, and her cheeks had a sunken, gaunt appearance. She resembled one of those *Walking Dead* people—half asleep, half awake—yet, as she looked at Julie, a flicker of life came to her eyes.

"Won't you come in?" Dina said, her voice weak. She guided them into her living room and gestured for them to take the sofa, while she walked to a high-backed chair in the corner. She didn't sit all the way back, comfortably, like most people do when they receive visitors, but she perched on the edge of the seat as though ready to run, if needed. In her hand was a lace-trimmed handkerchief, which she twisted and scrunched into a knot.

They sat in awkward silence., then Dina started to rise. "Would you like something to drink? A Coke? Some water?"

"No, thanks," Julie said before Mark could respond. "We came to talk, Mrs. McAndrews, that's all."

The older woman settled back on the edge of her chair. Her back was rigid. Only her fingers moved as they mauled the handkerchief in her hand. Tears came to Dina's eyes. The defeated woman bore no resemblance to the angry shrew who had hurled accusations at Julie on the church steps, six years ago. This woman had suffered much.

On an unexpected impulse, Julie got up and walked over to Dina. She placed a hand on the woman's shoulder, bent close, and kissed her on the cheek.

"You don't have to say a word, Mrs. McAndrews. You said it all in your letter to me. I came by today to tell you one thing. I forgive you. Nothing more needs to be said."

By uttering those compassionate words, Julie felt a rush of relief flow through her, like she, herself, had been freed from guilt and shame. She was in control of her emotions again. The truth was, in freeing Dina McAndrews, she'd also released herself from a prison of her own making.

Dina's red-lined eyes filled with more tears. She began to sob. "I—I don't know what to say." With her wrinkled handkerchief, she mopped rivers of pain from her cheeks.

Julie knelt to the floor. "Your reaction, back then, was understandable. You had to support your husband. Any woman might have done the same."

"But—but, those terrible things I said to you—"

"Forgiven." Julie said.

"The gossip I promoted."

"Forgiven."

Dina shook her head. "The years of grief I gave you."

"Forgiven," Julie said, her voice firm. "I've forgiven you, Dina. For *all* of it. And I'm certain God has too."

Julie glanced at Mark, still seated on the sofa. He gave her an encouraging nod, and she turned her attention back to Dina.

"My sister told me you'd stopped going to church, Mrs. McAndrews. You should go back. It's where you need to be. Your friends will welcome you. My mother will welcome you."

"I—I don't know. It's been so long. After Ben went to prison, I couldn't face those people again. Some of the members called on me, but I felt so ashamed."

Again Julie responded to a surprising impulse. "Why don't you come to church with us? Tomorrow morning."

Julie was stunned at her own behavior. She hadn't come to the McAndrews house with the intention of inviting that woman to church. Yet, in this moment, it seemed like the right thing to do.

"Really? You would do that for me?" Dina said. She stopped twisting the handkerchief and searched Julie's eyes.

"Of course."

Dina doubled over and put her face in her hands.

"I *want* you to come with us," Julie said. She rubbed Dina's back.

Once again, Yanno's face came to Julie's mind, along with his command to *love your enemies.*

The idea was more realistic here, in Dina's living room, than it had been when the old man first spoke those words. Julie took Dina's hand and lifted her to her feet. They embraced in the quiet of the living room, and the chains that had kept Julie bound for so long began to fall away as she expressed a sincere compassion for another human being.

39

FOURTH OF JULY

Mark was elated by the way Julie handled her meeting with Dina McAndrews. She had proven to be the right girl for him. Not that he was testing her, because from the beginning he knew in his heart that he could love no other. Now that the stress was gone, he was ready for an evening of relaxation at her family's Fourth of July celebration.

It was late afternoon when they arrived at the lakeside picnic area. They parked the two cars side-by-side and began to unload the trunks. Each member of their party grabbed what they could handle—blankets, coolers, bags of food, beach toys, folding chairs—and set up camp on a grassy knoll not far from the beach.

While Julie's dad got the grill going and her mother spread a plastic cloth on a picnic table and began laying out supplies, Mark and Danny pulled off their T-shirts and started a game of Frisbee. The two girls, clothed in their swimsuits, quickly joined them, giggling and flinging the Frisbee in random directions. An amazing peace washed over Mark.

He'd spent so much time at work lately, he hadn't taken time to play. He breathed in the salty air and relished the caress of the setting sun on his back. Somehow, he managed to leap, dodge, and chase the Frisbee, until he wore himself out and had to take a break.

He dropped onto a blanket and propped himself up on one elbow. Danny and the girls headed into the surf. Mark gazed after Julie frolicking with her sister. The love of his life looked like a little girl out there. Her ponytail bobbed like a dancing flame and her bubbly laughter carried toward him on a breeze from the lake. At last, Julie had forgotten her troubles and was having fun.

On an impulse, Mark leaped to his feet and rushed into the surf between the two sisters. He stomped his feet and sent a spray against Julie. She shrieked, spun toward him, and scooped water into his face. He reached out to grab her arm, but she evaded him and ran off, squealing and laughing. With three long strides, he reached her and pulled her down into the waist-high water. Then, he slid his arm underneath her and held her head above the surf. For a moment in time, they both froze. Neither spoke. Julie stared into his eyes and grinned. Mark thought his heart was about to jump right out of his chest.

Julie's dad broke the spell by calling out that it was time to eat. Julie slipped free of Mark's grasp and ran toward the shore. His heart still pounding, he went after her. When he reached the picnic table, his appetite took over. The romantic interlude faded from his mind as he consumed two hot dogs, a healthy serving of potato salad, and a huge slice of watermelon.

By the time the meal ended, the sun was low on the horizon. The final rays cast long shadows on the beach. Julie and her sister spread another blanket on the sand for Rita and Danny. Bill and Margie set up two folding chairs facing a dock in the middle of the lake, where firefighters had set up their pyrotechnics.

When darkness settled on the beach, the fire crew ignited their rockets, ground level spinners, sparklers, and fountains.

Mark stared at Julie. A blast of color lit up her face. Patriotic music poured from loudspeakers, and people all around them uttered the expected "Oohs" and "Aahs."

At one point, Mark snuck a peek at Julie's parents. Her dad had moved his chair close to his wife's and he'd wrapped his arm around her. Their intimacy created a different image than Julie had described to him.

Then Mark caught Danny planting a kiss on Rita's lips. He glanced back at Julie's parents. They were in their own world, their faces pointed to the sky.

Mark turned his attention to Julie, surprised to see she had raised her chin and was gazing into his face. Her soft green eyes conveyed a message of acceptance. As Mark leaned toward her, she trembled against his arm. Then she shut her eyes. He kissed her gently. She responded. Then, he gathered her in his arms and held her close to his chest.

Please, God. Let her stay with me. Forever.

Sunday morning, when Julie walked into the church with Dina McAndrews on her arm, amazed whispers echoed off the plaster walls and stained-glass windows. Dina hesitated in the doorway. Julie gripped the woman's elbow and guided her to a pew about half-way down where the other members of her family were already seated, along with Danny and Mark.

This time, Julie held up her head and sang the hymns with renewed passion. She was surprised at how the words of praise came flooding back from her past. Then Pastor Harmon took the pulpit and gave a sermon about life's twists and turns. He emphasized that God never leaves or forsakes those who belong to him. Ironically, that was the question that had plagued Julie for years, *Where was God when I needed him most?* Because of Yanno and Mark and all the twists and turns in her own life over the last few weeks, she now had the answer. *God had been there all along.*

Pastor Harmon began with a reading from the book of Hebrews. *"... for he hath said, I will never leave thee, nor forsake thee. So that we may boldly say, The Lord is my helper, and I will not fear what man shall do unto me."*

Was she wrong, or did the minister keep looking at her when he mentioned the theme of his sermon, *Why do bad things happen to good people?*

"Entire books have been written on the subject," Pastor Harmon said. "Yet, no one has ever come up with a satisfactory answer to that question. I think of Joseph who went to jail for something he didn't do. I think of Moses who led the Israelites through the wilderness for 40 years, then he himself couldn't enter the Promised Land.

"I think of King David, a tremendous soldier and a man after God's own heart. Yet, he had to entrust building the Temple to his son, Solomon. And I think of the apostles who walked with Jesus. They suffered horrible punishments and died as martyrs."

Mark leaned toward Julie. "All except John, that is," he whispered.

She chuckled softly.

Pastor Harmon continued. "On this Independence Day weekend, I can't help but think of the servicemen and servicewomen who risk their lives to make America free, particularly those who are even now serving in dangerous situations throughout the world. Their sacrifice will always be appreciated.

"And," the preacher concluded, "most of all, I think of our Lord Jesus Christ, the King of the universe who came down to earth and lived a humble existence, only to suffer persecution and then die on a cross. And for what? So we can have eternal life. The perfect One dying for the imperfect. Now, I ask you people, does *that* seem fair?"

Pastor Harmon paused and swept his eyes over the congregation from one side of the sanctuary to the other. His gaze landed on Julie.

"No one will ever know why bad things happen to good people," he said. "That is, not until we're in the arms of our loving Savior. But, we don't have to wait for heaven to get to that comforting place."

Another pause, and he hit them with the climax of his message.

"We can go to our Savior right now, because he has spread his arms..." The old preacher extended his hands to either side of him. "Like this," he said with finality.

Though she tried to keep her emotions in check, Julie couldn't stop the flow of tears that surfaced unexpectedly. She wondered if Pastor Harmon suspected how much his message meant to her. She let out a muffled sob. Dina also was weeping quietly.

Without saying a word, Dina and Mark each grabbed one of Julie's hands. She basked in the comfort of Christian love. God had worked in her life in an amazing way. He hadn't struck her with a lightning bolt, hadn't forced her to accept him, hadn't chained her to the Bible. Instead, he had revealed himself to her a little at a time, through wonderful people—Yanno, Mark, and now Dina.

The three remained locked together when the concluding

hymn began to play. When the pastor gave the altar call, Julie and Dina slipped out of the pew and headed for the front of the church together.

That afternoon, Julie handed Mark the keys to her car.

"You drive," she said, then she put her seat back, shut her eyes, and smiled with contentment.

"What's so funny?" Mark asked.

Julie kept her eyes closed, and kept smiling. "Nothing."

"Sure. You and Rita probably stayed up half the night talking about me and Danny."

"You'll never know," Julie said with a giggle.

Mark started the car and cued in a music station on the radio. They drove without speaking for a while. Julie mulled over many of the events of the last couple of weeks, including the pastor's sermon that morning. Yanno would be pleased.

She opened her eyes and sat upright. "Have you stayed in touch with Yanno?"

Mark nodded. "We emailed back-and-forth a couple of times after we left Patmos, but our correspondence has kind of tapered off. I assumed he was busy. I got involved in my project and, sorry, but I let the emails go for a while. But I'll contact him again soon."

"Did you tell him about our decision, that we won't publicize anything about him?"

"I did. He wrote a thank you message."

"That's nice."

"I told him you lost your job. He said he knew you'd make the right choice, and that you had, in a way, laid down your life for him."

Julie's eyes stung and a lump settled in her throat. "Anything else?" She choked on the words.

"The last time he wrote he was still ministering to the villagers. He said he was getting ready to take a short break—maybe a motor bike ride around the island."

Julie laughed and tears gushed out of her eyes. She reached for her purse and pulled out a wad of tissues.

"I'll never forget that wild ride on his Vespa," she said, as she blotted her face. "What an amazing guy."

"Yeah." Mark nodded. "You know, we should go back to Patmos some day and visit him."

"I'd love to. And the Petras—Damien and Sofia. I want to tell them about our decision and set their minds at ease. Maybe they won't resent us anymore."

"I imagine Yanno has already told them."

"So, everything has worked out for the best," Julie said with a sigh. "Yanno and his people are safe. But, I still don't have a job."

Mark patted her hand. "It'll work out for you too, Julie. You have to believe that God has a better plan."

She turned to look out her window, gazed past the branches of trees that lined the highway, past the rooftops, past the parting of the clouds above.

"Right, God has a better plan," she said with conviction. "Even for me."

When Julie arrived home, she found out that God *did* have a better plan for her. After unpacking her things, she went to her computer, checked her emails and found a correspondence from a Mr. Ian Fairchild, editor of *Great Destinations*.

Julie was familiar with the elite San Diego-based travel magazine.

Ms. Peters, the message began. *I was fascinated by an online version of your recent travel piece, and I ordered a hard copy of the newspaper that ran it. Members of our editorial staff at 'Great Destinations' also were impressed. They agreed with me that we should offer you an opportunity to write for our magazine. I don't know what your situation is, but if you're not obligated to the newspaper, I wonder if you might consider doing a series of articles based on the same premise you used in your story, 'In Search of the Beloved, In the Footsteps of John the Apostle.' We at 'Great Destinations' want to have your subsequent articles start with the same words 'In Search of …' We also came up with a list of potential subjects, such as Ernest Hemingway, Pablo Picasso, Frederic Chopin, and several others.*

Julie pushed back a stray lock of hair. She moved to the edge of her seat and continued to read.

The job would require you to travel to various locations in the footsteps of these famous individuals, with a full expense account, of course. You would write about the historic significance of the sites, while also including travel tips for our readers. Let me know if this appeals to you and we'll discuss the contract, salary, and job benefits.

Sincerely, Ian Fairchild, editor.

Julie let out a shriek.

The email had several attachments, including the magazine's submission guidelines, a contract form, and a pay scale that caused Julie to gawk, speechless, at her computer screen. The proposed salary was three times her salary at the newspaper.

Julie sat back in her chair, unable to move for several minutes as she read and reread the offer.

Then a thought struck her. The magazine was published in San Diego, thousands of miles from home. She slumped forward and put her face in her hands. As much as she wanted this job, she couldn't relocate. Not now.

What about Mark? And Lakisha? And Rita? Julie feared she'd have to give up too much if she accepted the magazine's offer. She needed to address her concerns immediately.

Dear Mr. Fairchild, she wrote. *I'm excited about your offer, however, I was wondering if this position requires a move across the country? Do you have offices in other states where I might be able to fulfill these assignments without having to relocate?*

Though Julie feared her request might sound unprofessional, she *had* to ask. She hit *send.*

Fairchild's response came later that day.

Dear Ms. Peters, There is no need for you to relocate. The job requires some travel, but your base of operation can be your own home office. Several of our writers already work from their homes throughout the country. We only ask that you make an occasional trip to our office in San Diego, so we can discuss upcoming projects. I hope that satisfies your concerns. Sincerely, Ian.

Julie couldn't wait to tell Mark. She phoned him immediately.

"We need to go out and celebrate," Mark said. "How about the Red Lobster? I'll be getting off work soon. Pick you up at six-thirty?"

"Yes, that's fine," Julie replied. "See if Greg and Lakisha can meet us. Don't say anything. I want to see Lakisha's face when I tell her."

"Right," Mark said. "I'll call Greg right away."

Julie then called her sister and told her the good news. Rita shrieked with delight.

"Be sure and tell Mom and Dad," Julie said. She realized she had inadvertently dropped the formal word "Father" in favor of the more personal label, "Dad." Perhaps the healing of their relationship had already begun.

Julie hung up the phone and glanced at the kitchen clock. She had less than an hour to get ready. One thing was certain, Mark was never late for dinner.

Julie took a quick shower, then slipped into a pair of white Capri pants, a green silk blouse, and a pair of sandals. She swirled her hair into a bun, donned a pair of faux pearl earrings, all the while with thoughts of the new job swirling through her head. In a couple of weeks, she'll be boarding a plane bound for San Diego. Ian Fairchild had assured her a round-trip ticket and her hotel itinerary would be in the mail within a few days.

A job like this, Julie mused, *can open so many windows.*

Two days passed and Julie hadn't come down from the clouds yet. As Ian had promised, her airline ticket arrived with a complete itinerary of his planned meetings with her. She began to create her own list of famous people she could use as subjects for her travel stories. *Mother Teresa, Martin Luther King Jr., Anne Frank*, and a half-dozen more. The list would take her to such places as Calcutta, Amsterdam, Paris, London, and various parts of the United States. With each personality, Julie put together a brief synopsis that might help her editors approve of her ideas.

She spent all of Friday prepping for her trip to San Diego. Mark called with dinner plans. She turned him down and ignored the disappointment in his voice.

"I have too much to do to get ready for this trip. Call me early in the morning," she said. "I'd like you to help me with something."

At six o'clock the next morning, Mark knocked on Julie's door, rousing her from a peaceful sleep.

"How about breakfast?" he said. He held up a bag of donuts and a paper tray bearing two cups of coffee. "We can eat in the car."

Julie scrambled to get ready, threw on some clothes, and grabbed her coffee from him on her way out the door. "Take me to your secret hideaway," she said. "You know, that secluded place on the hill."

They drove for twenty minutes, then turned off on the dirt road that led to Mark's favorite hillside retreat. He pulled the car onto the grassy knoll.

Julie was out of the car ahead of Mark. She walked to the crest of the hill and looked down at the rippling landscape below. A scattering of lakes glinted like pieces of broken glass in the early morning sunlight.

"I've been thinking about Yanno," she said. "He showed me that if I forgave others I also would be able to forgive myself. He was so wise, Mark. I felt like he could see right into my heart, like he could read my thoughts. He was always one step ahead of me."

Mark nodded. "I have to admit, a part of me wanted to believe he was John the apostle, still waiting for Jesus to return." He looked at her tenderly. "It sounds like he made quite an impression on you."

"He did," she said. "Only a few weeks ago, I went searching for John the apostle, but I found so much more. In the end, I found the Beloved—but it wasn't John. It was Jesus.

Yanno helped me find Him, and, in the process, he helped me find you."

Her eyes filling with tears, she reached inside her purse and withdrew the small plastic bag that contained Yanno's hair clippings. A muffled sob escaped her lips.

"Let's finalize this, once and for all," she said. "If I don't do this, there will always be the temptation to have them tested. And, to be honest, I don't really want to know."

"I'm with you, Julie." Mark placed a comforting hand on her shoulder.

She opened the bag, turned it upside down high in the air, and shook it. Yanno's hairs poured out and were caught by a gentle breeze. They drifted upward and danced on a current of air. As the strands scattered in the sunlight, they turned into a scintillating spray and fell like a shower of diamonds from heaven.

With a sigh, Julie started to turn toward the car, but Mark grabbed her hand and held her fast. Puzzled, she faced him. He dropped to one knee and pulled a tiny box from his shirt pocket. Julie caught her breath. A tear ran down her face, followed by another. Mark opened the little box, a wrinkle of hope creasing his forehead. This time, she didn't run away.

RESOURCES and ACKNOWLEDGEMENTS

Having never visited Ephesus or Patmos, I depended on input from people who had been to those locations, including Linda K. Dwyer who provided photos and information on Ephesus, and columnist and award-winning author Marilynn Preston, a frequent visitor to Patmos.

I received on-site logistics from Theologos D. Gryllis of the Skala Hotel in Patmos, as well as reviews by several visitors to the location. I got a crash course in conversational Greek from Lucy Athanason and the owners of Laki's Restaurant in Ocala, Florida, also from Irene Manosi, a servant at St. Mark's Greek Orthodox Church in Belleview, Florida.

Through email communications I was able to get information on epigenetic testing from Connie J. Mulligan, PhD. Associate director of the University of Florida Genetics Institute; Kris Rebilliot, director of communications at Buck Institute for Research on Aging; Steve Horvath, PhD, professor of human genetics and biostatistics at UCLA; and Richard Stepp, PhD, Department of Anthropology, University of Florida.

My local library provided helpful video documentaries and written materials, and I was able to experience several online virtual tours provided by videographers. I am grateful for fellow members of the Ocala Chapter of Word Weavers International, particularly Delores and Chuck Kight, who encouraged me through the entire writing of this book.

Many thanks to Mike Parker, my editor and publisher, who makes me feel like my writing has value. And, last but certainly not least, I am eternally grateful to my Lord and Savior, Jesus Christ, the true Beloved we should all be seeking.

ABOUT THE AUTHOR

Pulitzer Prize nominee Marian Rizzo has written four contemporary novels and two biblical era novels. She's been a journalist for twenty-five years with the Ocala Star-Banner Newspaper, part of the Gatehouse Media Group. Now retired, Marian has continued to work with the Star-Banner as a correspondent. She's won numerous awards in journalism, including the New York Times Chairman's Award and first place in the annual Amy Foundation Writing Awards.

Marian lives in Ocala, Florida, with her daughter Vicki who has Down Syndrome. Her other daughter, Joanna, is the mother of three children. Grandparenting has added another element of joy to Marian's busy schedule, which includes workouts five times a week, lots of reading, and lunches with the girls.

Visit her online at Marianscorner.com

Also Available From

WordCrafts Press

A Purpose True
    by Gail Kittleson

End of Summer
    by Michael Potts

Odd Man Outlaw
    by K.M. Zahrt

Maggie's Song
    by Marcia Ware

The Awakening of Leeowyn Blake
    by Mary Garner

Home
    By Eleni McKnight

www.WordCrafts.net

Made in the USA
Columbia, SC
03 July 2019